MY SAVAGE EMPIRE

A DARK GANG ROMANCE

STEFFANIE HOLMES

MY SAVAGE EMPIRE

Let them hate me,
as long as they fear me.

I've ascended my throne.
I wear my crown of thorns.

Fancy that? I'm Queen of the August crime family.
I'll rebuild my father's kingdom in blood and fire.
With three broken princes at my side.

I've been betrayed, shot, hunted, and forced into a loathsome
marriage.
But I'm still here, still fighting for them.
For Noah, Gabriel, and Eli.

I love them too much to chain them to my savage empire.
No one will take them away from me.
No matter the cost, my broken princes will be free.

I've sharpened my sword.

I made my sacrifices.
I'm unleashing *war*.

Drink and be merry, for tomorrow we bathe in blood.

From *USA Today* bestselling author Steffanie Holmes comes the chilling conclusion to this dark and gritty contemporary high school romantic suspense.

Grab a free copy *Cabinet of Curiosities* – a Steffanie Holmes compendium of short stories and bonus scenes – when you sign up for updates with the Steffanie Holmes newsletter.

JOIN THE NEWSLETTER FOR UPDATES

Grab a free copy *Cabinet of Curiosities* – a Steffanie Holmes compendium of short stories and bonus scenes – when you sign up for updates with the Steffanie Holmes newsletter.

www.steffanieholmes.com/newsletter

Every week in my newsletter I talk about the true-life hauntings, strange happenings, crumbling ruins, and creepy facts that inspire my stories. You'll also get newsletter-exclusive bonus scenes and updates. I love to talk to my readers, so come join us for some spooky fun :)

A NOTE ON DARK CONTENT

This series goes to some dark places.

I'm writing this note because I want you a heads up about some of the content in Stonehurst Prep. Reading should be fun, so I want to make sure you don't get any nasty surprises. If you're cool with anything and you don't want spoilers, then skip this note and dive in.

Keep reading if you like a bit of warning about what to expect in a dark series.

- This book contains scenes of on-page torture – not of our heroine or her men – and extreme violence.

- There is some bullying in the first book, but our heroine holds her own. No heroes in this story threaten or are involved in physical or sexual assault of the heroine.

- Claws is a sexual abuse survivor and she references this past trauma in this book.

- Claws also experiences a sexual assault in *My Stolen Life*, but it is stopped by one of her boys.

- There is also a scene where a beloved animal is attacked and hurt. In *My Broken Crown*, animals are shown living in appalling conditions. I want you to know that these animals survive and the people responsible will be punished.

- All books contain violence, human trafficking, organised crime, drug use, murder, further examples of animal cruelty (not by Claws or her boys), and further references to sexual assault.

Claws and her boys are deep in a cruel, bloodthirsty world. It's not pretty, but I promise there will be suspense, hot sex, and beautiful, violent retribution. If that's not your jam, that's totally cool. I suggest you pick up my Nevermore Bookshop Mysteries series – all of the mystery and hot book boyfriends without the gore and trauma and violence.

Enjoy, you beautiful depraved human, you :) Steff

*I*Utinam populus Romanus unam cervicem
haberet!
Would that the Roman people have but one neck!

– Gaius Caligula, Suetonius, *The Twelve Caesars*

It's my birthday.

I stare at the open book in my lap, thinking that I have to go to work at the diner in a couple of hours, thinking that if things were different – if my mother hadn't been sliced to pieces, if my father hadn't died suffocating in a coffin – I might have a birthday celebration to look forward to, instead of another day of endless, numbing *silence*.

From her spot on the arm of the sofa, Queen Boudica raises her head and regards me with a stoic nod. Even though she's only lived with me for a couple of months, it feels like we've known each other my whole life. She seems to sense when the darkness of my solitary existence threatens to consume me, and chooses those exact moments to remind me that she's *here*, she's a cat so she doesn't *need* anyone, but she quite likes me, and could I open another can of tuna, please?

Queen Boudica pads over my book and slumps across my legs, exposing her belly for rubs. I stroke her silky fur as a hard lump rises in my throat.

Daddy always took the day off work on my birthday. No matter what was going on in his empire, he made the time for me. We'd do something together as a family, just the three of us. Sometimes Daddy let me invite Antony along, too – like that time he took us both to this crazy ranch in the middle of nowhere where we threw axes at trees and ate rabbit stew. It was one of my favorite birthdays ever.

For my ninth birthday, Daddy rented an entire rooftop restaurant and hired a team of chefs to make me anything I wanted. I asked for lamb chops and strawberry ice cream sundaes, and the four of us had an epic food fight, coating the walls in strawberry sauce that dribbled like blood after a massacre. That one was pretty cool, too.

I often wondered if Daddy had the chefs killed after that party, since they had seen my face.

But for my seventh birthday, I asked if I could have a party at a fast-food restaurant with a playground and a ball pit, like the kids I saw on TV. So Daddy emptied our pool and filled it with balls, and had his chef prepare gourmet burgers and truffle-butter fries. I cried the whole day.

Daddy tried. But it was never about the ball pit.

It was about being the only kid at my birthday party.

And here I am again, the only human guest at my lame-ass pity party. I mash the buttons on the remote, and Gabriel Fallen's voice rises through the opulent ballroom, singing of broken wings and avenging angels. I feel his own broken wings wrapping around me, the feathers tickling my face.

> Memories assault me,
> I curl my back against the onslaught
> of you
> Memories are for sharing.
> Forgetting is a refuge.
> Pain is a weapon,
> Sharpened to kill.

> This pain I carry,
> Into battle, toward death.
> I carry for you.

How does he do that? How does he reach out of the speakers and squeeze my heart until my ribs feel like they're going to collapse?

I slam the book closed and throw it across the room. Queen Boudica gives me a sharp 'mew,' reminding me that the company of a cat should be all I ever require to be happy.

Solitude is fine and dandy, except when it's not.

Antony bursts into the ballroom just as the book clatters against the wall, leaving a dent in the plaster. He's dressed for the club in his favorite suit, and holding a couple of white takeout boxes. He stares at the ruined book a moment, the corner of his mouth twitching into a smirk. "I see the birthday's going well."

I hiss through my teeth. Queen Boudica sits up, peering at the boxes, her whiskers twitching with anticipation.

"Don't be like that. I didn't forget about you. We're going to have our own celebration." He sets down the boxes and opens them for me. Fried chicken tacos from one of my favorite places (and a couple of fish ones for Boudica), and half of a pink frosted birthday cake, the swirls of icing like the lace of a prom dress. Gabriel's voice swirls around me.

> ...there's a hole in the world where you used
> 　　to be...

"There's only half a cake in here." I frown at the box. I want to hate Antony for something, because my veins hum with rage and if I don't get it out of me I'm going to implode.

"It's just the two of us." Antony makes a big show of

unfurling an oversized napkin and tucking it into the collar of his shirt. He picks up one of the tacos and takes a bite, juice dribbling down his chin.

"Three of us." I press my finger into the frosting and give it to Queen Boudica to lick off. Who gives a fuck about being civilized? Who am I saving my mother's immaculate manners for? "It's always just us in this big, creepy house. Except when it's just me and the cat."

"We're nearly halfway through your five-year purgatory," Antony says, his mouth full of chicken. "I didn't say it would be easy. You have to be patient."

"Easy for you to say – you get to go outside. Smell the roses, stick your dick in someone warm and living. All I've got is ugly statues and Howard Malloy's porn collection, which let me tell you is not to my taste. I've been hiding away most of my life, and I'm fucking *done*. I'm going crazy in here." I roll my eyes at the ceiling as Gabriel lets out a tortured scream. "And with those fuckwits crowded at the gate, I feel like I'm an exotic fish or a creepy doll trapped in a glass cabinet."

"If you were a doll, you wouldn't be nearly as creepy as the ones upstairs." Antony reaches for another taco. "You need a hobby that's not listening to emo music and simmering existential rage. I'll bring you some crochet supplies. You can make a hat."

"Only if you want a crochet hook up your asshole."

"Such a mouth on one so young and beautiful." Antony nudges the box. "I'd be nicer to me if I were you. We're going out tonight."

"We are?"

"We are," he grins. "But you'll have to go in disguise. Can you do that?"

We finish off our tacos and cake, and I skip upstairs and throw open Mackenzie Malloy's closet. I've already raided Ainsley's for her comfy designer loungewear and garish evening gowns, but Mackenzie has some slutty dresses appropriate for Antony's club. She only disappeared two years ago, and as well as being similar looking we seem to be the same dress size, so they fit okay.

Antony watches from the bed as I perform my own fashion show for him, trying slutty dress after slutty dress until he nods. "That's the one. It's just slutty enough."

His throat sounds tight. I glare at him, arms folded across the tight black bodice. "Don't get all fatherly on me now. I need to get out of this house, and you'll be right there beside me if anyone tries anything."

I twirl around, admiring the way the flared black skirt swishes around my knees. It fits so snug and perfect it feels like it's made for me, which I guess is kind of true. This is Mackenzie Malloy's dress, and she looks an awful lot like me.

"You need a wig," Antony says. "And to shave those gorilla legs of yours."

Ainsley Malloy has an impressive fashion wig collection. I select a black one and do my face with dark, smoky eyes and plump red lips. I look like a goth whore, but I also don't look anything like me. Perfect.

I tuck my arm into Antony's as we head down to the garage. I know exactly where we're going. He's taken me to Colosseum before, as a treat. He doesn't like to do it because he spends all night worrying about me, and he needs his head in the game when he deals with club stuff.

But I love everything about Colosseum. The crunch of arena sand – pink-colored particles coating every surface and glittering under the floodlights. The smell of sweat and sex and blood heavy in the air. The crowd a many-limbed monster, writhing and undulating as it gorges itself on a feast of debauchery.

Antony grips the steering wheel so hard his knuckles glow white. He keeps looking over at me, frown lines etched across his face. He's starting to regret taking me out, but it's too late to turn back. We pull into a space behind one of the abandoned warehouses and walk out to the old roundhouse.

As soon as we enter the crowd, I'm swept up in the hum of anticipation. All around me, people mill in small groups – the men in dark, expensive suits, the women resplendent in figure-hugging gowns, their throats dripping with diamonds. Cigarettes and glass pipes are shared freely. People rush to Antony, talking a mile a minute about all sorts of things I'm not familiar with. Some he greets in friendship, others he brushes aside as he leads me behind a velvet rope and up a narrow staircase.

He has a whole life here, a whole world of responsibilities and friends, that I'm not part of. Why can't I have that too?

Antony settles me into a table at the rear of the VIP area. Waiters and staff bustle around, setting the tables. No one gives me a second glance. I'm just another of Antony's nameless dates. How many women has my cousin sat in this very same chair? I shift my ass, trying to get comfortable.

Antony plonks a blood-red cocktail in front of me and goes off to tend to his duties.

As the moon rises over the mangled railway tracks, the fairy lights illuminating the audience dim and people take their seats. In front of me – in the prime spot directly overlooking the arena – are the tables reserved for the Imperators. Nero Lucian bends to whisper in the ear of Marion, his second wife. No one knows what happened to the first wife, but everyone agrees she was annoying and her three sons by Nero are as much use as a hedgehog at a condom factory. Two of Marion's sons and her daughter are here tonight – they're about my age and are both staring at their phones, looking bored. They're hardly an improvement in the brains department.

At the second table, Constantine Dio sits with a group of his top assassins. They sip their drinks, eagle eyes surveying the room. Constantine's back is to the staircase, but there's an edge to his posture, an ease in the slope of his shoulders that implies he'd be impossible to surprise. Constantine isn't married, and is rarely seen with a female date. The gossip around my father's house parties was that he's gay, but it's never been proven. Gay or not, he'd better find a woman quick, or he'll be without an heir. The life expectancy of crime lords isn't exactly stellar, and a dead Imperator without an heir will leave the entire system unstable, vulnerable to a coup.

At the third table, accepting a plate piled high with creamy spaghetti, is Brutus.

Brutus the betrayer.

Brutus the *murderer*.

Cold rage settles in my stomach. I grip the edge of the table, breaking the edge of my nail on the cold metal. I repeat Gabriel's lyrics over and over in my head, reminding myself that my pain can be a weapon. A single line repeats over and over again.

Drink and be merry,

for tomorrow we bathe in blood.

My time will come. One day I will bathe in that man's blood.

But it's not today.

Today, I watch my uncle Brutus sling his arm over the back of the chair Julian August should have occupied. Today, soldiers I remember from my father's office jostle each other to kiss his feet. Today, he bends over and snorts a line of cocaine through a small straw. The light illuminates the back of his hand – the skin puckered around an old injury. My father's *sacer* mark, now so mangled with scar tissue it's unrecognizable as the August sword and laurel. Brutus dares to wear it with reckless pride. I'm surprised he hasn't had surgery to hide the *sacer* we *do* live in Emerald Beach, home of the best plastic surgeons in the world.

It must serve his purposes to have it on display, a sign that he's beaten death.

I'm so busy glaring at the back of Brutus' hand, twirling my butter knife around in my trembling fingers, that I don't notice the fights have begun. First up is a couple of bouts between condemned men – disgraced soldiers from Lucian and Dio fighting to the death. One is a man named Cicero – a loyal soldier of my father's, a man whose voice always sounded kind. Was his only crime loving my father?

The Imperators and their entourage show no respect for the men circling each other in the ring – they call out friendly insults to each other, placing wagers on which man will win his freedom.

Cicero gets in a few decent punches, but is stuck in the guts by his opponent's trident and collapses in a pile of blood. Brutus pounds his fist in triumph as Cicero's opponent hacks off his head and lobs it into the crowd.

After that, they bring out the lion.

I grind my teeth, dig my nails into my skin – anything to hold back my scream. The poor creature circles the ring, ribs sticking from his emaciated frame, his shoulders hunched and malformed from being kept in a too-small cage. He lifts his nose high, his dirty mane streaming behind him, and licks at the dried blood around his mouth, baring his terrifying teeth. The front rows of the audience lean away from him, unable to bear being so close to such beauty, to be confronted with what they've done to a graceful creature in the name of entertainment.

This close, they can smell the decaying human flesh on his breath.

The lion turns its head toward me, and all I see is my kitten. My Queen Boudica's defiant yellow eyes peering back at me from the darkness behind the dumpster. This lion will do what it has to do to survive.

My father banned the beasts from the ring. It turned his stomach to see beautiful creatures reduced to this... this *baseness*... for entertainment.

But my father isn't in charge anymore.

Brutus and Nero laugh and cheer as the lion stands on his hind legs and roars with wild hunger. A man is tossed from the gangway into the ring. He barely has time to stagger to his feet before the lion is on him.

When there's nothing left but bones and gore, and the lion lopes away to fall asleep, they prod him back into his trapdoor, scoop out the carcass, and call for the night fight to begin.

Antony marches into the ring, his arms raised as the applause washes over him. I raise my hands to applaud too, even though I want to turn away in disgust. My phone – hidden in my bra – buzzes.

I slide the old iPhone from my bra, tracing the sparkly pink heart on the case. A notification flashes on the screen – a new SMS. The only person who messages me is Antony. Mackenzie Malloy used to get a few SMS messages from old school friends, but they stopped... except for...

Jace.

This guy must've been someone special to her, because he kept texting long after the others gave up. A few times I've almost been tempted to answer him. He seems so desperate for answers, I want to do something to put him out of his misery. But of course that's insane.

My finger trembles as I tap the notification.

"Wherever you are, Mackenzie, I'm thinking of you."

I'm thinking of you.

I choke back a sob. Today of all days it's exactly what I need to hear. Somewhere out there, someone cares about me.

Except that this message isn't for me. Except that Jace is thinking about a dead girl and the life I stole from her.

I wonder why he chose today, of all days, to message her?

I toss the phone on the table, trying to fight back the tears stinging the corners of my eyes. *I'm not going to cry. I refuse to waste a single moment of my one night of freedom feeling sorry for myself.*

I snap my fingers for the waiter to bring me another drink. As I sip, I focus back on the arena. It's hard to see what's going on because the crowd is on their feet, waving their fists in the air and chanting, "Barbarian! Barbarian!"

I stand and move to the edge of the platform, only a few feet behind Brutus' table. The bastard is telling a story to his admirers, and they're all cracking up as if he could possibly say something worth laughing about. If I'd brought a knife, I could twist it into his kidney before he even saw me coming. I've been practicing. I'm quite good.

The locked box in my mind rattles its chains. The darkness inside longs to be unleashed.

I force myself to angle my body away and focus on the arena. Two men lock together in battle, naked except for horned masks and tight athletic shorts that reveal hard, muscled thighs. They fight bare-knuckled, with no weapons apart from their bodies. There are no rules. They fight having decided that only one of them may go home at the end.

The older fighter is drenched in blood. He has some fancy footwork and a mean left hook. But it's the other – the one they call the Barbarian – who arrests my attention. He's young – around my age, I guess – with hard shoulders and the kind of long, delicious legs I want wrapped around my body. But it's not his youth that captures me, it's the way he moves. He throws his whole being into every punch, every kick and grapple, as if he knows it will be his last and he intends to make it count.

This boy is *wild*. He bites, scratches, roars, and rains down blows like he's an avenging angel. He fights like someone who has gone numb on the inside. He needs the taste of blood and the bite of pain to feel alive.

It's hot as fuck.

I press my thighs together, aware that the slap of skin on skin as the Barbarian pummels his opponent flares heat deep in my core. Aware that even though I've never slept with a guy before, that the last person who touched me did so without my consent and is sitting ten feet away from me *right now*, I'm not immune to the raw, feral scent of *lust*.

Of longing.

My breath catches in my throat as the Barbarian goes for a chokehold but ends up slammed against the wall of the arena. Blood spurts from his nose, drenching the wall, but he whirls around and attacks like he doesn't even notice. He moves... exactly like Antony. I know it's not my cousin beneath that mask, because I can see him standing on the end of the gangway, watching intently. But this Barbarian has Antony's same desperate energy, his wanton revelry of pain.

He's been trained by the best.

What could have driven that boy into Antony's hands? What's happened in his life that makes him come here and throw himself into the fray?

Applause erupts from the crowd as the Barbarian knocks out his opponent with an uppercut so fierce I half expect brains to fly out his ears. Antony walks down into the ring, shakes his bloody hand, and lays a laurel wreath around the horns of his mask. The crowd roars as the Barbarian glares blankly into their depths, still swimming in the adrenaline haze of his fight.

Antony wraps his hand around the Barbarian's wrist and raises his arm in a salute to the Imperators. The Barbarian looks up then, right at me. From behind the mask, his eyes graze my face before falling to my body. A shudder rocks through him like he's seen a ghost.

The Barbarian turns to Antony and slams his fist into his nose.

What the fuck?

Antony's head snaps back. Chaos erupts as the crowd reels, as soldiers storm the arena. They try to pull the Barbarian off Antony, but he's unstoppable.

I can't watch any longer. I fling myself away from the edge, spilling my cocktail down my dress. I run for the stairs. I shove my way through the heaving, cawing crowd, into the train sheds.

Antony... is he...

I can't get any closer. I'm hemmed in on all sides by people. The crowd has become a wild beast – a herd that's scented a predator on the breeze and are stirring to bolt in a million directions. I hug my arms to my chest. If I'm not careful, I'll be crushed.

As I try to shove my way toward the arena, I catch a glimpse of a blonde head moving the opposite way. Toward me. I start at the sight of her. It's not just that she's young to be attending the fights. It's not that she's beautiful, although she is.

She's a mirror image of me.

In every way.

Except...

Except for the blood streaked across her face.

"Hey, wait!" I try to push myself toward her, but by the time I've broken through a wall of men, she's gone. Sucked back into the crowd, or never there at all.

A memory made real. A birthday gift from Brutus that I will never, ever forget.

1

———

CLAUDIA

A killer is *in my house.*

I reel, squashing down the panic that threatens to overwhelm me. I reach through the absinthe haze that's swallowing me, punching my hand through air thick as molasses to close my fingers around my knife. I know they say you should never bring a knife to a gunfight, but *they* haven't crossed Claudia August.

The fire flickers higher, licking at the edge of the table where Gabriel still sits in his absinthe stupor.

"Take that!" Gabriel springs into action. He tosses the first thing he gets his hands on at the flames. Unfortunately, that's the bottle of absinthe. He grins in triumph, clearly expecting the liquid to douse the fire. Which it doesn't, because science. Instead, the flames roar to life – a column of blue fire that sizzles as it climbs the wooden table leg and reaches for him.

"Get away from it." Noah shoves Gabe aside. George hits the lights. The chandelier flickers to life just as Eli whips the purple cloth off the table and uses it to smother the flames. Gabriel's got his neck bent up, peering around the room with detached interest, but I grab him and yank him under the table, searching everywhere for our attacker. Yara and Madeline have taken cover under the day bed. Noah crouches behind the sofa, his gun poised at thin air.

Where's the shooter? I cast my eyes around the room, but no one could have done it. We were all around the table. There's no one else here.

Odette lays across the rug, her chest blooming with blood. Gabriel must have only just seen her, because he scrambles out from my grip and is at her side in an instant, trying to hold one of her purple scarves over the wound. I know it's too late.

"Gabe." I tug his arm. He doesn't move. "Gabe, there's no pulse. She's gone."

"Fuck." His chest heaves. "Fuck."

I wrap him in my arms. I know he's slipping into a dark place, the place I'd been fighting to keep him out of all this time. This is another friend dead after a night partying with Gabriel Fallen. He'll blame himself.

"There's no one here," Noah says. He's right. There's nowhere to hide in the sitting room. Cautiously, he creeps around the side of the couch, checking behind the curtains and in the cupboard of the antique liquor cabinet. No shooter.

I crawl out from beneath the table. My hand lands in the pool of Odette's blood. I wipe it on my dress. "The door?"

"It's locked." Noah turns the handle to check. "From this side. And we didn't hear it click. The shooter never left this room."

My throat scratches and my eyes water as I try to squint through the haze of smoke. I *taste* the aftermath of this attack – singed carpet and fresh blood. Eli rushes to open a window, coughing as he leans out to gasp in fresh air.

I peer down at Odette. "Then who the fuck shot her?"

I glare at Noah.

He holds up his hands. "Don't look at me."

"You're the only one in this room with a gun." I don't believe he did it, but I need to say something, *do* something. I need to think, but I can't think because my veins are soaked with absinthe and adrenaline and someone *was in my fucking house* and they've vanished into thin air. "Otherwise, the only explanation is that someone just snuck into my house, shot at us *badly*, and disappeared."

"That's impossible."

"Exactly. I thought you and Tiberius had this place locked down tighter than a medieval chastity belt."

"We do." Noah stares down at his gun like he doesn't know how it got into his hands. "So how the fuck did they get in?"

"That's what I need you to tell me."

"This is going to sound insane," George pipes up, "but could it have been a ghost? Like, a real ghost? Maybe the spirits of Malloy Manor didn't want us being all up in their business—"

"You're right, that *is* insane."

"Sorry, I just know this right now feels like the part of a horror film where someone says 'I don't believe in ghosts,' and the next thing they're decapitated at the foot of the stairs, and I'm a big fan of keeping my head attached to my shoulders."

George lets out a little squeak – a laugh to cover up her terror. I want to go to her, but there's no way I'm breaking my grip on Gabe. He feels impossibly light in my hands, as though he might trickle through my fingers like grains of sand and be blown away from me.

"We've got to call the police," Gabriel cries.

"Fuck no." I nod at George. "We've got our very own CSI: Emerald Beach right here. George, can you give us a time of death?"

Noah stares at me like I've gone nuts, but George gets it. She lets out another high-pitched laugh-squeak, but she bends down to inspect Odette's body.

"Time of death is, ah, about four minutes ago. I recall three distinct shots, but only two went into Odette and the other is... look there." George points to a bullet embedded in the wall. "This one missed all of us. Noah, hand me one of those envelopes on the table. Claws, I need your knife."

I hand her the blade I still grip like a vise. George accepts one of the purple-lined envelopes Odette brought along for creating spells. She jiggles the bullet from the wall so it falls into the open envelope. "I'll have a look at this under my microscope. I might be able to figure out the type of gun, but if it's something generic it's not going to help us much."

Next, George creeps forward and leans over Odette, examining the wound and the position of the body. "It's hard to be exact because it was so dark and I didn't see what direction Odette was facing when she fell. But assuming she was looking into the center of the table, it looks like the shots came from over there." She points a trembling finger at the bookshelf.

"But how did someone get over here..." Eli waves his arms to clear the smoke. He stops in his tracks. "Claudia, look at this."

Eli drops to his knees and peers at the books on the lowest shelf.

"You think the killer stopped to consult Churchill's biography before they took their shot?" My brain swims with absinthe dreams, half-formed visions of Eli growing horns out the sides of his head and George crawling around on the floor like a panther, tail and all.

"Just shut up and get down here."

I glare at horned Eli, but I obey. I untangle myself from Gabriel (whose arms feel stretchy like rubber bands. Boy, absinthe *fucks you up*) and drop to my knees in front of the shelves. I stare at the spot Eli's pointing at, but I can't see anything other than an ugly Persian carpet and a few errant drops of Odette's blood.

"The rug is pulled in the opposite direction here." Eli runs his fingers over the fiber. His nail becomes a claw. "I'd never have noticed it because the pattern hides it, but when you touch it, it's obvious. Something heavy's been dragged across here."

My heart quickens as I feel the edges. *He's right.* "It's a half-circle pattern, like... like a door swinging out."

Our eyes meet at the same time.

"What?" Noah barks. "What's going on?"

We start yanking the volumes off the bookshelf. Howard Malloy's Churchills and Sun Tzu and leatherbound volumes of the *Decline and Fall of the Roman Empire* are tossed carelessly aside. Eli presses his fingers into every corner of the shelf, frowning when he doesn't find a spring. We move to the next shelf. I grab a figurine – an Egyptian *shabti* – but it's stuck fast.

"It won't move," I grumble as Eli slides his hand around the ancient painted figurine depicting a servant carrying a platter of food. The Egyptians left whole armies of these painted *shabti* in their tombs, believing that the tiny clay figures would magically come to life and serve their ruler in the spirit world.

"That's because you're not meant to move it." Eli twists the figurine sharply to the left. There's a clicking sound, and a section of the bookshelf swings out toward us. I peer into the dark void – a gap in the walls large enough to admit a person.

A secret passage.

"This must be one of the escape tunnels Howard Malloy was rumored to have installed in the house," Eli says, his horns bouncing.

I nod, but I'm left wondering how our intruder could possibly know about this tunnel. I remember when the family disappeared and people started to see glimpses of the Malloy ghost (i.e., me), all these articles were published online about the manor's secrets. There were rumors of secret escape tunnels and underground torture chambers. But they were just that – rumors. No one could find a worker who'd admit to installing such things, and although ghost-hunters scanned the outer perimeter with all kinds of detectors and devices, they never found an alternate entrance or secret torture chamber.

Hell, I've lived in the house for more than four years and I never found this hidden door.

A random killer didn't just stumble on this secret passage.

There's only one person I can think of who might know this house better than me.

"I can't believe you have a secret passage." George leaps over, her eyes shining. "Your house is *so cool*."

"Careful." I throw out an arm to hold her back. "Remember our gunman escaped out there only a few minutes ago."

Or gunwoman.

One look at Eli's furrowed brow, and I can tell he's thinking the same thing. And something else occurs to me through my absinthe haze – when we had the break-in where Queen Boudica was attacked, I assumed the intruder was Alec LeMarque. I branded his face in punishment before figuring out it wasn't him. Then I assumed it was Brutus. But what if I was wrong? What if the intruder knew about the maintenance shed because they knew this house as well as I do? And I watched the intruder escape by vaulting the wall like a gymnast.

Or a head cheerleader.

And the person who shot at me and Noah outside the front door... the person who was such a terrible shot they missed with a sniper rifle. What if they're the same person who couldn't kill me from fifteen feet across the room?

I stare into the gloomy abyss of the passage. What waits for us down there? What secrets does Howard Malloy have to reveal?

Eli holds out his hand to Noah. "Give me that gun."

"No fucking way." Noah holds the weapon across his chest. "I'm not letting the two of you go down there by yourselves."

"The tunnel is narrow. No way are your monstrous shoulders going to fit. Besides, I'm a better shot than you. Give me the gun."

Noah frowns, but he hands Eli the pistol. I slide my second knife out of my shoe, ignoring the handle turning into a snake that wriggles in my fingers. *No absinthe for me ever again.* I nod to Noah and Yara and Madeline. "Call Tiberius. We need him to keep an eye on the perimeter in case she's escaping on foot. And you'd better tell Antony, too."

"She?" Noah looks confused. I can't believe he hasn't figured it out.

"Yes. My sister's the only person who could have done this."

Eli enters first, and I follow him into the dark tunnel. It's a nice piece of work – the walls plastered and finished. I rap the wood with my knuckles, and find the sound muffled. The tunnel is heavily insulated. Whoever installed this wanted to be able to come and go as they pleased without anyone in the house being aware of them.

The tunnel turns left, then right, following the line of the walls. I can't believe I never noticed how thick the walls were in this part of the house. There are a lot of shelves, cupboards, and storage on this floor that disguise the tunnel's path. It's cleverly designed, even if it does feel like a set piece from a horror film.

After about thirty paces, Eli stops. "There's a ladder leading down," he says. "I need you to hold the gun."

He presses the weapon into my palm as he swings out over an empty space where the passage passes into the floor below. I keep the gun trained into the dark hole as Eli descends. When he reaches the ground, he thrusts up a hand and I give him the weapon, then follow him down.

We walk along another short passage, then descend another

two ladders. The temperature drops. The hairs on my arms stand on end. Here, the walls are rough, hewn from the bedrock itself. I wonder if this section of the tunnel is structurally sound, if we're just one wrong step away from being crushed by falling stones.

"It smells strange down here." Eli's fingers reach for mine, squeezing tight. He speaks in a whisper. He's thinking about cave-ins, too.

It does smell odd, kind of sickly sweet. The smell gets stronger as we walk deeper into the cave. We walk and walk and walk. There's no way to tell how far we've moved away from the house, but I feel certain we've no longer beneath the Malloy property.

"This is the kind of tunnel you build if you know you might need to make a quick escape," I whisper as we turn yet another corner. The smell is stronger here, hanging in the damp air like something living. "Legitimate businessmen don't build secret escape routes from their homes."

"I think it's firmly established that there was nothing legitimate about Howard Malloy," Eli says. "Do you think the family used this to make their escape four years ago?"

I shrug, a pointless gesture since Eli walks ahead of me, shining his phone's flashlight into the gloom. "Who knows? Maybe they assumed new identities and are living it up on some tropical island. But according to George, someone drove the Malloy's car out of the house. If it wasn't them, who was it?"

The tunnel widens out, and we emerge into an underground chamber. I breathe a sigh of relief to see the hewn-stone walls propped up with steel supports. High on the wall opposite us is the entrance to another, smaller tunnel. There's no way to reach it from where we stand – supposedly, our intruder used a rope or ladder to enter through that tunnel, and pulled it up after they fled. The cloying smell hangs thick in the air.

Eli's phone beam shines on two long wooden boxes in the center of the room. I swallow as the shapes resolve into long boxes, with dark stained surfaces and ornate brass handles. *I know exactly what they are—*

Coffins.

Two coffins just hanging out in a secret tunnel beneath Malloy Manor.

What.

The.

Actual.

Fuck?

"I'd recognize this design anywhere." Eli bends down in front of one, wiping his finger over the filthy brass plating. "Walter Hart originals. They're DIY kits. One of Dad's clever ideas – flatpack funerals. All the gravitas and grandeur for half the price."

"I guess that explains how they got down here." I can't imagine how someone could get two coffins down the narrow tunnel and around all the tight corners into this room, but it would make sense if they were assembled here – as much sense as any of this made. *Why are they here in the first place?* "You know we're going to have to open them, right?"

Eli staggers to his feet. "I feel like we're at the point in the horror film where the audience is screaming at us to turn back. So yes, sure. Let's take a look."

I move along the side of the first coffin, my finger tracking the dusty edge. It may be the remnants of absinthe in my system, but I fancy I see tendrils of inky black miasma curling from beneath the lid. I want nothing more than to run from this room and never, ever return.

But Claudia August ain't afraid of ghosts.

It doesn't take a genius to figure out what the smell is – the lingering of decay, of organic remains returning to the earth.

There's no ventilation down here. That smell will hang around long after these coffins become ashes and dust.

"At the same time?" Eli raises an eyebrow. I nod. His fingers curl around the handle. "Three, two, one..."

I heave up my lid and shine my phone's flashlight into the gloom.

I see... exactly what I expect to see. A mostly decomposed human body – bits of flesh and other gross *stuff* clinging to a skeletal frame. The silk coffin lining is stained with all manner of dark liquids and secretions. A lone rat scurries through the eye socket. Broken bones reveal the story of violent death.

Eli's coffin contains a larger skeleton with the tattered remains of a black suit still clinging to the shoulders. More broken bones. The skull has been staved in.

Two bodies, both brutally murdered. My eye catches a glint of metal on the finger of the larger skeleton. I pinch my nose and bend down to inspect it. It's an ancient signet ring carved with an elaborate M, in the same font as the one carved into the gates, or the stamp adorning the stationery in my office.

M for Malloy.

We've found the final resting place of Howard and Ainsley Malloy.

2
______

GEORGE

"It's definitely Howard and Ainsley. They're the right ages, and aside from the signet ring, I can match the clothes they're wearing to the last pictures we have of them alive."

Claws taps her fingernails on her arm as she watches me work. I circle the coffins. It's weird – after what happened to my dad, death should completely freak me out, and yet there's something about holding the ashes of a gerbil instead of your father that makes you realize death's nothing to be afraid of.

That, and helping Galen perform that autopsy on Brutus has destroyed any squeamishness I might've had about getting elbows deep into a corpse.

Claws needs answers, and we can't exactly take these bodies to the cops. That would mean exposing the fact Claws has been living in the house these last four years, not to mention her current employment as one of the city's foremost crime lords. (Crime lass? Crime lady? Crime Mistress? I'll have to ask her for the correct term.) In our family, everyone has their job – Claws runs the show, Eli's the heart, Noah's the mathematical genius and the muscle, Gabriel causes chaos and provides a killer soundtrack. And I've got to roll up my sleeves and get cozy with Howard and Ainsley's bones.

"You okay if I head up?" Claws asks a few minutes later. "The smell is making me sick."

I read between the lines. She might not have known them in life, but these corpses *are* her parents. And I think it's clear to all of us who murdered them – her sister. Mackenzie Malloy.

Not everyone's as comfortable around corpses as I am, not even crime lords.

I nod, and she heads upstairs. I get back to work, jotting down my observations in the Notepad app on my phone. The bodies were never embalmed, just shoved in these coffins and placed down here so no one would discover them. I take some samples of the... *goo...* dried on the silk linings. Galen will help me figure out if there were any poisons or other substances present in their blood when they died. Howard Malloy was a big dude – I'm curious how Mackenzie overpowered him and dragged his corpse all the way down here. I can't see any signs that they were killed in this chamber.

When we found Brutus, he was high as fuck on Grey Death. I think that's how she kept him pliant. Did she do the same thing to her parents?

As for how they died, that's easy. Howard Malloy's face practically doesn't exist anymore – multiple blows have turned the bones to splinters. Added to that, his ribs have been broken in three places by something sharp – maybe an ice pick? One of those blows would have been fatal. Ainsley isn't in nearly as bad a condition, but she had several broken bones and a wound to her skull that looks like it might've come from hitting a hard, flat surface like a floor or table.

The killer beat them to death using a variety of implements. It looks as though they took great pleasure in choosing different weapons – the killer dropped one object and picked up another, and chose targets on the body that would maximize pain before death finally overcame the couple.

I know Mackenzie is fucked up. That girl made it her life's mission to torture me, and she had a talent for cruelty. But this...

This is next-level hate.

I finish my observations and carry my vials upstairs, the sickly sweet smell lingering in my nostrils. I emerge from the bookshelf just as Antony thunders into the room. He steps right over the dead, still-oozing-blood body of Odette and frowns at the singed rug, which tells you everything you need to know about Antony. "What the fuck happened here?"

Claws leans against the wall, a joint hanging from her fingers as she glares at her cousin with those terrifying icicle eyes. "I knocked over a candlestick. And then Gabriel tried to put it out with absinthe because he's a fucking idiot. We were lucky Eli is such a Boy Scout; he knew exactly what to do. Oh, and someone broke in and shot at us." She laughs, but it sounds a little high-pitched, manic. She's more shaken up by this than she's showing.

I don't blame her. I mean, Mackenzie was literally right *in the room* with us. A cold chill creeps up my spine. It's a fucking miracle Odette is the only one who got hit.

Why *did* Odette get hit?

Why Odette and not Claudia?

"Did you get a look at the intruder?" Antony demands.

"No. But it's Mackenzie. I'm sure of it. No one else could know about that tunnel."

"Can we get out of here? This place stinks." Antony marches out of the room. We trail after him into the ballroom. Tiberius is already there, holding Ms. Drysdale against his chest as he fingers the pistol at his belt.

"I've checked all around the house," he says. "I didn't see

anyone come or go. I don't understand how this fucking happened."

Noah and Eli flank Claws. They sweep across the room as a pack and stand by the window. Claws stares across the empty pool to the high garden wall. She takes the last drag from her joint and grinds the roach into the marble beneath her heel. Gabriel flops down on the opposite sofa. He pats the cushion beside him and beckons to me. My heart does that annoying skipping thing it does sometimes around Gabe – it's not a crush, exactly. It's more a... sense of awe. I've been at school with Gabriel off and on since he moved to LA (mostly off, since he's always on tour) and I've never been able to say a word to him because I'm afraid what will come out is a random stream of nonsense about how much I love his music, how much his songs meant to me after Dad died. And now we're friends. Now we have in-jokes and banter, and I've seen him at his absolute worst and it's... it's a *lot* sometimes.

Antony slams the door behind him with such force the entire wall rattles. Queen Boudica looks up from her bed on the cat tower and shoots him a withering look. Claws' cousin collapses onto the sofa and puts his feet on the table, scattering chess pieces everywhere. He's usually so put-together with his sharp suits and sardonic smile, but tonight he looks... disoriented.

Antony runs a hand through his short hair and glares at Claudia. "Who was that dead girl? Why are you bringing more randoms into this house?"

"She's a friend of mine," Gabriel says. His fingers tremble around the joint in his hand. His other hand is still gripping the absinthe bottle, and I can see the alcoholic glaze over his eyes. *This is going to send him spiraling again.* "She *was* a friend. Was. She was helping us celebrate Claws' birthday. And now she's... fuck."

"Based on the angle of the shot and position of the killer, I think the intended target was Claudia," I say. I pry the absinthe bottle from his fingers and grip his hand in mine. Antony's gaze falls on me, hard as nails, and I swallow. "In the dark, her purple dress would look similar to Claudia's red one. And their hair is the same length and color."

"Claudia's is prettier, like spun gold," Gabriel slurs.

"What are we going to do with her body?" Ms. Drysdale asks, her lip quivering.

Claudia flicks her gaze to Tiberius. "You'll take care of it? We can't have her death traced back to us."

He nods.

What about Odette's family? I want to ask. *What about the people who care for her? Don't they deserve closure? Doesn't she deserve a proper funeral where all her friends weep over her grave?*

But this is about our family. Claws is trying to keep us all safe.

"And the tunnel?" Antony sounds resigned.

"Contains the bodies of Howard and Ainsley Malloy," I say when Claws doesn't speak. I don't like the intensity of Antony's stare. I remember the comfort of his hands around my shoulders in gym class, where he taught me how to throw a punch, how to break bones. He's looking at me now the same way he looked at Alec LeMarque while I kicked him. I know he's just trying to protect Claudia, but it makes me nervous. "They were beaten to death and hidden in those coffins so they couldn't be found. I think driving their car away and the phone call to the maid was to make the world believe they left, when really they've been here all along."

"We need to find my sister," Claws says. "This has gone on long enough. She's somewhere in this city, and she's got a murder wish. I'll talk to Constantine. He'll give me someone who'll help us get rid of her—"

"We can't bring anyone else in on this," Antony says. "Not without revealing your secrets."

"Then do your fucking job," she screams at him, her whole body trembling. "Find her. Take her out. No fucking around. I don't want to talk to her. I don't want to see her. I want someone to bring me her fucking heart on a silver platter."

I know she's shaken by how close we all came to death. But I've never seen her go off at Antony. *Never*. And judging by the look on his face, he's never seen it, either.

"Fine," he barks. "I'll get right on that, *Imperator*."

He stalks out of the room. The door slams again, and Gizmo dives under the sofa.

Grim silence hangs in the air. Claws glares at Antony's indentation in the couch cushions. I can see the cogs turning in her brain. I expect her to go after him, but instead, she turns to Noah. "We need to locate the end of that tunnel and block it the fuck off. This house has to be a fortress or it's useless to us."

Eli turns to Noah, his hand sliding over Claudia's clenched fist. "I saw some climbing equipment downstairs. I think we can rig a ladder to get into that hole and follow it out."

"Get it done. If you need me, I'll be in my office." Claws shrugs off his hand and starts for the door. "I have an empire to run. I don't have time to deal with this shit."

"Birthday girl, what should I do?" Gabe calls out.

She glares at him. "Sober up."

The door slams again. Gabriel winces, as though her words were a physical punch.

"You can help me," I say, holding up the vials. "I'm going to talk to Galen. I want him to test these. I'm curious how Mackenzie managed to overpower her father. Remember how Brutus was high on Grey Death? Well, what if we find out they were given the same drug..."

I trail off as Gabe shakes his head. "I'll just get in your way. I know nothing about chemistry and forensics and all that bollocks. But before you go, I have a present for you."

"It's Claws' birthday, not mine."

"I know." He whips a brochure from the pocket of his designer jeans and drops it in my lap. "But Gabriel Fallen can spread the love."

I stare down at the brochure. It's about a scholarship program that helps kids all over the world study abroad in Britain. I stare at the name. "The Blackwich Foundation?"

"My father's charity." Gabe grins. "The old man may be a piece of work, but he knows how to bury his assets. Only super-genius overachieving nerds get these scholarships, so I immediately thought of you."

As I scan the list of qualifying institutions, I think of another brochure I keep hidden in my science textbook. *Blackfriars University*. One of the most prestigious and unusual arts programs in the world, housed in an old Catholic monastery in northern Britain. All my life, I've longed to be anywhere but Emerald Beach. All my memories of this place are shit – my dad dying, Walter Hart's court case, the years of bullying and torture at school, Alec LeMarque and what he did—

My whole plan was to finish school with the grades I needed to get the fuck out of this town. But now there's no way I can even think about leaving Claws. Not when our family is still in danger. Not with Mackenzie Malloy running amok. Not while strange men are breaking into my house and spraying blood and brain matter across my mom's vegan kitchen.

I don't see this turf war ending any time soon. Claws needs me. I've never been needed before.

But then I look up at Gabriel. Beneath the haze pooling in his dark eyes is the gleam of understanding. We've lived completely different lives he grew up in a *literal* castle with parents who made him hide who he was, while I'm the daughter of a vegan food truck owner and a B-movie director who always encouraged me to wear my weirdness on my sleeve. He's a multi-gazillionaire, and whatever money my father left us got spent fighting Walter Hart in court. He's a talented musician, and I made a podcast about my father's ashes. We're not the same, and yet... and *yet*.

We both know what it feels like to be trapped.

To be caged in on all sides with no way out.

That's why I love Gabe's music so much. He can capture with a haunting riff and a few lines of poetry what it feels like to be trapped inside a house that's on fire while the fire department has gone on strike. Claws says he can sing the stars, and she's right – when I listen to Octavia's Ruin, it's like I can suddenly see the sky through the bars of my cage, and they're the same stars Gabriel Fallen sees.

Gabe drowns himself in alcohol until he can't see the walls of his cage anymore, and I put my head down and study as if I might one day be able to *think* my way out. And maybe that's what he's offering me.

He grabs my shoulder and gestures shakily at the room – the cat castle, the rack of knives and swords set up against a target, Tiberius stalking in front of the French doors, his finger tapping the stock of his weapon. "This is Claudia's life now. She had the chance to walk away from the August family legacy, and now she's ruling it. The moment she made that choice, she changed the course of my entire life, all our lives. I may be useless dead weight to her, but I'll follow wherever she leads, even if that makes me no better than cannon fodder in a gang war."

"You shouldn't say that." Absinthe churns in my gut, and I know it's partly the fact I'm tipsy, and when I'm tipsy I'm always desperate to talk, but I *must* convince him of his importance. It feels somehow *essential*. "It's not as if you planned your life based on needing to be useful to a mafia queen. Claws chose you because she needs art and music and poetry to make sense of the bloodshed. What you do *is* important, and she would never want you to stop."

"I know," Gabriel says this with sadness, and I'm not so sure he does know. "I had my choice, too. I chose her. And I'll choose her a hundred more times. But you're different, George. You have more to do than cleaning up the trail of bodies left behind by a mafia queen. But if you keep getting your hands dirty, there will come a time when you can't wash the blood away. If you want to escape Emerald Beach and the Triumvirate, your window is closing fast."

I stare at the list of prerequisites for the scholarships. Candidates can't simply have perfect grades – they need to excel at extracurricular activities and show themselves to be outstanding leaders in the community. "I don't see how I could possibly qualify for this scholarship. I can't exactly put 'performs underground autopsies for criminal organization' under extracurricular activities."

"No, but you did make a world-famous podcast and put a con artist behind bars. You've already done so much in your life, George. Don't throw in your lot with us when you can do so much more." He nods. "Think about it."

Gabe snatches the absinthe bottle from my fingers and tips his head back, draining the final few dregs. I fold the brochure and shove it into my pocket, where it burns blue-hot against my skin.

3

____

NOAH

*I*n the basement, Eli yanks open a large storage cupboard. Random sporting equipment tumbles out. He ducks to avoid being decapitated by a set of skis, and drags out a large bag containing ropes and harnesses and other climbing equipment.

"I can't imagine any of the Malloys using this stuff," he muses as he digs through the bag.

"You ever used this type of gear yourself?" I peer at the bag with trepidation. Felix did a bit of climbing with his friends over the summers, and he'd always invite me to come along, but I preferred to spend my summers in the pool. I think about how I gave up swimming to switch to track because I wanted my father to look at me the way he looked at Felix, and my hands clench into fists and I want to smash that rogue ski through the big screen TV.

I wasted far too fucking long offering the best of myself to my father and it still not being good enough. And all that time, he was the one who destroyed our family. Every shitty thing that's happened to me is on his shoulders

I'm done.

I'm fucking *done*.

If I find out he's in any way connected to this attempt on Claudia's life, I'll squeeze the life from his body with my own hands.

"Nope, but it can't be that hard." Eli pulls out a tangle of rope. "We'll find a YouTube video. All we need is for one of us to climb up into that hole, then we can rig a permanent ladder or something, in case we need to get in there again in a hurry." He starts dragging the bag toward the stairs, his brow furrowed. He's in problem-solving, protector mode, which is a good thing because I'm in punching-holes-through-the-walls mode, which gets nothing productive done except better indoor-outdoor airflow. But I know Eli well enough to see that he uses it to hide from what he's truly feeling. And maybe I want to see Eli lose his fucking shit for once. Maybe I don't want to be alone.

"Eli."

He looks up. "Yeah?"

"You okay?"

Mackenzie fucking Malloy, the girl he's been crushing on since before we were friends, just broke in and shot someone dead under our fucking nose. Eli might not have seen Mackenzie in the dark, but she was literally breathing down his neck. That's gotta do a number on him.

I'm not exactly sunshine and roses myself. That bitch might not have had as much to do with Felix's death as I thought, but she's trying to kill Claudia. And I'm gotten too damn good at imagining what it will feel like to wrap my fingers around her scrawny neck and squeeze until she's no longer our problem.

I want to choke a lot of people. Every time I close my eyes, I see visions of violence etched on my eyeballs. I'm jittery, on the edge of fucking losing it.

I need to get back in the ring. It's been too long since I washed this poison from my veins.

Eli runs a finger through his hair. "She smells the same."

"Huh?"

"I thought it was a hallucination. You know, from the absinthe? Odette was rambling on about spirits and I could *smell* Mackenzie – violets and bubblegum – just the way she used to smell when we were kids." He shakes his head. "She was right *there*, in the room with us. We could have reached out and touched her."

Rage coils around my heart to think about it. "What I don't understand is how could she miss at such close range."

"I think George is right, that she mistook Odette for Claudia," Eli points out. "It was too dark to see faces or distinguish the dress colors. We got lucky, is all."

"We need to find her," I growl. "Emerald Beach is only big enough for one Malloy daughter, and I know damn well which one I want to triumph."

I don't add what we're both thinking. *If Mackenzie is this bold, this fucking unhinged to just walk into her sister's space and start shooting, then what will she try next when she finds out Claudia isn't dead?*

We leave too many things unsaid and get to work. Eli does indeed find a YouTube video, and in minutes he's got the harness on and is scrambling up the wall of the underground room, placing nuts and cams into the bedrock to build a safe route up to the tunnel entrance. He drags his arms over the lip and shines his headlamp inside.

"There are hooks up here – nice, solid steel ones," he calls down to me. "Mackenzie probably had a rope ladder she took with her. Throw me that rope."

I do it, and Eli loops the rope through the hooks. Now, it's easy for one of us to climb back up if we need to. I grab the rope and pull myself up behind Eli.

This tunnel is so low, we have to crawl on our hands and

knees. Damp clings to the rough bedrock walls. We follow the tunnel at an upward angle for quite a distance. It comes out in a hidden rock-shelf near the boundary of the Beaumont Hills cemetery. Eli and I duck around the crumbling graves of less-prosperous individuals as we clamber up the rocky cliff-face to the flatter ground.

At the top of the cliff, I lean against an obelisk and catch my breath. Here, the heart of the cemetery has been manicured within an inch of its life. It's crowded with elaborate-looking tombs and monuments that lord over the more modest memorials dotted further down the cliff toward the bay. Even in death, they command the premiere view of the emerald waters below. They're all treated equally by the elements, though – the elaborate carvings blasted flat by the ocean winds, the relentless salt spray obliterating names and dates. Discarded ribbons and flower petals scatter around my feet, torn from the hands of mourners before they can be placed on the ground.

Nothing lasts forever.

"Noah, look," Eli calls from further along a meandering path that leads to a jacaranda tree, bent and twisted by the ocean winds. Its lower branches sag under the weight of purple blooms that dangle like forlorn trumpets over a pair of crumbling tombstones.

Eli stares at the graves like he expects a zombie hand to shoot from the ground at any moment and drag him down into the depths of hell.

When I look at the graves, I don't understand what he's so freaked about. Maybe they're relatives of his. But Eli moved to Emerald Beach from Tennessee, and I didn't think he had family in the area...

"The names," Eli whispers.

I stare at the names on the graves. ARCHIBALD CLARENCE

and his wife GERALDINE CLARENCE. "Dude, what about them?"

"I remember the Clarence family," Eli says. "They were Dad's clients. Died in a boating accident. They had a Nautical-themed funeral – remember, from the reality TV show? Dad dressed up as a pirate... that was about four and a half years ago. The timing makes perfect sense. Their graves would have been freshly dug. I think we're standing on the spot where..."

He can't bring himself to finish the sentence.

The truth slams into me like a fist in the arena. Archibald and Geraldine – I don't know who they were, whether they were good people, whether they loved each other, but I want to dash their gravestones on the cliffs below and salt the earth where they lay.

This is the spot where Claudia was buried alive.

If we dug up these graves, we wouldn't just find the earthly remains of this deceased couple – we'll find an empty second coffin in one and, in the other, the remains of Julian August.

My blood boils with a rage so all-consuming it burns my soul clean. I am washed of my sins, born again baptized in bloodshed. Born again as her soldier, her knight in battle-scarred armor.

Claws could have been killed tonight, just as she was nearly snuffed out that night four years ago, the night that changed everything.

We weren't there to protect her then, but we're fucking here now.

Eli looks up at me, and his eyes are hard as stone. "At the prison, they said Brutus visited my father several times. Dad was terrified of Mackenzie, because he thought she was six feet under. Because he *helped put her there.* We *have* to find Mackenzie. We have to make sure no one ever gets the chance to hurt Claudia again."

"We'll do more than find her," I growl. "I'll pull every bone from her body out her asshole, one by one."

———

THE SUN RISES over the ocean by the time we crawl back into the tunnel – a flaming chariot fighting back the darkness, tearing the sky open to spill blood across the horizon. I find Claws in Howard's office, upending drawers and flinging papers into a messy pile on the floor. I run to her and wrap her in my arms, pulling her away from the bookshelves before she tips them over and buries herself under piles of her father's old junk.

"What are you doing?" I murmur into her hair, holding her so tight I know I'm cutting off oxygen. But I don't care. I need to feel her in my bones.

"I missed something. I know I did." Claws kicks a pile of books, then winces, rubbing her toe. "You blocked off the tunnel?"

"We followed it out to the cliffs at Beaumont Hills cemetery. We can't do much in the daytime, but we're heading back tonight with some quick-set concrete to finish the job," I say. "Tiberius is picking some up on the way back from his little chore."

"Good." Claudia clings to me like I'm the only thing keeping her upright. "That's good."

The sun's heat stretches through the open French door, lighting my skin, reminding me that I've burned up on the battlefield of my own rage. Two modest graves blot my vision, but what surges in my veins isn't rage – because the rage that's lived inside me since my brother's death is only destructive. It takes and takes and takes, eating me from the inside until I was nothing but an empty, bitter husk.

But seeing love and tragedy exist in harmony at those two

tombstones has burned away the rage. A couple who wanted to spend eternity together had their final resting place corrupted by a blood feud without end. The knowledge of it gives my rage form, substance, *life*.

What flows in my veins now is only *her*. Only love.

And I want to say this, but I'm no Gabriel Fallen. I'm no fucking poet. I don't have pretty words and sweet melodies to offer. There's only one way I know how to say what I need to say.

"Turn around," I growl.

"Noah, don't—"

"You need this. Don't deny it. Turn around. Hands on the desk."

Claudia bites her lip. But she knows I can read her like a book. Those ice-cold eyes alight with something feral – her own rage flickering to life at my command. She drops the papers in her hand with a flourish and spins away from me.

She plants her hands shoulder-width apart, her fingers curling around the edge of the desk. Her back curves as she peers back over her shoulder with a defiant glare, hair spilling over her shoulders in golden waves. She may do what I command, but I'll never have dominion over her.

I'd never even dream of wanting it.

I press my palm into the small of her back and bend her over the desk, dragging the slinky red dress up her thighs. The hem is streaked with Odette's blood. *My savage queen.* I almost lost her. This could've been her blood on my fingers right now, her blood staining the rug in the drawing room.

But she's alive. Because she's Claudia fucking August.

Alive, and *mine*. And I'm utterly hers.

Claudia trembles beneath my palm. She needs cock so bad right now. She's afraid for our family, and she's like me – she doesn't know what to do with fear except burn it all away. And nothing makes my Claws feel powerful and in control like riding me until neither of us can breathe.

I'm happy to oblige my queen.

I roll the dress over her hips, exposing the globes of her ass and that tiny bit of pink skin between her legs that glistens with her juices. She bites her lip, tilting her hips back to give me an even better view. My breath catches. My cock strains against my zipper.

Claudia August has never been more beautiful, more gloriously *alive*.

I drop my pants to my ankles and step out of them. The tip of my cock is already wet with pre-cum. I can hardly breathe for what I want to do to her when she's like this, ass in the air, submissive in pose, if not in nature. I run my fingers over her ass cheeks, sliding underneath the thong she's wearing, peeling it back and then snapping it taut, enjoying her yelp as the fabric teases her skin.

I lean down and kiss her exposed skin, drawing her into my mouth to bite her ass. Hard. Claudia yelps again, and I almost come right there.

"I could have lost you tonight," I murmur as I lean over her, bunching her dress up higher until it exposes her breasts. They topple from the dress, braless and perfect, the nipples hard and begging to be pinched. I cup her breast in my hand, circling her nipple with my finger before pinching it hard enough for her to grit her teeth. I rasp in her ear. "I hate losing."

"I know," she glares at me, her eyes the cold blue of the ocean at sunrise, when the brisk chill hits your skin just before you dive and discover how warm she is underneath. "You act like a real bitch about it."

The sound of her voice is heaven come to earth. *I nearly lost her. I nearly lost all of this, but I didn't. She's right here.*

Claudia August isn't like every other person I've loved. She's not going anywhere.

"I just know that's important in life. So I'm not going to lose again." I tug the dress over her shoulders and toss it at a bust of Caesar. The Roman emperor wobbles a little on his stand, but remains upright. I lean forward further, pushing Claudia into the desk, making her breasts splay out so I can play with her nipples. I roll the other one between my fingers as I reach between her legs with my other hand to cup her pussy. I love how wet she is. How needy. "Right now, you're mine, and I'm going to fuck you until you scream my name, until you tell the whole world who you belong to."

I snap her throng, tearing the flimsy material from her and tossing it into the mess. Claudia makes a beautiful little mewling sound as she grinds herself back into me. Her golden hair tickles her bare breasts as she tilts her head back, her mouth searching for mine.

I fuck her mouth with my tongue as I drag her thighs back, plunging inside her with one stroke. Her whole body bucks as I enter her, and I'm enveloped in her hot, slick folds. She melts into me, taking everything I have to give and throwing it back. My queen. My mirror. The only one who sees who I truly am, who will never dream of running, of turning away, of telling me I'm not good enough, because denying me means denying part of herself.

Fuck, she's amazing.

I plunge inside her, again and again and again until my balls are hot coals of need and every atom of me brims with her. Holy fuck. Every time inside her feels like the first time, like I've been waiting my whole life to feel Claws' walls clamp around me and her body melt into my touch.

I slam her into the desk. Pens and Post-it notes go flying. Caesar wobbles before crashing to the floor. Ceramic shards dig into my feet, but I can't stop, *will never stop* fucking Claudia August until she's been thoroughly worshipped and utterly undone.

"Noah," she cries out, her arms flailing, swiping Howard Malloy's designer pencil holder off the edge of the desk. A framed picture of a thoroughbred horse falls off the wall, glass shards twinkling in the shaft of sunlight. I reach around to rub Claudia's clit – not softly the way Eli would, but with all the power and fervor she deserves.

She comes apart in my arms, her whole body lifting off the table as she screams her way through an orgasm. Her pussy squeezes around me, milking my cock until my stomach leaps into my throat, until it's too fucking much and I fall over the edge with her.

Stars dance across my vision.

I think my cock might've exploded.

No, no. It's still here. Thank fuck for that.

Fuuuuuck.

We sink together onto the desk, our bodies no longer supporting our weight. My dick still shimmers with whatever sinister pussy magic she pulled on me. My balls have never felt this empty or my chest this full.

Claudia's the first to move, rolling away from me and grabbing for my boxer shorts. I expect her to toss them to me, but instead she pulls them on, yanking her dress down on top of them.

"Hey, those are mine."

"Yeah, and you don't need to get to the bathroom with someone's cum dripping out of you, so shut it. Stop tearing all my underwear, and maybe you'll get them back," she glares at me as she twirls around The boxers bunch up around her narrow thighs beneath the dress. It looks ridiculous, but I'm not about to point that out to my queen. She shuffles outside to use the bathroom down the hall. When she returns, I'm sitting in the middle of the floor, shuffling papers around my feet.

"I hope you're not touching any important documents with your bare ass," she says, flopping down beside me.

"Unlike Howard Malloy's finances, my ass is perfectly clean, thank you." I stare at the mess around our feet. "You're trying to figure out what his shipment could have been."

"Sort of. I keep coming back to my price," Claws says. "I *know* Julian. He may have lied his ass off about my true lineage, but in his personality – his *essence* – he was truthful about who he was and what he stood for. He was so against trading in skin, and yet he must've paid a hell of a price for Howard Malloy's child. I feel like that price is the key to the whole thing, and it's sitting right under my nose and I can't *see* it."

My father said Malloy came to him about an important shipment that disappeared from under his nose. Shortly after that, Malloy himself disappeared. We were positive this shipment was the treasure Julian August traded for my life thirteen years previously. What we didn't know was what the fuck that treasure could possibly be, or how Malloy managed to lose it at that precise moment.

"Hunting down Mackenzie is more important than this treasure," I growl, my fingers tightening around Claudia's arm as it all floods back to me, how close we came to losing her.

"They're the same thing. Mackenzie's after the treasure, too." Claudia looks up at me, her icicle eyes hard, crystalline. "I've been wrong about so many things. It wasn't Brutus who broke in. It was Mackenzie. She's an accomplished cheerleader – she can vault a fence without batting an eyelash. *And* I bet she was the one who shot at us by the front door."

That makes sense. Mackenzie has shown herself to be a reckless, lousy shot.

"She kept Brutus alive for days with that Grey Death," I say.

"She broke his legs. She *tortured* him. She probably thought he had the treasure, especially since he's the only other person alive who knows what Claudia August looks like. It would certainly explain how he managed to hold on to his empire."

"If that's true, the treasure is long gone. He'd have spent it, sold it off, traded it for drugs and whores like he did with every penny in my father's accounts. But something about this doesn't feel right – if Brutus captured a treasure he knew Julian traded for my life, why not use that story to bolster his claim? Why keep quiet about it? There's never been any talk in the underworld about the treasure during Brutus' reign, and things are still silent now. If Brutus had the treasure, he didn't spend it or tell anyone about it, and that makes me think he never had it at all." Claudia continues, "I can't stop wondering about that first break-in. Why did Mackenzie want to get in this house so bad?"

"Because she's fucked in the head. Because she wanted to frighten you. That shit gets Mackenzie Malloy wet. Ask George – she'd back me up."

Claudia flashes me a cruel, dazzling smile. "Those are my genes you're talking about."

"My comment still stands."

"Fine, fine." Claudia glances up at Howard's shelves, crowded with leatherbound volumes and artifacts. "But seriously, why did she come here? Was she trying to frighten me out of the house, stop me from finding the bodies? Why bother with all the pageantry, when she could have gone to the police or City Hall at any time and got my squatting ass kicked out? So why didn't she? Why did she wait and hide in Germany instead of claiming what's hers?"

"Because Brutus saw your face," I say. Claudia's nails dig into my arm. I know she doesn't want to think about that night, so I rush past it. "Not to get all Eli on you, but I think we can deduce from the fact she captured Brutus that Mackenzie knew at least a little about who you were and what her father had done. Mackenzie knew she wouldn't be safe while Brutus lived, in the same way Antony didn't want to risk you exposing yourself as Mackenzie Malloy until Brutus was dealt with. Maybe she wanted to start a new life, I don't know. But your face is her face, so you starting at Stonehurst Prep set this whole wild ride into motion."

"True. But if Mackenzie killed Brutus so no one could associate her face with Claudia August, why break into the manor?" She taps her chin. "I get killing me. It ties up loose ends. But the break-in doesn't make sense. What did she achieve by trashing my room and hurting Queen Boudica?"

"It's almost as if..." My mind whirs. It doesn't make sense and yet... "Howard's shipment disappears a few days before Mackenzie kills him. What if Mackenzie's after the shipment? What if she thinks it's in the house, or maybe that you have it?"

"I don't understand. Why would she think it's in the house if Howard lost it?"

"I don't know. Maybe she doesn't know he lost it." I stare at the pile of papers. "But today we have evidence that Malloy Manor holds all kinds of secrets. What if Howard Malloy built some secret compartment where he was hiding his shipment? Mackenzie might've seen him hide it there, watched him check on it over the years. Maybe it was a giant treasure vault he swam in, like Scrooge McDuck. So she thinks it's here, safely hidden away until she's ready to walk in and take it, but she also doesn't want to alert my father or Brutus to her existence, so she decides to wait until the situation is more stable. But then *you* start telling people you're Mackenzie Malloy, and she knows the truth. She knows you're living in her house, and she doesn't want you to get your hands on what's rightfully hers. So she breaks in to check her treasure is still intact."

Claudia's eyes twinkle like shattered glass. "Do you think she took it with her?"

I shrug. "It's possible, but no. If she has the treasure, what possible reason would she still have to be in Emerald Beach? Brutus is dead; she could pay for a new face, a new life." I stare down at the broken bust of Julius Caesar. A jagged crack runs along his aquiline nose. "If I'm right, Mackenzie Malloy believes Howard's treasure is in this house, and she's not going to stop until she takes back what's hers."

4

———

ELI

*T*iberius offers to drop me off at my job at Nero's club. I should have been suspicious when he mentions we need to make a stop first, but what can I say? I'm new to this whole running a criminal empire thing.

I should have protested when he heads along the highway out of town and turns off onto the dirt road leading to the Everlasting Hart Ranch. But there's only so much a scrawny, smartass runner like me can do against a three-hundred pound wall of muscle. What was I going to do? Knock him out with my witty repartee and take the wheel on a dangerous gravel road?

"What are we doing here?" I ask instead.

"I've got two shovels on the backseat and a body in the trunk. What do you think we're doing here?" Tiberius grins. "I thought you were the Sherlock Holmes of the group."

We pass the tattered sign, kicking up a cloud of dust that obscures the grand gates. I swallow. "I'm not sure how I feel about bodies buried all over my dad's ranch. Isn't that going to be easy to trace back to us?"

"Look at this place." Tiberius waves a hand at the crumbling house and broken fences. "It's a dump. No one's looking for bodies here. And besides, if they do, they won't be able to trace them back to Claws. It'll drop your pops deeper in the shit, though."

"His appeal is coming up, but there's no way they'll let him out early. Not after all the negative press about the case." I shrug, trying to appear as though I don't give a shit either way. But it's not true. I care about what happens to Dad, and I *hate* that I care.

On the one hand, I want my father to stay locked up. He did a horrible thing, and he should stop pretending he's the victim and accept justice for all the hurt he caused. And, selfishly, I want to get out from under the shadow of his legacy. I want to do my own thing, but I can only do that if Walter Hart is not actively in my life, trying to groom me as his successor and choose what's best for me.

But there's a part of me that feels the tug of loyalty. He's a piece of shit crook, but he's my dad. He's the one who stood on the sidelines of my track events, cheering the loudest of all the parents as I racked up the medals. He's the one who always pushed me to do well at school. He didn't just want me to take over the business, become the next Walter Hart. He wanted me to *surpass* him. I admired him for that, loved him even.

And now?

Now I have no fucking idea.

I turn to Tiberius. I've never talked to him much before – he's in the background, the friendly muscle who drives us around and shows up just when he's needed. But I know he has an Ivy education and Ms. Drysdale fell hard for him, which means there must be a soul beyond that scarred face. Maybe it's time I paid more attention. "How did you get tied up in this whole thing?"

"The same way anyone does," Tiberius shrugs, following the drive around to the outbuildings. "It's easy money."

"I don't buy that. You have a degree from an Ivy League college. You could have joined Wall Street or become a lawyer, made just as much money going legit. Why bury bodies in the desert and sit outside our house every night?"

"Wall Street brokers and lawyers are just as crooked. At least this way is honest." Tiberius drums his fingers against the wheel. "Open the glove compartment."

I pop the compartment. Inside is a handgun, and a faded photograph of a smiling girl taped to the lid.

"That's my Angel." Tiberius smiles down at the picture. "My little girl. She's twelve years old now and she's the light of my life. Angel's mother was hooked on Grey Death when she gave birth."

"Oh." I can't think of what else to say. I've read about what drugs like that can do to a fetus.

Tiberius nods. "She needs special schools, medical treatment to reset her bones, all kinds of equipment that doesn't come cheap. If you want to know why I do what I do, it's because I want to see her smile, give her everything. Just because the sun shines out your asshole, don't think for a second you're better than me. I may have killed a few evil men, but I've never given jars of cement to grieving families."

"You know about my dad?"

"You kidding? Your daddy's famous in Tartarus Oaks. Who do you think was selling on all those organs and body parts he stole?" He grins at me. "You're looking at one of his delivery boys."

I already knew my dad was a cog in Brutus' machine. That was why the FBI was involved in his case, and why they leaned on him so heavily. They saw Dad as a pin that, once jammed, could upset the entire mechanism. I think about that photograph George found – my dad and Brutus hanging out at Nero's club like they were the best of buds. Maybe Tiberius can fill me in on some of the details I don't know. "Brutus was visiting my dad in jail. Any idea why?"

"You really want the answer to that question?" Tiberius yanks the wheel hard around, pulling in behind the last of the outbuildings – the lean-to where we found Brutus trussed-up and waiting for us.

"I know my dad's a scumbag. I doubt anything you say will surprise me."

"You sure about that, kid?" Tiberius sighs. He tucks the gun into his belt and slams the glove compartment. "Your dad wanted in with the Augusts."

"More than he already was?"

"Sure. He wanted to be a proper partner in the business, not just an outsider making a little extra cash on the side. Walter Hart saw the money, the danger, the women, and he wanted it. His business was in peril, and he saw crime as a fast way to an easy fortune. Only problem was, Julian August had a standing business arrangement with Howard Malloy, and Malloy refused to work with Hart, which meant Hart would always be on the outside. And then Julian dies and Malloy disappears, and suddenly your father sees his chance. He was negotiating with Brutus when your friend blew the case open with her podcast. That's probably what they were talking about in jail – Brutus paying for Walter's appeal, maybe keeping his debtors at bay. At least until Claudia killed him. Which is too bad for your pops, because without Brutus' protection, there's too much of a risk he'll talk to the Feds."

I think of those two graves we saw at Beaumont Hills cemetery – the graves where Claudia and her father were buried. Anger blazes behind my eyes. "You're saying my dad's going to be killed?"

Titus shrugs. "Your dad knows where the bodies are buried. Which is probably why Nero has his eye on you. Keep your enemies close, your potential snitches even closer. Come on, let's get this over with."

I follow Tiberius around the car. He's parked up next to an old lime pit where we buried Brutus' remains. He pops the hood. We both pull on gloves. Tiberius cuts open Odette's stomach to speed up decomposition, and I help him throw her over the side and shovel lime, and then soil, on top of her body.

I guess I know where a few of the bodies are buried now, too.

Tiberius leans against the trunk of the car to admire our work. Somewhere in the distance, a coyote howls.

Even though I'm wearing a hoodie, I'm cold down to my bones. I don't think I'll ever be warm again.

"Plenty more space in this hole for Claws' enemies," Tiberius grins at me as he tugs off the gloves. We'll dispose of them back at the house.

My head buzzes as I climb back into the car beside him. He's right. Things have been so wild over the last few months that I keep thinking if we can just get to a safe place, this will all be over. But there will never be a place of safety. Claws runs a criminal empire. There will always be wolves at the door and bodies to dispose of.

I will do anything to keep Claudia safe, but the life I imagined for myself after high school – an Ivy League track team, the corner office, the wife, the two-point-five children – wobbles and fades, burning away in an inferno of vendettas and bloodshed.

"WHERE HAVE YOU BEEN?" Livvie demands as I trudge into the Vault offices. "I've been calling you for hours."

"Sorry. Something came up with—"

"He sold Casper. I thought you'd want to know." Her lower lip trembles.

I stop short, barely registering her words. I've never, *ever* seen Livvie lose her composure. But she loves the animals, especially Casper, the mischievous white tiger cub.

No. Nero can't sell Casper.

He can. He's Nero fucking Lucian and he brought and paid for every one of those beautiful, wretched animals. And I promised I'd help them, and I can't do shit to stop this.

My head spins. "I thought he was going to keep the cubs for entertaining his club guests?"

Livvie shakes her head. "Now that your Imperator is closing the skin business and disrupting his contracts, Dad needs cash more than he needs a bunch of animals to feed. He found a buyer – some rat-ass Arkansas hillbilly with a private zoo. He's going to take Casper and his brothers, feed them terrible food, make them pose with tourists ten fucking hours of the day, then kill them when they get too large to manage."

"Over my dead fucking body." I have to fix this. It's the most important thing in the world that I fix this. Everything in my life has spun completely out of control. I have Odette's dried blood under my fingernails. But if I can save these animals, there's still hope. "Is Nero in his office? I'll talk to him—"

"It's too late. The hillbilly is already on his way. He's going to take the monkeys, the bear, and some of the snakes, too." She hugs her snake Essie to her neck.

I make a split-second decision – I know it's a terrible decision even as I'm making it, but it's also the only possible answer. "That's not happening. We're getting them out of here. All of them."

Livvie's head snaps up. Her eyes are rimmed in red, her mascara streaming down her cheeks. "Don't be ridiculous. This isn't as simple as rehoming a cat. They require proper facilities, a budget for food, specialist veterinary care. There's no one in this state who will be able to take these animals that I'd consider selling them to. And Nero will never consider a shelter—"

My mind whirs. There is a way to solve this. It's going to bring a mountain of trouble down on my head, but what else is new? "I have an idea."

I get on the phone to Claws. She sounds groggy, and I know I've woken her up. At least she's in bed, not pacing in her office or out trying to hunt down Mackenzie on her own. I hear Gabriel's voice in the background. I feel a rush of gratitude. It's weird – I never thought I'd want to share a girl with a couple of other dudes, but just knowing someone's always able to be with Claudia gives me the breathing space to leave her side and do other shit... like completely fuck up her life, as I'm about to do.

"Eli, what is it?" She sounds breathless. "Did Nero do something?"

In a breathless rush, I explain what's happening to the animals and what I want to do. She sighs. "You know this is going to bring a mountain of shit down on my head that we don't need right now?"

"I know."

But she doesn't say no. Because she's like me – she knows that humans are scum but these animals are innocent, and she won't let them become some attractions in a roadside zoo or playthings for a rich asshole. She listens as I outline the plan, and as I hang up I can hear her scrambling out of bed and barking orders.

"Well?" Livvie shakes my shoulders. "What did she say?"

"She'll do it. She's pulling her dockworkers in to help. We just need to talk to Nero."

Her jaw tightens. "He'll never go for it."

"We need to find the right angle. Don't pitch it as bad news. Nero doesn't care about these animals. To him, they're assets to be brought and sold. He's still getting exactly what he wanted.

We don't want him to look too closely at the deal – we just need him to get the hillbilly to back off. Do you want me to do it?"

Livvie tears a tissue from her desk and starts blotting at her makeup. That familiar fiery determination lights up her eyes. "No offense, Captain America, but you are dating Nero's fiancee, who's currently in the midst of fucking up yet another one of his business lines. He's gonna suspect an ulterior motive. I think I know how to play my daddy."

It's the middle of the day, so there's hardly anyone in the Vault – a couple of cleaners working their way through the private rooms, two of Nero's staff in offices upstairs, and Nero himself. The guy doesn't seem to sleep. He's always annoyingly around, hovering over my life with that cheery, sadistic smile of his.

Livvie knocks on his office door. "Father, it's me. Are you available for a talk?"

"Come in," Nero's voice booms. Livvie flashes me a thumbs up and swings the door open. We step into his office, which is no less intimidating with daylight streaming through the windows. I hang back by the door as Livvie approaches the desk.

"Olivia, Eli, what can I do for you?" Nero's features break out into his wide smile as he meets my eyes. That smile is so fucking unnerving. I feel like he can see through me, right into the deepest recesses of my heart, and what he sees there makes him want to burst out laughing.

Livvie stands straight and tall. "Father, I wanted to keep you apprised of the situation with the animals."

Nero lifts an eyebrow. "I wasn't aware there was a situation. My buyer is on his way now."

"The lion has caught a parasite, probably from one of the scumbags he ate at Colosseum. You never know what those lowlifes have in their systems when they enter the ring. Anyway, this parasite has spread through the entire basement – every animal has it, even Casp— even the white tiger. The vet informs me it won't jump to humans, but the infected animals must be euthanized. It's no problem—" she holds up her hand as Nero rises from his chair, a touch of color flaring in his cheeks. "—I've sold them to a collector for taxidermy. He's offered the same amount of money as your buyer. I know he'll be disappointed but—"

"That's fine. We must all learn to live with disappointment in business. Excellent work, Livvie. Eli." Nero steeples his fingers. "This solution has your name all over it – neat, precise, imaginative. You know, once I marry your girlfriend, you may wish to have a family of your own. And I have a daughter who will need a husband."

Livvie glares at me, her eyes begging me not to bite. I force a smile, hiding my hands behind my back so Nero can't see my fists burning to make contact with his face. "I'd definitely consider it."

"It's a pity Olivia was born with tits and that ass," Nero muses, sinking back down into his chair and reaching for one of his always-on-hand cigars. He addresses me, as if his daughter isn't even in the room. "She's by far the most brilliant of my children. She has a real head for the business. If she had a dick I might've made her my successor. But that's a decision for another day. I have plenty of life in me yet."

He dismisses us with a wave.

Outside in the hallway, I fume on Livvie's behalf, but she brushes it off. "That's not important now. All I want is to get the animals to safety."

"Who is Nero's successor?" I ask as we descend to the basement to start preparing them for transport.

She shrugs. "I don't know. He hasn't made an official announcement. I assume my older brother, Cassius. He's the cleverest of the lot, which isn't saying much considering he's a few feathers short of the whole duck."

I laugh at her description. "How many kids does Nero have?"

"Fourteen, by last count. Eight of us between his two wives, the rest illegitimate. It's part of Nero's image – he's the father figure, the head of the largest dynasty, the family man looking out for everyone in Tartarus Oaks. We all have our roles to play." She smiles, but there's a bitterness behind it. "Apparently my role is to marry you and cement the ties between our Imperators."

"It's not going to happen."

"Of course it's going to happen. Your woman may have temporarily waylaid Nero's grab for her empire, but she's no match for the power of Lucian, especially not with Constantine agreeing to this double marriage."

Livvie clearly doesn't know about the secret meeting Claudia had with Constantine. He could be a more powerful ally than we give him credit for.

"Seriously, Golden Boy, I'm fine. I don't give a shit about my father's empire. Now, stop looking at me like I'm a problem to solve." Livvie throws open the basement doors. When he sees us, Casper mews and scratches at his cage, eager to get out and play. Livvie strides past him, dangling the key to the veterinary room, a savage glint in her eyes. "We've got a lot of animals to move."

5

———

CLAUDIA

For the first time since I've lived at Malloy Manor, I throw the gates open wide.

I've dreamed about the day I might be able to come out of hiding. Things haven't worked out the way Antony and I planned – instead of claiming ownership of the house, selling it for a fortune, and living out our days in opulent obscurity, I've rebuilt Malloy Manor into my own private fortress, protecting my family from the cutthroat world of the Triumvirate.

And now, my family includes several mistreated and dangerous animals.

Fuck my life.

The first truck's tires squeal in protest as it rounds the sharp corner into the driveway. One of its huge wheels goes up on the garden and flattens an ugly succulent, which honestly I'm not sad about. I wave to the driver – my man Po – as he backs right up to the front door. Eli jumps out of the cab, waving at Po to start unloading.

Eli rushes over and wraps his arms around me. "Thank you, thank you. You don't know what this means."

"Yeah, yeah." I scowl, but secretly, I'm a little giddy with love for him right now. What we're doing is fucking *insane*, but it's also so completely *Eli*. He's always had to be the protector, to stand up for what's right, especially for those who can't stand up for themselves. And I know a lot of what he feels for these animals is about his guilt over everything he *hasn't* been able to protect me from, including Mackenzie entering our home.

I'll be damned if I don't love his gorgeous, do-gooder ass.

"They are your responsibility." I give him my best Ice Queen glare. "I need you to call every animal rescue and wildlife reserve in the country and get them out of here as soon as possible before the neighbors complain and the police or animal rescue get on my ass."

Eli plasters my cheeks with kisses, then rushes off to help move the monkeys.

Animals screech and howl as Po and his team unload their crates. They must be waking up from the sedatives Livvie administered. A second truck arrives and waits on the street until the first is cleared. The scent of shit and rotting meat wafts over the neighborhood as cage after cage is lifted into my house. My neck scratches with nerves standing out in the open like this, in the exact spot where Mackenzie shot at me and Noah. There's nothing I can do to help, so I wander back inside.

Bad idea. Malloy Manor is a disaster zone. There are terrariums stacked in the lobby, piles of shit on the hallway rug where the cages were tilted around the corner, and the whole place stinks like a zoo. Which I guess it is now. We have turtles in the downstairs bathroom, a lion in the swimming pool, and monkeys swinging around the basement gym.

"You sure he can't jump out of there?" I ask Eli as the lion paces around the bottom of the empty pool, his mane matted with dried blood. I hated looking at him dragging his feet down there – he should be lording it over his pride and living out his old age in dignity, instead of pawing at a half-deflated pink flamingo pool toy.

"It's deeper than the arena, and I've never seen him jump this high," Eli says. "But we're building a wire cage over the top, just in case."

I want to say that I'm not sure this is much better than living in Nero's basement, but that's unfair. Their stay at Malloy Manor will be temporary – as soon as we find them homes at properly-resourced animal sanctuaries, these animals will be on their way to living their best lives.

But the noise...

Roars and scritches and warbles and shrieks echo through the house. The walls tremble every time the lion opens his mouth. I lay a hand across my throbbing temples as I follow Eli back inside. How is a crime lord supposed to think? I retreat inside to my ballroom, but even my most private sanctuary isn't free of interlopers. Queen Boudica glares at Casper from the top of her tower as Eli sets up a run for the white tiger outside the ballroom window. Her tail bristles. I collect her into my arms and bury my face in her fur.

"I'm sorry, girl," I whisper. "I don't like change, either. But this is the right thing to do."

Queen Boudica hisses at Casper. She disagrees.

I take Queen Boudica into the kitchen and open a can of tuna for her. I call Gizmo, but she doesn't appear. She's probably hiding from the chaos. Smart cat. I stroke Queen Boudica's fur and watch as the second truck pulls up the drive. A girl slides out of the passenger side of the cab, looking fierce in designer overalls, stiletto heels, and wavy hair that must've taken hours in a salon to perfect. A large python coils around her shoulders, its head resting on her breast. It looks asleep, but I know better than to underestimate it.

This must be Livvie Lucian.

I lock Queen Boudica in the kitchen so she doesn't decide to play bat-the-string with the python's tail, and open the French doors for Livvie. She steps inside, extending a hand to me. The snake lifts its head, flicking a forked tongue as it regards me with cool indifference.

At least, I *hope* that's indifference.

"We meet at last." I shake Livvie's hand, squeezing a little tighter than I normally would. She doesn't bat an eyelash as I crush her tiny, perfect fingers.

"Thank you for doing this." She strokes the snake's head. "I don't say this lightly, because I know what it means in our world. But I owe you a favor."

I nod. "You do. And I'd like to cash in as soon as possible. Would you care to step into my office? It's far away from this madness."

"Lead the way."

I show Livvie into Howard's office and motion for her to sit. She steps gingerly around the pile of broken drawers and torn file folders. The snake raises its head and surveys the room with a lazy reptilian glare, then settles back down on her breast.

"I'll get right to business. Your father expects me to marry the two Imperators at Lupercalia." I sit on the edge of the desk, right in the spot where Noah fucked me last night. I shove my hands under my ass so Livvie can't see them trembling. I pretend I can still feel the warmth of Noah's body rising through the wood. That knowledge gives me strength. I try not to watch the snake as I continue. "Marriage to two men won't be legal, but that doesn't matter if it's done in front of our people. Nero designed this move to cripple my family, to make me subservient to the other two Imperators. Obviously, I don't want to go through with it. I'm looking for leverage. Or a loophole. Something I can use to get out of the bargain I made. If you've got something, I'll consider us even."

"That's a big favor to ask of Nero's daughter." Livvie rubs the snake under its chin, like it's a fucking cat. "What makes you think I'd be willing to help you pull one over on my father?"

I smile. "A white tiger is crapping in my ballroom."

A cruel silence falls over the room. My implication is clear. Either she helps me, or I'm under no obligation to keep these animals safe. I'd never actually do anything to hurt them, but Livvie doesn't know that.

Eli may be the bleeding heart, but I have to be all business.

"That's fair." Livvie crosses and uncrosses her long, shapely legs. She gives nothing away in her face, but I sense she's having an internal debate with herself about something. I wonder if I've overplayed my hand. Can she somehow read that I'm not simply interested in avoiding Nero's marriage? Does she sense that I want to take him out? That I plan to make his empire mine?

"I'm not asking you to hold a gun to his head. You'll have deniability. I think you know what I'm up against as the only woman at the table – all I need is something to even the playing field."

Livvie leans forward. "Okay, I have something. It's not a secret about Nero, but it's something I've been saving for a rainy day. I'll give it to you, but I want something more in return."

6

———

CLAUDIA

*C*leo doesn't show up at school.

It's probably for the best, because after we finished dealing with her, I snapped a couple of pics, which I've circulated to my soldiers. The spoiled social media influencer wearing my *sacer* has quickly spread through the underground. Cleo's helping my street cred – if people know I'm willing to condemn someone that famous and well-connected, they won't want to cross me. And it helps breed loyalty – whoever eventually kills her will earn major respect from me.

If Cleo shows her face in the wrong part of Emerald Beach again, she's a dead woman walking.

So I'm surprised when George hands me her phone in History class, a concerned look on her face. The screen shows a photograph posted to Cleo's social media. Our favorite spoiled princess has her forehead covered with a baseball cap so no one can see my mark. She wears a trendy cropped hoodie and leans against a crumbling stone wall. A very *familiar* crumbling stone wall, complete with battlements and Romanesque folly peeking through the trees beyond.

She's returned to Blackwich Castle.

The caption reads:

Whatup, bitches. School is for pussies, and this cat is free of that shit and ready to roam. Who needs a degree when you have a million followers? I'm staying with a friend while I figure out the next steps for my career. Like the view? Watch this space.

Irrational anger bubbles up inside me. Is this bitch for real?

This is the duke's doing, I'm sure of it. Gabriel's dad has the fucking *audacity* to toss him out without a penny, to break up Gabe's band and break his heart by having Cleo *murder* Dylan, and then to demand he marry that she-devil so he can have his heir, and all this time he was running the Grey Death trade through Emerald Beach?

And now he's got the nerve to keep that rat safe from my wrath? *And* she's on social media, posting about moving to England and living in a palace, as if her life is just peachy. I bet he'll get her in for surgery, too, to erase my mark. Make her good as new again.

Nope. Not happening.

I glare at the picture, trying to focus my rage into a solid plan of action. *What would Julian August do?*

It's simple, really. Julian August would clean house.

And that's exactly what I intend to do.

7

GABRIEL

"I need you to set up a meeting with your father," Claws says.

She lies across the bed in my room at Malloy Manor, watching as I strum my guitar and sing under my breath. I've been working on a song for her, fine-tuning the lyrics, getting it to where I know it has an emotional punch. If Noah Marlowe hears this song and weeps like a baby, I'll know I've done my job.

Holding the guitar in my hands feels strange – it's been so long now that I'm a little afraid of it, of the power it has to coax hidden things from inside me. But in many ways, it's like the music never left me. This song falls from my fingers and my lips like it always existed, like I'm simply plucking the lyrics from the universe and giving them form and substance.

But a song is a fragile thing. One mention of my father and it's gone, snuffed from existence like he's choked it out with his cruelty. Reluctantly, I set down the guitar and meet Claudia's icicle gaze. "Why?"

"Because we need to have a little chat about Grey Death." Claws flips her golden hair over her shoulder, her eyes boring into me.

Yeah. Fair enough.

I knew this was coming. I thought that if I distracted myself with Claudia's birthday, I could escape the truth. But I should know by now that I can't outrun my legacy. I may have taken the name Gabriel Fallen, but my father's blood still flows in my veins.

No matter how many times I go over what Cleo told us, I can't reconcile my dad the stodgy duke who disowned me for bringing shame upon the family as the kingpin of the growing Grey Death epidemic.

And maybe a bit of George's and Eli's Sherlock Holmesing has rubbed off on me, but I can't help being curious about how he ended up on this path. When did he go from the glory of the empire to hawking A-class drugs? But I also know all too well that where Grey Death is, *real* death soon follows, and I don't want Claws anywhere near him.

"I'll talk to him for you," I say.

She shakes her head. "This has to come from me. The Triumvirate has never included a woman before, and old school assholes like your dad will want it to stay that way. He can't believe for even a moment that I'm not in complete control."

"I can ask for a meeting, but I can't guarantee he'll speak to me."

Her eyes flash, and her mouth turns up at the corners with that dazzling half-smile she gets when she has a plan brewing. "He will if you tell him you agree to have his heir."

I drop the guitar on my foot. The pain doesn't even register as my heart leaps out of my chest. "You're pregnant?"

Holy shit. Holy shit.

Claudia's going to have a baby. We'll be a proper family and...

Is it mine? Please let it be mine—

"Why are you looking at me like that?" She pats her smooth

stomach. "Of course I'm not. We've all been careful. But I'm not above using my womb to get what we want. After all, that's what Nero's trying to do. You tell your father that we will get married and give birth to a Blackwich child. That'll get his attention now that he knows who I am, and then I'll hit him with my real reason for calling."

"That's fine but..." I touch her hair. "Can we make a baby? For real?"

She purses her lips. "Gabe..."

I push her back into the bed, cradling her in my arms and pulling her lips to mine. Everything about this woman is perfection – her bangin' body, her clever mind, her big heart, her delectable lips that yield for me as I kiss and caress. My cock strains against my jeans, and a giant fluttering bird tries to burst out of my chest as I speak my wish against her lips. "I want a baby with you."

Claw's hands close around my shoulders. I think she's pulling me closer, but instead she wriggles away and leans back on her elbows. She bites her lower lip, and I get the feeling she's choosing her words carefully. "Gabe, where's this coming from?"

"From me, the magnificent creature prostrated before you, who wants to give you beautiful babies." I wiggle my hips so she can feel how ready my cock is to take up the challenge.

For a moment, she falters. Her eyes cloud with lust, and her hips rock up to grind against me. I take that as my cue and reach down to push up her skirt, but Claudia circles my wrist in an iron grip and clamps my hand to the bed. "We're *eighteen*. We're so young. Do you really want to bring a child into the chaos that is our life? Not to mention the fact that you're in no position to be a stable father."

I jerk back, the fire in my veins stilled to ice. "What's that supposed to mean?"

I wince at the harshness of my words. But I won't take them

back. I'm shaking, knocked off balance. If I open my mouth to speak, I will scream.

She doesn't think I'll make a good father.

Claudia's face crumbles. She can see she hurt me. "Gabe, that's not what I meant."

"It is." Of course I won't be a good father. Look at the shining example I grew up with. Look at the brilliant mess I've made of my privileged start in life. I've had everything handed to me – all the things other people had to work and slave and kill for, and I still can't get my shit together.

Claudia has fought for everything she has. She's lived and died a hundred times, and she's only eighteen. And she's never – not for a single moment – let her pain and her rage break her. But I, I am utterly broken. I will always be a screw-up, an embarrassment, a liability. What was I thinking? I can't have a child. I'm like a child myself, a burden to everyone I love.

I'm supposed to stay sober for her, and I've already had two drinks this morning, and if I don't get to kneel between her legs and worship her soon, I'll need another.

"You look heartbroken." Claws strokes my cheek. "I didn't mean the way that came out. You just surprised me, is all. I didn't know you wanted kids. After your father, I didn't think... but of course you want kids. You have such a big, open heart. You'll be an amazing dad. I'm not saying *no*. I'm saying, not right now. I need to stabilize our empire first before I can even think about an heir. And you need to get your shit sorted out. You know that. Show me the brilliant, beautiful Gabriel Fallen underneath all the booze, and then we'll talk about babies. Got it?"

Her words *cut*. They slice and tear at the bullshit stories I've been telling myself, leaving a gaping hole in my heart through which Dylan's scathing words escape. I swallow down the emotions welling up inside me. She's right. Of course she's right.

She's Claudia. My Claws. She's the only person who's ever seen me.

What she's asking is next to impossible. Because the truth is, in all the drink and partying, the schemes I've fucked up, and the songs that no longer have meaning, I haven't seen the real Gabriel since Dylan was alive. I'm not sure he's worth digging through the bullshit to find.

I'm not sure the real Gabriel Fallen is worthy of Claudia's love.

I'm terrified to lay myself bare, to open my despair so she can flay my insides with her icicle eyes.

But I have to try.

Because she's worth it.

"I'll set up a call," I promise. Claudia smiles. She tries to wriggle out from beneath me, but I crawl back on top of her, clinging to her with a desperate ache that burns in my chest. I'm too afraid that if I let her go now, she'll float away, so high above me that I'll never be able to reach her from down here in the mud. I press my lips to hers. "Later. Right now, I have other duties to perform for my queen."

I expect her to protest, but I fail to remember the impact I have on her. Claudia is so strong-willed that it's easy to forget the woman who carved a bloody path to the top of the August empire and the one who comes undone for me between the sheets are one and the same. I can't believe how lucky I am to see this side of her – the quiver in her lips as she meets my kiss, the way her eyes cloud over as she sinks into the moment, the rise and fall of her breath in her chest as I kiss away her troubles.

Claudia fists my collar and drags me down into the pillows. Her schoolbooks topple over the side of the bed. I straddle her, pushing her top up to reveal her tits. Fuck, she's so fine. I've seen a lot of tits on tour – half the time girls have their tops off before we even get backstage. I've become blasé about tits – they are the bouncy, fleshy wallpaper of my life – but then I pushed Claudia into the pool at that party and... fuck me sideways, her tits are magnificent. Because they're hers.

I bend and suckle one of her nipples, rolling my tongue until she cries out. She wraps her arms around my neck, dragging me closer. There are bruises around her waist where fingers have dug into her flesh. I'd be worried if I didn't know they belonged to Noah. That boy wouldn't know gentle if it smacked him across the face.

Those two don't do tender. They fuck like animals, all scratching and biting and gnashing of teeth. But I get the Claudia who needs to be overwhelmed with her feelings, the Claudia who *surrenders*. And I've never seen her more beautiful or more powerful than when she arches her back and surrenders to me.

"Gabe," she cries as I move to the other nipple. It hardens in my mouth, and I nip and tease and suck, relishing the taste of her sensitive skin, my eyes locked on hers as she sinks into me, as I pull her under, as she relinquishes her fight.

I wrap my hands around her thighs, pushing her legs apart as I sink back to lie between them. I slowly flick my tongue across her clit, lapping and tasting her until she curses my name. Until her back begins to arch and her eyes roll back in her head.

Touching Claudia is like playing music. I coax melody and heart and emotion from every caress. I know what she needs, and I play her until the music hums inside her, until she sees the stars shatter across her eyelids.

When she's recovered enough to move, she tugs my belt, her touch demanding. But even though my dick is so hard and my balls are squeezed in a vise, I slide off the end of the bed. "I can't put my dick inside you. Not until I've made things right. Otherwise, it's too easy to convince myself that everything is okay."

"You're fucking serious, Fallen?" she cries. "I want you to give up drinking, not become a monk."

"I know, but this is the way it has to be." I shrug, even though all I want to do is fall to my knees for her and make her feel so good again. "I need added incentive, and if thinking about sliding into your warm pussy won't keep me from the bottle, nothing will."

"But where does that leave me, you selfish prick?" She throws a pillow at me.

I nod sadly. "I'm sorry. I'll send Eli in. He'll be happy to oblige."

I turn. I leave the room on shaking legs. She screams at me to come back, demands that I fuck her, and even though every fiber of my being longs to run back to her, to sheath myself inside her and forget the world for a moment, I won't be weak.

I'll earn the right to be in my queen's bed.

The next time we fuck, it'll be to make our baby.

8

CLAUDIA

*M*alloy Manor is being torn apart from the inside.

The monkeys escaped and broke several expensive, ugly statues, shat in a wall sconce, and chewed through the wires in the media room, nearly causing a house fire. Casper refuses to stay in his run, and only stops crying when Eli brings him into the ballroom so he can chase Queen Boudica's toys. And the turtles chewed off one of the taps in the bathroom and now half the downstairs is flooded.

And that's just the animals. The humans aren't doing much better. George is obsessively poring over Howard's documents, convinced she can figure out what the treasure is and where we can find it. Eli's moping about his father's involvement in burying me alive, Noah's raging because we still haven't ferreted out Mackenzie's hiding place, and Gabriel's refusing to fuck me out of some twisted need to prove himself. It's enough to drive a crime lord to the bottle.

When I brave the ballroom to drown my stress in top-shelf Scotch, I discover the worst possible disaster has befallen us – the alcohol supply has run out.

This is all a metaphor for my fucked-up life.

I think Gabriel's been drinking in secret, which is fucking concerning, not least because I've just mixed vodka and ouzo together since that's all he left me. The boys are out – Noah training with Antony for the upcoming Lupercalia fight, Eli at Nero's, and Gabe to talk to the police about Odette, who's just been reported missing by her family. Going to the store on my own is a giant hassle since Tiberius insists on shadowing my every move. And did I mention the zoo in my house? I need the sweet sweet release of liquor or I won't get any shit done tonight, and my disgusting vodka/ouzo shot isn't going to cut it.

There has to be alcohol in this house.

Gabe and I have already stripped bare the cellar and bar in the basement. But I definitely remember a few cases of wine stacked in that weird eyrie in the master suite. I moved some bottles there in case I needed projectiles to hurl at the barbarians storming the walls. But now I need sustenance more.

I climb up to the master suite and slide the door shut behind me. It's blissfully quiet in here, away from the squawks and howls and chirps and the endless parade of shit that needs to be dealt with. I flick the light switch, but nothing happens. *That's right, I turned off the circuit breakers for the master wing to save on the electricity bill.*

I click on my phone's flashlight and move through the enormous room. My gaze falls on the four-poster bed covered in a thin layer of dust, perfectly made up like its last occupants will return at any moment.

The last people who lay on that bed were my parents. My *real* parents.

And now they're dead.

I wish I could go back to seeing Howard and Ainsley as the evil rich strangers who built this freakshow of a house and have no impact on my life beyond their taste in stuffy designer furniture and weird modern sculptures.

But I can't go back. Because they are my parents. *Were* my parents. They made me, birthed me, and sold me to the highest bidder. Was it a complete fluke that I ended up with the Augusts? Was I just the first baby they grabbed out of the crib? How easily could Mackenzie's life have been my life, and hers mine?

What would I have done in her shoes?

I rub my eyes, but I can't stop those open coffins from searing across the inside of my skull. My parents and their horrific injuries, inflicted by someone whose heart has been burned up by hatred. Could that have been me?

I think about Brutus, about the locked box bobbing around in the ocean of my memories. Yes, it could have been me. I might not want my sister to win this particular battle, but I understand her need to fight it.

When the Malloys built this house, did they have any idea it would become their tomb?

Could it become mine?

Gabe wants to have a child. I know not to take half of what Gabe says seriously. But he looked so earnest and excited, and then so hurt when I turned him down. But... a *baby*. I can't be a fucking mother. I don't exactly have shining fucking examples of great parents. None of us do. How could I bring a new life into this mess? What legacy would I be giving a child?

I'd fuck it up. All I can offer a kid is a baptism in blood and fire and a lifetime of looking over their shoulder. My love gets people killed, or fucks up their lives. Just look at Gabriel, drowning himself in alcohol. Look at Noah, hardened to cruelty, ready to throw his lot in with my nefarious schemes. Or Eli, the Golden Boy of Stonehurst Prep working for a crime lord instead of preparing for college.

For all I tried to find a light at the end of the tunnel, I know that light is a freight train bearing down on us. We have no options. Our futures are bathed in blood.

In the end, if my child wanted to be free, they would have no choice but to beat me to a pulp and leave me to rot in an underground cave.

I shine the flashlight around the room. I've never taken the time to look around in here before – just gone straight to the eyrie or Ainsley's closet. But now, in their most intimate sanctuary, I hunt for a sense of who they were. I already know more than I ever need about Howard Malloy from Mackenzie's diary. I mean, that girl is stone-cold crazy, but she wasn't born that way – she was *made*. And maybe I – the adopted daughter of a crime lord – shouldn't cast aspersions.

But Ainsley is a mystery to me. Apart from her immaculate closet, which I've raided more than a few times over the years, I know nothing about her. What kind of a mother was she?

What kind of a mother would I be?

I walk over to the vanity, running my hand across the marble top until five streaks appear in the dust.

Is this where Ainsley sat the night before her wedding to Howard? What did she think about when she held that white dress against her body? Was she a pawn in rich men's games?

Just like me.

With a roar, I swipe the dusty tubes of lipstick and crystal vials onto the floor. Several smash, spreading broken shards and colored dust across the pristine rug.

I won't be their pawn.

I won't play the role I've been cast.

I'll burn the whole fucking game to the ground.

I can't stand to be in the room a moment longer. Not without my liquid courage. I reach the narrow staircase and scramble up into the eyrie. It's dark inside, the only light from the pale moon and the smudge of city lights glowing an unnatural green against the churning ocean beyond. The wraparound window looks straight down the ridge of the hill, out to the end of the bay and the Beaumont Hills Cemetery that guards it. The dead farewell their spirits as they glide over the water.

I swallow once, twice, three times. I taste the grit of my grave dirt.

Is the fact Howard Malloy's tunnel emerges into the very cemetery where I was buried alive, where my father still remains buried, a coincidence? Or does it have a deeper meaning? This thread connects my two fathers – the man who purchased me, who raised me, and the man who sold me, who gifted me his cruelty.

I stand with my toes pressed up against the glass, staring down at the hideous succulent garden so I don't have to look at the cemetery. I let vertigo wrap its trembling wings around my body and draw me close. My arms spread wide, and I imagine falling through the window and taking flight, soaring over the city and far far away from my murderous sister and my boyfriend who wants to have a baby.

I remember the night I came up here and talked to Eli while he sat on the wall, back when he thought I was Mackenzie. A sob claws its way up my esophagus and trembles from my lips.

I wish Eli was here right now.

I wish they were all here.

My boys. My princes. My loves.

I wish they could hold me and tell me everything would be okay. I wish they could push back the night and sing the stars into existence again, because everything I see is black and cold and absolute.

But the path I've chosen is a lonely one. My father taught me that. Even with great love at your side, you still had to walk alone.

So morose. What did I come here for? That's right, alcohol.

I grab a few bottles from an open crate and stack them under my arms, then scramble back down the stairs and head for the door. *Once more into the chaos—*

Wait a second...

The drawers in Ainsley Malloy's bedside cabinet are hanging open.

I didn't leave those drawers open. I've never even approached that side of the bed – not tonight, nor any other night. I hardly ever go into this room, and when I do, I don't hang around their bed. Gross.

Except for tonight, where I sat at the vanity, I always go straight for Ainsley's closet or the eyrie.

So who the fuck opened those drawers?

It's possible one of the others was snooping around up here and left them open. Eli does love to learn secrets, and George is too curious for her own good. But... I just didn't believe it. No one in this house would come up here without telling me.

I swallow down the panic that swells in my chest as another memory assails me. My beautiful, brave kitty with a slash in her side. GO AWAY written on the wall in her blood. Mackenzie's old bedroom trashed. Statues broken, dolls with their heads staved in.

Did I check this room after the break-in? Were the drawers open then?

Was Mackenzie in here, looking for something?

I yank out the drawer and slide my hand around inside. It contains a jumble of items – discarded jewelry, pill packets, more makeup and hair curlers, spare watch straps, mobile phone chargers. Flowery notecards with phone numbers and notes from friends. Nothing that would tell me what the intruder might've been looking for or what they might've taken.

And I wonder...

I pull back the covers on the bed, trying not to think about what Howard and Ainsley might've done on those sheets. I slide my hand behind the headboard, feeling the velvet for discrepancies. I find a hard lump in the far corner. I slide my knife from my wrist. *Gotcha.*

I cut open the material and pull out a slim, leatherbound journal.

A hidden diary.

Like mother, like daughter.

The diary feels like lead in my hands. I know I've found another of Malloy Manor's secrets. I prop my phone on the bed to give me enough light, open the book, and start reading.

It's... a lot. Ainsley Malloy is the epitome of a vapid, rich housewife. In the childish scrawl of a woman whose sum total of handwritten discourse was signing her prenup, she details page after page of petty drama – which friend's husband is sleeping with a new mistress, some nonsense about their holiday bookings being canceled, and how she got the manager at the golf club fired after he brought her a vodka martini instead of gin. And then, a gap of three months, and...

She announces she's pregnant.

With twins.

I clutch my fingers to my smooth, flat stomach as I scan the entries. Ainsley Malloy records her pregnancy here in lavish detail – the midwife appointments, the health supplements, the pre-natal yoga and designer stroller purchases. Ainsley Malloy was excited about raising her two baby girls to be the envy of Emerald Beach society. Until this entry:

Howard says I'm not allowed to tell any of my friends that we're having twins. He wants me to pretend we're having only one child. I'm only to purchase one crib, one stroller, one changing table. "I want to surprise them all," he says, with that familiar glint in his eye.

It makes no sense. It's not practical to buy one crib when we need two. It means I'll have to rush around getting everything after the birth. But I know that glint. It says, 'do what I say, or you'll get the weed killer again.' So I do what he says.

At least he's given me a new credit card for the baby things. Shopping spree!

I know I should stop reading, but I can't. I can't tear my eyes from what I know is coming.

The next few entries are lists of items purchased for the new baby. Ainsley must've burned through her black card pretty quick with Gucci pacifiers and Versace onesies. How is she not questioning Howard's demand she pretends they're having one child, not two?

I guess when weed killer is used as a threat, you develop some sick coping skills.

Or maybe it's better to live in luxurious ignorance than to risk losing everything. *I'm glad I didn't have you as a mother,* I want to scream into the diary. *You didn't even try to save me.*

Finally, I reach it – an entry dated a few days after my birthday.

We arrived home from the clinic today. Howard is being lovely, fussing over Mackenzie, counting her ten tiny toes. He had the nursery decorated while I've been away. An adorable border of dancing teddy bears. He even put together the crib. Everything is absolutely perfect.

Except... except it's not.

Except, I remember two heartbeats. Two sets of tiny onesies. Twenty little fingers and twenty little toes.

They keep telling me it's the drugs, that of course I only had one baby. My friends tell me I've only ever talked about one baby, I only purchased clothes for one baby. But when I look back through these pages, I see it's not true.

Howard may have forced me to set the stage for my own deception, but he doesn't know about this diary. He doesn't know I kept a record.

I know what he's done.

I gave birth to twins. And my daughter – my other daughter – she's disappeared.

She didn't know. She wasn't in on it.

Tears pool in my eyes. I don't know why I'm crying. This changes nothing. I don't give a shit about Ainsley Malloy. From everything I read in Mackenzie's diary, her mother could be just as cruel, just as evil, as Howard. I was the *lucky* one to be sold to the Augusts.

But I can't wipe the tears away fast enough. I have to blow my nose on the corner of the sheet before I can read the next page.

Howard sold my baby girl.

I don't have any proof. Nothing that I can use to go to the police. But my baby is missing and he's dancing around the house, talking about a deal that will make our fortunes.

I want to scream. I want to smash his face in. But I can't do a thing. He won't hesitate to kill me.

But I won't let this stand.

I will never forgive him.

I'll bide my time, but I'll get him for this.

I turn the pages with trembling fingers. The entries here are spread over several years. They're numerous but short – a couple of lines of jagged handwriting peppered with exclamation points. Sometimes she presses the pen so hard it tears through the paper

...Mackenzie broke all my nail polishes...

...Mackenzie threw my Versace gown into the swimming pool...

...Mackenzie puked in my purse...

...we took her to Disneyland and she told Mickey Mouse we kidnapped her, so the police dragged us off the Jungle Cruise ride with all those people watching...

...I can never show my face at the club again, and it's all her fault...

...I hate her. I hate my own daughter. She's ruined my life...

...Howard sold the wrong child. He got rid of my precious angel and left me with a demon.

Like father, like daughter. The Malloy house is a toxic hell-hole. I check the date on the last entry, my heart stuttering as I see it was written only a couple of weeks before Mackenzie murdered her family.

Howard's been talking about this deal for weeks, unknowingly letting little details slip. He thinks I'm too stupid to understand what he's talking about, but I've been waiting for this chance for years.

Biding my time.

Letting every attack from his little she-demon go unpunished.

Letting them both think they've won.

Howard thinks I don't care where his money comes from, as long as I have my perfect house and my dream husband and my little girl.

He underestimates me, and it's cost him everything.

I did it.

I made my plans so carefully. He didn't suspect a thing. Tonight, I waited until he got the call to go to the docks. The she-demon was at cheerleading practice, so she couldn't see me get in my car and follow him. I parked a little way away and hid in my pre-designated spot. I watched him load the box onto the ship – the payment he received for our daughter all those years ago. I don't know what's inside, but I know that he uses it as collateral for his deals.

My husband's treasure travels all over the world, but it always returns to him, like a boomerang.

Not this time.

It's nice to know I've still got it. All it took was a bat of my eyelashes to have Howard's shipping captain completely under my spell. The wad of bills I stole from Howard's safe helped, too. He'll never even notice the money missing, and he'll never know it was me who arranged for that box to be lifted from the boat before it left port.

He'll never know as he rants and rages and starts wars with his clients that the treasure more precious to him than his own daughter is right under his roof. By the time he figures it out, I'll be long gone.

I'm going to find my baby girl, my angel, my heart. I'll tear her from the evil people who bought her like she was a Gucci handbag. And the two of us will make a new life for ourselves, far away from this nightmare.

Holy shitballs.

Ainsley Malloy didn't forget about me. She didn't merrily go on with her perfect life knowing her husband sold me to a crime boss.

The badass bitch got *even*.

She stole Howard's treasure.

She was coming to get me.

She really is my mother.

Another piece of the puzzle slots into place. All this time, I'd been ignoring Ainsley Malloy as the clueless trophy wife under Howard's thumb. But she had been forced to give up one of her children, and tricked and drugged in an attempt to stop her from making a fuss. So she hit Howard where it would hurt most – by taking his prize.

She was going to leave him. She was coming to get me.

But she never got to me. My sister beat her to death first.

My heart thuds against my chest. Conflicted emotions swirl in my brain. I can't process this, can't reconcile that this ugly woman might have loved me with such violent passion that she crafted this scheme to save me, and what my life might've been if she'd managed to pluck me from Julian August's arms and make her escape. It's too much. It's too close to ripping my heart out and splattering it across the floral duvet.

So I focus on the tangible, the here and now. The treasure.

This explains why neither Howard nor Mackenzie knew where the treasure is. They both believe the other stole it when all this time Ainsley Malloy kept it hidden.

In this house.

Noah was right. The treasure is *here.*

I peer over at the open drawer, my mind reeling. If I'm right about this, the treasure should still be wherever Ainsley hid it, and Mackenzie doesn't know that. My sister certainly believes the treasure is somewhere in this house. But she thinks her father hid it, and she doesn't know where it is.

We've got to find it before she does.

"George," I yell as I race toward the stairs, the diary clutched against my heart. "I'm going to need you to tear Malloy Manor apart."

9

MACKENZIE

I lower the binoculars and lean my cheek against the rough bark of the tree. This spindly bitch of a tree isn't exactly designed for climbing, but I've been keeping up my gym training all these years and I'm still as sprightly and sure-footed as a spider monkey.

I'm not supposed to be here, climbing the trees surrounding Malloy Manor so I can see over the wall, watching my sister pulling something out from behind our parents' marital bed. It's a diary, hidden in the identical place where I used to stash mine. It figures Ainsley Malloy never had an original thought in her head.

I'm not supposed to be here, and that makes it even more delicious to raise the binoculars to my eyes again and watch my sister chew her lip in concentration as she scans the pages. She's searching for answers. She's so fucking clueless.

I'm not supposed to be here.

No one tells Mackenzie Malloy what to do, not when this bitch is the interloper in *my* house.

I touch the gun on my hip. I'm not supposed to have that or use it, either. I'm *supposed* to stay silent, sit back and let the men handle this. As if. I've been on my own, sorting my own shit out, since I was thirteen. Before that, even. I lived in that dilapidated castle in Germany and a bombed-out factory in Russia. I've done things that would blow my sister's fragile little mind. I'm not taking orders any longer, not even from—

My phone vibrates against my leg.

As I shift my weight so I can reach for it, Claudia leaps up from the bed, her face white like she's seen a ghost. I worry that she's seen me, but she's not looking out the window. Her little friend George comes running in. George is the real brains of the operation – she and Noah are the only real threat to me. Eli's too nice and Gabriel is too drunk, although I am going to enjoy breaking him over my knee.

Claudia jabs her finger at the book and they start talking at each other. I wish I could hear what they're saying, but I didn't think to hide microphones in the house.

Actually, I did, but I was outvoted.

Certain people should just listen to me. I'm obviously right.

Claudia and George disappear down the hallway, but they're back in view a moment later, through the French doors in Howard's office. Claudia pulls out drawers and raps on the inside of bookshelves while George spreads out the house schematics on the desk.

They're searching the house.

They can only be searching for one thing.

The treasure.

My treasure.

The diary must've had some new information. Interesting. I tortured Howard for hours and never got the location out of him. He claimed he lost it. What a joke. I knew he'd never tell Ainsley a thing, so I killed her in front of him to make him pliable, but maybe I should have leaned on her a little? I could have popped out her big, bimbo eyes one by one. Such a shame.

Let them search. It's about time my sister did something other than lie around wasting precious oxygen and getting cat fur all over my clothes. She can find my treasure, and then I'll take it from her.

My phone vibrates again. I stare down onto the back patio. No one's outside, so my voice won't carry. I pick up the phone and jam it on my ear. "Yes?"

"Where are you now? Please tell me you're not at the house."

"How little you think of me. Of course I'm not. I'm at a cafe, having a Danish. It's terrible. Americans can't do pastries like Europe." I hold the binoculars up again. George and Claudia are inspecting a china cabinet in the dining room.

It's not in there, you fools. I already looked.

"Good," the deep voice on the other end says. "We can't risk her seeing you. There've been too many close calls. I'm on my way to your place. Can you bring me a Danish when you head home—"

I hang up the phone. I'll go back to my place when I'm good and ready. I hate the way he calls it *home*. The dingy one-room apartment in the worst corner of Tartarus Oaks isn't my home.

My home is right here – Malloy Manor.

My home is in the arms of three beautiful, utterly clueless princes.

My home is Claudia August's life.

I let the binoculars drop against my tits. I blow a kiss in the direction of my clueless sister. "See you soon, Claws."

10

GABRIEL

"Hello, Your Grace. It's lovely to speak again."

I stand behind Claudia as she sits at Howard's desk, making sure my father can see me in the shot. He frowns at us from behind his enormous inlaid desk – the monstrous piece of furniture apparently used to belong to Winston Churchill. Even though he's thousands of miles away, just seeing him on the video sucks the air from the room.

The duke steeples his fingers and peers at Claudia over the end of his nose like she's a curio in his private museum – something to be put behind glass and admired for its beauty, but too old-fashioned, too obsolete, to be any further use.

He underestimates her.

That will be his downfall. And I can't say I'll cry when she finally spills his blood.

"You say you will marry my son and provide me an heir," the duke says. "But I've had word from my people in California that you're to marry the heads of the Lucian and Dio families. Which is it to be?"

His people.

My father has *people* in this city of sin and depravity, a city he would never deign to visit because the very idea of it offended him so.

I came to California to escape the Duke of Blackwich's poison, and all this time, he's had his talons sunk into the very fabric of Emerald Beach.

I can't escape my father. He's in my blood, my marrow. His poison eats away at me from the inside out.

Claudia twists a lock of hair around her perfectly manicured finger. "If you're referring to Cleo, I know she's with you. The silly bitch has been posting on her social media. You should probably tell her to stop, lest *my* people figure out where she's hiding. Don't think the walls of your castle will protect her from my wrath."

I watch the duke's face carefully. He remains perfectly stoic, refusing to give anything away. But I think I can just see the vein above his eye throb with rage. *I bet he didn't know about Cleo's post.*

But all he says is, "Your authority doesn't stretch across borders."

"Doesn't it now?" Claws smiles. From the outside, she appears a glamorous Emerald Beach teenager, all golden hair and Ice Queen eyes, but I see she's in scorpion mode. She has her pincers bared to distract her quarry while she raises her poison tail. "Let me get straight to the point, Blackwich. You know who I am, and I know who you are – you're the one bringing Grey Death into Emerald Beach. You were also the one who had Dylan O'Connor killed. Did Cleo tell you that she gave away that little nugget? I have enough evidence to go public with Dylan's murder – what a fun scandal that will be for your gutter press."

His nostrils flare. "It would be unwise to threaten me, Claudia August."

She smiles at his use of her real name. "You may be right – I have secrets that can destroy you, but you hold my secrets, too. What happens next is up to you, and what you believe I'm capable of. Perhaps I'm just crazy enough not to care about our stalemate. Perhaps I have the police in my pocket, and I'll get off scot-free if you try to dob me in. Perhaps no one will believe you that an eighteen-year-old Valley girl is the head of a crime empire. You'll have to take your chances. Or, we can accept our mutually assured destruction and reach an amicable agreement."

The duke steeples his fingers once more. "I'm listening."

"Nero Lucian has been funding your expansion into Emerald Beach. Don't deny it – Cleo told me everything. Nero had been using his chokehold over my predecessor, Brutus, to muscle in on the drug trade, which is Lucian territory. That's over now. Here's what's going to happen – you no longer deal with Nero. If you want to sell in *my* city, you go through me. My cut is fifty percent of profits. I won't accept any less, and I'll need to have my accountant look over your books. If I find out you're short-changing me, my vengeance will be swift."

"Fifty percent?" The duke's nostrils flare. She's got his attention. "What makes you think for a moment I'd agree to these terms? Nero is more powerful than you."

"Is he now?" Claudia smiles again. I love watching her work over my father, taking his carefully laid plans and throwing them into the sun. "Ask *your people* what happened on New Year's Eve when Nero found himself without a shipment of women for his clients. Without the support of Lucian's trade routes, he's not as powerful as he thinks he is. *I* control the flow of goods into and out of this city, which is the key to expanding your drug trade in the US. I may be little, but I'm mighty. Remember, *Duke*, Lucian and Dio are fighting over who will marry *me*. They don't know yet that I'm going to marry your son.

Your heir will inherit the empire we build together. What do you say to that?"

I purse my lips, trying to hold in all the things I want to say. I can't bear to listen to Claudia talk about a child, *our* child, so callously. Not after she promised me that she'd consider it if I could get myself together.

I've been so, so good. I haven't caved on my celibacy, even though my balls have shrunk into my body from underuse. I haven't had a drink in over a week, unless you count the three shots of ouzo I had needed to get to sleep last night. Which I don't count, because everyone knows that Jesus himself drank wine so he could sleep, especially when he was forcing himself to remain celibate and his rock-hard cock didn't know when to quit.

Jesus and I have a lot in common.

I've been doing everything *right*, hoping she'll see that I could be a good father, trying to resist the pull of sweet substance oblivion to be there for my queen. But she's been so busy helping George bust down walls and rifle through closets looking for treasure, I don't think she's even noticed my new leaf.

I know what she discovered about Ainsley Malloy has freaked her out, but that doesn't mean she has to follow in her father's footsteps. I'd rather not have a child at all than let my father use them as a pawn.

The duke leans back in his chair. It takes everything I have to remain casual and not to leer at the computer and scream in his face.

I could use a drink.

"We're not interested," he says. "We will take our chances with the status quo."

A figure walks around my father's desk and drapes herself over his shoulders. It's Cleo. She's wearing another cropped designer hoodie and a wide-brimmed straw hat that hides her *sacer*. She waves into the camera and blows me a kiss.

"Claudia, Gabriel, hiiiiiii," she drawls. "So cool to see you again."

Claudia hisses through her teeth.

The duke turns to Cleo, and with a tone like he's discussing the weather, says, "I think it's time you told them our news."

News? What news?

"You should have taken the duke's offer to marry me while you had the chance, boo." Cleo places her hand over her flat stomach and flashes me the look of a snake closing in on a tasty mouse. "You're too late. I just got back from the doctor. I'm pregnant with the duke's child. As soon as we're wed, my baby will inherit the title and the Blackwich estate, and there's nothing you can do about it."

11

CLAUDIA

"I can't believe she's going to marry that old goat," George says as she stuffs a second candy bar into her mouth. It's lunchtime at Stonehurst Prep, and she's flipping through Cleo's social media and the UK papers, where the headlines loudly proclaim the impending divorce for the Duke and Duchess of Blackwich. George shows me a selfie of Cleo and the duke sitting on the edge of the artificial lake. Gabriel's father almost looks *relaxed*.

I'd be relaxed, too, if I was fucking someone fifty-five years my junior. I'd be peaches and fucking cream.

"I didn't want that shitty pile of rocks, anyway," Gabriel declares as he does battle with a package of corn chips. "At least Malloy Manor has *personality*. It may be the personality of an evil old goat with no taste in art, but it's still a personality."

He's not wrong. Unlike the stuffy, cold halls of Blackwich Castle, where the weight of Gabriel's lineage crushes his beautiful spirit, the manor is the vision of one man, and Howard Malloy knew what he liked.

Gabriel's trying to pretend he's perfectly okay about Cleo becoming his new stepmother (gag me). So, of course, it's obvious he's *not* okay. Noah told me he saw Gabe get a bathroom pass first period. When he came back, his breath reeked of alcohol. He's making a big show of refusing alcohol when he's around us, and drinking in secret. That's not an improvement.

The worst part is that Gabe's distress isn't even about losing the Blackwich estate to Cleo and her gross demon child (which is a pity – I was looking forward to solidifying my rule with an actual *castle*). He's upset because I waved the marriage-and-baby thing in his dad's face. Because I told Gabriel I didn't want to have a kid with him and then pretended we were all ready to conceive.

It was a tactical move. Nothing more. Surely he can see that?

"You know," Eli says, stirring his zucchini noodles around his plate. "An heir might be one way out of this marriage mess."

I turn to him with interest. *Did Gabe tell him about the conversation with the duke? Is he going to back me up on this?* "Explain."

"This whole marriage thing is about heirs, right? Nero and Constantine – whichever one puts a baby in your belly first, they'll be the one with the power to claim a true alliance. But that only works if there's no other heir to claim the August empire. So we make an heir."

I hold out a hand. "Stay away from my uterus. I'm not getting pregnant just go fuck up Nero's plans."

"We don't have to actually *give* you a baby. Just get Galen to fake scans or something. It could buy us some time—"

"I'm leaving." Gabe stands up. "I've got songs to write."

"Gabe—"

I reach out to grab his arm, but he darts away from me and slips into the cafeteria crowd. Noah watches him leave, his coal-eyes wreathed in orange.

"What's up with him?" Eli asks as Gabriel pushes his way through the crowd in the cafeteria and heads out toward the bleachers.

Ah, so he hasn't said anything. Guess we're having this conversation, then.

I shovel a mouthful of kale salad. "Oh, he's mad because I told his father we're getting married."

Eli drops his fork. Noah's hands ball into fists as he swivels his intense eyes toward me. "You did what?"

"I'm going to... go over there." George quickly snaps up her tray and races off, leaving me alone to face the wrath of Eli and Noah.

"So, tell us about this marriage." Eli gives me a wobbly smile that doesn't reach his eyes.

"It's basically exactly what you were talking about a few minutes ago. If Gabe and I married, we align ourselves with a powerful family, get me out of this stupid wedding with the Imperators, and take another valuable market away from Nero. And any child we *might* have would inherit his father's estate. It was a good idea – how was I to know it wouldn't work because the randy old goat was screwing Cleo?"

Neither Eli nor Noah picks up on my Cleo news. Noah's eyes narrow. "You were just going to marry Gabe without talking it over with us?"

"What about Nero and Constantine?" Eli says. "What will your *other* husbands say about that?"

"I don't give a fuck what they say because I'm getting out of that. And this thing with Gabe isn't a real marriage," I say. "I mean, it would have to be real in order to claim the estate, but it's not about me choosing Gabe over either of you. If I *wanted* to get married now and I had a choice, I'd marry all of you. But that's not a legal option, and if I marry Gabe and string the duke along thinking there will be an heir, we'll get possession of his estate, and I take the Grey Death business away from Nero, which is another massive blow right in his cajones—"

"I'm going to find Gabe." Noah rises.

"Noah, what the fuck—"

But he's gone, his huge shoulders shuffling away from me. Seriously, what the hell is going on?

I turn back to Eli. "So this is it? I spend every moment of every day trying to figure out how to keep this family safe, and instead of discussing your problem with my plan like adults, you act like spoiled children being forced to share a toy?"

"You're not a toy, Claws. You're our girl." Eli frowns. He reaches across the table and places his fingers tenderly over mine. "I get what you were attempting; really, I do. But you're thinking like Claws the mafia queen. Just for a moment, can you see this as Claudia, our girlfriend?"

I shove his hand away. "I don't have that luxury anymore. If I want to keep you safe, I have to make hard decisions. We all do. You all said you were in this. You all agreed to wear my mark with pride. Well, this is what it means to be with me. It means that everything is up for negotiation, even my fucking womb if it means my family will live another day. So what is it, Eli? You still want in?"

I don't wait for an answer. I shove my own chair back and storm out.

12

CLAUDIA

*T*HWACK.

Plaster rains down on me as the sledgehammer connects with the wall. The drywall caves in, leaving a fist-sized hole.

Adrenaline courses through my body as I swing again. It feels good to smash shit. Better this wall than three stupid boy faces. I can't believe they're having an emo moment about me marrying Gabriel and a baby that doesn't even *exist*.

And what's the big deal for Gabe, anyway? He *wants* to marry me. He said so literally the day before. As if I don't have enough to deal with, I've now got to add three fragile male egos into the mix.

I yell as I bring the sledgehammer over my head and pummel the wall again, and again, until the drywall is sagging and riddled with holes and cracks. I drop the sledgehammer and George hands me a crowbar, which I use to tear out the remaining drywall.

I've had plenty of practice in my rage room. But today, I'm not just venting my frustration on a perfectly innocent wall. We're looking for the secrets hiding behind it and—

"Argh!" I cry as a stream of water hits me in the face, sending me reeling. George leans in to look. She's blasted backward as a second leak tears through the wall, spraying filthy, stinking water all over the basement. And me.

George flails her arms as she tries to stand on the slippery tiles. "I was sure there would be a compartment behind that wall."

"There is," I yell as I try to beat my way out of the stream of water. "For pipes and shit. But no treasure."

George crawls across the basement floor toward me. She grabs me under the shoulders and together we stagger over to the steps. We climb, squeezing water out of our soaking clothes, and collapse in a heap in the hallway.

"Shall I call a plumber?" George asks.

"I'll take care of it." Yara appears from out of nowhere. "I took a course on plumbing as part of my degree. I bet I can patch up whatever mess you've made."

"I don't know what we even need boys for," I grumble to George as we drag our sodden asses down the hall. Yara heads off to the garage to find some tools, whistling under her breath.

"You don't mean that." George looks terrified.

"They're acting like babies."

"They're acting like three guys madly in love with you who are trying to sort out their shit," George says. She trembles a little as she shoves open the ballroom door. I'm not sure if it's the freezing water dripping from her clothes or the fact that this is the first time she's ever contradicted me. "Gabriel is trying to banish his demons for you. He wants to prove that he's worthy of your love. And you saying you'd marry him just like that..." she snaps her fingers. "It made him feel like you don't care. And..."

She freezes. I glare at her. "Out with it, Fisher."

George looks away. "And I've heard them talking about you,

late at night, when you're holed up in your office. Talking about the future. About marriage and babies and college and shit."

My heart thuds against my chest. "What did they say?"

"I think you should ask them yourself."

George shoves me forward. I stumble over the threshold into the ballroom, expecting her to follow. Instead, she slams the door on me.

Traitor.

I swipe a stand of matted hair from my eye and find myself staring into four sets of eyes – my three princes draped over my sofas, and the wide sapphire blue orbs of Casper the tiger, who darts around Queen Boudica's cat castle like he owns it.

Gabe grins at me and makes a comment about a wet t-shirt contest, and Noah threatens him with evisceration. They're all behaving perfectly normal, as if that fight we had at lunch never happened.

But I know it happened.

And we're dealing with this shit *right now*.

"So, I hear you've been discussing our future without me." I yank off my damp t-shirt and reach for Gabe's big, cozy Octavia's Ruin hoodie. As soon as I tug it over my head, his pagan scent slams into me.

My breath stutters.

Am I wrong?

I'm backed into a corner by Nero and this fucking sham marriage. Am I doing what I always do lashing out like a caged animal, a wild heart desperate to kill the hand that feeds? I bury my face into Gabe's hoodie, sinking into myself like a cat crouching low before it strikes.

Am I wrong?

Am I trying to love them the only way I know how to love, with claws and teeth, with possession and control?

"I told you George overheard us," Eli says to the others. In their shared glances I catch their unease, their fear.

No, no, this isn't love. They shouldn't be afraid of me.

Eli smiles at me, but it's wobbly.

"What's going on?" I meet each of their eyes with my patented Ice Queen glare. Only Noah can hold my gaze for longer than a moment. I pull the hoodie over my knees. My armor in place, I cross the room to get all up in their grills, allowing their individual scents to reach me through the invisible bars of my cage.

I touch my finger to the August tattoo on Noah's wrist, and even he flinches.

"I thought we were a team," I whisper. "I thought we took an oath to protect each other, to be with each other always. And here you all are, making plans without me."

"You made plans without us," Noah says. He won't look me in the eye. "You decided to marry Gabriel. That's a pretty big thing to fucking spring on us without discussing first, especially after you told him you weren't ready."

"I was *trying* to de-escalate the duke situation. It's got nothing to do with what I want or what I'm ready for. In my job, I don't always get that luxury. And besides, it didn't work, so you can stop harping on about it and tell me what the fuck you're all planning behind my back."

They look at each other, guilt written all over their faces. My hands ball into fists. I want to knock their beautiful, stupid heads together until little birds dance around their skulls.

Only the ones you love can truly betray you.

"We weren't trying to leave you out," Eli says. "That's exactly why we were talking. We all wanted to make sure we're on the same page about certain things so that we can work together to be the best tribunes for you."

"We weren't holding a war council," Gabriel pipes up. "Not without our favorite queen."

"And what have you decided?"

"That Eli will go to law school," Noah says, resting a hand on Eli's shoulder. "He'll learn the ins and outs of international law so he can find the best ways of circumventing it, and maybe he'll also make some contacts that will come in handy. I'll leverage my father's name into a career in politics – that will give us further advantages. Gabe will quit music and work full time as your assistant. He'll help you use social media to raise your profile in the criminal underworld, make working with the August family a desirable goal for any discerning criminal."

My mind reels at their vision for our future, at everything they're willing to sacrifice for me, for the glory of the August name. "You three... this is too much..."

Noah cracks that heart-melting half-smile of his, the one where a faint hint of sunshine bursts through the darkness. "And we were thinking that maybe one day in the future... you and Gabriel will get married."

My stomach contracts like I've taken a punch. "Let me get this straight, after all your tantrums, you *want* me to marry Gabe?"

"Just for the legal benefits, and the social clout. And only if you want to, of course. The ceremony could be for all four of us," Eli adds. "Because we're all fucking nuts about you."

"You all want to marry me?"

They nod.

"But Eli has to be the wedding planner," Gabe adds. "He has very specific ideas."

Eli's cheeks flush with color. "All I said was that I wanted a church service, and white lilies in the bouquet, and blue flowers on the tables to match Claudia's eyes. *You* can plan the wedding if you have a problem with—"

"*Please*. I'll be too busy planning the wedding night," Gabriel grins. "That's my department. Noah can take care of chair bows."

"As long as he's not in charge of the cake," Eli says with decisiveness.

I can't hold it in any longer. I burst out laughing.

It's like a cork pops inside me and healing balm pours into my veins. All the tension of the last few weeks is sloughed away by their declaration. I look at their three perfect faces – at Eli's too-pretty smile and Noah's coal-black eyes and Gabriel's shit-eating grin – and I see how truly wrong I've been.

I can't believe I thought they betrayed me.

All this time, I've been so worried that they weren't truly *in* this, that they were holding on to the broken shards of their old lives. But they're willing to raze their futures to the ground for me, and from the ashes something new and fierce and brilliant will emerge.

I topple forward and they catch me, pulling me into their arms, laying their kisses on my skin, linking their hands around me to hold me upright, to keep me strong. Tears scratch my eyes. *I needed you, and you came through for me. You always come through for me.*

"I'm sorry," I sniff, burying my face in Gabriel's shoulder. "I'm so sorry. I shouldn't have sprung the Gabriel wedding thing on you without discussing it first. I was in problem-solving mode. I didn't think that it might impact all of you. I know I've been acting like I'm in this alone, like nothing I do is above scrutiny, but I'm just so fucking *scared*. And I'm the one who's supposed to be strong. I have to hold it together but... Mackenzie came into our *house*. She was right there in the room with us. It could have been any of you bleeding out on the floor, and the thought of that makes me ill—"

"It could have been *you*," Noah growls, brushing his lips across my forehead. "You're not the only one who feels trapped or afraid. That's why we have to stick together. Because all we have now is each other. And if we have to marry you off to Nero and Constantine at Lupercalia, we won't even have that—"

"I told you, I'm making a plan to get out of that."

"Then you need to *tell us the plan*, Claws." Noah sighs. It's the same sigh he uses when he tutors me and he thinks I'm being really fucking dim. "You're not alone anymore."

You're not alone anymore.

Fuck, if any four words could break me, those are the ones.

The tears I've been holding back spill over. I'm so used to being alone, first when my father hid me away from the world to protect his legacy, and then for four long years in this big, silent house while life went on outside the walls. I'm not used to letting people in. I'm supposed to be strong enough to survive on my own.

But I don't have to. Not anymore.

I start crying harder as Eli adds, "We're here to help you. And if you truly think it's the right thing to do, we'll help you marry Gabe now—"

"I was wrong about that plan," I smile sadly. "As it turns out, it's a fucking moot point, since Cleo and her demon child are going to swipe Blackwich Castle out from under us."

"Wait, Cleo's pregnant?" Eli's brows knit together. "With Gabe's father's kid? She's going to be Gabe's *stepmother*?"

Noah makes a gagging noise.

"Maybe that's for the best," Gabe says quickly. He leans against me, snuggling his head into the crook of my arm. He feels so tiny, so vulnerable like this. "Nothing good has ever come out of that castle. We don't need my legacy – we're building our own right here."

I gather them to me again, holding them so tight I hear Gabe's spine crack. I've been such an idiot. I've been like a tiny bird pecking at the bars of my cage, completely oblivious to the fact I've got three lovers who'll help me smash down the door.

I love that they have our future mapped out. That's adorable. But their plans are small. They're right – I can't run this family on my own, especially not once I dethrone Constantine and Nero. I'll need my own Triumvirate in place. Gabriel will run the entertainment side of the business, and Noah will be in charge of Dio's assassins. Eli shall remain by my side as my advisor, although I do like the idea of arming him with a thorough knowledge of the law.

But for now, I keep my plans to myself. This isn't a time for plotting, it's a time for kissing my loves and feeling their still-beating hearts in their chests and remembering that today, this day, we're still alive. We're together. And we are invincible.

A WHILE LATER, Yara barges into the ballroom (thankfully, we're all buttoned and zipped up by then), with a damp t-shirt of her own, a grease stain across her brow, and a self-satisfied smirk on her pretty face. "All fixed."

"You're a genius." I pat the sofa beside me, where only fifteen minutes earlier, Eli had thrust inside me so hard he jerked the sofa leg across the marble, leaving behind a permanent scratch. Yara dumps her toolbox on the table and drops into the pile of cushions.

"I know," she grins. "What the fuck were you trying to do to the wall, anyway?"

"I thought the treasure might be hidden there." George follows her into the room, her head in her hands. "But I give up. I've scanned and measured every inch of this house. Unless Malloy Manor is secretly on Ash Tree Lane and is bigger on the inside than it is on the outside, there's no hidden treasure room or secret stash."

"Points for the *House of Leaves* reference," Yara nods to her. They're both huge horror geeks.

George slumps further into the sofa cushions, looking sorry for herself. Queen Boudica, the lap-seeking missile, leaps up and makes herself a comfortable nest between George's thighs.

"We're missing something," I say. "We know the treasure is in this house."

"I'm telling you, I've measured every wall in this house against Howard's schematics. There are no other secret passages apart from the one Mackenzie used to escape," George says. "Maybe Ainsley moved the treasure before she was killed? Or maybe we're wrong, and Mackenzie really does have it already?"

I shake my head. "Mackenzie thinks it's here. Otherwise, she wouldn't be on my ass about the house. There are no other clues in the diary?"

"I've scoured that thing from cover to cover. All that the last entry tells us is that the treasure is in this house. But I'm telling you, it's not here."

"Maybe it's under the marble in the entrance hall?" Noah says.

George shakes her head. "Please don't start guessing. Trust me, I already thought of everything. It can't be under the floor because lifting these marble tiles would take a team of guys days to do and it would create a lot of dust and mess. Ainsley might've had help, but she'd have to work quickly."

"Maybe we're thinking about this in the wrong way," Eli says. "We don't even know what this treasure is. We're assuming it's something big – like, gold bars and statues and stuff, because it's shipped in a crate. But Claws' father is the person who gave Howard this treasure, right? And it had to be something worth giving up for the child he always wanted. So we've got to think like Claws' father."

"What are you saying?"

"I'm saying we should challenge our assumptions. Until we know what the treasure is, we can't find it. And if we want to know what it is, we need to think like Julian August. Maybe the treasure is actually tiny. If it was small and fragile, it might've needed cushioning during storage," Eli says. "Or Howard might've hidden it inside a shipment of something else."

"But what's tiny that could be valuable enough to exchange for a daughter?" I ask. "A check?"

George shakes her head. "If it was a check, Howard or Ainsley would have just cashed it in. No need to hide it. A check also couldn't be used the way Ainsley described, as collateral for illicit business deals. But Eli makes a good point. If the treasure is tiny, it could be anywhere in this house – hidden in a drawer or stitched into a headboard. It could even be something on paper – property deeds, maybe? Or a really valuable diamond?"

I shake my head. "If we're thinking like... like Daddy, then Julian August wouldn't have batted an eye at a diamond. But you might be onto something with the property deeds. That might have value to my father. We should check Howard's office again, maybe something will pop up."

13

CLAUDIA

*B*ut nothing pops up. And I'm getting more and more desperate.

Cleo and her baby, Nero, Constantine, the Lupercalia wedding, Grey Death, graduation, the guys acting weird, monkeys in my closet, a lion in the swimming pool. Mackenzie and her scattershot bullets of Damocles hovering over my head.

Around and around they whir. All my problems. All my fears. All the evil that could befall my family if we don't hold back the onslaught of bullshit. The weight of my savage and precarious empire is stacked on my shoulders like Mackenzie's dolls in that closet upstairs. If one piece slips out of place, the entire stack comes crashing down, limbs everywhere, glass eyes shattering.

I've got 99 problems but at least Brutus ain't one.

Thank fuck that bastard is dead, his body burned away, my father's murder avenged. I take some comfort in that. It's cold comfort, because the clock is ticking on my impending marriage and I still have no idea what the fuck I'm going to do, and around every corner I expect to find Mackenzie spraying bullets everywhere.

The next week of school passes in a blur. Alongside the rest of the senior class, Eli and Noah sent in their college applications a few weeks ago, so there's this restless hum in the air while they wait for results. No one sits still in class. Ms. Drysdale is showing movies in English, and Mr. Dallas teaches us how to make molecular cocktails in chemistry. There hardly seems much point attending any longer.

They only have a few more weeks to wait to see if their hard work will pay off.

I give up on any pretense that I give a shit about school. I didn't apply to any colleges. I never saw myself strutting around an ivy-covered campus, reading glasses dangling from a perfectly manicured fingernail. I sleep through my classes and wander the halls in a daze. It's as if school is the dream – the alternate reality of parties and finals and SATs from which I'll soon wake up.

My real life begins when the sun goes down. When the monsters of Emerald Beach come out to play.

At the rate I'm going, I might not even get my high school diploma. Luckily, qualifications count for shit in my world. I may not be able to name all the Founding Fathers, but thanks to Noah's excellent tutelage, I understand complex shipping forecasts and ship's manifests. Piece by piece, I'm putting my father's empire back together, winning over his old alliances with new deals, playing off factions against each other.

But I need more.

If I want to get out of this marriage, I'm going to need something I can sell other than myself. The secret Livvie gave me is good, real *good*, but it's a last resort – I'd be taking a huge risk revealing it, and I only want to play that card if I have no other choice.

When I crashed the Saturnalia council, I promised Nero and Constantine secrets. I promised an advantage they didn't have –

the face of Mackenzie Malloy. A face that can unlock doors to the elite in this city. And I need to use that face to get them something.

On Friday, I wait for George outside her art class and yank her into a supply closet.

"Ow." She rolls her shoulder. "We can talk at home, you know. You don't have to yank my arm out of its socket."

"This can't wait." I'm too amped up, too desperate to act. I hate sitting around in this annoying school, knowing Mackenzie is out there, plotting her next move. She could be watching us right now, her sights trained on me. "You said you had secrets on people in this school. Important families, YouTube stars, etc. I need you to start spilling."

"I keep it all right here." George taps the side of her head. "I've been saving things up for years in case I need them. Sometimes, just knowing you can destroy someone with a well-placed media leak makes it easier to endure their bullying. What are you looking for?"

It figures George is too nice to make use of anything she knows. Luckily for us, I'm not nice. "I need something I can bargain with. An opportunity that the Triumvirate can exploit."

"Okay. Well, turns out that Amanda Siegal's mother's Gulfstream G5 is actually a rental."

"What else is new?"

"Um...Tyson Gray's father paid twenty million dollars to charter an expedition vessel to hunt for the Loch Ness Monster."

"Hilarious, but not of interest to the Triumvirate."

"Okay, then... you've got Cleo's friend, Daphne Ballantyne. Her father got into some trouble three years ago. He had a gambling problem, was embezzling money from clients to pay his debts, all the usual stuff. The whole thing came out in the media and he committed suicide." George grins. "Supposedly."

A faked death. That's perfect.

If this bastard had gambling debts in Emerald Beach, I know exactly who he owed money, and who would have been hired to ensure those debts are paid.

"George, you genius. You got proof?"

"Always." George taps her phone screen a few times, then hands it over. A video plays, timestamped over the summer, showing Daphne embracing a man who I'm guessing is her father.

"This isn't good enough. We need to know where this guy is hiding out."

"I don't have that information…"

"Can you get it?" I tap my chin. "Never mind, just get me in a room with Daphne, away from school, away from prying eyes and security cameras, and I'll get it out of her."

"Daphne's going to be at that Stonehurst Prep alumni party Noah's going to this weekend." George taps her phone. "You're already on the guest list, but I've just added me and Gabriel. It's one of those things where we need to attend in pairs."

I tap my finger on my chin. "How convenient that the event is at Vault. I'll make sure Eli leaves one of the private suites available for us. We're going to need a soundproof room. And I'll have to figure out how to get my knives past Nero's security."

George's face collapses with panic. "Wait, what do you need *knives* for?"

"What did you think I was going to do, tickle the answer out of her? We need to find out where Daphne's hiding her father. If Constantine can collect on this job, he'll be happy. It's a win-win."

"It's not a win for Daphne," George frowns. "I thought we were just going to, I don't know, blackmail them. I'm not sure I'm happy giving up her dad to be slaughtered by Constantine Dio."

I wrap my arms around George. "And that's why you're *CSI:*

Emerald Beach and I'm the crime lord. Now let's go home. Who needs last period when we've got to find outfits for this party."

14

ELI

Claws and George disappear last period. Claws texts to say that they've gone home to find outfits for the alumni party. I'm not sure why George thinks she's getting in, since she's a scholarship student at Stonehurst Prep, but I don't bother questioning it. I trust Claudia, especially after our talk. *Especially* if George is involved.

After school is indoor track practice. Noah's given up the team, thank fuck, so I'm no longer spending all my time trying to coach him out of mediocrity, and I can focus on my own times. I've been so distracted this year that I've missed opportunities to be scouted by the Ivies, but my performance as team captain should give my college applications the boost they need.

For two hours I focus on nothing but my stride and my breathing. As I unlace my running shoes and joke with the other guys on the way to the showers, I can almost pretend I'm a normal teenager with boring concerns like getting into the right college, instead of worrying about my dad's upcoming appeal and whether my girlfriend will be gunned down by her psychopath estranged twin sister.

But that all changes when I drop my gym bag into the

passenger seat and pull the Porsche out of the school parking lot. My fingers tighten on the wheel as I drive the ten blocks to Vault and my other life as Eli Hart, tribune to the notorious Claudia August and assistant to an entertainment kingpin.

I don't know what's waiting for me beyond the gilded doors of the old bank building. Last time I was here, I tricked Nero into selling Claudia his entire collection of exotic animals. Another lucrative business line that's been stripped from him. If he's watching Malloy Manor, he has to know we have the animals, that the whole thing about the parasite was a ruse. As I wait at the last set of traffic lights, I touch my fingers to the gun strapped beneath my suit.

Am I driving to my death?

I park up in Vault's underground parking and head up to the main bar. I'm relieved to see Livvie standing on a table in the VIP area, arms raised above her head as she directs her dancers through a new routine. *She's alive. That's got to be a good sign.*

Tension fizzes in the air, and I notice there is double the number of security wandering around the building. One of the girls misses a cue, and Livvie barks a reprimand with an unusual venom. We may still all have our heads, but something's afoot in the land of Lucian.

"Nero's not happy," Livvie whispers to me as I grab drinks for us both and join her at the table. "He's been on the warpath all week, so watch your back. I don't think even the Golden Boy will be immune."

My stomach drops into my shoes. "So he knows, then?"

"Nope. He forgot about those animals the minute we took them away. I told you he wouldn't give a shit. He's having trouble with the snooty British duke who—"

"—deals Grey Death?"

"How'd you know?" Livvie hisses. "That's a big secret. Do *not* let on that you know. The duke's connections are what makes the business so lucrative. Grey Death isn't for the plebs; it's not a street drug. That product goes straight to the most elite clients."

I roll my eyes. "The duke is Gabriel's father."

"Your lover's other lover? The bad boy musician one?" Livvie licks her lips. "How intriguing. So Claudia knows, then?"

I nod.

"Well, I wouldn't let on about that if I were you. The duke is using the current instability in the Triumvirate as an excuse to drive up his prices. Nero has clients waiting on product, and without the profit from the skin deal, the duke is withholding his next shipment. He says he has another buyer who's willing to make him a better deal."

I bet that other buyer is Claudia.

I guess this is how things work in this world. The duke may not need Claudia and Gabe's heir, but he's not above taking her deal if it works out better for him. He's hedging his bets in Emerald Beach, stringing both Nero and Claws along while he sees how this whole thing shakes out.

"If Nero loses Grey Death on top of the skin trade, it puts all his plans in jeopardy." Livvie downs her Old Fashioned in one gulp and slams the glass on the table. "I hope your girl knows what she's doing. A lion is at its most dangerous when backed into a corner."

My head spinning, I leave Livvie to manage the dancers, and head upstairs to get some of the accounts done. I'm learning an awful lot about moving illegal money around different holding companies and offshore accounts, hiding Nero's fortune from the Feds. It's like a game, staying one step ahead of the authorities. I've been showing Noah some of the tricks so he can start squirreling away Claudia's illicit profits. She doesn't have much yet, nothing like Nero's resources, but so much of his money is tied up in deals. He doesn't have much available cash to settle with the likes of the duke—

"Eli."

A familiar voice calls me from the bottom of the stairs. My chest soars at the musical sound. She brightens the entire space just by opening her mouth.

"Claudia?" I rush down to her, sweeping her into my arms. She's wearing a short blue sundress, despite the cool weather. It matches her eyes, making those pools of blue appear even deeper and colder than usual. "What are you doing here? I didn't know you had a meeting with Nero today."

I can't talk about what I know, not in the open like this where Nero's security system will hear every word, but I try to convey with my eyes that she's in danger, that I need to get her away from here.

"I don't have business with Nero," she smiles, tossing her golden hair over her shoulder. Something about her smile is a little off, and I wonder if she already knows about Nero's issues with the duke, if this is a calculated move. *You're supposed to talk to us about what's happening.* "I came to see you. I have something to ask you. Is there somewhere private where we can talk?"

"Um..." I can't exactly take her down to the basement – someone will notice that on the cameras and report to Nero. It has to be somewhere they'd expect me to take my Imperator. I have an idea. I lead her up the secret elevator to the private rooms, and hold open the door to a plush suite. Claudia enters, her eyes widening as she takes in the BDSM gear scattered around the opulent bedroom.

"Eli Hart, you've been hiding your kinky side."

I pick up a remote from the end of the bed and turn up the sound system. Claudia tries to push me into the St. Andrew's cross, but I yank her down onto the bed, laying beside her and cupping her cheek to mine. I expect to feel the fizz of our attraction as our skin touches, and that giddy adolescent flutter in my chest I get every time I'm near her. But all I feel is a sick churning in my stomach. "If we talk softly, they won't be able to hear us on the tape," I whisper, trying to distract myself from this strange vibe. "What did you want to ask?"

Something's gone wrong, I just know it.

"Oh, silly, it's nothing so clandestine as all this." She trails her fingers along my arms, the tips of her nails raising goosebumps on my skin. Something... something's not right. It's not a new threat. It's something about *her*, but I can't put my finger on what. "The Valentine's dance is coming up, and I wanted to ask if you'd be my date."

I blink. *Valentine's dance? Does she mean the one at school?*

"Why?" I draw my arm away. My skin feels like it's been scraped raw. "I mean, sure. Of course, I'll be your date. But you shouldn't have come *here* to ask me. Nero's on the warpath. It's all to do with Gabe's father, but I can't talk about it—"

She cuts me off with a fierce kiss. The minute her lips brush mine, a wave of repulsion rockets through my body. I know exactly what's wrong.

I'm not kissing Claudia.

Her eyes remain open, that icy stare locked on me. She watches for a sign that I've seen through her disguise. Even though it makes bile rise in my throat, I kiss her back, giving her just enough to make her believe I'm taken in, that I'm just a guy hopelessly in love kissing his girlfriend.

She tastes like violets and bubblegum.

The gun digs into my thigh. My heart hammers in my chest. Can I reach my hand down and grab it without her noticing? What will Nero do if I blow her brains out in his luxury guest suite? If I kill her *here*, this girl who looks exactly like my Imperator, how will we prevent Nero from figuring out the truth?

Mackenzie's tongue wraps around mine, like a witch trying to suck my soul out through my mouth. I swallow the urge to gag, and press hard against her as I angle my torso backward, trying to surreptitiously slide my hand down between us without her noticing.

Can I even do it? Can I look into my girlfriend's eyes as I decorate the wall with her brain matter?

I loved you once, I want to scream into her open, moaning mouth. *I would have gone to the ends of the earth for you, if only you'd asked. And now I have to kill you. You're too much of an unknown to be allowed to live.*

Just as my fingers brush the holster, she pulls back. The hunger in her eyes makes it clear she wants to kick things up a notch. She's weighing up the chance to bounce up and down on my cock versus the likelihood that I'll catch on to her deception.

I tuck a strand of golden hair behind her ear, trying not to flinch as I touch her. "As much as I very much want to continue, Nero's going to come looking for me. And we probably shouldn't be caught in here today."

She pulls back, her eyelashes aflutter. She trails a finger across my jaw and down the center of my chest, leaving a line of fever in her wake. "Sure thing. We can finish this at home later."

"You bet." I fold my lapel back over the holster and give her a peck on the cheek. Do it, Noah's voice echoes in my head. *Take her out. We'll deal with the fallout later. She's too dangerous to walk out of here alive.*

As soon as I escort Mackenzie outside and shut the door behind her, a wave of nausea slams into me. I double over and throw up.

"You okay?" Livvie rushes over. She rubs circles on my back as I cough and spit acidic bile. "You don't look so good."

I rest my spinning head in my hand. "I think I ate something bad."

Ain't that the truth.

"Go home. You're in no state to work, let alone deal with Nero."

I don't go home. I peel out of the parking lot and head deep into the old industrial district of Tartarus Oaks. The acid taste burns in my mouth, but it can't disguise the violet and bubblegum scent that clings to my skin.

I burst into Colosseum just as Noah and Antony begin a practice bout. They circle each other, their steps wary, before Noah throws an exploratory punch and Antony bursts into action. Within minutes, he has Noah in a headlock. From the gangplank above the arena, Claws cheers and calls down advice like an overbearing soccer mom.

"Hook your leg around him, Noah... no, not like that... argh, sure, that's right, lie down and play dead, that will help... Eli? I thought you were at Nero's—" Claudia's face crumples when she sees me. "What's wrong? What did that bastard do now?"

"Not him. Mackenzie." I collapse into an empty table beside the stage, my head in my hands. "Mackenzie came to see me."

"*What?*" Claudia's screech could break windows.

"She did *what?*" Antony drops Noah, who lands on his face.

"What the fuck?" Noah cups his nose, which is pissing blood.

Claudia races off the gangplank and plonks down beside me. She pries my hand from my face. "Eli, look at me. I need you to tell me everything. Is she working with Nero? We have to figure out what they're planning. I'll get George to sort you out with some hidden microphones and—"

"No." The word comes out harsh. I need... I need to get the words out before I go insane. I grip Claudia's hand so hard she winces. "She didn't come to see Nero. She came to—to ask me to the Valentine's dance."

"I don't understand."

I swallow. "I thought she was you at first. She was pretending to be you. But when we kissed, I *knew*—"

"Hang on, you kissed her?" Murder burns in Claudia's eyes.

"She kissed *me*. We were hiding in one of the private rooms because I didn't want Nero to overhear our conversation. I thought you – she – came to tell me about the duke, but instead—"

"Wait, what about the duke?" Antony demands. He unscrews the cap on his water bottle and dumps the contents over his head. Noah limps over to our table and takes the chair opposite, pinching his nose and tilting his head back in an attempt to staunch the bleeding.

I take a deep breath and explain everything, even the bit about how I couldn't bring myself to shoot Mackenzie. By the time I'm done, all three of them are staring at me like I grew a third arm. I brace myself to be berated for cowardice, but that's not what happens.

"This is next level insane, even for Mackenzie," Noah says.

"You can say that again," Antony growls. He paces between the tables, his hands in fists at his sides, the vein above his right eye throbbing. "What the *fuck* is she playing at?"

"She must've known we'd figure this out," Claws says. "Eli would get home and quite quickly figure out we'd never had that conversation at Vault. She's taunting us, making it clear that she could be anywhere in this city at any time, pretending to be me, fucking up my plans. That I'm only holding on to my crown by her pleasure. One word to Nero from her and I'm toast."

"What do we do?" I ask. "There's no counter to this move."

"Leave it to me," Antony says. "I've had a lead on where she might be hiding. I'll take the boys in before Lupercalia and sort her out."

"Count me in," Noah growls.

"Thank you." Claws squeezes my hand back. Her shoulders sag with relief, but her eyes betray her unease.

We're not out of the woods until her sister is dead and buried.

15

———

NOAH

"I don't understand why we have to do it *here*," I complain as we slide out of the car and move along the red carpet toward the entrance of Vault.

"Because parties like this are the perfect places to gather secrets." Claudia smiles, waving to the cameras that line either side of the carpet, snapping away at celebrities and their spoiled offspring. Stonehurst is *that* kind of school. A long line of hopefuls from school who don't have alumni connections wait at the door to the club, calling out to me and Gabe and Claws in the hope we'll invite them to join our crew.

"Then why is Gabe with us? He can't even keep his fly closed. No way is he good at secrets."

"I'm here because you have the personality of a sledgehammer." Gabe claps him on the shoulder. "This kind of work requires a little finesse."

I punch Gabe in the shoulder. It's meant to be a friendly tap, but I've been hanging out in the ring too much lately, and I send him sailing into velvet rope. Real fear flashes in Gabe's eyes before he rights himself, smoothing down the lapels of his pinstriped suit and flashing me that shit-eating grin of his.

"I'm sorry, man." I hold out my hand as the cameras snap merrily away. "Don't know my own strength."

Play it cool, Noah.

I'm on edge tonight. Jumpy, fueled by the knowledge of what we've come here to do. I'm liable to put someone through a wall instead of shaking their hands. Good thing Claudia clings to my arm, her sleek, don't-fuck-with-me attitude keeping my simmering rage under wraps. For now.

After my uncouth display, I half-expect us to be turned around at the door, but of course we're ushered right inside where a smug waiter takes our coats. We join the flow of eager college hopefuls and their parents as they swarm into the club. The stage has been dismantled to make way for round tables and some college displays.

The ceiling drips with strings of golden beads and crystal chandeliers, and everywhere I turn my head I see the glitter of gold and diamonds adorning blueblood necks and wrists and ears. A string band plays in the corner, their soporous music drowned out by the hum of networking and backhanded compliments.

"Who are all these people?" Claudia asks. "I see hardly anyone I recognize from school."

"This party isn't for us, it's for our parents. It's where the ultra-rich meet to grease the wheels of capitalism," I murmur. My father has been dragging me to parties like this since I could walk – it's in rooms like this that he makes the friends who've built his political career, and who he hopes will one day carry him to the White House. A waiter appears at our side, holding out a tray of drinks. I mean, we've obviously both under twenty-one, but who cares? The cops won't be breaking up this party. I throw mine back as I search the crowd for my father. I see him in the corner, chatting to a hedge fund manager and a big-shot film producer, and Vincent Bloomberg.

"Who's he's talking to?" Claws asks.

"Members of the Eldritch Club. It's one of those super-secret elite societies that control the world," I explain. "Pretty much everyone in this room belongs to one of those, but the Eldritch Club is the *worst*. If I didn't know better I'd assume they really did make human sacrifices to some cruel ancient god."

We move deeper into the room, scanning the crowd for our intended target. A group of girls from cheerleading and their mothers stand around beside the Harvard display. I spy Daphne's signature pink hair.

Target acquired.

We saunter on over, inserting ourselves into the group.

"Hi, Noah." Brandy bats her eyelashes at me. Beside her, Daphne makes a disgusted face, probably out of loyalty to Cleo. "So good to see you. Isn't it wonderful that your dad is helping those poor, innocent women start their new lives in America?"

"Oh, sure, Dad's a saint," I hiss through gritted teeth. Claudia digs her heel into my foot, reminding me in the most painful way possible that I need to pretend to like these people. "Are you ladies enjoying the party?"

"Yes, we—"

"Daphne, darling." Her mother elbows her way into our conversation, the glint of a cougar in her eye as she sweeps her gaze over me. "You must introduce me to your friends."

"Why don't you just do it yourself, since you're going to drool all over them anyway?"

"Daphne, *please*." Her mother digs her talons into Daphne's arm. "That's no way to talk to your peers. No wonder Stanford turned you down. At this rate, I'll have to beg Brandeis to take you, and I don't know if we'll ever live down the shame."

"*Fine*, Mom." Daphne glares at us, like it's our fault she didn't get into Stanford. "This is Noah Marlowe and Mackenzie Malloy."

"Oh, *Mackenzie,* it's so good to see you." Mrs. Ballantyne forgets all about drooling over me as she latches on to the juiciest bit of gossip to have walked into the party. She leans in to kiss Claudia's cheeks. "I used to be close to your parents, such a shame to hear they disappeared. Tell us, because we're all just *dying* to know, what have you been doing with yourself all these years?"

"I've been relaxing on a deserted island of the coast of Belize." Claudia hugs my arm and flashes her Ice Queen glare. "Waiting for Noah Marlowe to come of age so I could snap him up."

"And who is this delightful creature?" a very familiar British voice drawls. "Daphne, darling, where have you been hiding this ravishing woman?"

We're saved from further interrogations by Gabe and George, who join our group. Gabe wastes no time turning up the British charm to eleven for Daphne and her mother. We leave them to it and make another circuit of the room. I notice familiar faces from school – Chad and Brenda and Finneas, all being dragged around various groups by their parents, desperately trying to get their kid into the right school or the right internship.

"Oh, there's Grace." I spy my stepmother over by the food table. Regret stabs at my chest as I watch her lean heavily on a cane – I should have gone to see her more since she's been bedridden, but with everything happening with Claws I just... I ran out of time. I didn't want to step foot in that house again. I was afraid. Name a shitty excuse, and I made it to myself. Nothing changes the fact that I left her alone in that house with Dad when she didn't have the strength to defend against his temper.

Yet here she is, standing – albeit shakily – on two feet. Grace was always a fighter.

I drag Claws toward her. Grace is speaking to a group of over-Botoxed ladies-who-lunch. She sees us pushing through the crowd, and she waves us over. The women look like they're ready to pounce on Claudia and pepper her with more questions about deserted islands and the status of the Malloy fortune, but one hard look from me and they scurry away like the rats they are.

"You came." I lean in to kiss her cheek. "I was so worried you'd be stuck in that bed for a while longer."

"I wouldn't miss the chance to see you shine," she beams. I notice she sways a little on her feet, and grips the edge of the table with her free hand, like it's holding her upright. "Every school representative in this room is eager to talk to you. Your mother would be so proud. Thank you for saving me from that horrendous conversation."

I choke up a little at the mention of Mom. In all the chaos of senior year, I've thought of her less. There are even whole days that go by now when I don't remember her bright smile and kind voice, or her blue skin and how cold she felt when we pulled her out of the pool. Yet another thing to feel guilty about. "Always a pleasure."

"Your father abandoned me the moment we walked through the door. I'm so happy to see you. You scrub up so nicely." She leans in to kiss my cheek, but before I can pull away she catches my arm, her grip shaky but firm. She whispers, "There's a small anteroom off the coatroom. Meet me there in fifteen minutes."

I'm too stunned to reply. *Did she really just say that?*

Grace pulls away and starts chattering to Claudia about school and the cheerleading team. I notice how heavily she leans against her cane. Is she still struggling after the scare? I know Grace has neurological problems; it was one of the reasons she quit her job as a journalist. But did Claudia's revenge prank scare her that much?

Should I be worried?

Maybe that's what we're going to discuss in the cloakroom.

My father pulls Grace away to talk to some of his Senate buddies. He gives Claudia a nod of acknowledgment, his hard eyes reminding us of our agreement to remain silent in exchange for new lives for Yara and her girls. I don't even get a nod, not a wrinkle of his nose or a disgusted curl of his lip. I'm still nothing to him. The son he didn't want.

A year ago that rejection would have sent me straight to Antony's club to burn away my rage by beating some poor guy nearly to death. But now, I feel nothing. John Marlowe is *no one* to me. He doesn't deserve my hatred.

I lean in close to tell Claudia about Grace's whispered invitation.

"Oh, intrigue." She glances over her shoulder at Gabe and Daphne. He leads her through the crowded club toward the bar. Her face glows with joy to be on Gabriel Fallen's arm. "It looks like Gabe has everything under control out here. We can spare a few minutes to find out what Grace wants."

We circle around the food table, stuffing our faces with tiny foods until the fifteen minutes are up. I check that my father is occupied with Eldritch Club members, then we slip away into the coatroom. There's no attendant on duty – in this den of thieves, there must be a semblance of honor. *Thou shall not steal thy neighbor's Burberry coat.*

We hunt around behind the jackets, but can't find the anteroom Grace told us about. I'm starting to panic when an arm waves at us from behind a mink.

"Pssst. In here."

Grace ushers us into a narrow door disguised in the paneling. She pulls it shut behind us, plunging us into darkness. I pull out my mobile phone and flick on the 'fireplace' app, and a flickering pixelated fire lights up a small storage area filled with boxes and racks of skimpy costumes for the club. Grace sinks into a pile of peacock-feather fans, her eyes closed as she takes the weight off her legs. Her hands tremble around her cane.

What's wrong with her? That doesn't look like nerves. It looks like she's really fucking sick.

"That's better," she says. "I can hear myself think in here."

"How do you know this room exists?" I ask.

"Nero invited me and your father to tour the new club while it was being built. I happened to notice this little room." She taps her forehead. "I guess he didn't expect I'd have such a journalist's memory for details."

"Grace, are you okay? You look really sick—"

"We don't have much time." She glances at the door. "I need to get this out. You're going to find out tomorrow anyway, but I... I couldn't go through with it without telling you in person. You need to hear this, too, Mackenzie. It concerns your late father. And my sister."

Fear churns in my gut. "Grace, what are you talking about?"

"Harriet didn't kill herself." Her breath comes out in ragged gasps.

I know.

We figured this out weeks ago, but hearing Grace speak it aloud brings it all rushing back – the memory of finding her, of clutching her suicide note in my hands. *First Felix left me, and now you. Everyone I love leaves me to face the darkness alone.*

The rage clouds my vision. I don't want to sit in this tiny room for another second. I want to storm into that party and tear my father's face off with my bare hands. I glance at Claudia, needing her presence to steady me. She plasters a look of shock on her face. "Are you sure? What makes you say that?"

"When I started seeing John after Harriet's death, he made me feel close to her. You both did." The tenderness in Grace's gaze makes my dark heart hurt. "I felt that by being with him, by loving him, by loving *you*, I could keep a piece of my sister alive in my heart. I even quit my job at the newspaper because you both needed me. And I was struggling with the stress, too. That was part of it. But mainly, I wanted to be there for you."

I remember it all so clearly. Grace worked for the *Emerald Beach Examiner* covering local stories. My parents actually met through her. My mother, Harriet, accompanied Grace to some event she was covering where my father was speaking, and they got to talking during the cocktail hour. Grace used to laugh when she told their friends the story. "Here was the up-and-coming politician in a room with all these influential people – the kind of connections that could make or break his career – and he ignored them all to hide in the coatroom with my sister."

As a kid, I always loved this story. It gave me a sick, sad hope that beneath my dad's tempestuous exterior was an actual *person*. But now I see the truth behind Grace's sunny version – that my dad spied a woman who was pliable, naive, and who would fit the wholesome image he wanted to portray. And he pursued her with the full force of his personality until she was powerless to resist him.

And as a cynical, broken teenager, I watched Grace fall for the same shit – his surface charm, lavish holidays, and grand gestures that hid the reality of living with his anger. Through her eyes, my father became the hero once again – the family man looking after her widow's sister, finding love again in the darkness. All the while, behind the doors of our gilded prison, he was as cold and remote as ever. Never violent, but cruel beyond words.

I swallow back the bile as I think about everything Grace gave up for two men who never appreciated her. "If you're telling me that you're leaving him, I'll help you pack your bags."

She shakes her head sadly. "That's not it. I wish that was all it was. The truth is, Noah, for a long time I've wondered about Harriet's death. I stayed with your father long after his grief made him ugly because I wanted the truth. And this week, I found an old laptop hidden at the back of the closet. It's your mother's laptop. One she was using to write her romance novel. I don't think your father knows she hid it there."

He doesn't. I remember Mom laughing as she lay on the sofa with an iced tea, the keys clacking beneath her fingers. Writing the romance she didn't get to have in real life, then shoving the computer under the cushions when my father entered the room. She couldn't bear the scathing cruelty he'd lob at her if he knew she was writing something so *frivolous*, and I couldn't bear the idea of him taking this joy from her, too. She smiled when she wrote, and her smile was so rare and precious.

"You're going to publish her novel?" I guess.

"*No,* omigod." Grace grabs my wrist. "Harriet was many things, but a skilled wordsmith she was not. Just give me a second to get this out, okay? I boot up the laptop and connect it to the WiFi and I find your mother's second email account, the one she used to use for things she didn't want your father to see. There's an email in the draft folder that she wrote to me but never sent." She swallows. "She wrote it the day before she died."

My mouth dries.

"In this letter, Harriet told me that Howard Malloy stormed into the house a couple of days prior, demanding to speak to John. Apparently, Howard was trying to move a large shipment out of the city when it was stolen from under his nose. He seemed to think it was John's problem. He kept saying 'if this gets out, you'll be on the hook just as much as me.' Your father told him to leave, and he did. But Harriet was worried about what she heard. She wanted me to look into it. She couldn't think what business Howard and John could possibly have together, and then..."

And then I found her face down in the swimming pool.

Grace's eyes flutter shut again, and I know she's thinking the same thing as me, remembering that awful sight. Why can't I remember my mother alive and happy? Why does my brain fixate on her blue, bloated body? "If only Harriet had sent that email, I'd have looked into this much sooner. Better late than never. It wasn't hard to get the key to your father's office while he was out and dig around. I've found some pretty horrible things. Your father was accepting large campaign donations from Malloy – way in excess of his other donors. Bribes to make sure Malloy's company was allowed to continue doing what they were doing. But I think it's more than that – I think John was in business with Malloy. That's what Malloy meant when he said 'you'll be on the hook just as much as me.' Plus, John took out a large sum of money right before the Malloys disappeared. You don't take out that kind of cash unless... unless you plan to do something illegal with it. And there's more... paperwork from the trial was fabricated. It looks as though your father made *certain* that Howard Malloy could never go to jail. I think he did it to save his own ass, to cover up whatever he and Malloy were working on together. And then Malloy disappears, the only person who knew about John's involvement... and Harriet started to figure it out and then..."

This tracks with everything my father has already told us, except... except that he said *Malloy* killed my mother to get back at him for the treasure going missing. But what Grace is saying...

...is that my father might've killed my mother to keep her quiet.

He didn't know about this unsent email, but she could have said something that tipped him off. Maybe she confronted him about her suspicions, and he... and he...

I'll kill him.

Claudia's hand clamps on my shoulder, reminding me that I can't go postal in the middle of this party, that we've got a job right now and that needs to be done before I eviscerate John Marlowe and choke him with his own intestines.

Grace coughs into her hand, her whole body racked with pain. She wipes her mouth on the back of her hand. "Noah, you look ready to murder him. Please, don't touch him. It's not your job to take care of this. It's my job to look after you, to get justice for my sister. I sent everything I found to my old boss at the paper. The article comes out tomorrow. And then... I don't know what will happen. Your father will know I was the one who did it. He will know what I suspect him of. Things will get ugly, Noah. I'm afraid I've blown up your life, but—"

"He'll pay." I can't help the grim smile that tugs at my lips. "You're going to burn his entire career to dust, everything he's worked for. And it's exactly what he deserves."

As much as I want to feel my father's life slip through my fingers, what Grace has done is even *more* satisfying. John Marlowe got involved with a crook and killed his own son, then put my mother through the pain of a sham trial before killing her to cover up his crimes. He made me believe she abandoned me, that I was so unloveable that she'd rather die than carry on without Felix. And all to save his precious reputation, to keep his illicit activities out of the press.

And now, the tough-on-organized-crime senator will reap what he's fucking sown.

He's done for. He's hung himself by his own noose.

Only when he's reached absolute rock bottom, when he's died a thousand deaths in the media for the evil he's done, will I kill him for real.

"Veritas liberabit vos," Claws whispers, reverting back to her father's Latin lessons. "The truth will set you free."

"I needed you to know," Grace whispers, her hand curling around my arm. Her skin feels too hot. It's sheened in sweat despite the cool air in the club. "I wanted you to hear it from me.

Your father will fight back with everything he has, and I couldn't stand it if you thought I wanted to hurt you after everything you've been through."

I gather her in my arms. She's skin and bones, a shadow of the bubbly, vivacious Grace I remember. "I'd never believe that. You've been more of a parent to me in four years than he ever was."

"Are you safe?" Claudia asks Grace. "You shouldn't be anywhere near him when this story breaks. Come to Malloy Manor."

"That's sweet, but I have a plan. I need to go home with him tonight, or he'll suspect something is up," Grace says. "But you know how heavily he sleeps, Noah. I'll be long gone by the time he wakes up. Old newspaper friends in New York are helping to hide me. I've got it all worked out. I'll call you as soon as I can."

I hold her tighter, never wanting to let her go. I want to insist that she comes with us instead. We have Tiberius, and Antony, and all of Claudia's other soldiers. We can protect her. But she's right, she's probably better all the way across the country.

"We should get back out there," Grace says, pulling back abruptly and smoothing down her dress. "I don't want him to see me talking to you, in case he thinks you have anything to do with it."

He's going to think that anyway. But I don't know if it matters. John Marlowe is going *down*.

Grace leaves first, stumbling over the lip of the paneling. A hard lump forms in my throat as I watch her go.

Claudia turns to me, icicle eyes blazing with blue flame. "You okay? If you want to, we can skip the trial by public opinion, and I get Antony and Tiberius to kidnap him for a little personal revenge."

Yes. My fingers curl into her soft skin, imagining digging into his neck, squeezing the life from his despicable lungs. "No.

Grace is right. The media will do it for us, and it will be all the more enjoyable watching him brought down in public. When that story breaks, his career is over. He'll go to jail, and they won't be kind to him in there."

"That's my dark prince talking. Can you go back out to the party?" she asks. "Can you smile and shake hands with his sycophants and do what we came here to do, or do I need to get you home?"

"I can do it." I'm here for her. We need to get the information out of Daphne to have something to bargain with, so we can get Claudia out of this fucking marriage.

"Good." Claws holds up her phone. "Because Gabriel has got her in position. We've got work to do, and I want you by my side. I don't know if any of the others have the stomach for this."

I hold out my arm for her – outwardly, I'm the perfect gentlemen, but inside my beastly heart races at the thought of what's to come. "After you, Mackenzie Malloy."

Claudia rolls her eyes as we step out of the hidden room and push our way through the coats. Back in the club, the press of bodies is even more intense than before. I spy my father in the far corner, smiling broadly as he chats to Chad's parents. No one notices as we slip through a door into a short hallway leading to a single elevator.

Our feet sink into thick burgundy carpet. A large man who makes Tiberius look like a teddy bear guards the elevator, arms folded and frown directed at me. His eyes widen when he sees who's on my arm – every crook in this city recognizes Claudia August.

Claudia smiles at the operator. "Gabriel Fallen came this way with two women. Which room are they in?"

"I gave them fourteen, ma'am." The man pulls open the elevator cage for us and presses a key into her hands. "Have a good night."

"I intend to." Claudia's smile could melt butter.

We exit the elevator three floors up into another plushly-carpeted hallway. Gold-flecked wallpaper and gilded portraits adorn the walls. From behind the row of closed doors come moans and cries.

It's hard to believe just a few days ago, Eli was here with the *real* Mackenzie Malloy. I glance down at the woman on my arm, confident that I've got the right twin, and damn she looks fine tonight. Brutality never looked so good.

We locate room fourteen. Claudia slides the key into the lock and sweeps inside. I follow her, closing the door behind me with a click.

"I thought you'd never get here." Gabriel swigs from a silver flask as he luxuriates across the gold-flecked bedspread. George sits stiffly in a velvet chair, her nails digging into the arms. Scattered around them is a plethora of BDSM gear – floggers and leather collars, whips and handcuffs, and several oddly-shaped implements I don't want to inquire about, all thrown about as if there'd been a grand struggle. "I was just about to start my own unique brand of torture by singing Justin Bieber songs horribly off-key, over and over and over until I drove her insane. She's practically begging for Noah to take over."

I peer around the room until I locate our charge. Hanging from the Saint Andrew's cross is a woman, naked except for a pastel pink lace bra and matching thong. Her hands and feet are shackled to the apparatus, and a ball gag muffles her cries.

Claws slips the gag from her mouth. "Hello, Daphne."

16

GEORGE

"It was too easy." Gabriel leans against a sex swing, his hands patting his pockets, looking for the weed I swiped earlier and dumped in the trash. Sad to waste good grass, but Gabe needs an intervention, stat. "All I did was *mention* that George and I were looking for a good time away from the stuffy parents and she melted like butter, practically led *us* up here. And who am I to turn down such an enthusiastic fan?"

Gabe's features are relaxed, but I notice his eyes dart nervously around the room. He pulls a silver flask from his pocket and takes a huge swig. He's supposed to be sober. He *promised* me and Claws he'd stay sober. But I get that he needs to obliterate the memory of what he's done.

What *we've done.*

Daphne jerks her head back as Claudia leans in close. Even through the haze of alcohol, she's terrified. She screams for help, and Claudia chuckles, slapping her cheek lightly.

"Scream all you want, princess. Anyone outside these walls will only believe Gabriel's working his magic on your body." She licks her lips. "Tsk, tsk. If only you remembered that his demon tongue is for my pussy only."

Claudia slaps her other cheek. Daphne's head rolls back. "What do you want?" she cries, tears streaking makeup down her cheeks.

I did this.

Gabriel might've been the one who manhandled her into place, but I clamped the restraints shut. I pushed the ball gag into her mouth.

I told Claudia everything she needed to know to kill this girl's father.

I have no love for Daphne. She's tormented me since grade school. And everything I read suggests her father is a complete scumbag. The world won't miss him.

But... I lost my dad.

I know the pain that cuts open your chest and twists into your heart. I know that grief is endlessly bleeding through that open wound, and you walk around trying to act normal with a fuck-off big gaping hole in your chest. Eventually, you get so good at pretending that people stop seeing your blood and guts spilling all over the floor, but the hole is still there. Always.

I don't know if I can live with carving that same hole into someone else's heart.

"Get out of my face, bitch." Daphne switches tactics, going from sniveling victim to bitch princess.

"Manners, Daphne." Claws strokes a nail along her cheek. "We're not here to hurt you. We just want to have a little chat about your father."

"My father?" Daphne's jaw sets. "What does he have to do with anything? He's dead."

"That's not true, is it?" Claudia crosses the room and throws an arm around my shoulders, pulling me in close so I can smell her heady perfume. She's wearing something of Ainsley Malloy's tonight – some vanilla and floral scent that reminds me of Mackenzie wafting past me in the halls before she slammed me into a locker. "You see, George here has learned that your old man is very much alive."

Daphne glares at me. "I never thought a goody-goody freak like you would do something like this."

I swallow. I never thought so, either. I don't say anything. If I open my mouth, I'm going to scream.

"You know I'm going to sue you when I get out of here, George Fisher. Your poor freak hippie mother won't have a single thing left by the time I'm done."

Claudia tsks. She slides the hem of her dress over her thigh in a slow, languid motion that makes Gabe moan. From the leather sheath strapped to her thigh, she draws a thin, silver blade. Claudia turns the point on the pad of her finger, drawing a droplet of crimson blood. "If you want to make it out of this room alive, insulting my best friend is not the greatest way to start."

Daphne's eyes widen as she watches the knife. Her whole body goes rigid. Claudia stands and crosses the room again. Blood rushes in my ears. Claudia bends over her captive. I taste acid in my mouth. I want to scream, to hurl myself across the room and stop this, but I'm frozen in place.

Why don't Gabe or Noah stop her?

Noah stands behind Claudia, beefy arms crossed over his chest. He peers down the cross, dark eyes narrowed with hunger. Gabe lies across the bed, chin resting in his hands, gazing up at Claudia like she's a goddess come to life.

They won't stop her.

Gabe's words thrum against my skull. *If you want to escape Emerald Beach and the Triumvirate, your window is closing fast.*

Claudia leans over and draws the flat of the blade across Daphne's naked skin. Daphne's eyes shudder closed. Claudia hums to herself as she winds Daphne's long, perfect hair around her wrist, pulling it taut until fresh tears stream from Daphne's eyes.

"Your father owes money to people I know," Claudia says.

"Newsflash, you psycho," Daphne hisses. "Tell me something I don't know. He owes a lot of people money. Why do you think he... he offed himself."

"Still lying, I see." Claudia yanks Daphne's hair, tipping her head back and stretching her long neck. Daphne whimpers as Claudia swipes above her fist. Clumps of Daphne's hair tumble to the floor. "All we want is a location so we can go and collect on his debts. That's not too much to ask, is it? Now, answer the question, or the next swipe will take one of your pretty little fingers."

"You wouldn't dare," Daphne spits.

"Wouldn't I?" Claudia grabs her wrist, flattening her hand against the edge of the cross. Daphne's jaw works as she stubbornly and stupidly remains silent. She still thinks Claudia is bluffing.

Claudia swings her arm. A half-circle of blood splatters the wall.

Daphne screams.

And screams.

And screams.

A bloody finger joins the clumps of hair on the rug.

The tiny food I ate rises up inside me and ends up in a pile on the floor.

"Shit." Claudia tosses the knife to Noah. "Take over. I need to get George out of here."

She grabs my arm and yanks me from the room. I close my eyes, but I can still see that half-circle of blood. My stomach gasps and twists, but there's nothing left to come up.

In the hallway, Claws shoves me into one of the velvet

armchairs. She kneels at my feet, taking my hands into hers. "What's going on with you?"

"I didn't know..." I shudder as the blood forms a half-circle across her face. I survived Galen's brutal autopsy and watching Claudia bury her knife into that boy's head. Brutal killings are easy for me now. I feel weirdly comfortable around death and gore. But this is a girl I've known since grade school, and now her finger is lying on the rug. And as soon as Claws is done with her, she's going to lose her dad.

"You're the one who gave me the information about her father." Claudia's fingers stroke my cheek. "You had to know what might happen."

"But her dad..."

"George, I know you don't believe in an eye for an eye. And that's exactly why you need me. If anyone, anyone, ever tries to hurt you, I'll do worse than cutting off their fingers, got it? You never have to feel afraid or alone again."

I nod, drawing her words inside me and holding them against the gaping hole in my chest.

Claws continues, "But you *also* don't have to become me. One bloodthirsty mafia queen is enough for any friendship. You don't have to tough it out because of some sense of loyalty. We're ride or die, got it?"

I nod, still not trusting myself to speak.

Claudia glances back at the door to room fourteen. Daphne's scream mingles with the other moans and cries – just another of Nero's clientele at the mercy of a lover. Only this time, it's Noah Marlowe kissing a blade to tender flesh. I know Claudia wants to join her lover, wants to wield the knife herself and feel the moment of triumph when Daphne caves.

"Come on." She drags me to my feet, punching the button for the elevator. The doors swing open and she pulls me inside. "Let's see if we can't find you some of those tiny profiteroles."

"I do like profiteroles," I murmur, leaning my head on her shoulder as the elevator doors close on us. Claudia kisses my forehead. *We're ride or die.*

I think of Gabriel's scholarship brochure burning a hole in my bookbag.

How can I desert this girl? How can I leave the best friend that's ever happened to me?

The elevator doors open, and the guard holds the door open for us to re-enter the party.

But if I stay, what happened in that hotel room *will* become my life. I won't be able to help it. And I don't think I can hold my father's memory in my punctured heart while turning into the monster from one of his films—

My whole body goes rigid.

No.

He can't be here.

He can't.

But he is. My body recognizes him before he even turns toward us. I stagger away, my back slamming into the elevator, my veins sparking with adrenaline as I fight my instinct to run.

He's here.

Alec LeMarque.

17

CLAUDIA

That bastard. That fucking *bastard*.

Beside me, George is as white as a sheet. She's never told me what Alec did to her, and she doesn't have to. We've been friends long enough that I can read between the fucking lines, and it doesn't take a best friend to see that Alec LeMarque messed her up.

And for that, he will die.

I slam my fist in the elevator buttons, closing the doors behind us and sending us back up to the private rooms. George's eyes cloud over. Her nails dig into my arm, biting my skin.

"George?" She doesn't register my voice. I shake her arm, try again. "George, listen to me. I know what he did to you. I *know*. I thought we dealt with Alec LeMarque, but he's like a fucking whack-a-mole. We knock that fucker down and he keeps popping up again. Now he's here, and I can't allow that to stand. So let's play this out. We could go to the police. That's a possibility. We could tell our stories. You could submit yourself for whatever evidence they require, open your entire personal life up for scrutiny. His lawyers will paint you as the weird loner chick wanting to get some leverage from the up-and-coming actor, probably trying to promote your podcast. 'Hasn't Alec been through enough without these baseless allegations?' they'll say. Nod if I'm right."

George nods. Her eyes dart to the doors, and a tremor shakes her whole body.

"So that's not an option. You went to the authorities when you found out about your dad's remains, but they didn't want to know, so you got justice for yourself. But you're not on your own anymore. We're ride or die, remember? So, my friend, that fucker is out there laughing and eating profiteroles like every-thing is right with the world. He hasn't learned a thing, and I won't abide that. Not for another minute. So what I want to know is, do you want justice? The kind of justice only Claudia August can deal out?"

The doors open onto the private rooms. Daphne's screams echo along the hall, mingling with the other moans and grunts. The boys are busy. We girls can handle this for now. I shove my foot into the elevator door, blocking it from moving. When George looks back at me, her eyes harden.

"Make sure he never hurts anyone again."

"There's my George." I kiss her forehead. I let my foot slide out of the door, and I punch in the floor for the bar. The elevator jerks back down. "I'm going to ask you to do something, and it's going to completely suck. It's the worst thing I'll ever ask you to do, and I'm so sorry. But I need you to go back into the party and get Alec LeMarque alone."

George bites her lip as the doors open. "Why?"

"Because if I go over there, he's going to make a scene. He won't come with me willingly. But you…"

"He won't believe me, either," she says. "Not after Antony's PE class."

"He will if you tell him you were jealous of the attention he gave me." I grab her shoulders. "I know it's fucking disgusting.

But can you dig down deep and find the words to convince him to follow you into the backstage bathroom? I'll do the rest."

She shakes her head. Tears pool at the corners of her eyes. "I'm sorry, Claws. I wish I could, but I can't face him…"

"For fuck's sake, I'll do it," another familiar voice says. "What am I doing?"

I whirl around to see Yara, standing in the hallway wearing a server's uniform, a tray of profiteroles perched on her arm.

"What are you doing here?"

"I wanted to see you in action, and I thought you could do with an extra pair of eyes, so I got myself hired by the catering company," Yara says, like it's obvious. She holds the platter out to George, who's nervously stuffing profiteroles into her mouth. "So tell me what I'm doing."

"Seducing a bastard rapist scumbag so he follows you into the backstage bathroom."

"To be honest, I'm a little offended you didn't think to ask me in the first place." Yara yanks George into the bathroom. "I'll need to borrow your dress."

They emerge five minutes later, wearing each other's clothes. George picks up the tray, while Yara sashays her way over to Alec's group. Within moments, she has them all laughing, and she steps close to Alec, touching his arm as she smooths down his tie.

"Holy shit, she's doing it," I whisper to George, who nods. One of the Eldritch Club members snaps her fingers at George, and she hurries away, platter in hand. I cast one last look over at Yara, who's touching Alec's arm and smiling in all the right ways, and sneak back upstairs to see how the guys are getting on with Daphne.

I turn the key in the lock and poke my head in. Noah appears in the doorway, the front of his shirt splattered with blood. Daphne's head is slumped against her shoulder, her body limp.

"We got the location. He's living in a vacation house they own in Nantucket, purchased under a fake name."

"Good. I need you both downstairs."

Noah peers down at his bloody shirt. "What's going on?"

"Alec LeMarque is here, and we're going to make him pay."

18

NOAH

We leave an unconscious Daphne tied to the cross for Nero to deal with, and follow Claws back down to the party. I'm barely off the elevator when I spy the bastard. Alec has peeled Yara away from his group, and he has her back up against a pillar, one elbow leaning close to her face, hemming her in. Yara tugs on his shirt collar, looking as though she's exactly where she wants to be.

Damn, that woman has a natural gift for subterfuge.

Beside me, Claudia beams her cold smile. I think she sees a lot of herself in Yara. Her nails dig into my arm. "We should get in position."

The two of us move toward the backstage door, sliding past George on the way. Claudia gives her wrist a squeeze, alerting her that shit is about to go down. We slip through the hidden door into the backstage area, pushing our way through racks of costumes, disassembled stripper poles, and piles of sky-high pumps. At the back of the room is the bathroom for Nero's dancers – one row of stalls, another of sinks and lighted mirrors, with hair straighteners and makeup scattered across every surface.

I take the stall second from the end, while Claws squeezes herself behind some boxes underneath the sinks. I see the glint of her second knife as she slides it into her hand. Her other knife is tucked in my belt, still stained with Daphne's blood.

We wait.

The silence builds. Blood pounds in my ears. All I can see is Alec's twisted face as he held Claudia down on the hood of his car.

Voices, laughter. The bathroom door creaks as it swings open. I watch through the crack in the stall door as Yara pulls Alec inside. Her fingers tangle in his hair, and he clamps one beefy hand over her tit, the other frantically tugging at the hem of her dress. This guy thinks it's his lucky day. The bathroom door swings shut behind them.

We're alone.

"Come here, baby," Alec purrs, cradling her body against his. "You know you want this."

I remember that day in the desert when he threw Claws on the hood of the car. I thought she was Mackenzie then, but even though I hated her for her part in my brother's death, seeing what he intended to do made me realize I could draw a line across my rage.

This guy tried to make me into a rapist.

He tried to take from Claudia what wasn't his, and George... sweet, kind George...

For years I've been friendly with Alec, playing on the same teams, going to the same parties, listening to his inane stories about being on set for all his bit parts and TV commercials. Alec the actor. Alec the friendly, popular guy everyone loved. And all the while George was alone, carrying the memory of how he hurt her. And all those other women who came forward after we trashed his car. And if I'd known... if I'd fucking *known*...

Tonight's retribution was a long time coming.

Yara pulls Alec into the stall next to mine. Their bodies slam against the wall. She lets out a loud, fake moan.

As silently as possible, I climb up on the toilet bowl, leaning well back so Alec can't see me as I peer over the side. He has Yara pinned in a corner, his hands struggling under the tight fabric of her dress. Yara tilts her head up, and her dark eyes meet mine. She smiles.

Showtime.

Claudia slinks like a cat from her hiding spot. She kicks the stall door open, slamming it into Alec's back. Alec whirls around, his face a picture of surprise. "What the fuck are you—"

His words cut off into a scream as Yara twists his wrist and slams his hand into the tiles, pinning him in place with her body. Alec's too dumbfounded to react. Claudia seizes her chance – she reaches up and snaps three of his fingers.

Pop pop pop.

The pain takes a moment to register. When it does, Alec thrashes wildly. "Bitch, get off me or I'll call security."

"Now, now, Alec," Claudia smiles. "Where's the fun in that?"

She flicks the knife across his cheek, making a deep cut that weeps blood. Yara's fingers dig into his wrist as she works to trap his leg with her knees. Alec rolls his shoulder forward and slams Yara into the opposite wall, his good hand going around her neck.

"You two runty girls don't stand a chance," he growls. "First, I'm going to choke the life out of your friend here, then I'm going to finally do what I should have finished in the desert. You're going to get what's coming to you, Mackenzie Malloy."

That's my cue. I lean over the stall, wrapping my tie around my fingers. Alec peers up at me as I come for him. "Marlowe," he croaks out, his grip loosening on Yara. "These crazy bitches fucking broke my fingers. Get me out "

I fling the tie around his neck, twisting the ends until he

stops fucking talking. Alec claws at the silk, but I have the better angle. I brace my weight against the stall, lifting him off the ground. His eyes bug out and his feet scramble for purchase. One lands in the toilet bowl, splashing water everywhere.

"Gross." Yara wrings the hem of the dress. "This is *silk,* and now it smells like a toilet."

"Don't kill him," Claudia reminds me. "Not yet."

One of the tricks you learn in underground fighting – especially if you're up against a buddy and you've both decided to throw the fight for a bit of extra cash – is how to choke someone out until they lose consciousness. I hold on until I feel Alec go limp in my arms, then I drop his body. Alec slumps, his head banging against the toilet bowl.

I jump down and crowd into the stall, ready to drag him out. Claudia bites her lip as she throws out an arm to hold me back. Her chest heaves as she stares down at him. She draws back her foot and kicks him, again and again and again, her stiletto making a bloody mess of his face.

"How does it feel?" she yells as she pummels him with her fists. "How does it feel when you can't fight back?"

Alec doesn't answer.

I let her do her thing until her shoulders sag and she slumps against me. "Yara, get George and Gabriel," Claudia says, her body trembling as the adrenaline dissipates. "We're going to Colosseum. I have just the thing for our friend Alec."

CLAUDIA

When we arrive at the club, Colosseum is packed with the usual Saturday crowd. Antony greets us at the rear entrance as Noah drags Alec's unconscious body from the trunk of his car.

"You'd better have a good reason for pausing tonight matches," he growls as he lets us in through the old locomotive shed he uses as a staging area for his fighters. "They're baying for blood out there."

"Good." *They shall have it.*

We come out in a large shed that must have once housed a locomotive and now serves as a locker room and training space. A couple of fighters warm up in a makeshift ring, while others sit around drinking and doing lines of coke. An old trench extends from one end of the shed to the other – once a space for the engineers to work under the locomotive, it's been turned into an underground tunnel connecting this room to the arena, so the fighters can come and go without having to walk through the ravenous crowd. The room reeks of old sweat and blood. Noah props Alec up on a stone bench in one of the cells we reserve for prisoners, and shackles his arms above his head. The other fighters look on with interest. A few call out insults of Alec, but they return to their card game. They're used to sharing their digs with the damned.

Antony's lip curls back as he recognizes Alec. He looks to me, and understanding flickers in his eyes. "How the fuck did you get him out of Vault without anyone seeing you?"

I pat George's shoulder. "It was all George's idea. She pulled the fire alarm. We snuck him out a side door in the chaos. Right now, Nero's people are too busy dealing with the fire department to notice a missing guest. The firefighters are going to insist on searching every room, which means that when they find Daphne he'll have a hell of lot of explaining to do. He's gonna be so pissed."

Behind me, I hear a whoosh of water as Noah upturns a bucket over Alec's head. I wanted to be in the room when he woke up, but I've got plans to make. The work of an Imperator is never done.

I take George's hand and place it in Gabriel's. "You don't have to stay for this," I tell her. "I won't fault you if you leave. But I want you to know that I'm doing this for you. I am a shit best friend. I'll probably forget your birthday. I won't reply to texts. I'm flaky and damaged and self-absorbed and a general bad influence. But I can give you this. I can give you the justice you can't take for yourself. Do you understand?"

George nods.

"I can get Tiberius to take you home if—"

"I'll stay."

My eyes narrow. "It's not going to be pretty—"

Her eyes narrow right back. "Make him suffer."

That's my girl. I kiss her cheek, then touch my hand to Gabriel's, rubbing my finger across his jaw. "Your job is to look after her," I whisper. "Be your big-hearted, beautiful, broken self.

Let her fall to pieces with you, because I don't have it in me to be human tonight. Not where he's concerned."

Gabe nods. He leads George off toward the staircase leading to the private area reserved for Imperators. Noah drags a struggling Alec from his cell while I whisper my plans to Antony. He whistles. "And I thought the beating we gave him in class was brutal. I'll make the preparations, cousin. This will be fun."

I leave Alec in Noah's capable hands and take Yara with me. We don't follow George and Gabriel through the private entrance. Not yet. Both Nero and Constantine and their people are here tonight. I want to make an entrance. I want to make it clear just how much of a threat I am.

I drag Yara into one of the guest rooms, and we touch up each other's makeup. Alec tore the hem of Yara's dress, and I have his blood speckled up my arms. I don't bother to wash it off. Let them see that their Imperator will get her hands dirty.

We link arms and emerge at the back of the crowd just as Noah enters the ring, his barbarian mask firmly in place. People leap to their feet, cheering for their favorite fighter, knowing they're about to see something special. But no opponent enters the ring. Noah stands still as a statue, his naked chest glistening with sweat beneath the harsh floodlights, the mark of August clearly visible on his wrist. Yara and I start to walk toward him. Women gasp as Noah drops to one knee, his head bowed in reverence to me.

Slowly, heads turn toward us. I hold my chin high. The crowd parts. Men stare at Yara with hunger in their eyes, but no one dares to make a move.

Every eye in the place is on me.

I raise my chin to the VIP area, where George and Gabriel sit at the August table, a bottle of something between them. George nods to me. Beside them, the other two tables are full of people, but I'm only interested in two men.

Constantine stares down his long nose at me, his eyes dancing with the promise of blood. If I were into older guys and didn't already have three boyfriends I'm totally crazy about, I might've been into him. Bloodlust looks good on him.

Nero grins, his whole body shaking with suppressed laughter. But it's a ruse – I can read his rage in his eyes. I've dealt him too many blows – freeing his shipment of girls, swiping the animals he intended to use to sell his entertainments, and right now the fire department is around at his new club. To add insult to injury, I've hijacked our people at their most bloodthirsty to deliver some kind of message.

I surprise him. And for all his false mirth, Nero Lucian doesn't like surprises.

Eli's mother sits beside Nero, scowling at me. She hates me because if I marry Nero, she won't be able to. Well, she's welcome to him.

Beside me, Yara holds her head high, holding the crowd back with nothing but her remote, penetrating stare. I hear whispers about her. Word spreads through my people that she was one of Nero's girls, and now she walks by my side, reinforcing the law I've laid down. The August family doesn't deal in skin, and in this new world, anyone can rise in favor. They don't know how special Yara is – she wasn't born for this life, but Nero's cruelty *made* her, shaped her into a brutal and calculating ally, a woman I'm proud to have at my side.

By the time I walk onto the gangplank atop the arena, the crowd is on their feet, roaring and baying for blood. An Imperator interrupting the entertainments unannounced? They know something very special is about to happen. I raise my hands for silence.

"Hello, everyone. Are you enjoying the fights?"

I'm met with a roar of assent.

"Good. My cousin Antony works hard to give you the violence and bloodshed you crave.

I know you're sad that we lost our beloved lion. I want to promise you that you'll still have your bread and your circuses. Tonight I have a special treat for you. Tonight, you will bear witness to our own brand of justice."

I gesture to Noah. He rises from his feet and enters the tunnel, dragging out Alec. Alec's awake now, his head flailing in all directions as he takes in the blood-soaked arena, the baying crowd, and me.

I point to Alec. "This man is a rapist. He thinks he's entitled to the bodies of women without their consent. He tried to rape me, your Imperator."

People are on their feet again, bashing the tables with their fists, stomping the concrete, roaring their outrage. It's addictive, their righteous anger. It burns in my veins like a drug. They may be my subjects, but I want to please them, I want to give them what they want.

And they want blood.

"But most importantly, he tried this on my closest friend." I stare out into the crowd, pausing to meet as many eyes as I can. Men who may take lives but who do so with honor growl their disgust. Women glare back at me, hissing their own stories of abuse. Too many women in this audience have been hurt at the hands of men like Alec.

Tonight is for them.

"We are family," I say. "All of us. When you sign your name to the Triumvirate's ledger books, you receive the protection of this family. Tonight, I want you to know exactly what that protection offers. And I want anyone out there thinking of hurting my family to see what happens when you cross me."

I take Antony's arm and allow him to lead me off the podium. The crowd gasps as I step down into the arena. Imperators rarely touch the blood-soaked sand. We like to remain remote, above it all.

But not tonight.

Tonight I want to be close enough to *smell* his fear.

Noah kicks Alec. He trips over the shackles binding his ankles, and topples forward to land facedown in the sand. Noah reaches down and grabs a fistful of hair, yanking Alec's head back so he stares into my eyes.

"Bow before your queen," Noah roars, the mask muffling his words so that only Alec and I can hear them.

Tears stream down Alec's cheeks, mingling with the blood. I look down my nose at him, and my body hums with power. "You're a weed, Alec LeMarque. You grow through everything, choking away all that's beautiful. If the gardener wants a beautiful garden, she must pull out the weeds and burn them, and scatter the ashes back into the earth to feed new growth."

I nod to Antony on the gangway above. He signals to his people. Two men wheel out a large bronze sculpture of a bull. As soon as the crowd sees the bull, they go absolutely *wild*. They rush from their seats, their bodies slamming against the wire fence around the arena, desperate for a front-row seat to the spectacle. They cry and chant and roar with bloodlust.

It's been a long, long time since they've seen the brazen bull.

This punishment is reserved for only the worst offenders, for those who threaten the sanctity of the Triumvirate itself. Many of the people here tonight know of the bull only as a rumor, as a myth told by our veteran soldiers to frighten new recruits into loyalty.

It hasn't been used in my lifetime.

Until now.

It takes Antony's men a long time to get the bull into the center of the arena – even on wheels, the bronze effigy is heavy and ungainly. Once the brakes are set and the bull locked in place, the men busy themselves stacking wood underneath it.

Two more men disappear backstage and return carrying a leather armchair with beautifully carved arms. They set it down in front of the fire, and I sink into the cushion, my fingers curling around the carvings. Noah and Yara stand behind me. Noah's fingers tangle in my hair. The men bring me a drink, which I sip while we wait.

All the time I watch Alec's face, dim with fear and confusion. I savor every moment of his distress.

With Brutus, I robbed myself of my rightful vengeance. He died too quickly, too painlessly, because I would not lose the chance to put him down by proselytizing like a comic book supervillain. But a little pomp and circumstance feels right for Alec. I turn my head to meet George's gaze. She's still on the balcony with Gabriel, still watching with an intense expression.

Antony nudges me. "The fire is ready now."

I rise to my feet. The crowd falls silent.

The door in the bull's side is so heavy I need both hands to swing it open, revealing the hollow chamber inside – just large enough for a man. The exterior of the bull has been shined so I can see my reflection in it, but the inside is a gaping black maw.

I address the crowd, but my eyes never leave Alec's face.

"Perillos of Athens invented this device. It's called the brazen bull. The story goes that when he presented the bull to Falaris, the tyrant requested Perillos demonstrate its workings. Perillos climbed inside to demonstrate where the victim would lay, and Falaris slammed the door down on him and lit the fire beneath."

The bull gleams golden beneath the floodlights. Alec's fear scents the air. It hits my veins like the best drug in the world. I revel in it.

"It's said that Falaris described the screams of his victim, 'as the tenderest, most pathetic, most melodious of bellowings.'" I settle into the armchair. "Let's find out."

Alec's eyes are wide. He's too petrified to put up much of a fight as Noah and Antony stuff him into the bull. Alec reaches out to grab Noah's collar. The look in his eyes is of hope dying. "Help me. She's mad... she's going to kill me—"

"Damn right." Noah slams down the heavy door, jamming Alec's hand and severing three of his fingers. They drop onto the ground. Blood spurts from the door, and Alec's words break into screams.

I lean back in the chair and cross my legs. The crowd has gone eerily quiet. The only sound now is the crackling of the fire and my own blood roaring in my ears. The bronze bull groans and creaks as it slowly heats up. Smoke curls from the nostrils of the bull – faint tendrils at first, then great puffs of smoke, reminiscent of the steam trains that once used this roundhouse.

After a time, another sound reaches my ears. The sweetest sound I've ever heard.

Alec LeMarque screams.

His screams become more than screams – they are inhuman, otherworldly, rising from a place of essential truth within him.

Even though I'm watching Alec die with hundreds of other people, this feels strangely intimate. Noah's fingers stroke my scalp. As Alec's screams wash over me, there's only one face I see.

George.

She leans against the railing, the flames reflected in her green eyes. Can she smell him burning? Can she taste his death on her tongue?

Does she love the sweet sounds of retribution?

Noah remains beside me, his hand in mine. Gabriel films the whole thing. Later, I'll send it in an anonymous text to all the girls at Stonehurst who Alec victimized. Let everyone in this town know what the August family does to rapists.

Let bad men tremble before me.

It takes a long time for Alec to die. The bull glows. His screams pour over me. Falaris was right – it's the sweetest melody.

When it's finally done, I exit the arena to stunned, reverent silence. Tiberius drives us home, and I gather the three princes into my bed. That night, for the first in many nights, I sleep with peace in my heart.

20

NOAH

*N*o.

I throw myself out of bed with such force that I send Gizmo flying across the room.

She hits the curtain and bounces to the floor, shaking her head and peering up at me with wide, terrified eyes.

"I'm so sorry, girl." I pick up the tiny kitten and settle her back in beside Eli's sleeping head. I stand at the window, sucking in breath after breath, trying to disgorge the nightmare from behind my eyelids.

But there's no getting rid of it. Because my nightmare is my reality.

I boiled Alec LeMarque to death last night.

Every time I close my eyes, he screams inside my skull, the way he screamed inside the bull.

I don't regret it. Not for a single fucking second. What a way to spend my last night of freedom.

Because the *real* nightmare is about to begin.

Grace's story will hit the media this morning, and it will burn my life to ashes. I'll be shoved back into the media circus I lived through when Felix died. My life won't be my own until the media drags all of my father's sordid deeds across the coals.

He deserves every bit of the shit that's about to be flung his way, but it feels like history repeating itself – too much like last time, and last time ended up with my mother floating in our swimming pool.

Back then, during Felix's trial, I only had one person left on this earth I cared about, and she left me. This time, I have Claudia, the guys, Grace, George, Yara, even Tiberius and Ms. Drysdale. I have a real family. And the thought of losing them makes me sick.

Last night when I watched the brazen bull glow, when Alec's screams scoured my soul clean, I wished they were my father's screams instead.

There's still time. But let the press pick the meat from his bones first.

I go downstairs to Howard Malloy's gym, lock the monkeys in their pen, and run on the treadmill until my legs wobble and I can't hold myself up any longer. I deliberately don't turn on the TV or look at my phone. Maybe I'll be able to get a few blissful hours of ignorance before I have to deal with this new wave of bullshit.

Fat chance. When I head upstairs to the kitchen, Gabriel has the news blaring. The others sit around the table, glued to their phones. Every station, every paper is abuzz about Grace's article. "...residents of Emerald Beach have woken up to an exposé that's turned their world upside down. The beloved Senator Marlowe – who won his seat for his tough stance on organized crime – has been unmasked accepting dirty money from the billionaire Howard Malloy to fund illegal performance-enhancing drugs – the very same drugs that killed his son, Felix Marlowe. Following Felix Marlowe's death, Senator Marlowe sued Malloy in civil court, all the while fabricating evidence that extricated himself from blame, and our sources indicate he also put out a hit through the notorious Dio family for—"

"Turn that shit off," I growl. But as I reach for the coffee pot, I catch a glimpse of my father's face as he's led from our house in handcuffs. Something like happiness twists in my stomach, pulling my facial muscles in directions I'm not familiar with.

"Look at that." Gabriel grins. "Noah's actually *smiling*."

"They arrested him already?" I grab the phone from his hand. The camera scans our house as armed police swarm through the front door. The DEA is there with drug-sniffing dogs, and the FBI. *Holy shit, this is big. Grace, you're amazing. You blew this wide open. Maybe it'll save another athlete from ending up like Felix.* The announcer continues her commentary in a chipper voice. "—, while the body found inside the house—"

My heart sinks. *Body? What body?*

Everyone has gone silent, except the reporter, who keeps on talking as if her next words aren't going to ruin my life. Her voice has become a vacuous siren, a witch's wail.

Eli grabs his keys from the table and tugs my arm. "Let's go."

I DON'T REMEMBER the car ride over, or how we talked our way inside the secure perimeter. The next thing I know, I'm marching up the marble steps toward the gaping front door just as the paramedics wheel out a tiny, frail body strapped on a stretcher, an oxygen mask pressed over her face.

Grace.

My whole world stops.

Not Grace.

Please, no.

I can't lose her, too.

She was supposed to be with her friend, she promised us she was safe.

"What happened to her?" Eli demands.

"We don't know yet, kid," the paramedic says as she shoves him out the way. "We found her in a bedroom upstairs. She wasn't breathing. We think she might've overdosed on something. We've given her oxygen and restarted her heart, but until we know what she's taken, there might not be much we can do."

"I'm her son," I choke out. "I'm coming to the hospital."

He helps me into the van. Claws climbs up beside me. The ambulance screams as we tear out of the driveway, but I don't know if I'm hearing the siren or the screaming inside my head.

21

CLAUDIA

race dies in the night.

The doctors do everything they can. They pump her stomach, give her charcoal, and run test after test after test to try to figure out what made her sick. Eli thought to head up to her room and shove every pill bottle he could find into his bag and bring them to the hospital, but nothing matched the symptoms she demonstrated.

I think back to the way she acted at the party, how she leaned hard on her cane for support, how her glassy eyes swam with pain and determination. And I think of Brutus's glazed eyes peering up at me, baring me to end it all. A horrible, sickening feeling clutches my stomach and won't let go.

Noah holds Grace's hand as she closes her eyes for the last time. His face is desolate. Noah is gone. In his place is a monster.

Two orderlies hover in the doorway, waiting to wheel her away to the morgue. "What the fuck are you looking at?" Noah roars, flinging himself at them. He kicks their gurney against the wall. They scatter in terror, and I know it won't be long before we've got security on our asses.

I call Galen. "I need you to pull some strings for me."

My loyal doctor comes through for us. An hour later, another pair of orderlies knock on the door. "We're here on Galen's orders," one says. Noah turns, his fists curled, but I throw myself in front of him.

"They're going to take her to Galen. He'll give us the answers we need. Then you can give her the funeral she deserves."

Noah sags against me. The fight hums inside him, the monster begging to be unleashed. But he lets them take her.

Tiberius drives us across the bridge to Tartarus Oaks. Galen has set up shop in the basement of the largest veterinary clinic in the city. Upstairs, unknowing citizens bring their sick pets to the best vets in the city, who earn a top salary as long as they don't ask questions about the locked basement door and look the other way when medical supplies go missing. Tiberius leads us down a hidden stairwell into the basement.

Galen has an impressive setup – the veterinary clinic is housed in the one remaining wing of an old hospital building. Galen's makeshift infirmary, laboratory, and morgue stretches the entire length of the old hospital. I can see him and George in the morgue through the glass that separates the areas, moving around the body on the table, making notes, taking samples. Noah paces across the floor, his body rigid with hate.

I lose count of the hours. My ass is numb and Noah has worn a hole in the carpet by the time Galen approaches, his face grim. Noah lunges at him, grabbing his collar. "What happened to her?"

"She was poisoned," Galen says.

"The fuck?"

"There's a small needle mark on the inside of her arm. She's been injected with a drug. Grey Death, but not a kind I've ever seen before. It also contains high amounts of deer antler velvet."

Noah's head snaps back. He drops Galen and staggers away, his eyes wide as saucers. I know exactly what he's thinking.

Galen continues. "This injection probably happened fairly recently – sometime this morning. The dose would not usually be enough to kill a human, but when it's on top of the regular amount of this drug she's been taking, it's caused a toxic build-up that stopped her heart."

"What the fuck did you just say?" Noah yells.

"That this woman has been using this deer antler velvet concoction on a regular basis, most likely daily, for months. If she wasn't on some kind of illegal sports enhancement, then it's likely someone was trying to poison her."

Noah cries out. He lunges at Galen, who darts away just in time. Instead, Noah grabs a trolley of medical implements and hurls it across the room. An expensive-looking microscope follows, crashing into a filing cabinet and shattering to pieces.

I probably shouldn't let him turn Galen's lab into a rage room.

"Noah. Noah, look at me."

Noah gasps as he hurls a computer screen into the wall. I catch him as he reels, grasping his face in my hands. Anguish rakes her poisoned claws across his skin, opening deep wounds that he will never, ever be able to heal. He will bleed forever because he has already lost so much. Because even a soul as strong as Noah's can only endure so much heartache before his humanity is burned away to ash.

I know this, because I'm made of ash and vengeance.

Noah struggles against me, but some part deep inside him recognizes me, sees his own hate reflected back at him. It calms him a little, only enough so I can get through.

"Noah." I whisper his name, call him back from the brink.

"My father did this." Noah's face burns red. The anguish lives in his bones now. "He did it to send a message to us. We meddled in his shit and he *killed* her to make me stop. All those drugs he had her taking, pretending he was caring for her..."

"If he thought this would make you cower, he doesn't know

you at all," I say. "You give me the word and I'll have his throat slit by tonight—"

But Noah wasn't listening, not really. He was throwing himself against the walls of the cage his father created. "Grace knew what he was doing to her. She never intended to leave that house. She knew she was already dying."

"We don't know that."

"I know it," he says bitterly. "I saw it in her eyes at the party. Why didn't she let me help her?"

Why couldn't I save her? The wildness in his eyes keens. *Why does everyone I love have to leave me?*

"You did help her," I say, thinking of Grace's hand on Noah's arm at the party last night, the fire in her eyes as she watched him. "You gave her a reason to fight, to be braver than a person should ever have to be. So let's get him, for Grace. For your mother."

Noah's fingers crush my arm. His eyes are no longer two dark coals, but fathomless black orbs – windows into the coldness of space. "I don't want to kill him. Not yet. I want him paraded in the media as an example of corruption. I want him to have to stand before his peers in court and get fucked in the ass in jail by the criminals he put there. I will kill him, but first, I want him to *suffer.*"

"You sure that's what you want?" Eli asks. I know what he's thinking – that every day Noah will have to see his father's face on the news. It will be like living through Howard Malloy's trial all over again – a daily reminder of what had been stolen from him.

"It's what I fucking want," Noah growls. I know him, my mirror. I know that it'll be hard, but he will endure it. He'll be strong, for Grace, for his mother, for Felix. He wants to watch his father's downfall. He wants to revel in the punishment that will never, ever bring back his mother or brother or stepmother, but will drive a hot poker into the gaping wound in his heart.

His father's suffering will make Noah strong. That's how we are, him and me. Only when we are utterly broken can our true potential be unleashed.

Eli frowns. "But your future—"

"My future was dead to me the moment Felix died," Noah whispers. He shoves Eli toward the door. "Now, don't take this the wrong way, but get the fuck out."

Eli looks at me with concern, but they've been friends for too long for him to speak his fears aloud. He knows that the dangerous look in Noah's eyes will never be directed at me. He ushers Galen and George and the others out of the lab, leaving the two most dangerous animals behind, their cages unlocked, their malice unchecked.

"Don't wreck anything," Galen yells as he slams the door behind him.

I'm alone with Noah.

And his stepmother's corpse.

I back away from the mess of sharp objects on the ground, into the morgue. Noah stalks across the clinic, shoving a rack of implements out of the way in his haste to get to me. He slams me against the glass and crushes my mouth with his.

The kiss sucks every last piece of humanity from me. I drown in Noah's grief, his rage. I taste the blood and tears that pour from the hole where his heart should be. He demands, he *takes*, his hot mouth all over me as his wounds split open, as he bleeds his anguish into me.

There's no kiss deep enough to fix us. We're both beyond saving, beyond redemption.

We'll have to drown together.

We tear at our clothes, shredding my beautiful dress and ripping the seams of Noah's suit. I wrap my legs around him as he grinds me into the glass. Noah's eyes flicker to a spot over my shoulder, to the freezers in the morgue where his stepmother's body lies. I claw at his skin as if my own talons might somehow mend his unseen wounds, as if two broken people can somehow put each other back together.

Noah breaks the kiss with a ragged gasp. He staggers back, his lip puffy and red where I bit him. His jaw hardens as he grabs a scalpel from the tray.

"Noah," I say. My tongue darts out to lick the speck of his blood from my lip.

Noah's eyes narrow, his shoulders tense. He takes the scalpel and draws it across his chest. I bite my lip as the blade cuts his flesh. Blood trickles over his skin, then flows steadily as he draws the scalpel in a circle. He grunts as his hand trembles; the blade slips, but he doesn't put it down.

When he's done, he throws aside the blade. He doesn't look down, but at that spot over my shoulder, where he can see his handiwork reflected in the glass.

My heart stills as I see what he's done.

"I've been baptized in bloodshed," he says, his throat catching on the words. "I'm born anew, born to be your disciple, your servant, your blade."

It's a little lopsided and hard to make out through the blood dripping from the cuts. I swallow the lump of emotion in my throat.

He's carved the August symbol, the sword and the wreath, into his chest.

A symbol that he's leaving his old life. He has nothing left but his hate, and he lays that at my feet – the greatest gift he can possibly give.

Nothing has ever turned me on like this.

I throw myself at him. I'm not human any longer. We're frantic, crashing through the lab in our need to crawl inside each other. Scalpels and forceps and other medical shit topple from racks and scatter across the floor. I'm covered in Noah's blood, and he tastes of copper and rage and it's *so fucking hot.*

My fingers claw at his chest, drawing lines of blood that decorate his new wound. He lifts my ass onto the morgue table, the one where his mother lay only minutes ago. *We're sick. There's something wrong with our heads.*

His teeth scrape my nipple, and I don't fucking care. If what Noah and I have is a sickness, then I'm down with it.

The stainless steel is cold against my bare skin but Noah... Noah is pure fire. He fists himself in his bloody hand and takes aim at my entrance. I lay back and wrap my legs behind him. Blood smears across the sterilized table.

He slams into me. I gasp as my body jerks against the cool metal. I feel him *everywhere* – in my spine and in my elbows and scratching and scarring inside my skull. Noah Marlowe is part of me now – he's more my twin than Mackenzie ever was.

Noah cups my breast, smearing a bloody handprint over my heart. An offering to his queen. A mark of his loyalty. This man who thrusts inside me like a wild animal will die for me. He'll burn the whole fucking world for me.

He comes with a roar that tears through my soul. Noah Marlowe has always worn a veneer of civility over his brutish heart. But finally, *finally,* all of that's been stripped away, and the monster beneath is free.

I fucking *love* it.

22

CLAUDIA

oah's father's arrest may have the attention of the news outlets, but Alec LeMarque's death rules the gossip mill at Stonehurst Prep. By now, the video Gabe took of him burning is circulating freely. Eli's made sure none of our faces are visible, so we won't be connected to it. Apparently, Alec's father saw the bull's door close and threw up. The police are investigating, but I'm not worried. I've got people inside city hall who will make sure my punishment stands unopposed.

No one has noticed that Daphne hasn't been at school. According to Madeline, she'll be completing her schoolwork online. I know she's gone to warn her father, to move him to another safe place before I send someone after him, but she doesn't know that while Gabe had her tied to that cross singing Justin Bieber songs, George put tracking software on her phone. I've got Yara following her, keeping tabs on her movements. She and her dad won't get far.

Even though the senator's arrest has dragged Howard Malloy's name into the headlines again, no one dares say a word to me about my father, not with Noah Marlowe glowering at any student who steps near us.

They don't know their queen walks in their midst.

In the end, I have a lot to thank Alec for. After my show of brutality at Colosseum, I've won back even more of our soldiers. Antony has been fielding requests from anyone shifting their allegiance to us, while Eli takes the testimonies of those who wish to exchange information and services for my favors. Claudia August has shown she's more than a chattel bride – and I'm setting new standards for what's acceptable in our world. Men will think twice before assaulting a woman in Emerald Beach.

Now, I need to solidify my power.

LIKE EVERY OTHER wild story that's done the rounds at Stonehurst Prep, Alec's brutal death fades into legend as the next big thing takes over. And the next big thing is Valentine's Day and the associated dance.

The halls of Stonehurst become awash in red hearts. Eli's hardly in class because he's so busy helping the student council deliver roses to students and teachers. Noah should be helping, too, since he's class president, but he hasn't been back at school since Grace died.

I receive over fifty roses – from my three guys, from George, from Ms. Drysdale, and from anonymous classmates who got sent the video. *I know you had something to do with Alec's death,* one note says. *From the bottom of my heart, thank you.*

I can't get behind all the excitement, because Valentine's Day means something much darker for me. Lupercalia is the second event celebrated in the Emerald Beach underground on February 15th of every year. But unlike Valentine's Day, it's a blood-soaked, orgy-fueled celebration of loyalty. As well as the usual fights, games, and sacrifices, it's the time when family ties are cemented – my new soldiers will officially take their oaths of loyalty, and it's considered the luckiest date for a wedding.

It's the day I join in unholy matrimony with Constantine Dio and Nero Lucian.

At lunch, I swirl my zucchini spaghetti around my plate, my stomach twisting. I have a plan, but it's precarious. I need to play my hand carefully, or I could end up losing all the ground I've gained against Nero.

"You don't want your lunch?" George asks, wiping a smear of vegan pesto from her chin.

"It tastes like ass," I mumble, sliding the tray across to her. "Why can't this damn school give us food with actual carbs?"

"Blame Cleo. She campaigned for healthy food options in sophomore year."

I moan. Cleo. Yet another problem we need to fucking deal with. Cleo's blowing up social media with all her baby talk. A lot could happen to her before that baby's born, like a bullet between the eyes. I've put notice out with some of the British gangs in my father's network, but none of them are interested in fucking with the duke. So she's safe, for now. But I know the duke sold Senator Marlowe the Grey Death he used to kill Grace, which means he's probably also mixed up in Howard Malloy's pharmaceutical company. For that, he will die. When it's convenient for me.

Right now, I have bigger crime lords to fry.

"Come to the dance with me," Gabe begs, startling me out of my thoughts. "You've got to be a normal teenager some of the time."

"I'm not sure it's a good idea," I yawn. I'm barely scraping through my schoolwork as it is. I don't need a dance to think about, too. "Mackenzie might see it as the perfect opportunity to take me out. Remember, she asked Eli to go with her."

"I saw Tiberius in English class, and he mentioned he and

Antony are in charge of security," Gabriel says. "That catering company Yara works for is going to do the food, so she'll be there. Eli has to go, because he's on the dance committee. And you know Noah's not going to leave your side. I'd like to see Mackenzie get through them. Besides, I have a surprise for you." When he sees the look I give him, he pouts. "I promise this is a fun thing. No spirit mediums will be harmed in the making of this surprise."

I can't say no to that pouty face, so I agree to go with Gabe. And I wait in the stupid line with Gabe and George for stupid heart-shaped tickets, listening with half an ear as George brainstorms my perfect dress. When we get to the front, Brandy frowns at me and waves us away. I assume this is out of loyalty to Daphne, but when Gabe pushes her, she gives us an answer I don't expect.

"You already have a ticket."

"Nope." What is this shit? "I only just agreed to be Gabe's date. We've been standing in line for twenty minutes. Gabe may relish a good line because he's British, but do I look like the kind of girl who queues for fun?"

"I could have sworn I already sold you a ticket..." Daphne taps her iPad. "Yup, I've got you down here – one for Mackenzie Malloy. You picked it up from me yesterday."

My blood runs cold. "I didn't."

"You did. Are you high or something? I *remember*. We have a five-minute conversation about whether a red cocktail dress would be too predictable." Brandy rolls her eyes.

"Well, I lost it. So can you void that ticket and give me another, I'd be *super* grateful." I bat my eyelashes.

"No can do, I'm afraid." Brandy folds her hand across the iPad and gives me a satisfied smile. "Health and Safety, you see. Each ticket has to have a student's name, and I can't sell the same student two tickets."

I lean across the table, ready to put her head through that iPad, when Gabe plonks down his Visa Black. "I'll have three tickets – one for me, one for George, and one for my date, Claudia Jones."

"I've never heard of Claudia Jones." Brandy taps the screen to bring up the card reader.

"She doesn't go to this school." Gabriel winks at me.

We get our tickets and head outside to the bleachers. "You look like you've seen a ghost," Gabe wraps a hand around my shoulders and pulls me close. "Relax, she probably just forgot who she was talking to or wrote the information down wrong. Brandy isn't exactly batting a full wicket."

"I'm Mackenzie Malloy," I snap. "People don't *forget* me. *She* was here, I know it."

Mackenzie Malloy has been at Stonehurst Prep, walking the halls like she owns the place. Like this is her fucking school.

She has a ticket to the Valentine's dance.

That means one thing.

Bad shit is about to go down.

23

CLAUDIA

I spend the last two periods mentally running through what Mackenzie Malloy could possibly have planned for the Stonehurst Prep Valentine's dance. She's made it perfectly clear she's willing to open fire in a room full of strangers. Should I call in a bomb scare to the dance, or find some way to get it canceled?

Or do we use the dance to lure her from her foxhole? Is it the perfect time to spring a trap and finally get rid of my batshit crazy sister?

All thought of Mackenzie vanishes when I see the package waiting for me on the steps of Malloy Manor. When I harass Tiberius about letting delivery men get so close, he fixes me with a terrifying stare. "These weren't the kind of men you turn away."

I take the package inside and lift the lid. Inside is an exquisite white silk gown, encrusted with thousands of tiny diamond beads. I hold it up against my body. It's the perfect fit.

The perfect dress for a white wedding.

I swallow. It would be the easy path to just agree to this fake marriage. To grit my teeth, open my legs, and go through with it for Queen and Empire. It would keep Nero distracted while I built up enough power to squash him forever.

But for how long? I know Nero Lucian. He wants my empire – every inch of my father's legacy I've managed to claw back. And he knows my weak spots – my family. If I'm tied to him, he'll have all the leverage he needs to force me to do his bidding. The only way I can ensure their safety is to own this town.

And if he tries to force me to go to be with him, I'll cut his dick off, and that'll bring a world of hell down on us that we don't need right now.

I call out for Antony. He appears in my doorway in a flash, his mouth a hard line. He smirks as he sees the dress in my arms. "Planning your upcoming nuptials?"

I throw a shoe at him. "Instead of being a smartass, how about lifting a finger to help me get out of this?"

He folds his arms and glares at me. "I *had* a plan. It was called 'protect my cousin from being dragged into the criminal underworld.' *You* chose to claim your father's legacy. You made that deal with the Imperators. I don't see why you can't just follow through. What's it to you to add two horny old goats to your harem?"

"Slut shame me again and I'll boil you in the bull." I waggle my finger at him. Antony smirks. He knows I'd never hurt him.

Antony stalks into the room and sits on the corner of the bed. "While we're on the subject of fucking with the plans, there's something I should tell you."

My stomach clenches. Just what we need, more bad news. "What?"

"Lately, I've been having a bit of a hard time with my eyesight."

I snort. "You serious?"

"'Course I'm fucking serious," Antony glowers. "Galen thinks I might've knocked something loose in the ring. Anyway, I'm wearing contacts and they help, but it's getting worse and it's possible I won't be able to do a lot of the stuff I'm used to. So if you see me fucking up, now you know why. It's why I couldn't shoot Mackenzie at the ranch."

I remember Noah mentioning something about that. At the time, I'd been too busy *not dying* to give it much thought, but it *was* odd. In Germany, Antony had been swerving all over the road. I put it down to him being a boy on the autobahn, but when I think about it, he'd had Tiberius drive him everywhere since we got back.

I feel a pang of sadness that he hadn't been able to tell me. Having the guys around had put a wall between us. I pat Antony's leg. "Thanks for telling me. I guess we haven't really had much time to hang out since all of this went down. I know things have turned out different than we planned."

"Don't worry about me, cousin," Antony squeezes my shoulder. "I have a feeling everything will work out in the end."

"That's the spirit." I grin at him. "Now, get your blind ass in gear and secure me a meeting with Constantine Dio. He and I have some things to discuss."

24

CLAUDIA

Tiberius drops me and the guys at Constantine's fight club. I don't worry about a disguise – Claudia August visiting a fellow Imperator is nothing out of the ordinary. The *maître d'* of the Korean restaurant doesn't bat an eyelid as we walk in. "Your table is waiting, Ms. August," he says as he leads us upstairs.

There's a Krav Maga class going on in the main dojo. Constantine leads the demonstration. He drops his opponent, then extends a hand to help him to his feet. He's drenched in sweat when he comes out to meet us. "You won't be offended if I don't offer to shake your hand."

"Not in the slightest. We need to talk. Somewhere private." I glare at his students, who are staring at us from inside the dojo. "I can't have anyone overhear."

Constantine leads me to a small room divided by Japanese screens. He slides the screens back against the wall to show me no one is hiding in the space. "The walls are soundproofed," he says. "I assure you, we are secure. But don't take my word for it. Station one of your men in the hallway, and have them check every corner."

Eli moves into the hallway, and Noah walks around the perimeter of the room. He nods to me, and I beckon Gabriel to come forward. He carries a large box, which he hands to me. I step forward and drop the box at Constantine's feet.

"Nero left this on my doorstep yesterday."

Constantine kicks the lid aside, frowning as he reveals the glittering beads of my wedding dress. There's no mirth in his eyes as he says, "Thank you for this, but it's not really my color."

I roll my eyes. "I didn't know I was talking to a comedian. Nero's message is perfectly clear. This may be a marriage between the three of us – an outward show of unity. But Nero intends to form an alliance between Lucian and August." I kick the tulle. "If I wear this dress, it says to our people, 'I am the wife of Nero Lucian.' I can't come back from that statement, and neither can you."

Constantine frowns at the dress. He's difficult to read, but I think he's come to the same conclusion. "You've made yourself more popular in such a short time than either of us anticipated. That stunt with the brazen bull has taken you from a vassal bride to a real Imperator."

The implication hangs in the air between us. We don't need to speak it to know it's true. Nero wishes to shift his alliance from Constantine to me. Instead of the two of them pushing me out and dividing my empire, it will be Nero and I eroding the Dio family.

But while I'm Nero's wife, I will always be under his thumb. And once Nero has brought Constantine to heel, the August empire will be next.

"Why are you showing me this?" Constantine frowns at the dress. He knows as well as I do that it's in my best interests to accept Nero's offer. He's by far the most powerful of the three of us, and if our standoff becomes an all-out gang war, Nero can call on more soldiers.

"I have a proposal." I fold my arms. "The two of us need to make our alliance official. Individually, we're no match for Nero, but together, we're stronger. Nero knows this, which is precisely why he's trying to divide us. So, here's my proposal. If you support my opposition of this double-marriage, I'll marry you."

Constantine lifts his eyebrow.

Beside me, Noah doesn't say a word. This isn't like last time. I talked to the guys about this. We all agreed this was the best course of action.

"In name only. Don't get any ideas." I wiggle my finger at him. "And I'm not touching your gross old-man dick, got it? You'll get the protection of the August name, but not my cunt or my womb."

"I stand by what I said earlier," he says. "I don't touch women unless they're begging for it."

"Good. That's how you stay out of the bull's belly."

He smiles at that. "You do realize that by challenging Nero, we might be heralding the end of the Triumvirate?"

I nod. "Maybe it's time for it to die. Maybe this empire isn't big enough for all three of us, and I'd rather rule with you at my side than Nero."

He laughs. "Such youthful arrogance."

I shrug. "I prefer ambition. My father trained me well, and Brutus' betrayal has only fueled me."

"And what's to say I help you get what you want, only for you to turn on me?"

All in good time. "I'm not strong enough to rule on my own. August and Dio need each other more than we need a turf war, especially if Nero refuses to accept defeat. Things could get ugly before we push him out. To seal our agreement, I've brought you a gift. A good-faith gesture to show how August and Dio might work together in the future."

"I'm listening."

I tell him about Daphne's father's faked death and his current Nantucket location. "You'll be able to collect on that high-profile debt."

Constantine frowns again. "This is good, but one little collection is not exactly going to win me back soldiers who've defected to Nero."

I suck in a breath. I was hoping I wouldn't have to use this, that I could save it in my back pocket for the future, but it's clear that Constantine is demanding more. His position in the Triumvirate might be precarious, but he knows now how much I want Nero out. He thinks he can get more from me for his trouble. Well, his wish might be a double-edged sword.

"I'm a holder of many secrets," I smile, all sweetness and violence. "I know about the chemical vat. I know you can't have children, either."

I suck in a breath as Constantine's head whips up. Even Noah looks to me in surprise. I hadn't told him this.

The chemical vat – the secret Livvie revealed to me because I saved her animals. Livvie had access to all the security footage at Nero's clubs. One day, she was bored so she decided to look back at old content from when Nero had the bright idea to manufacture sex toys. He built a manufacturing plant in a warehouse across town, and one night Julian and Constantine snuck in after hours to teach a disrespectful soldier a lesson. Constantine wanted to drown him in an open vat of chemicals, but the guy struggled and managed to pull both of them into the vat with him. They held him under until he drowned, then crawled to safety. But the exposure to the chemicals left both of them impotent.

You'd have to know about the scientific properties of certain chemicals to make the connection. But Livvie is *way* smarter than Nero gave her credit for. She saw Constantine's lack of an heir, and some of the weird details around my birth, and put it all together. She's known from the very first day I showed up on the scene that I wasn't biologically related to Julian August.

I'm taking a big risk here. By admitting I know about the vat, I'm also admitting that I'm not Julian August's true biological daughter. But Constantine's known all this time, just like Livvie. He could have shut down my claim in an instant, could have insisted on me presenting DNA evidence, but doing so might mean revealing his own impotency. And he couldn't risk that in front of Nero. That would be handing Nero the sword to stab him with.

But now we're bound together by our secret.

"*Touche*, Ice Queen." Constantine smiles sweetly, the kind of smile that would make tough men quake.

"You have no heir. You have no wife, and you've been able to get away with it so long because you can slice the throat of anyone who questions you. But you're not a young man anymore. You know that Nero has already begun the Chinese whispers – 'maybe Constantine isn't man enough to sire a son,' 'Perhaps a man who doesn't think of his legacy isn't right for the Triumvirate.' You know what he's saying. You know that people don't believe it, yet, but whisper it enough times and they'll start to see the pattern. The way I see it, we can destroy each other with this secret and let Nero win, or we can help each other."

"And what help do you think you can offer me?"

"I have a womb. And three lovers who are interested in putting a baby there. And if, *IF* I decide I want a child, as my husband, you could declare it as your own."

Beside me, Noah shifts. I can tell he wants to say something, but he can't risk making me look weak. We didn't discuss this, because I was hoping I wouldn't have to use it. There's a reason I sent Eli into the hallway. If he heard what I planned, he'd have something to say. I can deal with him later, in private.

But Noah... I don't expect him to react so viscerally. I dare a glance over at him. His eyes remained fixed forward, at some point over Tiberius' shoulder. He exudes that barely-contained brutality I so love about him, but the slight twitch in the corner of his eye tells me he's a hair's breadth away from unleashing that brutality on *me*.

What's he so wound up about? It's the perfect solution to our problems. Yeah, none of us want things to go down this way, but it's better than being dead in a ditch.

"Galen will fudge whatever medical records we need as evidence. He's done it before." I point at my own chest, doing my best to ignore Noah's shifting demeanor. "This way we'll both be able to hold on to our empires, to build an alliance between Dio and August that will supersede Nero Lucian's grand schemes. I'd do the same if you have a child by a mistress, but it'll be harder to pull off."

"That's a big promise you're making, Ice Queen." Constantine drums his fingers on his chin. "What do you want in exchange for this boon?"

"It's pretty simple, really. Protect my family from Nero. Help me take him down for good. It's time the Triumvirate became an alliance of two."

Constantine's eyes glint with interest.

"Oh," I can't believe I nearly forgot. "And tell me the price Senator Marlowe paid for Brentwood's hit on the Malloys."

Constantine taps his fingers on his arm. "A fuckton of cash."

"Wrong. I know you wouldn't waste a bargain with the senator on cash. You asked for a secret. And I want to know what it was."

Constantine meets my eyes.

"I see your father in you, Claudia August," he grins. "You were never going to be content to be one of three."

"Not if it means making nice with Nero Lucian."

"A woman after my own heart." He smiles broader. "The

senator told us how Malloy was funding his business. The sports supplements were just a front, which from stories splashed all over the papers today, I'm guessing you already know. His real business was performance drugs made to order – if you wanted to be bigger, stronger, faster, and you didn't want anything to show up in a drug test, you went to Malloy. The kind of work he was doing had to be top secret – scientists, supply chain, chemical manufacturers on the take, all of them only making part of a recipe so they couldn't steal his formulas. That kind of secrecy requires deep pockets and a fuckton of collateral. That's why he had a business relationship with your father – Julian could get the materials Malloy needed into the country, and the drugs back out. And he offered something else Malloy couldn't get anywhere else – collateral."

"How do you mean?" Malloy was a rich fucker. Surely he didn't need my father?

"Senator Marlowe informed us that Malloy had a cache of ancient artifacts – apparently these were found sealed in an underground chamber in Alexandria, Egypt, about eighteen years ago. The cache went straight onto the black market, never saw the inside of a museum." He flicks an invisible speck of dust from his shoulder. "Your father might've had something to do with it landing in Malloy's hands."

My veins buzz with energy. *That's it – that's what Daddy traded for me.* His most valuable treasure.

Of course, Daddy would consider ancient artifacts more valuable than cash or jewels. And if it came from Alexandria, that could mean items from... from the period the emperor Augustus fought Marc Antony and Cleopatra for control of the Roman Empire.

Daddy would lose his *shit* over treasure like that.

"Of course, you can't sell crap like that," Constantine says. "It's too unique, too priceless. But you can use it as collateral when you make the kind of deals we make. It's easier to move old junk than millions of dollars in cash. If Malloy's collection was worth anything like what Marlowe claimed, that kind of collateral could secure decades' worth of deals, which is exactly what Malloy was doing with it. So why had Julian given it to Malloy instead of keeping it within the Triumvirate? Malloy was getting too big for his boots, making all kinds of demands on Julian, starting to insert himself into Triumvirate decisions. I think he fancied himself a future member, and it's my humble opinion that Julian was allowing him too many liberties. Julian turned down a perfectly good business relationship with Walter Hart because Malloy refused to work with him. So Walter went to Brutus to establish the body brokering ring, and that's where Brutus started to build support and funds to make his move against your father."

Shit, shit, shit. All the pieces are coming together. It's all connected – every horror in mine and Noah's and Eli's and Gabriel's lives comes back to the bargain on my life. In exchange for me, Julian August *made* Howard Malloy. My fake father gave my birth father everything he needed to design the drug that would take Noah's life, put Eli's dad behind bars, and put Grey Death in the hands of the Duke of Blackwich.

I glance over at Noah again, and I can see he's thinking the exact same thing.

"Why did you want to know how Malloy was funding his business?" I ask. "If Malloy was weakening my father, wasn't that good for you?"

"Julian couldn't see Brutus' betrayal coming, but I could. *And* I could see Nero licking his lips with excitement to get his hands on the August empire." Constantine shrugs. "Nothing much has changed since then. So yes, I was interested in the treasure. Malloy was about to be feeding the worms and I wanted to get my hands on it before the Augusts or Lucians."

I lean forward. "And did you?"

"No. All I know is that Brentwood was supposed to get the location out of Malloy and then kill him and his wife. But he came back and said someone got to the treasure first and cleared it out. Only it turns out Brentwood was a lying sack of shit, told me he finished the job when really he blubbered like a baby because he's afraid of your sister, and left without the cache. I sent a few men to search the house back when it was empty, but they couldn't find anything." He shrugs again. "I assume whoever killed the Malloys got away with the treasure, but if they did, they're keeping it quiet. We'd all know if something like that was floating around the market."

But she didn't. Because she never thought to ask her mother. And now she's after me because she's convinced I've got it.

But I don't.

Not yet, anyway.

"Thank you. This has been enlightening." I step forward and hold out my hand. "I look forward to a fruitful alliance with you."

"To our nuptials." Constantine wraps his long fingers in mine. We shake. I don't exactly feel good about this, but I feel... confident.

My confidence lasts until I turn to leave and something heavy drops on me from above. I slam into the floor, the wind driven from my lungs.

Someone digs a knee into my spine, yanks my hair back, and draws a blade across my neck.

25

NOAH

*S*hit.

I lunge for the figure holding Claudia, but I'm not fast enough.

Everything happens in a flash.

A thin line of red wells at Claws' throat as the blade bites her skin. Claudia reaches behind her, slides her own knife from her sleeve, and jabs it into her attackers' thigh.

Her attacker screeches, rolling to the side to claw at the knife in her leg. I recognize her now – Cali, Constantine's tribune and Brutus' ex-girlfriend. Her romance cut tragically short by Claudia putting a bullet in her lover's skull. I guess she wants to even the score.

"Let me help you with that." Claws yanks the blade from Cali's leg. Cali howls as blood squirts from the wound, splattering across Claudia's face. My girl staggers, one hand clutching her throat, the other wrapping around the blood-soaked knife handle. Her face sets with grim determination.

Get her.

I'm mad as fuck at Claws right now, but I still want to see her kick Cali's ass.

Claudia lunges. Cali swings her injured leg with surprising force, and swipes Claws' legs from under her. I'm flying toward them, but I seem to be moving in slow motion. Cali's body unfurls, like a panther pouncing on its prey, her hands outstretched to scratch and gouge. Claws lands good and rolls, crouching low and using Cali's own momentum to shove her off balance and flip her onto her back. They crash to the floor, rolling as they claw and hiss and bite at each other. Claudia slams her fist into Cali's nose, and Cali rakes her nails down Claudia's face. It's blood and rage and carnage.

I grab Cali's shoulder and yank her off, aiming my pistol in her face. "Give me one good reason why I shouldn't shoot you for attacking my Imperator."

Behind me, Constantine cracks up laughing. I glare at him, and he shrugs. "Sorry, kid. You made an amateur mistake. You didn't secure the room."

My face reddens. I checked every fucking corner of the room when we walked in. I stayed at Claudia's side the entire time, but it never occurred to me to look up at the ceiling. I tilt my head back now and spy the narrow metal rafters, with a wide enough span between them to hold a body. Cali must've lay between them, holding her body weight by her hands and ankles, not moving, not making a sound, for the entire conversation.

Shit.

That means she knows everything.

Including who Claudia really is.

"Noah, let her go." Claudia sighs.

I don't want to. I want to wring her treacherous neck. But it probably doesn't help solidify our official alliance with Constantine when we follow it up by beheading his tribune.

I loosen my grip. Cali glares at me as she simpers away to stand beside Constantine. "You should have shot me."

Yes, I fucking should have. I tap the trigger on my gun. "Keep talking. I still can."

"I don't like shooting people," Claudia says. "Too messy."

"Agreed," Cali smirks.

Another flash. Cali slams Claudia into the wall. Fuck, she's fast. Cali leans in close, snarling in my girl's face like an animal about to tear out chunks of flesh. "I like to be right up close. I like to watch the life drain from their faces."

"Do it, and my people will put you down," Claudia chokes out.

Cali looks over at Constantine, who watches with his arms folded. He's not laughing anymore. Cali's shoulders slump, but she doesn't let go of Claudia.

"You killed my Brutus," Cali whispers.

"He killed my father. He buried me alive." Claudia sounds eerily calm, but I can tell she's dangerously close to losing her shit.

Same, Claws. Same. She shouldn't have done what she did. She should have told us that she might give our child to Constantine to claim. We don't even have a child, so why does it make my blood boil?

"Julian August wasn't your father, though. Was he?" Cali smirks. "I could gut you right now, but then the fun would be over. It'll be so much more interesting to kill everyone and everything you love first."

"You and Brutus were made for each other," I growl as I haul her off Claws and toss her to the ground. She leers up at me with something like admiration, swings her legs beneath her, and leaps at me. I duck the arc of her knife and slam the butt of my weapon into her jaw, sending her sprawling again. She lands with surprising grace and kicks out a leg and—

"Enough," Constantine's voice booms through the cavernous space.

Cali freezes. So do I.

"I ask you to lower your weapon." Constantine nods to me. "Cali is loyal to me. She knows that I do not want the Imperator or any of her tribunes dead, and that she cannot reveal this secret without also exposing me."

Cali growls at me – an actual *growl*, low in her throat. But she slinks away and goes to stand beside Constantine. It's weird, but I admire her. She is clearly unhinged. Her rage has consumed her, a feeling I very much relate to. But she won't betray Claws' secret. Oh, she'll stab my girl in a heartbeat, she'll use what she knows to destroy us, but this secret will die with her as long as Constantine is her Imperator. I know because I've seen loyalty like hers before. In Antony.

"It's a pity, Cali. In another life, I think we might've been friends. I was going to offer you a job, but if you're going to be like that..." Claudia dusts herself off and nods to Constantine. "I'll see you at our wedding."

26

CLAUDIA

Noah is silent in the car. I know he's fuming about what I agreed to do for Constantine. A million bitter words dance on my tongue, but I don't say any of them. I won't justify myself to a guy who fucked me on a morgue table. It's *my* body – my weapon of mass destruction in this fucking turf war – and I did the right thing. I did what any of them would do to secure the alliance that will keep our family safe.

Eli and Gabe don't ask what happened. The silence looms large in the tiny car. Luckily, Lamborghinis are notoriously speedy. In no time at all, we're screaming down the underground tunnel into the Malloy garage. As soon as I climb out, the screams and jabbers of the animals wash over me. I'm so fucking tired.

Before Noah can storm off, I drag all three of them outside. I need to be away from the animals. I need to focus.

But even out here, I can't be alone with my tribunes. The lion lopes in circles in the bottom of the swimming pool. When he sees Eli, he stretches his huge paws up the tiled wall and roars for food. The hunger in his eyes breaks something in me. It's not fresh meat he wants, but freedom.

Eli comes up beside me, holding packages of steak from the fancy organic butchery in Harrington Hills. He shows me how to toss the steaks into the hole in the center of the wire mesh covering. The lion leaps and twists to gobble the meat – the closest he'll get to a hunt.

"I wonder," I say aloud. "Does he know that he no longer has to eat men to survive? When he looks up at us, does he see the bars of a new cage?"

Eli rests a hand on my shoulder. He knows I'm not really talking about the lion.

Noah tears the steak from my hand and tosses it angrily at the hole. "Tell them what you did in there," his eyes flash. "Tell them what you agreed to."

I suck in a deep breath. I turn to face my three lovers, my tribunes. Noah's face is a storm. Gabe's face is open and earnest, ready to be hurt. Eli just looks... resigned. Like he knows what I'm going to say before I say it. Somehow, that's the worst.

"The good news is that I getting out of the marriage to Nero and Constantine." I stare at my hands. Blood from the steak runs between my fingers. *At least it's not their blood.* "The bad news is that I'll be marrying Constantine, which we knew was a possibility. I won't be trying to get out of it. For now. But he wanted more, and he knows he's got me by the ovaries. So I had to pull out my last bargaining chip, something I never wanted to use so we didn't discuss it. I said that if we have a child, he could claim it as his own."

Gabe's face crumples. He staggers back as though I punched him in the gut. Eli throws out a hand across his chest before he trips over the edge of the swimming pool.

Every broken, lonely lyric and sad melody he's ever written flashes across his face in an instant. The weight of it crushes me – in a single sentence I've done more damage than his father has done in his entire lifetime.

No. Gabe, I'm so sorry.

This is what it feels like to see a fallen angel lose his wings.

But I can't back down now. I can't be weak. This is happening, and I need them to understand. I need them to stand beside me on this.

So I take a deep breath and press on. "I know how you all feel about it. I'm not exactly thrilled, either. I feel like our lion friend here – I may have upgraded to a larger cage with a kinder master, but I'm still trapped. You don't understand that I'm the first woman to have this kind of power in the Triumvirate. They don't know what to do with me. I have limited options, and I need to use every weapon I have or we won't survive the year. This isn't just about me and what I want anymore. It isn't even about the four of us. It's about all the people who need me for their livelihoods, their lives. It's about how safe this city will be for women like me if Nero takes over the August empire."

I explain to them the terms of our agreement – that Constantine will offer us protection, he won't expect me to sleep with him, and we'll work together to overthrown Nero, provided that any child I had with my tribunes would be raised as his. "Remember, I'm not ready for kids yet, and a lot can change between now and when I am. I'll fight this, the way I fought the marriage, but not now. Not until we're safe."

"We'll never be safe," Eli says in that dull, resigned voice that makes my stomach feel like lead. "There will always be another enemy at the gates."

Gabriel's chin wobbles. "If we have a child, they'll never be able to know that I'm their father? They'll never call me papa or daddy?"

He looks so completely gutted. I wrap my arms around him, nuzzling my face into his neck. "Maybe if there are other children. But the first – the one who will inherit my empire – will be

Constantine's in name only. But we don't have to worry about this yet. We need to move forward, focus on Lupercalia and—"

"Does it not seem ridiculous to you?" Eli asks, his features shifting as an idea occurs to him. "Why leave the fate of empires up to the genetic lottery? Think about it. If Nero's sons are all morons, why doesn't he just find someone who isn't? Constantine is surrounded by viciously competent people, but he's supposed to force himself to sleep with a woman just so a baby has his genes, and then hope he doesn't get snuffed until the kid grows up. A blood dynasty seems awfully precarious to me. Isn't this why all the Egyptians went nuts? They were all fucking their siblings to keep the blood pure."

"The Romans were aware of this," I say. "It's one of the reasons why they started 'adopting' heirs. Only a handful of emperors are blood-related. The rest were adopted to ensure a smooth transition of power. Otherwise you end up like Egypt – a child ascends the throne and the nobility or priesthood could force their will through them."

"Exactly. I think if you asked your father, he might agree they had the right idea." Eli's eyes shimmer. He's almost forgotten about my announcement in his enthusiasm for this idea. "If he'd been allowed to pick someone from his ranks to train as his successor – like Antony – everything we're going through now might never have happened."

"Yes, but then I would have grown up with Howard Malloy for a father," I frown. I look up at the facade of Malloy Manor, trying to imagine what it might've been like to grow up here. I didn't have to do much imagining. The horrors of Mackenzie's diary are burned into my head.

This house really could have been my prison, and Howard Malloy's fists my jailors.

I squeeze Gabriel tight, wishing I could squeeze the hurt from his marrow. For all the shit mounting on our heads, I'm still glad my life turned out the way it did. He may not have been my biological father, but Julian August believed in me. My mother may not have pushed me out of her cervix, but she was kind and fierce and wonderful. They *loved* me. And looking between my three princes, I see just how rare and precious love like that can be.

"Even if you never were Claudia August," Gabe whispers, laying feathery kisses across my cheek, "even if you were a Valley girl who only cares about football scores and Instagram likes, we would still have fallen madly in love with you."

I look into his shadowed eyes, and in the depths of his despair, I see a flicker of hope – a life preserver I cling to, praying it will float me into shore.

"I never knew how much you wanted to be a father," I whisper, tugging his labret piercing until he gives me a sad smile. "I promise you that one day your child will be able to look you in the eyes and say, 'I'm proud of you, Dad.'"

It's exactly the right thing to say. Gabriel's eyes flutter closed, his eyelashes tangling together as he slips away into his own head. I kiss his closed eyelids, wishing I could follow him, wishing I could slip away from my life as Claudia August for just a moment and exist in the stars with him.

"Do you remember Mackenzie's twelfth birthday party?" Noah asks suddenly.

Eli nods. This is his territory. When I first met him, he lived in those memories. "Oh, absolutely. It was that pool party. She invited the whole class. Well, the whole class except George and a couple of other 'freaks'."

"Ooof. That Mackenzie was a real class act." I stretch out on the pool lounger, pulling Gabe down beside me. It's one of those double-width ones that can hold more than one person. Noah leaves and returns with two bottles of wine. He pops both corks and we pass them around, necking the sweet drink until we empty one of the bottles and a sugary buzz clouds my brain.

Noah holds up the empty bottle. "This was the *exact* spot at Mackenzie's party where we played that game of spin-the-bottle."

"Spin-the-bottle?" I glance at them incredulously. "Weren't you all, like, *twelve?*"

"People mature early around here," Eli says. He points to a spot on the patio tiles near the foot of the lounger. "Right there – that was where we had the bottle."

I scoot up, the wine dancing happily in my stomach. "Here? And where were you two?"

Noah looks thoughtful. "I was sitting over there." He points toward a long bench seat next to the outdoor table. "Next to Daphne. I had the biggest crush on her back then."

"And you?" I ask Eli.

Eli leans into me. "I was sitting at your feet. Of course." He sits on the concrete beside my lounger, his legs folded, his mouth curling up at the edge. "Mackenzie's feet, I should say."

We all look at Gabe. He grins. "I didn't live in Emerald Beach, obviously. But I've definitely played my fair share of spin-the-bottle. And if I was here, I'd be sprawled out exactly where I am, taking up as much real estate as possible, thus increasing my chances of a snog."

I punch him in the arm. Through the sadness, a hint of the real Gabe shines, like the first ray of sunlight after a violent storm.

Noah sets the empty bottle down on the tiles. We all stare at it.

"Ladies first," Eli says, his Adam's apple bobbing as he swallows.

I take the bottle and flick it with one hand. It spins in a few lazy circles. A thrill rips through me. I've never played spin-the-bottle, but I've seen it a hundred times in all those teen movies I watched 'for research.' And it always ends with an awkward teen makeout session, the kind of moment that makes me cringe while also pooling heat between my thighs.

I have a feeling our game is going to get significantly more R-rated.

The bottle lands on Eli. He swallows, and for a moment I see a flash of the boy he'd been the first time this game was played in this exact spot. Sporty, earnest, inexperienced, but trying to pretend he had everything under control.

It's not my memory – it belongs to my sister, the one who got to go to normal school and have normal friends and normal birthday parties and be around this perfect guy, who spurned his love for her revenge plot. But it feels good to think of Eli as my childhood crush – the boy who still loves me from afar all those years. And fuck it, I never got to have those teen-movie experiences, and Mackenzie squandered hers with bitterness, so I'm happy to steal this part of her life from her.

Eli studies my face. "Did you know I kissed your sister that day?"

"I figured."

"I had to kiss three other girls *and* Noah before the bottle landed on her," he shrugs. "I thought I was the luckiest guy."

Before I can ask some pertinent questions about this kiss with Noah, Eli kisses me, all slow and deep and oh so sweet. He rests his lips against mine, giving me a moment to feel the softness of them, to experience that wild teenage thrill of wondering if he'd try something, before he slips his tongue between my lips. Gently, oh-so-gently he pushes me open and tastes me.

Butterflies flutter in my stomach. It's so weird that after all the times I've kissed Eli, all those filthy nights where we've explored every inch of each other's bodies, he can make a single kiss feel new and exciting and wonderful.

I don't want our kiss to ever end, but that's not the game. Eli pulls back, his eyes closed. The air around us sizzles with unspoken truths, with promises and vows left unfinished. Gabriel and Noah watch us as a palpable heat thickens the air.

"Your turn, Hart," Noah says, his voice catching.

"Aren't we just making Claudia spin again?" Eli asks. "She's the one who missed out on this teenage rite of passage."

"Now, now, Captain America," Gabe waggles a finger. "You know those aren't the rules. Maybe you'll get lucky and you'll be able to tongue-fuck Noah again, now that he's all grown up."

Eli bites his lip as he spins. The bottle careens across the tiles as it spins, hits the leg of the lounger, and jerks to a stop facing Gabriel.

"Hey, the bottle hit the chair leg. I call a foul— mmmmmph." Eli's protests are stifled by Gabriel's lips on his. Eli tries to scramble away, but Gabriel holds him tight, the way I imagine he used to hold Dylan. I cheer, because seeing Eli bamboozled is completely adorable and okay, maybe I'm not a great ally by fetishizing my bisexual boyfriend for my own enjoyment, but I feel what I feel and my pussy clenches at the sight of Gabriel clearly enjoying his tongue down another guy's throat.

Noah laughs so hard his face goes red. Eli manages to wrestle Gabriel off him.

"Dude, that was your *tongue*." Eli grabs the wine from Noah and gargles, spitting onto the grass.

Gabriel leans back beside me on the lounger, his fingers playing innocently with the hem of my dress. He looks pleased with himself. "Homophobe much?"

"*Not* a homophobe," Eli says with force. "But that is way more of you than I ever wanted inside my body, thank you very much. Consent is important, you asshole."

Gabriel smirks at Eli as he picks up the bottle. He turns to

Noah and waggles his tongue piercing in his direction. "Pucker up, buttercup. I'm coming for you next."

Noah looks so visibly horrified I burst out laughing. They may be in a polyamorous relationship, but Noah and Eli still sometimes don't know how to handle Gabriel's bisexuality, especially since we all know Gabe would happily fuck both of them and make them love it.

Gabriel sets the bottle in motion with a flourish. The horror of my meeting with Constantine and what I agreed to forgotten as we let ourselves be swept away in the fantasy that we're perfectly ordinary teenagers with normal problems and overactive hormones.

The bottle spins and spins and Noah's face pinches with terror at the thought it might land on him, but the gods smile on him because it skids to a stop pointing at me.

Excellent.

"My turn to kiss Claudia," Gabriel grins. I roll over to kiss him, but instead of meeting my lips with his, he drops to his knees. His fingers slide up my legs to tug at my underwear.

"What are you doing?"

Gabe grins that perfect, chaotic grin as he pushes me back into the chair and slides my underwear down my legs, pushing my dress up around my thighs. The cool air hits my exposed pussy, dancing across that sensitive skin. I breathe hard, trying to control my racing heart.

His pagan scent hits me then, all tangled with the bracing heat of an Emerald Beach evening. I know I'm in for something magical.

"I never said anything about kissing your lips," Gabriel whispers as he buries his face between my legs.

He's slow, languid, making sure I feel every movement of his tongue as he drags it over my clit and teases my entrance. It's the same way he kisses me on the lips sometimes, taking his time, knowing he has the power to drive me absolutely wild. Gabe takes nothing for himself but the joy of serving me, of worshipping me. And what girl doesn't love a little worship, especially when it's Gabriel Fallen's tongue circling her clit with aching deliberation.

I roll my hips toward him, trying to make him go faster, chasing the heat pooling in my stomach. My veins are soaked in wine, heated to boiling point by the dry desert air.

It's been driving me insane not to have that glorious cock inside me lately, that piercing rubbing me in all the right places. But I'm not going to complain when he's rolling the ball in his tongue stud over my clit, burning away his heat with the coolness of it before dancing with his tongue.

The orgasm creeps up on me with stealth, the way Cali surprised us by leaping down from the ceiling. One moment I'm enjoying the swell of heat in the pit of my stomach, the wet glide of Gabe's tongue on my clit, and the next I'm lifted off the chair by the force of pleasure slamming into me.

I pull my legs to my chest. Gabe pushes them back down, holding me open so I have no choice but to ride my orgasm, to feel *everything* – every stroke of his tongue, every flick of that evil, evil stud.

My scream wakes the lion in the swimming pool. He roars along with me, calling for his own reckoning. His pain rumbles deep in my belly, drawing up something deep and primal inside me that has me clinging to Gabriel long after the last flush leaves my body.

Gabriel leans back and hands me the bottle. "Your turn now." His voice sounds a little ragged.

"Are we still playing?" I whisper, my body humming from the orgasm.

"Fuck yes." Noah's eyes are dark storms.

I set the bottle down and spin. There's a heaviness in the air as we all watch it, knowing that wherever it's going to land, this night has already been given over to sin and debauchery.

It lands on Noah.

"Come here," he demands, leaning back in his chair, his legs manspreading, his arm dangling carelessly over the arm to reveal an inch of tattooed flesh beneath the white cuff. In his pinstriped suit and slicked hair, he's every bit the dangerous gangster. I lick my lips and crawl toward him, climbing into his lap and straddling him. My dress rucks up around my stomach, and my wet, naked pussy grinds against his thigh. Noah groans as his hands slide up my back to cup my exposed ass.

Gabriel settles back into the lounger. He drapes his body in that easy way of his, but I can tell from the crease between his eyebrows that it's taking all his self-control not to join in with whatever Noah has planned. Maybe it's just the rules of the game, but I admire his self-control right now. Restraint is not exactly what Gabriel is known for.

Eli leans forward, his pretty eyes hooded with need. His fingers wrap around the remaining bottle of wine, drumming an agitated rhythm on the glass.

Noah reaches up, grabs me behind the neck, and pulls my head onto his, punching the air from my lungs with the force of his need. I love the way he takes control like this, laying those huge hands over my tiny body, manhandling me until I'm completely under his spell. We both know that I'm the one with all the power, but the way he dominates feels so protective, so safe.

This kiss... it's laced with the tension and danger we carried into Constantine's lair with us. Kissing Noah makes the blood rush in my veins, the same way it did when I had Cali under my power. There's a sense that we walk a knife-edge, that either of us might lose control at any moment, that fighting and fucking this incredible man are one and the same.

I fumble with Noah's fly, desperate to feel the heat of him. He lifts me easily as he pushes his pants and boxers over his hips, exposing his hard rod. I fist him, stroking my hand down his shaft until he bites my lip with a moan. His eyes roll back in his head, and the power shifts back to me.

"Oh, no you don't," he growls, thrusting his hand between my legs and shoving two fingers inside me. I yelp as he rubs against my G-spot – none of Gabriel's leisurely pace; this is hard, fast, *evil*. He's trying to get back at me for blindsiding him earlier. He'll drag an orgasm from me whether I want it or not. I sink my teeth into his lip as I stroke him harder, squeezing my hand so tight I half expect him to pop.

Fucking and fighting.

That's us. That's who we are.

We growl and thrust and grind and bite until I can't fucking take it a moment longer, and I come on his fingers. My walls contract around him as my whole body shudders and jerks. Noah flashes me that rare dark smile of his, the one I thought I might never see again after Grace's death.

"I'd slap that smirk off your face if I could move," I murmur as I grip his shoulders. My legs don't work anymore. He's the only thing holding me upright.

I become aware of the sound of the bottle spinning over the cobbles.

"Oh, look, I got Claudia again." Eli's breath rushes against my ear. He bends his body over me, notching his chest against my back like we're made for each other. His stiff cock rubs between my exposed ass cheeks.

"It's not your turn," Noah snaps, but he's not angry. He's *amused*. The two of them have been friends for so long, I think they quite like seeing each other like this – stripped away of their bullshit. Noah pokes his tongue out at Eli and shifts my hips forward, plunging his cock inside me. "I've got her now. What are you going to do about it, Hart?"

I want to laugh, but Noah starts moving his hips, and it's so fucking good I can't do anything except moan. My whole body is alive, and it wants to ride Noah's huge cock all night long.

I spy Gabriel over Noah's shoulder, fiddling in the bag. "Think fast, Captain America." Gabe tosses something through the air. Eli catches it and brings it in front of my face so I can see.

It's lube.

This game just leveled up.

But I'm not going to protest. I'm not going to do a thing except keep grinding down on Noah's cock, feeling his length touch deep inside me. Noah bites my lip again as he grabs my hips, forcing me to remain still. "She's all yours, friend."

Eli pushes a lubed finger inside me. He's not forceful like Noah. He takes things slow, moving his finger around my rim, letting me feel every delicious sensation as he rubs up against those nerve endings. My mouth hangs open. Gabe leans over Noah's shoulder and claims it, his tongue probing deep inside me, sucking out my soul through my lips.

I have so much of them inside me right now. Noah's cock, Eli's finger, Gabriel's tongue. It's like I'm made for them, and they are for me. Noah draws back and pushes deep, his cock pushing against Eli's finger, letting me get used to both of them moving inside me.

It's too much. I grind my hips against Noah, rubbing my clit on him. None of them move – they stay still, their eyes locked on me as I gasp and grind and take my pleasure. They don't say a word, don't move a muscle. As if the moment is too precious, too fragile to risk breaking.

They hold me as the orgasm claims me. It starts in my toes – a dark, hot ache that curls through my body. It pools in my stomach and reaches through my limbs before swirling through my skull. Every worry, every fear fades into nothing as pleasure pulses through me.

Eli's the first to move again. He removes his finger, and I hear the tear of a condom wrapper. Safe sex, always, with Eli. He kisses my neck as he braces himself against the chair with one hand, holding my hip with the other. He sighs as he pushes himself in – only an inch, a hot, stretched, glorious inch. He stops and waits, trailing kisses along my neck while I get used to him, until I'm squirming and murmuring for him to keep going.

Another inch.

Another inch. Noah's cock twitches inside me as Eli pushes against him through the thin wall. "This is so much more fun than spin-the-bottle," Eli whispers, his voice catching.

He pushes and kisses and digs his nails into me, and then suddenly he's all the way in. God, it's so... fuck, I can't describe it. You just have to experience it for yourself. It's like the tightest, warmest hug you've ever had, but from the inside out.

They start to move. Slowly, taking their rhythm from each other. The other times they've done this, the pair of them alternate strokes – one drives deep while the other pulls back. But this time, they thrust in unison, pulling out to give me this horrendous feeling of emptiness before slamming into me, filling me completely. Each time they do it it's like a mini-orgasm tearing through my body.

My feet slide out from beneath me. Eli braces me while Noah's huge hands hold me in exactly the right position. I can't do anything except enjoy the ride and feel every stroke of them inside me.

Gabriel watches, his hand fisting himself. His eyes don't leave mine and his lyrics burn into my brain, all those words that have kept me company in my loneliest hours. I don't need them anymore because I have him with me, and he is his music made flesh. He is the stars and the blood and the rain.

Looking at him like this – dark, pagan eyes hooded with need – sends me over the edge again. I fall into an orgasm that tears from inside me like a Xenomorph. My screams carry over the whole neighborhood. Sensing a kindred spirit, the lion roars his approval.

We'll get noise complaints before tonight is through, and it will be so, so worth it.

27

CLAUDIA

I don't want to go to the fucking Stonehurst Prep Valentine's Day dance. I'm a ball of fucking nerves about everything, and I'm worried Mackenzie Malloy will show up. She has a ticket. But I promised Gabriel I'd be there for his surprise, and I won't go back on that promise. Not when I've already taken so much from him.

So the night before Lupercalia I drag George and Yara up to my room so the three of us can get glammed up. Yara isn't at our school, of course, but the dance is actually a combined event for several of the swanky private schools in Emerald Beach. The organizers rented out one of Nero's downtown clubs. Some pretty big bands are playing, including Gabriel's friend's band, Broken Muse. We got Yara in as Eli's date from another school.

"You should have asked Isaac to come to the dance," I say to George as Yara rubs product in her hair. She teases George's short, feathery style until it perfectly frames her face. Is there anything Yara can't do?

"He's going with Malinda Hamilton," George says, her eyes not meeting mine.

Isaac was the sweetest stoner dude – he and George would

have made the cutest babies. But George threw in her lot with me, and she thinks being my friend puts those around her in danger. I'll admit that killing that guy in her kitchen did not help assuage her fears. She doesn't see that I can protect Isaac. If he's part of our circle, he'll have the power of my empire behind him, which is more than most people can say.

I haven't done the stats on this, but I bet Isaac is more likely to die in a car crash than he is to get shot in the crossfire of my silent war with Nero. But I can't explain that to my brainiac best friend.

We drive to the club. Gabriel rented a stretch Hummer for the occasion, and there's plenty of room and a fully stocked bar in the back. I stare at my reflection in the window, wondering if Mackenzie is lying in wait for me. Tiberius and Antony are already at the dance, acting as chaperones and briefing the 'security' team of August soldiers about the potential of a threat. I don't know how Antony intends to get around the fact that threat could look like their Imperator, but I had to leave that in his hands.

I have to focus on pretending to have a good time tonight, while I wait for the knife in my back.

We park at the club. I link arms with Eli and Noah, and Gabe takes George and Yara. Heads turn when we enter the room. Students from schools all across Emerald Beach gape at the Jesus-like Ice Queen who's returned from the dead, the girl with the three boyfriends and the penchant for violence who brings drama everywhere she goes.

The dance is 'Tunnel of Love' themed, with garish swans and kooky carnival decorations everywhere, totally ruining the actually-classy speakeasy-style decor. One-half of the room is dedicated to round tables covered in striped tablecloths. Magicians and fortune-tellers wander between the groups, and candy stripers deliver pink cotton candy on sticks. The other half is a heaving dance floor. My stomach clenches as I scan the room. Too many people, too many dark corners where Mackenzie can hide.

Noah stalks up to a table close to the stage, where a group of Emerald Beach sophomores is hanging out. "Move," he barks. They scatter. Eli pulls out a chair for me and I settle myself down, while Gabriel drags George and Yara onto the dance floor.

I watch my best friend dance with my boyfriend, my thoughts swirling. Mackenzie Malloy, Cleo St. James, Alec LeMarque, Daphne Ballantyne and their ilk made damn sure that George had as few fun high school experiences as possible. To see her having fun, with her shoulders relaxed and her arms waving about like a constipated chicken, makes me smile. This is what her life should have been. George is the best person, and she deserves to be happy.

Now all I had to do was get her laid.

A magician moves in front of me, offering to pull a rabbit out of a hat. After Noah shoos her away I look back at the dance floor, momentarily panicking I can't see my family. But no, there they are. Yara and George are dancing with a couple of guys from Gardin Academy. Gabriel is nowhere in sight.

Where is he?

I told everyone they had to stay close, in line of sight at all times. I *told* them.

I hope he hasn't gone off to spike the punch.

I told Gabriel he needs to sort out his substance abuse, and I truly believe he wants to do it. But I don't think willpower alone is going to get him there. I keep telling myself that as soon as we're out of danger, as soon as my empire is secured, I'll get Gabe the help he needs. But I'm starting to wonder if it might be too late by then.

If my fallen angel falls too far, I might not be able to drag him out of the abyss.

"I don't see Gabe," Noah whispers to me. Over his shoulder, Eli pretends to look interested as the magician pulls colored scarves from his ear.

"Me neither." I rise, scanning the room again. "I'll check the bathrooms, the bar. You text Antony and tell him—"

The lights dim. A single trembling note sounds from the stage. Students hush their conversations and turn to the lone figure standing beneath the spotlight – a girl with a waterfall of dark hair tumbling down her back, her eyes closed as she lets a note from her violin ring out.

A second blood-red spotlight flickers to life, and she's joined by a second violinist – an ice-haired man with a snowy-white violin. Fire and ice. Perfectly in harmony.

I want to find Gabe, but I'm rooted in place as the music swells, filling the club with somber, haunting notes, drawing all eyes toward the stage.

Red-tinted spotlights pulse on the sides of the stage, illuminating two other musicians – a guy with waist-length braided hair who looks like he could give Noah a run for his money in the ring plucks an electric guitar, and a raven-haired, too-pretty boy sits at the piano, cigarette hanging from his pouty lips, as he pounds the keys.

The crowd screams for Broken Muse – the same band who played at homecoming, only this time they're darker, more lush and haunted and ethereal.

I waver. The music fills me, and I can't tear my eyes from the band, even as panic about Gabe's whereabouts stabs at my chest. A fifth person joins them on stage, a shadow strutting through the classical instruments like he was born to be there.

Gabriel steps into the girl's spotlight, throwing his arms wide.

My panic turns to hot, needy addiction. I grab Noah and Eli

and surge toward the stage. What the fuck is he doing up there? Does he know how fucking incredible he looks?

The dark-haired beauty tosses him a microphone. Gabriel stares out into the crowd, searching the sea of faces. His eyes land on mine, and his labret piercing bounces as he flashes me a nervous, adorable smile.

"Hello," he says into the microphone, addressing everyone even though his eyes never leave mine. "My name is Gabriel Fallen. I know you didn't expect to see me here, and I hope you don't mind me ruining Broken Muse's set with my warbling. I've been mates with Dorien and the guys for a long time, and now that Faye's in the band, they've started experimenting with new musical directions. And one of those is letting a British tosser write lyrics for their music."

Lyrics?

Oh, Gabe. You beautiful creature. This is the best surprise.

"It turns out, we're quite good at working together. We're heading into the studio this month to record an album. And there will be a tour later this year, once I'm done with school. But I wanted to surprise you tonight with a special preview." Gabriel's grin is made of starlight. "I know you're all on social media, so you know I've been going through a rough patch. Someone I loved very much died tragically and unnecessarily, and I blamed myself. I thought the music had left me. I thought I didn't deserve the gift of your attention. But my girl set me right. That's why this song is for her."

He holds his hand out to me. To *me*.

In this room filled with screaming fans, the stars on his lips are for me.

I'm no longer Claudia August, notorious Imperator. I'm back to being the lonely, lost girl crying in an empty house while Gabriel sang my sorrows into a void. And here he is, my dream brought wondrously, perfectly to life, standing on stage with his hand held out to me.

I swallow the lump in my throat. Fuck, Gabe.

"Get up there." George nudges me, grinning from ear to ear.

I'm about to yell that I can't move in this crowd, but rough hands grab me from behind. Noah hoists me onto his shoulders. A spotlight circles the crowd before landing on me. Faces turn to stare. The room lurches and spins. I can't speak, I'm so mesmerized by Gabriel.

He waves at me and I wave back, shy now that the spotlight's on me. Gabriel winks. He opens his mouth and begins to sing.

> All I ever wanted was a knight in shining armor,
> To rescue me from your tower.
> All this time, the sword was mine,
> The clock strikes the final hour.
> Now the only weapon I have left,
> Is beautiful, damaging words.
> Words that cut,
> Words that kill,
> Words that blind,
> So you'll never see
> The broken boy you left behind.

Tears well in my eyes at his words. I know they're for his father. All the things Gabriel wanted to tell the duke but never could, he sings them into the starry night instead, for all the people in this room who can pluck their own truths from his poetry.

It's a song about betrayal, about what it means to find out your life has been a lie, that the king you desperately wanted to please was too busy burning his kingdom to ash to see you.

Every word drips with blood.

> The element of surprise,
> Is the deadliest blade,
> I see through your disguise,
> Your legend will fade,
> As my star lights up the sky.

The crowd surges, swirling and twisting in a hypnotic dance. We're carried forward by their tide. I squeeze my thighs around Noah's ears and grip for dear life as we're jostled closer to the stage. Gabriel leans one foot on the foldback and rests his hand on his knee, casual-as-you-please as he leans out over the crowd to deliver a gut-punch of a chorus.

> I've sharpened my steel,
> I've made my sacrifices.
> I'm unleashing war.

He screams the word war, pouring eighteen years of neglect into a sound that tears apart the room with anguish. His eyes reflect his love for Dylan, his love for me, and I know that even though we never met, the two of us will forever be linked in Gabriel's mind – the boy who gave his life for Gabriel's freedom, and the girl who will lay down hers to protect it.

A warm hand encircles mine. Gabriel yanks me on stage. I trip on some wires and fall into his arms. People laugh and cheer. He holds me, crushing me against him as he cries into the mic, stoking the audience into a frenzy. The noise rushes in my ears, and my heart is ready to leap out of my chest as Gabriel holds the mic between us so we can both sing. I can hardly hear our voices over the roaring of the crowd as they chant the words along with us.

I'm unleashing war.

I'm unleashing war.

I feel the music in my bones, my marrow. Lighters and mobile phones raise in the air. An ocean of flickering stars that swirl and sway to the music as the band takes over, the crunchy guitar riffing with the pianos while the two violins duel for supremacy. Only Gabe and I know that this song isn't only about personal triumph. It's our battle cry.

Gabriel holds me to his chest with one hand, the other raising the mic to his lips as his face breaks out into a wonky, genuine smile. "I've got you."

That smile. Gabriel's smile. It melts away the edges of my savagery.

"I've got you." He whispers the words into the microphone again, and the whole room goes mental. Gabe's eyes remain locked on mine, and I know he means those words only for me.

As Gabriel screams the last, lingering note, a hail of rainbow bubbles explode from the ceiling, It's so completely ridiculous and utterly Gabriel that I throw my head back and let the sticky bubbles pop over my face, soaking up the sheer seduction of the crowd and the music and his love.

As I stand up straight, a single face resolves in the surging crowd. The only person not singing. The only person standing still, icicle eyes watching me with cold, calculating glee.

The only person holding a pistol in her fingers, pointing directly at Gabriel's heart.

Mackenzie.

28

CLAUDIA

The sight of her freezes my blood.

The music dulls into background noise.

The band, the gyrating people, the flickering lighters fade and blur as every inch of her stands out in crystal clarity.

I can't move.

My eyes meet hers, and in that millisecond where we regard each other across the packed club, she hits me with an entire lifetime of hate.

It's like entering the fucking Matrix. I half expect streams of code to cascade over her cheeks. I know she must look like me, but seeing my own wavy gold hair, full lips, heart-shaped face, and cold, determined eyes reflected back at me is *creepy as fuck.*

Especially since she's holding that gun

People dance around her, oblivious to the danger. They probably think the weapon is fake, part of a costume or elaborate stunt. But it's real and it's pointing at Gabriel's chest.

No. No. This can't be how it ends.

Everything happens at once. Eli calls my name, his voice muffled like he's speaking underwater. Noah launches himself at

Mackenzie. I throw myself in front of Gabriel, my body shielding him. The bullet belongs to me and me alone.

There's a flash. I think that maybe the gun goes off, but she had a silencer so the sound doesn't register over the roar of the music. And Gabe, sweet oblivious Gabe, kisses my cheek and dives off the stage, his arms thrown wide.

The crowd raise their arms to catch him. He floats above them, his head tossed back in ecstasy, his arm raised and his fingers curling, beckoning me to fall with him. I can't see Mackenzie or Noah anywhere. Eli shoves his way through the crowd, his face panicked.

I have to get to them.

It'll take me forever to push my way through the crowd. Even under the glare of the stage lights, I feel the claustrophobia of them surrounding me, pushing and shoving, bodies hemming me in and preventing me from reaching my family. I'm trapped up here, and the gun went off. *The gun went off.*

A scream penetrates from the back of the floor. People start to turn to look. Fear and confusion scent the air. The band keeps playing, but the guitarist moves toward me, his features grim. "What's going on?" he yells.

I can't answer. I do the only thing I can do. I follow Gabriel over the wall, into battle.

I cross my arms over my chest like an Egyptian pharaoh. Even though it feels like a betrayal, I turn my back on the crowd, facing the four musicians who've welcomed him into their fold. The girl, Faye, waves at me, her eyes twinkling with mischief. But the pianist, Dorien, seems to have scented the change in mood. He yells something at me, but it's too late to answer him.

I fall.

I fall back into the stars, my eyes and heart wide open.

For a moment I'm suspended, falling through space and time. And then the crowd catch me. Hands clamp around my legs and lift my back, my shoulders, my arms. It's an incredible feeling. I would be on high on the thrill of it if I wasn't so terrified right now.

I allow the crowd to carry me along on a river of hands, trusting that they won't let me fall, trusting Gabriel to light the way through the darkness.

Trust. It's new for me, but I kind of like it – this clenching in my chest, this wild abandon of jumping into the void and feeling someone catch you. This resignation that even if your evil sister decides this is the exact moment she puts a bullet through your skull, at least you have been loved and held by the best people, and your family will make sure she never hurts anyone ever again.

I start to dip, but strong hands grab me and set me down on my feet. Gabe's here with me, all sparkling eyes and disgustingly self-satisfied grin. For the first time since I've known him, he looks honestly, properly *alive*, every atom of him in brilliant glow.

"I guess I can write songs again," he cries.

I wish more than anything that Gabe could have this moment for himself. He's fucking earned it. But his safety is more important. "Gabe, Mackenzie's here."

His smile freezes. His fingers clamp around mine. "Where?"

Our heads turn at the same time to a commotion behind us. At the rear of the room, where the crowd is thinner and spaced out, people have moved to the side so club security can drag away Noah. He kicks and yells, throwing a wild punch that knocks a burly guard to the floor. Blood spurts from the guy's nose, and I recognize him as one of my own soldiers.

Shit. What happened? Where's Mackenzie?

Gabriel holds my hand and shoves his way through the crowd, breezing past fans who tear at his clothing, desperate for a piece of him. His skin is sheened in sweat. *He's alive. I have to keep him that way.*

I reach Noah just as three of them get hold of him and start dragging him toward the exit. "What are you doing? Put him down this instant."

My men glare at me. I recognize one as Po, my man at the docks, a man who's proven himself resourceful and trustworthy. Until now. He frowns at me. "Fuck. How did you get back in here?"

I don't understand his question until I see another guard advance toward me, gun glinting in his hand. I grab Po's collar and shake him. "What are you playing at? I'm *Claudia*. You know, your fucking *Imperator*. Noah was after Mackenzie."

Bo's frown wavers as he looks me up and down. "Don't try to fool us. You're Mackenzie, the one we're supposed to take out if she shows up. You've been working with this guy – he lunged at Claudia, tried to kill her—"

"I told you, that was Mackenzie," Noah yells. He manages to pull one arm free and slams his fist into Po's face. Po's features crumble and he staggers back, cursing as blood pisses from his nose. I step between them before things get even more violent, and roll up my arm to show them the August mark tattooed on my skin.

"How can you not recognize your own Imperator?" I know we're identical twins, but they're not supposed to know that. They were supposed to be on the lookout for a girl who looks a lot like me. Panic bubbles in my chest as I realize how much time we've wasted already. Gabriel could've been *shot,* and my sister is still running free in this club somewhere and they're getting in *my* face?

Po's eyes bug out of his head. "How do we know you didn't just get that tattooed? Antony told us Claudia August was wearing a red dress."

I glance down at my beautiful deep emerald green dress. *Fuck, Antony's eyes.* In the dim light, he must've mistaken the color of my dress for red. And Mackenzie *was* wearing a red dress. I remember the flash of it under the lights. They must've seen Noah fly at her and assumed he was attacking me, and sprung into action like the good soldiers they are.

Po's eyes bug out of my head. He must've seen something in me – some mannerism that he knows I use, probably the way my eyes glaze over with ice before I wring his fucking neck – because his whole body trembles. "I'm so sorry, Imperator," Po cries. All three men drop their hold on Noah. "I truly thought the other girl was you. I thought you were in danger. She doesn't just resemble you, it's as if she's a carbon copy. I promise I'll—"

"There's no time," I snap, helping Noah straighten his suit. "Which way did Mackenzie go?"

Po points a shaking finger toward the bathrooms. I sprint over and slam the door, Noah and Gabe hot on my heels.

Tiberius stands in the hallway, tree-trunk arms folded across his barrel chest. He blocks the entire hallway to the bathroom and fire exit. No way could anyone get past him. *So where the fuck is Mackenzie?*

Noah looks up, checking the ceiling. He won't fall for Cali's trick ever again. No Mackenzie dangling from the fluorescent light.

"I'm Claudia." I hold up my arm to show Tiberius the tattoo.

"I know." His face collapses into a frown. "She got away."

"How?"

Tiberius scratches his head. The scar tugs at his skin, making him look like a fucked-up circus clown. "It was my fault. I was guarding this exit when the message came through. Mackenzie was up on stage. Antony's team was moving to intercept her. Noah attacked Claudia, and then everything on the comms went wild. Next thing, she struts down this corridor, red dress hugging that ass, casual as you like. 'Antony has Mackenzie cornered inside,' she says, giving me a smack on the lips as she saunters to the fire exit. 'He told me to leave by this exit and Noah will bring the car around.' She looks and sounds exactly like you. It was only after I let her out that Po sent through the message that *Mackenzie* was in the red dress."

"Fuck!" I tear at my hair. My sister was right under our noses and we let her get away. "How did this happen? So much for having this club locked down tighter than a nun's cunt. How did she get in past security?"

"She had a ticket. She looks like you. No one would have asked questions." Antony appears in the doorway. I lunge at him, ready to throttle him for making such a stupid fucking mistake, but he sags against the wall, his eyes round, haunted. I've never seen my cousin like this before, so... defeated.

He hates weakness. And tonight, he was our weakness. And his mistake almost got Gabriel killed.

No. It wasn't Antony who tried to open fire in the middle of a crowded club. It was my sister. She's the one to blame. She's the one we need to take down.

I collapse against the wall, my heart thudding in my chest. This was another insanely close call. Mackenzie was *here*. I literally looked her in the eyes as she held up that gun. She tricked her way into this club; she even tricked Tiberius.

How the fuck do I protect my family from someone who can disguise herself as me?

29

GABRIEL

The high of the show buzzes in my veins for the rest of the night. No amount of Claudia telling me she nearly saw me get shot could dim the buzz. If that was to be my last moment on earth, what a way to go. On stage with my girl, singing the song I wrote for her, for us.

Broken Muse return to the stage to perform another set, this time without me. There's nothing we can do to find Mackenzie now – she's slipped away into the shadows once more. So Claws and George and I ignore Antony's fatherly advice to go home, and we dance until the last trembling note, swept up in the raw power of the music until the lights go up and the spell is broken. The club is once again a big, echoing room with rubbish and bodily fluids caked on the sticky floor.

I want to chase the magic in my veins as long as I can – I want to believe I really am this version of Gabriel and not the fuck-up who lives inside my head and steals all the booze. I round up the family and shove them into the limo. Claws isn't even fully inside the car yet when I start to snog her. She tastes amazing, like Champagne and savagery. I want to crawl inside her skin and live there forever.

I'm starting to understand my place in Claws' world. I can't wade into bloody battle for her, like Noah. I'm never going to be the brains of the operation – that's Eli. But I can be the heart.

I can remind her what she's fighting for.

I sing to Claudia, letting my breath touch her skin as I slide the spaghetti straps over her shoulders. I kiss her forehead, my lips moving as I hum the melody under my breath. She moans, arching her back and clamping her arms around my waist to pull me closer. I will write the song of her body. I don't care that I've just elbowed Noah in the face or that George is cowering in a corner. I need this woman to know how amazing she is *right the fuck now*.

Yara bangs on the glass separating us from the driver. "Can you go a bit faster? I don't want to be stuck in this tin can when this lot start at it like rabbits."

I don't remember the rest of the car trip; I have my tongue buried in Claudia's hot, perfect mouth and nothing else matters. As we walk into the house, Eli looks at Claudia hopefully, but Noah shoves him toward the ballroom. "Tonight is for Gabe and Claudia. Go play with your kittens."

My friends have my back.

I sweep Claudia into my arms and carry her to her room. She clings to my neck, her eyes boring into my soul.

"You're unusually coordinated tonight," she murmurs. "You haven't stumbled once or knocked an ugly painting off the wall."

"I haven't had a drink," I reply, planting kisses on the top of her head. "A feat worthy of a fine medal, or at the very least to the right to call myself the singer of Broken Muse."

The singer of Broken Muse. It sounds strange and wonderful on my tongue. When I called Dorien a few weeks ago to play him my new song, all I was looking for was a bit of support from a fellow musician. Claws will like everything I write, and Eli and Noah are heathens when it comes to the arts, so I trusted Dorien to tell me if I have my mojo back or if I'd written the Gabriel Fallen equivalent of "MMMbop." He suggested I come into the studio and jam the song with the band. I thought he was just being nice, but I should've known Dorien doesn't do things just to be nice. The minute Faye picked up her violin and played my melody, we all felt it. The *spark*. The stars falling around us as the music flowed from our fingers.

I haven't felt that way about music for a long time, not since Dylan and I wrote our first songs hiding in the tower of Blackwich Castle. I didn't think I had the right to feel this way again, not after I took our pain and used it to make us famous, to get us record deals and groupies and drugs and shenanigans, so I never, ever had to deal with the growing gap between my heart and the boy I loved.

I don't think I've forgiven myself, but I think I'm starting to realize that regrets are meant to be *lived*. That instead of running from the pain of losing Dylan, if I run headlong into it, I won't crash and burn. Claws gave me the strength to carry it with me.

And the band is great – Dorien, Faye, Titus, Ivan. They *flow*. They're all in a relationship like I am with Claws, Noah, and Eli. They understand my life in a way I never thought possible. Titus is a beautiful soul, and Ivan has a dry Romanian sense of humor that cracks me up every time. All it took were three jam sessions and Dorien was arranging a summer tour. Every piece fit. *I* fit.

I know that part of the plan we worked out is that I quit music to be here for Claws, but I don't have to do that just yet, do I? She will sort out this shit with the Triumvirate, because that's what she does, and I'll have the summer to tour. Everything will be fine.

I kick the door of her bedroom – not Mackenzie's old room, but a guest bedroom downstairs she long ago claimed as her own. The wood cracks against the wall, sending Queen Boudica darting for safety. I lay Claudia down on the bed. She stares up at me like I'm a god, and my heart wants to burst out of my chest. I want to be the person she sees when she looks at me. I'm not there yet, but after tonight, I feel like I *could* be.

"Gabriel," Claudia reaches up and pulls me down to her. I'm surprised to feel tears streaking her face. "What you said on stage tonight, that was the most raw and real I've ever seen you. You showed me the real Gabriel. I don't know if I've ever truly seen him on display like that before."

I throw one leg over her, shifting my weight so I'm straddling her. I gaze down at the perfection that is Claudia August. My heart grows three sizes like a fucking Dr. Seuss character. I no longer feel the crushing weight in my chest of not deserving her. All I feel is this bright, brilliant love.

And horniness. My cock feels like it'd quite like to be inside her, thank you very much. I may be an immortal rock god capable of superhuman feats, but she's looking up at me all heavy-lidded and licking her lips, and 'restraint' isn't in this god's vocabulary...

I bend down and kiss her. Kissing Claudia August is like standing under the waterfall at my apartment – calming and grounding and also likely to drag me under. I drown in her intoxicating scent, in the way she mewls like a kitten when I stroke my stud across her tongue.

My hands roam over her body. Every touch is like touching her for the first time again. And I realize that so many of the times we've been together – including that first, magical night at Midnight Grotto – I've been drunk. I've had a screen of alcohol to shield me from her brilliance, but now that I'm sober(ish, let's not get carried away), it's as if I'm trying to stare directly into the sun – she *dazzles*. There's too much of Claudia to take in at once. I have to enjoy her in bite-sized pieces – the gentle slope of her shoulders, the dip in her collarbone that makes her squirm when I kiss it, the gorgeous dent under her armpit, the tiny swirl of skin in her belly button.

I kiss and touch and caress until she's writhing beneath me, until our touches are no longer tender but a needful grinding.

I slide my fingers under her green dress and push it up, tugging it over her head and tossing the offending fabric aside. Claudia watches me with an indulgent pout. I run my finger along her entrance, feeling the wetness already pooling there. The scent of her reaches my nostrils – heady and sweet, for me. For *me*.

Because I sing the stars for her.

And suddenly I can't take it anymore. We're talking about the real Gabriel Fallen tonight, the one I've been so afraid to let her see. Well, he's about to say something potentially very stupid.

"I want to have a child with you," I whisper. "I know you think I haven't thought about it, but I *have*. I hardly think about anything else. And if it has to go by some other dude's last name, but that means we can have a baby, a *family*, if it means that we're safe, then I'll do it. I'll do anything for you."

"Oh, Gabe." Claws holds my cheeks between her hands, kissing the tears pooling under my eyes. "I want a baby with you, too. I want you to see yourself reflected in our child, to know that you will always have a home to come back to, a compass pointing north. I know you're trying so hard to face your demons. You're not a fallen angel with broken wings. You're whole and complete, and you have such incredible strength and heart that our child would be lucky to have you as a father."

I know that in the years to come, when I'm at my darkest, I will repeat her words back to myself and find strength in them. "Is that a yes?"

She slaps my ass. "Get those sexy pants off and let's do this, Fallen."

"I don't mean we have to start right now."

"Why not?" She picks up her birth control pills from the bedside table and tosses them out the window. I hear a faint plink, followed by a low roar. They must've fallen in the swimming pool.

I hope the lion doesn't get sick if he eats them.

"You sure this is what you want?" Another thought occurs to me. "This isn't because of Nero, is it? Or my father? He hasn't made you some deal about my kid?"

"As far as I know, your dad is still playing house with Cleo and making Nero's life miserable. I haven't heard from him." Claws brushes her lips against mine. "This decision has nothing to do with them. It's because you're perfect and I'm badass and we'd make one amazing kid."

I slide into her heat, all the while thinking that despite what I know about birth control, and that we've only just decided to do this, that maybe, *maybe,* I might love Claudia August enough to create a spark of life.

Claudia clings to me, arching her hips to meet mine, her face twisting with ecstasy as my piercing reaches all the right places inside her. But this is more than sex. I'm cracked open, my heart raw and bleeding, but so imperfectly, gloriously *alive.*

A baby, a new life who will undo all the rotten things my father did to me. A child that would be mine – mine and Claudia's – that he could never touch. A child that would learn strength from Noah, fortitude from Eli, and heart from me.

30

CLAUDIA

*A*ntony outdoes himself with the Lupercalia party. I've set a high standard for bloody spectacle, and my people expect their bread and circuses. He knows he has to do something big to make people forget to be mad at me for taking away the lion, and I think he wants to make up for his fuck-up at the Valentine's dance.

So he rounds up all the men involved in Brutus' skin operation, and sends them into the ring, naked and without weapons. He walks out over the gangplank and calls down to them over the roar of the crowd.

"My cousin, Claudia August, is benevolent and kind. Even though you betrayed our family, even though you deserve no second chances, she offers you one. At the end of this bout, the last man standing will be granted immunity and given a place as an exalted soldier in the August family. The rest will have their corpses fed to the lion."

With that, Antony drops an armload of weapons into the ring. The men pounce. The fastest among them manage to pick up swords and knives and tridents and polearms. There's even a crossbow. They slaughter the unarmed, then turn on each other.

Severed limbs fly through the air, and by the time only three men remain, they're crunching the skulls of their fallen comrades beneath their feet.

I'm the only one in the VIP seats not watching the ring. Nero sits at the table next to me, one hand on Eli's mother's knee, every seat crowded with his numerous children (ex-wives of Nero don't tend to live long). Livvie sees me watching, and gives me a respectful nod. Nero laughs and claps along with the rest of the crowd, but I fancy I see a sheen of sweat on his fat brow. Those men may have belonged to Brutus, but they were loyal to him. I've thinned his ranks even further, and there's nothing he can do.

I'd heard through the grapevine (Eli, via Livvie) that the duke has put pressure on Nero to deliver payment, and Nero has sold. Gabriel's father hasn't come to me, so he's not yet willing to accept my offer, but he's making Nero squirm, and I'm here for it. My enemy's enemy is my friend, even if he's also my boyfriend's abuser. I'll make sure the duke gets his justice.

Good things come to those who wait. Usually, I'm an impatient bitch, but I need to play a long game here, let the duke believe he and that bitch Cleo are safe.

By the time I get my cue to descend to the stage, the entire ring is stained pink with blood, and the crowd roars for more, more, more.

The bodies are dragged from the arena and a red carpet laid on top of the carnage. Nero and Constantine descend first, moving through the crowd toward the arena, stopping to offer tokens – coins bearing their insignia that can be exchanged for small favors. They reach the arena and step onto the red carpet. My two husbands – polar opposites in every way. One jovial, the other every bit as ruthless as his countenance suggests.

Constantine stands mute, stoic. Nero grins and waves at the crowd, soaking up their adulation. He believes he still owns popular support in this town. I'm not so sure, but I guess I'm about to find out.

I stand to wild applause, my white dress flaring over my hips, and turn to my family seated around my table. Gabriel's made all the napkins into dirty shapes. Noah looks ready to smash heads together. George is tapping away on her phone. Yara is stealing everyone's untouched drinks and Eli... Eli keeps glancing over at his mom. At Nero's table, Darlene Hart scowls at me like I'm sour milk.

Don't worry, doll – after tonight, Nero is all yours. I sure as fuck don't want him.

The thunder of drums signals my cue. My family stands and flanks me, hemming me in from the restless crowd as we make our way to the arena. The dress swirls around my feet as I step onto the pink sand. The hem drags in the blood, staining the silk with pink droplets. Nero's eyes never leave me as he takes in the wedding dress – the dress he sent me.

The symbol of our alliance.

"I knew you'd come around to my point of view," he whispers as he takes my hand and places me between him and Constantine. "You and I will build the most beautiful empire the world has ever seen."

I nod, not trusting myself to speak.

Galen steps onto the stage, looking unusually dapper in a pinstripe suit instead of bloodstained scrubs. As well as being our resident medical professional, he performs wedding ceremonies for the Triumvirate and their soldiers. He winks at me and holds his hand up for silence.

"In a show of solidarity never before seen in our organization, our three Imperators have agreed to an unusual arrangement. I'll let Claudia August explain what's about to happen."

Galen passes the microphone to me. Nero beams at me, his

hand resting protectively on the small of my back. But behind his smile, he looks very, very serious.

"It's been a long, hard road to get to this point," I begin. "For years, I've lived in the shadows, unable to take over the empire that's rightfully mine because of a usurper, a traitor in our midst that first had to be expunged. A rabid dog that had to be put down. Now that that unpleasantness is behind us, your Imperators want to present a united front and a new dedication to working together to strengthen our position, instead of infighting. That was why both Constantine Dio and Nero Lucian proposed to me. A marriage between our three families would provide unity, certainly, and safety for all of you present tonight – a new era of peace."

A few people whistle and yell their approval, but mostly my words are greeted with silence. After years of rivalry, the idea of Imperators marrying, intermingling the families... it's never been suggested before. No one knows what to expect, or what this will mean for their livelihoods, their territories, their blood oaths.

In the end, it all comes back to blood.

This staunchly heteronormative world has never had to deal with the likes of me before. A female Imperator. A woman with inconceivable power, gifted by virtue of my blood. Even Constantine – the deadliest assassin in the city – has had to hide his true self. That's the price of his blood.

Maybe it's time to change things.

I fix my Ice Queen glare on Nero as I address the concerns of my people. "In our enthusiasm to force this alliance, we admit that as your leaders, we overlooked some of the more practical aspects. We all know that a wedding between one woman and two men isn't legal in this country. Making this arrangement public will invite scrutiny from the authorities, and this will bleed over into our business dealings. Marrying two men also causes succession issues for the August family. If I'm killed in the course of my work – as has happened to every Imperator before me – then the succession of the August empire cannot be certain. This makes us vulnerable to other forces who might try to usurp what's ours. For this reason, I am forced to accept that I cannot wed both these fine men. Although our alliance will still remain firm for the good of the empire, I must choose. And I choose..." I glance at Nero, longing to see the moment my betrayal registers on his smarmy face. "I choose Constantine Dio."

There's an audible holding of breath. No one expects me to choose Constantine, not when I'm wearing Nero's dress.

No one, it seems, except Nero Lucian.

He throws his head back and laughs. A merry, mirthful laugh that shakes and shudders in the vast space, a laugh that even the moon can't swallow. When he finally pulls himself together, he wipes tears from his eyes and shakes his head with mock sadness.

"That's too bad, too bad."

As quick as a snake, Nero slips a gun from his suit and shoots Constantine in the chest.

31

CLAUDIA

onstantine's eyes widen. He bends his long neck to peer down at the bullet hole – a circle of blood spreading across his pristine white shirt.

His face goes from detached interest to pale resignation. He flashes Nero a wobbly smile. "You got me," he whispers, extending his hand.

"Farewell." Nero takes Constantine's hand and shakes. With his other hand, he shoots Constantine between the eyes.

Blood splatters across my dress as my groom drops to the floor. His neck bends back, revealing blood bubbling from the neat hole in his forehead.

Well.

Fuck.

Blood pounds in my ears. I rush at Nero, but he keeps the gun poised on me, a fresh bullet in the chamber.

I stop in my tracks. *What the fuck is he doing?*

How the fuck does he think he's going to get away with this? He shot an Imperator in an arena full of witnesses. An arena full of angry fucking *assussins*. Any moment now this arena will erupt into a blood bath.

An angry rumble arcs through the crowd. Not even Nero's most loyal soldiers will be able to reconcile what he's done. I can hear my princes pushing through the crowd, trying to reach me. Constantine's people move swiftly, silently, into positions around the stage. At this moment there are at least twenty weapons aimed at Nero's head. *Take him out,* I want to yell. *Nero killed your Imperator.*

But they don't answer to me.

"Shoot him. Shoot the betrayer!" Cali screams. Out of the corner of my eye, I see her on the edge of the arena with the other tribunes. Antony holds her back, but the look he flashes me tells me that I better do something fast, or she'll go postal and we'll all end up dead.

I flick my focus back to Nero, who's still pointing that gun at my chest. The crowd, the arena, even the faces of my beloved family fade as my vision narrows on that barrel.

Is this how my father felt before Brutus laid him in a coffin? Am I staring down the barrel at the reaper?

"You are all welcome to take your anger out on me," Nero says, addressing our people without letting his eyes stray from me. He looks completely at ease. Does the man even sweat? "After all, I have broken our sacred rules and shot dead my colleague in front of you. You might think I've acted out of jealousy, that this was about a petty squabble for the hand of Claudia August. But before one of you puts a bullet between my eyes or stuffs me into the brazen bull, I ask for a few moments of your attention while I present the reasons why I acted in this most uncouth manner."

With his free hand, Nero opens the lapel of his jacket. Fingers twitch on weapons, but instead of drawing a gun, he pulls out a brown envelope stuffed with photographs. He pulls out the photographs and holds them up, shot after damning shot. Constantine's face is clearly visible talking, joking, passing documents to men we all recognize, men who work for the FBI. "Our good leader, Constantine, has been making plans in secret. He's working with the Feds. He was feeding them information about our operations here in Emerald Beach. Their men are likely planted in this audience right now. They will see what I've done here tonight and return to their masters to tell them that the Triumvirate stands strong against them, that their operatives will be rooted out, and their skin will boil for daring to cross us."

"How do we know those are real?" I snap.

Nero holds up a flash drive. "I have more than just photographs. All the evidence I've collected against him is on here. I *had* hoped to do this privately, between the Imperators after our wedding, but you forced my hand. I could not allow a man secretly working with the Feds to obtain such power over the August family, not without stepping in."

I grit my teeth. He's trying to undermine me, make it look like I'm the weak girl who needs his help.

Nero continues, "I'm sure Claudia August was thoroughly unaware of these facts. Please, do not assume she knowingly intended to align with this traitor. But I could not allow her to unwittingly sign her empire over to him. I had to act."

"Give me those." I snatch the photographs from his hand and flip through them. They're immaculate, I'll give him that, but that doesn't mean much these days. George could pull off 'evidence' like this in a couple of hours. "This should have been dealt with in a trial, as is the right of all Imperators."

"Do you mean the same courtesy he showed your father?" Nero sneers.

I drop the photographs into the sand. "What the fuck are you talking about?"

"Do you think Brutus pulled off Julian's execution single-handedly? How can you be so naive?" Brutus pulls out another envelope. "I have the documents right here. The signed contract between Constantine Dio and an anonymous party – for three bodies."

The guys reach me as I stare at the document in my hand – the scrawl of Constantine's signature smudged at the edge. My finger lifts the wax edge of the seal, where Constantine's signet ring has been pressed into the wax. An Imperator would never take their ring off or allow another to use it.

This is real.

All these years, Constantine knew Julian August's child wasn't legitimate, but that secret was his own personal sword of Damocles. When Brutus came to him with this job, he must've thought he'd been handed the keys to the August empire on a platter. He miscalculated Brutus' influence and Nero's cunning, and that miscalculation is the only reason I still have an empire left to claim.

Alea iacta est. The die is cast.

I think back to the night my life changed forever, to the rough hands pulling me out of bed, pinning my arms so they hurt. My mother, propped up in her favorite chair, knife handle buried in her neck and a pool of claret widening at her feet. My bloodied reflection glaring at me from the window. Waking up in the coffin, my throat closing from lack of oxygen, Antony pulling me from my grave, holding me while I gasped in fresh air.

I never saw Brutus that night. I assumed he had loyal followers who did the work for him. Followers like Eli's father who supplied the coffins and the graves. But I should have guessed he'd hire out the job. You can always find an assassin for any job if the price is right.

I see red. The paper crumples in my hands. I want to bring Constantine to life again so I can choke the life from him with my bare hands, then fuck his eye sockets with the handle of my knife.

Death is too good for him.

And Nero… fucking *Nero* robbed me of the satisfaction of killing him.

"Constantine has no immediate children," Nero says, moving things along as if my rage isn't a living, breathing thing that expands to fill the entire arena, crowding out the mundane concerns of succession. "The rule of blood decrees that his empire goes to the next in his line, which is his cousin, Marcus Dio. Marcus, if you would make yourself known."

A man shoves his way through the crowd, his hand raised. He's flanked by two burly bodyguards, their weapons trained on the crowd. His parade reeks of planning – he knew he'd be called forward tonight. The air crackles with tension as he tries to enter the ring, and Antony's guards stop them.

"I know that man's face," Eli whispers. "He's always at Vault. He's one of Nero's men."

And just like that, I know Nero planned this. All of this. The bastard knew I'd never consent to the double wedding. He anticipated that I'd make an alliance with Constantine. And he set about putting together this evidence to ensure we could never stand against him.

Nero reaches down and tugs the signet ring from Constantine's bloody hand. He holds it up, letting the harsh floodlights highlight the distinctive planes and dents of its surface, the eagle that symbolizes Constantine's line. Antony glowers, but he lets Marcus into the ring. He doesn't have a choice, and neither do I.

Cali steps in front of him, her knife pointing at Nero's throat. "Stop."

"You can't stand in the way of a succession," Nero says. "You've been an excellent tribune. I'm certain Marcus will give you an important role in his empire. But for now, you need to step aside and allow our sacred ceremony to continue "

"Marcus won't give me jack shit, and you both know it." Cali fixes Nero with a terrifying glare. "He has no right to the empire. I'm Constantine's rightful heir."

A rattle of unease settles in the audience. They know Cali isn't Constantine's blood.

What the fuck is she doing? She's going to get herself killed.

Cali reaches into her bra and pulls out a folded piece of paper, which she hands to Nero. "Check it. It's all legal. Constantine officially adopted me. As far as he was concerned, I am his daughter, his rightful heir."

"But you're not blood," Marcus splutters.

"What does blood matter if it isn't worthy?" she snaps. To prove her point, she spins on her heel and slices her curved blade through his neck. His head wobbles on his neck, his mouth open in a bloody scream before it topples from his shoulders and his headless torso crumples to the ground.

Checkmate, bitches.

As the crowd watch, stunned, Cali carves up Marcus, chopping his arms at the shoulders, his legs at the feet, then the knees. She tosses the pieces into the crowd, where her supporters dive for them like coveted trophies. The rest of the room remains bitterly, eerily silent.

"Anyone else want to challenge me?" Cali glares around her, her entire body drenched in blood. Every soldier in the ring takes a step back, stares anywhere else but the blood-soaked woman.

The crowd screams their approval, stomping their feet and waving their fists in the air. They're here for blood, and they want to be ruled by the bloodiest empress of them all.

Nero looks... *amused.*

I'm...

I don't know what I feel.

Tonight is... a complete fuckup. I walked into the arena confident in my alliance with Dio, ready to out-maneuver Nero and eat away at another slice of his empire. But all this time... I was signing my soul over to a deal with the Devil. And now my alliance is shot to shit and the woman who wants to rip my throat out is claiming charge of the Dio family.

Can Cali even *do* that?

I glance at Nero, watching the corner of his smarmy grin twitch. I guess if the Triumvirate agrees, Cali can do what she wants. It's not as if Marcus is in any state to dispute her claim. And I'm not exactly one to oppose, since I'm not technically Julian August's blood.

Nero watches his own carefully orchestrated plan fall to pieces around him. Not even he's been able to predict Cali. Now we have to decide what to do with her.

Cali is a complete wildcard. Nero can't manipulate her the way he could Constantine. But she hates me, so that's to his advantage. She represents chaos, and Nero adores chaos. He *thrives* in chaos. Plus, there's not much he can do with the whole crowd screaming her name.

He raises an eyebrow at me. "This is an interesting turn of events, wouldn't you say, Imperator?"

"Indeed." I raise an eyebrow in return. "I for one am ready to welcome another woman into our fold. What do you say?"

Chaos wins. It always does.

Nero claps his hands. Antony emerges from the wings, walking a pig on a lead – the sacrifice we give to the Gods for any big celebration. Cali slices its throat and collects the blood in the same small cup I drank from at Saturnalia. She raises it to her lips, only instead of drinking, she tips the blood over her head so it dribbles down her face, mingling with Marcus' blood and plastering her hair to her scalp.

The crowd cheer, although I notice a few sullen faces – Marcus' supporters, I'm guessing. Cali's move is going to tear Dio right down the middle. She'll have a hell of a job pulling them together under her banner. This is good, because if she needs to focus on solidifying her power she won't have time to kill me—

"As my first act as your Imperator," Cali runs her finger along the edge of her curved blade, "I challenge Claudia August to a fight to the death."

32

CLAUDIA

I snort. That's ridiculous. *She can't do that, can she?*

Cali continues, "Claudia August killed my love, Brutus August. Brutus August brought the August empire back from the brink after his brother's neglect. He deserved to die like a god, not to be slaughtered for some old, forgotten crime. For his death, I demand penance."

"Of course I killed him." The horror of that night stirs in my bones. My parents' deaths – my real parents, not by blood but by the gifts they gave me – are not a forgotten crime. Their absence is burned into my flesh. "Brutus *buried my father alive.* For his crimes against our family, he wore the *sacer.* I had every right to kill him." I glare at Nero. "She has no right to challenge me like this."

"As an Imperator, I have every right to question a decision, to demand satisfaction for a slight." Cali licks blood from her fingers. "And if I don't get what I want, I may be forced to reveal *certain other truths.*"

Of course. Cali was in the room when I revealed that I knew about the chemical vat. She knows my secret, and I no longer have Constantine's protection. Of course, it matters less now that we allowed her to be an Imperator without a blood connection, but having that secret will put me back in a precarious position again, this time with Cali's knife at my throat—

Fuck. Shit. Fuck.

Nero turns to me, his face lit up with amusement. "Your move, princess," he grins. "Surely, you won't allow this insult to stand?"

He's right, the bastard. The harsh lights burn against my bare skin. I blink. I can hardly see a thing beneath their onslaught, just the first row of tables beyond the stomping, roaring crowd. But I feel them all – their eyes pricking my skin, their skin straining over knuckles as they punch the air, the scent of blood hanging low and thick.

Noah strides across the arena, his body poised for a fight. Antony stalks after him to remind him of the rules of our organization. They argue over top of each other in harsh whispers, reminding me of every time in my life where men have made decisions for me.

"Fuck off," I shove them aside. "I'll fight Cali."

Eli's Golden Boy features darkens with rage. "Don't be insane. You're not getting in the ring with her. She can't just stomp in here and demand you fight her. It's not a fair playing field—"

"Listen to the crowd out there," I hiss back. "You think we can walk out of this now without spilling blood? This isn't a high school sports game. They don't give a shit about a *fair playing field*. They've just seen Constantine felled and Marcus chopped to bits. They want their bread and circuses."

"Fine. Then let Noah fight in your place." Eli balls his hands into fists. "Hell, give me a poleaxe; I'll smash the bitch's head in for you. But don't go out there—"

I grab his shoulders. "It has to be me. You understand that? If

I send one of you to fight in my place, I'll look weak, and someone will pick me off anyway. I can't look weak."

Eli lets out a strangled cry and tears himself from me, holding his head like it's in serious danger of toppling off his shoulders. "Please don't do this."

I look into those deep eyes and see the boy who never gave up on me, not in all those years when he thought his friend Mackenzie was dead. And she and I might not be the same person, but we're forever linked for him. He'll never give up on us, just like he hasn't given up now. He's still trying to find a way to save me.

Eli the protector. Eli the problem-solver. Eli the profoundly, utterly decent person who has found himself in love with a crime boss. And he has no idea how to think or love his way out of this mess.

I give him the only gift I have to give – the ability to turn away. I cover his eyes with my hand. "Don't watch."

Eli's face crumbles. And I know that in accepting this fight, I've severed something vital between us.

But I've also reclaimed a piece of myself – all these years I've been on my own, I've never needed anyone to look after me. It's fitting that I walk to my death alone.

If I fight with honor, Cali will spare my family. All I care about now, all I have left to care about, is keeping them safe.

Maybe it's good, and right, and proper, that it ends like this. Two broken women drawing blood for the entertainment of men. Maybe that's all my empire is – a house of straw that can be felled by a single flame.

Noah barges between us, his arms full of weapons. "This is everything in the prep room. If you use a long weapon like a staff, you might be able to hold her back before she can get close enough to use her blade."

I look up at him, my mirror, the one whose bloodlust

matches my own. He's not questioning why I'm getting in the ring. He doesn't need to. Instead, he's using every moment we have to prepare me for battle. We both know it's probably hopeless, but I'm not dead yet.

I shake my head sadly. "She's an assassin. She's trained to be an expert in every one of those weapons. I'd be better off with my knives."

Fuck.

I can't even look at Gabriel, or I'll burst into tears. He slides his arms around me from the back, pressing his cheek against mine. His heart thunders against my ribcage. "I've sharpened my steel, I've made my sacrifices," he sings softly in my ear. "I'm unleashing war."

My battle cry.

I slide every knife I can find into my boots and pick up a heavy sword – similar enough to the ones I'd practiced with that I think I can wield it. Antony nods to me. We've already said everything we need to say to each other. He can't save me, and I won't ask him to sacrifice himself for me. I've already asked so much.

I step into the ring. The crowd roars in my ears. Inside the bowl of the arena, the noise sounds strange, distant – like a thunderstorm rolling over the ocean. Blood pounds in my skull – a war drum counting down to my doom.

In here, there's only me. And Cali.

She's chosen no weapon. She cracks her bloody knuckles and smiles her white, toothy smile. "I'm going to enjoy wringing the life from you with my own hands," she says.

We circle each other – me in a crouched position, ready to dart away, Cali tall and lean and proud, her movements languid, like she's taking a casual stroll. She has the audacity to whistle a little tune.

I go on the attack, feigning a lunge for her. As Cali steps

easily aside, I sweep out my foot, whip a blade from my shoe, and let it fly. Cali pulls her shoulder back just in time. The edge of the blade kisses her skin. Her own blood joins the drying dribbles on her arm. She grins as she flicks the knife between her fingers.

Cali leaps just as I slide the second knife from my boot. Her elbow slams into my solar plexus, knocking the wind from my lungs. I fall hard on my back, kicking up a cloud of sand. It's in my eyes, my nostrils, my mouth. I swallow grit. My eyes weep.

Cali slams her fist into my jaw. I hear a crack that doesn't register as pain. Not yet. My brain rattles around inside my skull. The dull roar of the crowd dips and swirls, and my world greys at the edges. I'm aware, dimly, that I'm in a world of shit. But I can't seem to make myself care.

Every blow she lands feels like penance. Behind her shoulder, I see the three horrified faces of my guys as they watch me take the beating. I don't know if I actually see them or if they're a hallucination of my dwindling brain activity. *They'd be better off without me. They still have time to be free of this world, to start over.*

After a while, I don't feel Cali's punches. I stare up into her eyes and I see myself reflected there. I see my broken reflection as I gaze in horror at my mother's body, the window splattered with blood. The splatters bloom and grow, pulsing as they join together, as the entire world is soaked in crimson. I see generations of carnage and rage coalesced into this moment, this never-ending quest for blood.

A face breaks through the red veil. *Gabriel.* The shadows behind him look like a pair of dark wings unfurling from his body. His perfect lips move, and even though there's no way I can hear his words, they echo inside my head.

I'm unleashing war.

I swing my arm up. I mean only to touch Cali's cheek, to tell her that it's an honor to die by her hand. But I don't realize that somehow the sword is in my hand. The tip of the spiked pommel digs into her neck. Blood spurts from the wound. Cali's eyes pop open. She collapses, her hands clasping the wound.

Gabriel's face breaks into a smile. His wings glow with a shimmering light. And then he's gone. In his place is Noah, tall and dark and *quaking* with wrath. He's yelling at me, but I can't hear the words. I can't—

"Get up, Claws. You got her. Get up!"

I roll over. I'm moving through molasses. My arms are weighed down by all my guilt, all my regret. *They're better off without me.* Cali will recover, she'll hit me, and I'll be done.

But Cali doesn't hit me. She swings out at me with her foot as she scrambles for my discarded blade. Her ankle catches, knocking me off-balance. I spin as I fall, landing on top of her with all my weight. Instinct takes over. I jam my knee into her throat, the other pinning her left arm, the one that now has no hope of reaching a knife.

Thank you Antony for teaching me this move.

Cali can't move without my weight crushing her windpipe. Her eyes regard me with a serene calm as blood bubbles from the wound in her neck. She's not afraid of death. She's always known the reaper peers over her shoulder, and this is exactly how she wanted to go – in the hands of an enemy who bested her.

I press the tip of my sword against her throat. The crowd roars at me to spill her blood. I gaze down on my enemy one last time—

I see them.

The scars.

I remember the stories I heard about her, how she'd been a street kid abandoned by her parents, living on scraps and whatever she managed to steal for cash. How every person she turned to for help used her and abused her and left her broken. How she tried to jack Brutus' car one day and he caught her, and something of the fight in her eyes spoke to him. How he loved her as only the brutal know how to love, as only *I* can love. How he turned her brokenness into strength, nursed that flame of hate inside her until it burned bright and clear. He *made* Cali who she is. We weren't so different, her and I.

"What are you waiting for?" Blood dribbles from the corner of Cali's mouth. "You won, Barbie Bitch. Finish me off."

"I'm not killing a sister for the sport of men." I drop the sword. Gasps echo. I hear Noah yelling, but I ignore him. I slide my knee off Cali's throat and hold out my hand to her. "We're more alike than you realize. Join me, Cali. Join August in an alliance against Lucian, against the whole fucking world. We'll make a new empire, re-forged in our blood. Join me, and kill my enemies, and I will give you everything Brutus denied you."

Her smile is cruel, gleeful, her teeth dripping with blood. *Did she bite me?* "I imagine you have a lot of enemies, Barbie Bitch."

"Oh, countless."

"I'll enjoy spilling their blood for you, Imperator." Cali grins a wild, blood-soaked grin. "Especially your sister's."

"My sister?" Is she bluffing? How the fuck does she know about my sister?

Cali spits blood on the ground and lunges forward. I jerk my arm back, thinking she's trying to drive herself onto my sword, to give herself the honorable death she so craves. But she grabs my hand and shakes it so hard she nearly wrenches my arm from its socket.

"Mackenzie Malloy is closer than you think," she whispers. "You think no one can find her, but I can."

She grabs my hand and kisses my ring. I take her arm and raise it above my head.

"You wanted blood?" I roar at the crowd. "You shall have it. We are your Imperators and our rule over this empire is absolute. If you find yourself wishing for the days of Brutus, or asking yourself if you want to take orders from a woman, you will wake in the night to the blade of Cali against your throat."

The crowd roars their approval. Nero steps up beside me, wrapping his arm around my shoulders and waving to the adoring crowd. Anyone in the audience will see their three Imperators united. The promise of a new era of prosperity for the Triumvirate.

But they cannot feel Nero's fingers digging into my shoulder, or the way his voice drips with malice as he whispers, "If I were you, Imperator, I would sleep with one eye open."

33

———

CLAUDIA

"Of all the ways I saw that fight ending, this was not one of them," Noah remarks as he enters the ballroom a week later.

I look up from the sofa, where Cali has just painted my toenails a perfect shade of ice blue. She's a little sloppy – we're both still a bit raw from our injuries – but she has killer style. Behind her, George and Yara are flipping through fashion magazines, and Madeline Drysdale is trying on various dresses she nicked from Ainsley Malloy's closet for her date with Tiberius tonight.

I wave my hand at Noah. "Get out. Girls only. Feminist empire-building going on here."

"I'm sorry to interrupt this very important meeting, *Imperators*," Noah says with a cocksure quirk of his lips. "But Eli's just had a call from Livvie. Nero is giving testimony at Walter Hart's appeal. For the defense."

I leap to my feet. "What?"

Fuck. In all the mayhem, I'd completely forgotten that the scumbag Walter Hart is appealing his sentence. And I know

George's evidence is airtight, but if Nero's involved... that's not good.

Why is Nero getting involved in this? Hart's relationship was with Dio and Brutus, not him. He knows that hitching his cart to the Memories of the Hart horse is a PR nightmare. Too many gangsters trusted Walter Hart with their loved one's remains to welcome him back with open arms.

No, this is personal. Nero's only doing this because Walter is Eli's father, because he knows it will get to me. For some unknown reason, he's obsessed with Eli's family.

This is his next move – an indirect assault on my alliance with Cali, an attempt to undermine the solidity of my tribunes. I just don't understand why he's chosen Walter Hart to be his pawn. Is it because we already blew up Senator Marlowe's life? The guy is rotting in jail, waiting for his own trial while the press gleefully digs through his company records and reveals all kinds of nasty secrets. Noah's holding it together by swinging a sledge-hammer around the rage room every night.

"Eli?" I ask Noah, my heart stuttering in my chest. What's this news going to do to my Golden Boy?

"He knows. He's not great." Noah's dark eyes cloud over as he fists one of my knives. Nero is lucky he's not within stabbing distance, because Noah's ready to go nuclear. Despite the shittiness of the situation, my chest swells thinking that this guy won't hesitate to draw blood for anyone in this family.

I slide out from beneath Cali and go to find my broken Sherlock Holmes.

I LOCATE Eli in my rage room, throwing a set of Alberto Pinto china against the wall. I touch his shoulder and he whirls around, a gravy jug raised above his head like a weapon. His face crumples with misery when he sees me. I wrap my arms around him.

"It's going to be okay."

"Nothing's okay when Nero Lucian is involved. Why can't he just rot in jail like he's supposed to?" Eli yells. "Because he's Walter fucking Hart and even though he did everything George says he did, he still seems to expect the world to treat him like he's God's gift to the death industry."

I look over at Noah, who hovers in the doorway. "What grounds does he even have for an appeal?"

"Fuck knows. We remortgaged the house to pay our useless lawyer, Sanderson, to come up with some kind of case. I expected to spend a fuckton of money and lose, because Dad's guilty as sin and George's evidence supports that. I don't give a shit if we're destitute – that money was dirty, anyway. Why is Nero involved? It makes no sense. What's he going to be able to do for the case? He's not exactly a convincing character witness."

"He wants to fuck with me," I growl, thinking of the planted evidence Nero created to condemn Constantine. As for the seal on my father's death contract, I didn't know if it was real or not, but it didn't matter anymore. Brutus was dead. Constantine was dead. My father was well and truly avenged. Everything is about my family now. "Somehow, Nero is going to use this trial as a stage for whatever drama he wants to play out against us. I have no idea how you still have a job with him, or why Livvie is still talking to you if you're public enemy number one, but we have to use that. We have to find out what the fuck is going on."

34

CLAUDIA

I'm attending school now only to keep up appearances. Noah and Eli are finishing most of my assignments, Ms. Drysdale gave me top marks in her classes since I saved her ass, and Antony and Tiberius are letting us all skate in their classes with little work. It's a pointless waste of time. I have no intention of going to college. Why do I need a high school diploma when I already manage one of the most complex supply chains in the world?

To be fair, I'm not exactly doing a bang-up job. This shit is complicated, and Noah and my accountant David have to explain things to me over and over again. It's hard to focus on the actual business stuff when my precarious situation with the Triumvirate and Mackenzie's continued existence weighs on my mind.

Not to mention the fact that the streets of Tartarus Oaks are running red with blood. It's no longer safe to walk my city alone, with random fights and shootings breaking out every day.

The media is blaming the recent violence on the 'tough-on-organized-crime' senator awaiting trial, but I know the real reason – there are many in our organization who don't approve of my appointment, or Nero's slaying of Constantine, or Cali's claim to the Dio empire. There's an undercurrent of dissent running through my city, and if we don't quash it, it will burst its dams and sweep us all away.

All of this swirls around in my head as I move through the halls toward History. I wave to Eli, who is walking in the other direction. "You skipping class? Can I join? We're just going to be watching Citizen Kane again and I didn't understand that film the first time—"

"You can't come with me." Eli shifts uncomfortably. "I... I have a meeting."

My eyebrow arches. "Like with the police? About the trial? Don't you want me to be there?"

"No. It's a meeting with Berkeley about... about their law program."

His eyes dart away.

"Eli, you got into Berkeley? That's amazing." And it is. It *is*. But the words drop from my tongue like lead weights. I know this is what we discussed, that legal experience would be an asset to our family. But with this new violence and Cali in charge of Dio and Nero inserting himself into the trial... I don't think he should be so far from us.

He nods. "And Yale. And Harvard."

"Two Ivies? Holy shit. You're incredible." I stand on tiptoes to kiss his cheek. "But why didn't you tell me? Do you think going so far away for college is a good idea right now?"

"I didn't tell you because I knew you'd react like that," he frowns. "Because you're too fixated on Nero to see the bigger picture. That this is good for us."

"That's not fair." I shove my hands in my blazer pockets. "It's my job to fixate on Nero. There won't be a bigger picture if he slaughters us all, or if Cali kills me in my sleep. Is this even what *you* want? Wasn't being a lawyer your dad's dream?"

"Dad wanted me to take over the family business. I don't know what I want. That's why I'm going to this meeting – to see if it helps me make up my mind." Eli touches his finger to his wrist, where his August family tattoo is. "It doesn't change anything."

But it changes everything. And we both know it.

Eli drops his hands back to his sides. "I have to go."

I watch my Golden Boy walk away from me. And for the first time, I don't go after him.

35

ELI

From across the courtroom, Nero nods to me, his eyes sparkling. Beside him, my mother squirms uncomfortably in her seat.

As the hearing commences, I'm a ball of nerves. I hardly hear a word the lawyers say. All I can do is stare at my father at the defense table. He looks so different from the broken man I'd visited behind bars – his hair is slicked back, his suit is immaculate, and there's a little of his famous showman's swagger about him.

Walter Hart has to give the performance of his life today, and he's ready for showtime.

I watch every twitch of his eye muscles, every shuffle of his papers, waiting for the clue that will give me answers. *How did you get mixed up in this, Dad? What the fuck is Nero doing?*

I'm so busy watching him that I don't hear a word of the trial. Even Nero's testimony – a rousing speech about my father being a victim of an unscrupulous man named Constantine Dio – is swallowed by the hole in my heart. The only thing that breaks through is Claws jabbing me in the gut with her sharp elbow.

We haven't talked about Berkeley, or my other college acceptances, since that day at school two weeks ago. She gave me a cake from a local bakery decorated with the three college mascots and a 'bloody knife' dipped in strawberry coulis stabbing the center. "To help you decide," she grinned, licking icing off her finger.

I don't want to tell her that every time I get close to a decision, I can't pull the plug. Every answer is a betrayal of her.

I turn to Claws just in time to hear the judge utter the words.

"—free to go."

There's movement in the courtroom – harsh whispers, cries of shock and outrage. My father grinning his showman's grin. I tug Claws' sleeve. "Wait, what did he just say?"

"Weren't you listening? Didn't you hear Nero blame every aspect of the body brokering business on Constantine Dio?" She knits her fingers in mine. "Your father is free."

"What?"

That's impossible. He can't be free. He's guilty. He *did* this.

"His conviction is overturned with the court's apologies. I don't entirely understand the reasoning, but I don't think it matters." Claudia glances across the room. "I think we all know who's behind this."

Nero flashes us a wave and a dazzling smile. I ball my hands into fists, longing to punch that smile off his face but knowing he's untouchable.

"Why does he give a shit about my family?" I repeat the same question we've asked ourselves a hundred times already. "He can't possibly think Dad will be some kind of asset."

"I don't know what he thinks, but you'd better get over there before you become the lead story in tomorrow's paper."

I don't want to be anywhere near Dad, but Claudia's right. If I don't get over there, my snubbing of my father will be all over the papers, and things will get worse. My feet carry me onto the steps of the courthouse, where my father waits with a shit-eating grin on his pale face. "This is a good day for justice," he says to the cameras, pointing to the flag pin on his lapel. "I'm proud to be an American citizen, knowing that the truth will win out in the end."

Nero hovers beside him, his fat fingers sliding over his lapels. My mother threads her arm through Dad's, but she only has eyes for Nero Lucian.

I step over to the group. I'm not in control of my body. I'm back on the sofa in the media room at Malloy Manor, stuffing popcorn in my mouth as I watch the film of this horrific moment playing out in HD.

Cameras snap as Dad wraps his arms around me. "I'm back, son."

My hands move from my side to pat at Dad's shoulders in one of those 'man' hugs he taught me. He feels like he's made of cardboard. He's not real.

Dad says a few more platitudes, then the three of us crowd into the back of a limousine with Nero, his bodyguards, and Dad's lawyer, Sanderson, who is grinning like the Cheshire Cat as if he had something to do with Dad getting off scot-free. As if this wasn't all part of Nero Lucian's master plan.

Just as the driver starts to pull away, Claudia slides into the limo.

I expect us to drive back to our house, but instead, Nero takes us to Vault. He pats my father on the knee as we pull up. "I thought you might like to see where your son has been getting his lessons in business."

"Wow, son, look at this fancy joint. You're moving up in the world, eh?" Dad squirms in his seat like a kid in a candy store. Why is he acting all buddy-buddy with the guy who stole Mom from him?

I don't like this. I don't like it at all.

Claws grips my hand, squeezing hard. She's got my back,

always. That's what matters – not college, not Nero, none of this bullshit. Me and her and our family looking out for each other.

Nero leads our group upstairs to a private room. He takes our drink orders – a Long Island ice tea for Dad, dry martini for Mom, Macallan neat for Nero, nothing for me or Claudia – and rings down for service. I'm surprised to see Livvie arrive with the drinks, Essie wrapped around her shoulders. Mom startles when the snake turns her head toward her, and splashes her drink down the front of her low-cut court blouse.

Nero accepts his drink from Livvie with a fatherly smile. "I'd like you to stay."

I can tell by the way Livvie bites her lip that she's surprised, but she doesn't let on. Instead, she takes a seat on a round ottoman on the other side of me, crossing her ankles and staring up at her father with prim obedience.

"We have some matters to discuss," Nero says. "I've asked our women to remain because these matters concern them, too."

Oooh, what a feminist.

Nero sips his drink. "I believe it's best to be plain, so I'll get right down to it. Don't let my youthful exterior fool you – I'm not a young man. The expert surgeons of Emerald Beach have had their work cut out for them keeping this mug looking beautiful." Nero swipes a finger lovingly across his cheek. "Recent events have made me increasingly aware of my mortality, and what my heir will make of the Lucian legacy after I move on."

Here we go again.

The closest thing to being immortal is shaping a legacy. That's why the Triumvirate is so concerned with blood. Men with power over everything in their lives except death trying to outdo themselves in the only competition that still has meaning to them, the only game where they might actually lose.

"I have always been a family man, as you know. I have many children who are scrapping it out amongst themselves to earn my favor, to be declared the rightful heir to my empire. Every single one of them is an imbecile."

I dare a glance at Livvie, who's holding back a snort of laughter. *Not all of them.*

"I refuse to leave my legacy to an imbecile, which leaves me with a problem. I've been wrestling with the decision of my heir for some time." Nero steeples his fingers. "And then Elias Hart came to my attention."

Claudia's fingers gouge my thigh. "What?"

That's my name.

Why is he saying my name?

Nero's eyes hit mine, and when he sees my expression, he bursts into laughter. "My boy, don't look so flabbergasted. You've been on my mind for some time. When Walter Hart was sent to prison, it was a blow for the Triumvirate – he provided a valuable service we have greatly missed. I followed the trial with great interest, and it was there I was first introduced to you. The Golden Boy of Stonehurst Prep: that's what they call you. Straight A student, student council member, track star, bound for some fancy Ivy League college and a corner office. Clever, resourceful and, like your father, with the imagination to dream big. I simply had to meet you."

This is insane. I must be dreaming. That's the only possible explanation. Any moment Nero's going to turn into a T-Rex and I'll wake up with sweaty sheets and this will be nothing but a terrible nightmare.

"So, after the trial, I introduced myself to Darlene." Nero smiles across the desk at her. It's an indulgent smile, the kind you give to a favorite pet. The kind of smile that probably had my mother on her knees for him. (Gross.) But today, even she is too shocked by events to succumb to him. She throws her drink at him.

"You spent all that time wooing me – all those parties, the

boat trips, the nights in your private island – to meet my *son*." She jabs a frosted nail at me. "Him? But he's so... so *honest*."

Sticky gin dribbles down the front of Nero's suit.

"Exactly." Nero's smile fixes on me. "Eli is honest. He's affable. He has that all-American smile. He's the kind of person you trust implicitly, and that makes him the ideal heir to my empire."

Um... *what the actual fuck?*

A lot of things happen at once. Dad grins from ear to ear like I'd just been offered a track scholarship or a thoroughbred horse or an enormous monster truck. Darlene's on her feet, screaming at Nero. Livvie drops a glass, which smashes glittering shards across the rug.

He can't be serious.

Nero holds up his hands for calm, and the gesture is so mundane and yet somehow manages to convey all the power and menace of his position. Everyone freezes. An eerie silence blasts the room. "The more I've observed of Eli's work over the last few months, the more I'm convinced he's the perfect heir. He's loyal to a fault and always takes the time to think things through before he acts. He has a strict code of honor. And he won't hesitate to be ruthless when his family is in danger. If only he had been born of my loins!" Nero claps his hands over his cheeks in mock dramatics.

"Very well, I thought, if he cannot take over the family, then at least he could be my tribune, my trusted advisor. Perhaps he could even teach one of my sons to not be so fucking stupid. But that means I had to bring him into the Lucian fold. At first, I thought to do this by marrying Darlene. But then Eli declared his loyalty to Claudia August, and so I set about trying to form an alliance between our families, but she refused me. But Cali's ascent to Imperator has set a precedent that allows Imperators to adopt heirs who are not blood-related. This is fortuitous to all of you." Nero slides a leather-bound booklet across his desk and flips it open. "I have a proposal."

"What is it?" My father leans forward. Saliva forms at the corners of his mouth.

Nero addresses my father. "Eli will marry my daughter Olivia and inherit my empire when I die. He will take the Lucian name and I will officially adopt him as my son. In exchange for this, I will pay you the compensation outlined in that contract, and set you and Darlene up with the funds to rebuild your funerary business. This is with the caveat that of course you'll be available to the Triumvirate when we require your services."

He holds out the booklet – my marriage contact – and Dad takes it. His fingers leave sticky circles in the leather.

So this is what he was planning. All this time we thought he was after Claudia when really... he wanted me.

I can't wrap my head around it. Everything Nero said is insane.

"You can't be serious." I glare at Nero as I roll up my sleeve to show the August mark on my wrist. "I can't be your heir. I've already sworn my loyalty to the August family."

"I don't see this as a problem," Nero says. "As long as August and Lucian are in harmony."

In other words, no matter who is in control of August, the Lucian will retain ultimate control of the Triumvirate.

"But why this marriage?" Livvie asks, her voice rising in pitch. "If you adopt Eli, I don't need to marry him."

"There will be those who don't accept the adoption – namely, your brothers and their loyal soldiers," Nero says. "Cali is dealing with dissenters in her ranks now, and the violence is spilling over into the streets. Most unsavory. But then, I've always said Dio are only one step removed from savages. I won't have Eli stabbed the week he ascends the Lucian throne for one of my biological sons to take his birthright. His marriage to you adds legitimacy. And I've observed the two of you working together – you make a good match. I trust this is agreeable?"

He says it pleasantly enough, but Livvie's dead eyes tell me that she knows she must agree. In this world, a woman like her loses all autonomy. She casts a futile glance at me. "What if Eli doesn't want to marry me?"

"Nonsense. You're a Lucian, a wife to be proud of. He may continue to fuck whoever he likes on the side." Nero smiles at Claudia, who is shaking with rage. She hasn't said anything yet. I don't know if it's because she's biding her time, gathering all the details of Nero's plan before she tears him down, or whether she's silent because opening her mouth will endanger us all.

But time is running out. My father flips through the contract, his pen poised to sign my life to over Lucian on the dotted line. I knock the pen from his hand.

"I'm not doing it."

"Son, you're being emotional." My father bends to pick up the pen. "This is a great opportunity to build a bold future for all of us."

"I already have a bold future ahead of me." I stomp on Dad's wrist. He yelps as I grind my heel and crush his hand into the wooden floor. I link hands with Claudia, letting her strength flow through her fingers and keep me calm, brave. "I'm the tribune of Claudia August."

"There's no future for you with August." Nero smiles at me. It's not a smile of joy, but an open threat. "As Claudia has made abundantly clear, she cannot marry more than one man. She has been playing you off against the Barbarian and the Pretty Boy. And I think we all know who she will choose. Who is the one with the malice and brutality to match her, the one who she keeps by her side in all Triumvirate business? It's not you."

Noah.

I mean... Nero's right. Noah and Claudia are two sides of the same coin. They've taken to bloodshed like Gizmo's taken to Queen Boudica's cat castle. My morals have no place in her criminal empire.

And Gabriel keeps her sane. She needs his music, his emotion to ground her, to keep her from being utterly intoxicated with power.

Who am I to her? Really? I'm the problem-solver, the sensible one she doesn't even listen to half the time.

I'm the devil's advocate who always questions her and makes her doubt herself.

I'm the bastard who left her when she needed me most.

I'm the disloyal one who's considering starting a law degree at Berkeley when she needs me *here*.

I'm the fool who couldn't even tell her apart from her twin sister.

I glance at Claudia. Her eyes fix on Nero. She gives my fingers a reassuring squeeze, but I barely feel it. "Eli is eighteen. His father doesn't make decisions for him anymore. That contract is worth jack shit and you know it. If you want Eli to be your heir, you offer him the position yourself. But you know he'll say no – that's why you've brought us all here under the farce of family loyalty to try and guilt him into accepting. You're trying to play against his better nature, and I'm telling you it won't work. Because Eli Hart will never be for sale."

But I can see the cogs turning in her brain. I can see her thinking about the fact that if Nero declared me his rightful heir, she could bump him off and control the Lucian empire through me.

My skin prickles. My stomach squirms like Essie is slithering around in my gut. Claudia is right – I'm not for sale, because I already gifted my moral code, my future, and my life to her a long time ago.

But there's always a price, and I'll pay this one in blood.

"Elias Hart, you're doing this." My mother folds her arms and glares at me. "You and your woman stole my next chance at happiness. If I have to go back to your father I should at least get to do it bedecked in diamonds."

I glare at them all, starting with my shitbag father and gold-digging mother, moving to scheming Nero and his daughter who will doom us both to a loveless marriage rather than fighting for what she wants, and finishing on Claudia. My Ice Queen, the girl who owns my heart. She knows I would die for her. I will do anything for her, even this.

And she's going to ask me to do it.

I stride out of the room, slamming the door behind me.

Outside, I call an Uber. I tap my foot with impatience as I wait for it to arrive. Three minutes. I need to get the fuck out of here before someone in that room comes down here and—

My car pulls up. I jog over and reach for the door. It takes me three tries to get it open because my hands are trembling so much. "Hi, I'm going to—"

The opposite door flies open. Claudia rolls across the seat, bowling into me.

"Get off me," I growl. I plant my hands on her shoulders and try to shove her back toward the door.

"Not until you stop running away from your problems and listen to me," she shoots back, wrapping her fingers around my wrists. Her implication is clear – she's not letting go, so if I want to get away from Nero and my parents, I'm taking her with me.

"Lady, I'm not allowed to park here," the driver yells as a car behind him blows the horn. "Are you in or out?"

"Out," I yell, and the same time Claudia barks, "In."

The driver plants his foot and takes off before she's even shut the door.

36

CLAUDIA

"I know you're upset," I say as I lean across the seat and pull the door shut. "But you can't run away every time something happens that shatters your fragile reality. What are you going to do when you're at college and you get your first ever C on an assignment?"

"That would never happen." Eli sits rigid in the seat, back upright, hands folded in his lap. He won't look at me.

"I never told you to agree to Nero's bananas plan." I grab his arm and shake it, trying to get him to look at me. "But I need you to not shut down a potential opportunity like that before we've had a chance to explore all the options. Nero's showing his hand. I knew he had a weakness, and now we've found it. And it's you."

"You want me to do it," his tone is flat.

"Of course I don't want you to marry Livvie. You're *mine*. But I have to think about more than us. I have to consider the doors this might open." I tap a few buttons and hand him my phone. "You seen what's happening out there?"

The screen plays a video from in front of Constantine's restaurant and training club. A group of angry people armed with pipes, knives, and bats slam into each other. There's a sickening CRACK as a guy's head hits the pavement. Eli's jaw clenches as he watches the chaos unfold, as he sees the insignias worn by the mob.

Lucian. Dio. August. The three families turned on each other.

"What do you want me to do about this?" he says in that flat voice that tears my heart in two.

"Nothing. That's not your job. I'm the one that has to stop this because I'm the one who caused it. Mostly this is about whether Cali has the right to rule Dio, but it's about so much more. It's about Nero killing Constantine, and it's about two women having a seat at the most powerful table in this city. People's worlds are turning upside down, and they don't like it."

Eli stays silent. I search desperately for the right words.

"You think I'm throwing you away. You're asking yourself if I think you'd be more valuable to me if you were Nero's heir?" The quiver in his lip tells me I'm right. "You're my conscience, Eli. You're the moral compass pointing me north and the angel on my shoulder stopping me from disappearing into the void. I *need* you. I can't go into war without my guardian angel." I trace the line of the August tattoo on his wrist. My eyes cloud with tears. "Please come back to me. Daddy had a quote from some ancient philosopher for every occasion. He loved this saying from Plutarch: 'I don't need a friend who changes when I change and nods when I nod. My shadow does that so much better.' That's why I need you, because Noah will follow me into the abyss itself and Gabriel will sing my funeral dirge, but I need you to keep me away from the edge even if I'm the one pulling us all in. My father thought he knew what he loved until he was faced with the choice to give it up for me. If you ask it of me, I'll give everything up for you, but I have to make sure no one else dies for a pointless war first, okay?"

Eli wipes his face with his hand. "If your dad hadn't been a crime lord, he could have been a philosopher."

I dare a tiny smile. "Oh, I doubt it. He had this other favorite saying from Aristotle, about love being a single soul inhabiting two bodies. Which sounds lovely and like the exact kind of platitude Cleo would post on her Instagram, except Daddy would take great delight in telling you the rest of the story. Aristotle wrote this satirical essay claiming that long ago humans looked very different – we had large round bodies with two faces and two sets of limbs, and we'd wheel around like giant beach balls with doll legs and arms sticking out. We humans got cocky and tried to roll right on up to heaven, so Zeus got pissed off and chopped them all in half. And now we all wander the earth as these half-orbular beings, searching for the other half of our souls to put back together again and— holy shit," I breathe. "Eli, I've figured it out."

"What?"

I hammer on the back of the driver's chair. "Hey, you. Drive faster! We need to get to Malloy Manor."

"Claws, what is it?"

I throw my arms around Eli, plastering his face with kisses. "I know where the treasure is hidden."

37

ELI

Claudia refuses to sit still on the ride back to the manor. She calls the others – interrupting Gabe's practice session with Broken Muse and George's college interview – and tells them to get home immediately. She barks orders to the driver and keeps urging him to take dangerous shortcuts. She won't stop kissing me, which despite how angry I am with her right now, I can't help resist. I'm caught up in her excitement.

That's what Claudia August does to you – she dazzles you until you don't know which way is up.

Her face lights up like Christmas as we pull up behind the house. She tears off toward the maintenance shed. I jog after her, my head still spinning from the conversation with Nero.

She leaves the maintenance shed door hanging open – something she hasn't done since Brutus got into the house. I step into the car tunnel, but she's already disappeared.

"What is it? Claws, where are you?"

I follow the sound of her footsteps through the garage, up the stairs, down the hall, to the large display room beside Mackenzie's old bedroom where she kept most of her doll collection. I remember. Her father got her those creepy dolls –

one for every birthday and Christmas, and every time he made a visible mark on her body he needed her to cover up.

"He's trying to buy my silence," Mackenzie used to say, staring into the eerie, silent face of her latest acquisition.

I hated the dolls. Mackenzie kept some in her room, but her father made her display the rest in this room of horror. Sometimes she'd break one accidentally, and her mother would fix it for her. Ainsley loved those dolls more than she loved Mackenzie. I think she was the one who chose them from catalogs and auction houses.

I hang in the doorway, not wanting to step into that room of unseeing eyes and frozen smiles. "What are we doing in here?"

Claudia picks up one – a French bisque doll with a mop of golden curls. "This is it." She shakes the doll in my face. "This is the treasure."

I shake my head. "I'm sorry, Claws. George already researched the dolls. They're valuable collectors' items, but you couldn't secure an illegal trade with them. They're not the treasure—"

Claudia shoots me a triumphant glare as she tears the doll's head off.

I'm so shocked I can only stand with my jaw open. Claudia tosses the head on the floor. It bounces on its curls and rolls against my feet, the glass eyes peering up at me with silent accusation.

Claws digs two fingers inside the neck of the doll, biting her lip in concentration as she fishes around inside the porcelain and fabric. She tips the doll upside down and shakes it violently. An arm falls off. And a long metal cylinder slides out the neck hole into Claudia's hand.

What the fuck?

"Daddy's story gave me the idea," Claudia says. "Thinking about those orb people with their doll hands – one orb holding the souls of two people. And I thought this would be the perfect place for Ainsley to hide the treasure. Especially if it is what I think it is."

I hear footsteps behind me. George pokes her head in the room, and from the look on her face, I can tell she's immediately grasped the situation. "Of course." She slaps her forehead. "Why didn't I think of that? She hid the treasure inside the dolls."

"It's perfect, right?" Claudia looks down at the row of dolls in front of her. "What better way to get back at Howard than to hide the treasure right under his nose?"

George picks up the cylinder and frowns at it. "So what is it?"

"I've seen these before. Daddy used them to transport ancient documents to his clients. They're temperature and humidity controlled and you open them—" Claws flicks a clamp, and the cylinder pops open with a hiss, "—like that."

Claudia tilts the cylinder on its side, and a brown roll of paper falls into her hand. Noah, Gabriel, and Yara have appeared at the doorway now, and we all crowd around her as she unfurls the paper.

I don't know what I expect, but when I peer at the rows of Latin script scrawled in short columns across the page, I can't help but feel a little... disappointed. *This* is the treasure Julian traded for Claudia? Is a dusty old manuscript really worth all this pain and bloodshed?

"Any idea what this is?" I ask Claudia.

Claudia's eyes scan the document. "My Latin is a little rusty, but I believe this is the book called *Exhortations on Philosophy*, by the Roman Emperor Augustus."

"Oh, that explains it. No wonder Julian considered this a treasure."

"Eli, you don't understand," Claudia's icicle eyes sparkle with life. "This document doesn't *exist*. It was thought lost to time. But it's here in my hands. And I'm willing to bet it's not the only one."

Claws grabs a large stuffed teddy bear and tears off its head, pulling at the stuffing. She yanks out another cylinder and opens it. Another ancient scroll tumbles into her hand. Behind her, Noah smashes the head of a doll against the shelf and digs a cylinder from her innards.

Claws tears into the cylinders, unfurling the scrolls just enough to glimpse their titles. With each one, her eyes widen.

"Here's the second book of Aristotle's *Poetics*, and this is one of Cato's lost books on the history of Rome. And if I'm right and this is a page from the Emperor Claudius' Etruscan dictionary, then... holy shit." She looks up at me, her eyes wide. I'm surprised to see them brimming with tears. "Of course. Of course. Daddy's most precious treasure. These are lost scrolls – works of literature that have never been seen before. He must've found them in that cache in Alexandria."

"Alexandria?" George perks up. "You mean, like the place with the library?"

"I mean exactly the place with the library." Claudia stares at the object in her hands. "And I don't know, but a cache of work this valuable... perhaps the librarians hid these scrolls when Julius Caesar entered the city in 48BC, to keep them safe. The dates are right. We could be holding some of the lost knowledge of the Library of Alexandria."

All this time, the treasure was here with us.

Julian August was right – his daughter, my love, is worth the greatest treasure of all time.

38

CLAUDIA

*B*y the time we've torn off the heads and smashed open the porcelain stomachs of every doll, we have a total of eighty-six cylinders stacked on a towering pyramid in the middle of the room.

Eighty-six ancient manuscripts, each one a lost treasure from the Classical world. Each with the potential to answer questions scholars have debated for centuries.

My father's greatest treasure – until me.

Constantine was right – these scrolls would be impossible to sell. They're priceless beyond belief, and any private collector would have to be so careful not to alert authorities that they wouldn't want to touch them. Once a collection like this enters the underworld, it stays there – no museum displays, no scholars furiously translating and writing papers on the remarkable find, no earnestly enthusiastic *Discovery Channel* documentaries to make this remarkable find accessible from the living room of every house in America.

These cylinders have been back and forth across the world, never opened except to check their authenticity, prized not for their cultural and historical value but because they could facilitate Howard Malloy's shady pharmaceutical deals. They likely facilitated the trade of the deer antler velvet that killed Noah's brother.

The only person who might have seen this treasure for what it truly is, is Julian August. And now, me.

The daughter of the two men who stole this gift from the world, and the woman who hid it away.

This is my legacy.

"What do we do with them all?" Noah peers over the pyramid of cylinders.

I stare at the stack, the exact question buzzing through my head. This treasure is the key to securing my empire, to making certain I have the resources to topple Nero from his throne. But it also makes me a target. I have to be careful with my next move. No one can know about this treasure until we're ready.

"These should be in a museum," Eli breathes. He stares at the stack, eyes wide with awe. "I know some people at Berkeley. They have a world-renowned Classical archaeology department. I can call them to assess the collection and—"

I shake my head. "No. These scrolls are the key to our power. Brutus burned through my father's money, then Eli made me buy a ton of loud wild animals, and with Grace's article, Malloy Pharmaceuticals' assets are frozen, so I can't get access to that either. We need money to hold onto our empire and get the shipping routes working again, and this treasure will give us the collateral we need to make powerful alliances—"

Eli looks at me like I've sprouted two heads. "Hang on, you've only just found these documents again. You honestly want to send them back onto the black market? What about its historical value? What about the fact this is your father's legacy? What if you at least had them translated, or scanned? That way they could be studied—"

I shake my head. "We don't have time, and I can't trust a

bunch of scholars to stay silent. Not to mention the fact that I'm not the only one searching for this treasure right now. The sooner we get these scrolls out of this house, the safer they will be from Mackenzie."

"If you give them to a museum, the treasure will be lost to Mackenzie forever." Eli holds out his hands. "It sounds like the perfect plan to me."

"Exactly – if we give the treasure away, we lose our ticket to my sister." I grin. "I don't want her to think there's no hope. I'd like to draw her into a trap."

Eli's jaw clenches. "I can't believe after all the trouble this treasure has caused, you want to send it right out into the chaos again."

"How many times do we have to go through this? It's not a matter of what I want." I throw my hands up in the air. "It's a matter of what's best for our family. We have to make sacrifices. I don't think you understand that."

"I understand perfectly," he says through gritted teeth.

An awkward silence descends over the room. I glare at Eli. After everything I said in the car, how can he not understand?

"We don't have to make any decisions about this now," George says quickly. "The most important thing is that we store the cylinders where they won't get damaged and Mackenzie can't find them. Then we can hash out our next move."

39

CLAUDIA

We stack the cylinders in the panic room, which has a built-in temperature-control system and dehumidification system. George does some online research and comes back with an ideal temperature range (bless you, George), and we plug that in and close the door.

Gabriel goes out and comes back with a spread of food, and we have a celebratory meal. Everyone is excited, talking about the manuscripts we've identified so far, wondering what secrets they might reveal. I smile and clink glasses along with them, but my mind is a million miles away.

Eli's made it clear what he thinks. And under normal circumstances, I'd agree with him. But this isn't normal. Nothing in my life is ever normal. The safety of my family is too important to let this treasure fall into the hands of a museum or university. I hate the idea of sending those scrolls off to some Russian oil baron who could accidentally drop one in the ocean, but I can't think about myself. I'll do what I have to do.

But not right away. This treasure is my birthright. It gives us the perfect opportunity to do what has to be done. Brutus was right about one thing – my father became a victim of his own moral code. He allowed others to overtake him because he refused to do what was necessary. I won't make the same mistake, especially not when Mackenzie is so close. And so dangerous.

But how to use the treasure to draw Mackenzie out of hiding?

I slide out from under Noah's arm and head to Howard's office. Alone for the first time in hours, I drum my fingers on the desk as I turn over my idea in my head. I pull out my mobile phone and stare at it, my finger paused over Livvie's number. I drop the phone. Pick it up. Stare at it some more.

I hit CALL.

Livvie picks up on the seventh ring. "Claudia August," she says. "To what do I owe the pleasure?"

I hear noise in the background – glasses clinking, voices chattering, soft piano music. "Where are you?"

"At one of Daddy's restaurants with Eli's parents. We're celebrating Daddy's new heir." I hear a door swing. "I was at the bar when I saw your name come up, so they don't know I'm talking to you."

"How can they be celebrating? Eli hasn't agreed to be Nero's heir."

I can practically hear Livvie rolling her eyes. "Tell that to Daddy. Hold on."

I hear scrambling and footsteps and a door clicking shut. The noise disappears. Livvie flicks the call to a video screen. Her face is in shadow, sandwiched between chef whites and cleaning equipment. "I'm hiding in a closet now."

"Did anyone see you?"

"Let me check." There's rustling on the other end, followed by the creak of a door. Livvie returns to the phone a moment later. "We're secure. I'm intrigued to have a call from you after my father tried to marry me off to your boyfriend."

"Your father is a piece of work," I growl. The audacity of his trying to steal Eli out from beneath me sends a fresh wave of fury through my veins. And the fact that it could actually work in our favor makes it grate all the more.

"Tell me about it." Livvie's tone is bitter. I can't say I blame her. For all the effort Nero's put into choosing his ideal heir, he can't see what's right in front of him. "So what's up?"

"Hold on. I'm making this a three-way call."

I punch a couple of buttons, and in a few moments, Cali's face appears in the third window. There's a dribble of blood over her eye that I'm guessing isn't hers.

"I'm busy," she snaps, panning the camera around so I get a view of a man trussed up from the ceiling, soaked in blood. "This better be worth it, August."

"It is." I grin. "You said you might know where my sister is hiding?"

"I said I can find out." She twists the knife in her hand. "But it will cost you."

"I'll pay whatever you ask."

"Your sister?" Livvie asks. "You don't have a sister. Claudia, what's going on?"

"You want to show Nero how ruthless you can be?" I lean forward. "I have a proposal for you."

40

ELI

We don't mention the treasure again. It hangs over Malloy Manor like a bad smell, tainting every conversation, scratching at the back of my throat when I kiss Claudia goodbye. She's not even going to school anymore, instead spending hours in her office, on the phone, poring over the shipping data Noah and David compiled for her.

I fly out to Cambridge to visit Harvard and tour the law school. I wish Claudia could've come with me and seen the university – all those ivy-covered buildings and secluded court-yards, the ancient manuscripts on display at the Houghton library. I think it might've changed her mind.

The tour itself is a complete disaster. I meet with one of the freshman advisors and he asks me what I'm looking forward to most about Harvard and all I can think about is a lion tearing out a man's organs while a crowd roars for blood.

I fly home in a daze. I've still got a meeting at Yale next week, but is that enough time to sort my shit out? What's going to change in a week? Am I miraculously not going to be in love with a crime boss? Am I suddenly going to feel like I can brush off everything I've seen in the last year like it's nothing and step into the life of varsity track and fraternity stunts I was destined for?

I push open the garage door of Malloy Manor, stinking of anxiety and airline food. As well as the now-familiar waft of animal shit, I catch something delicious in the air, something that warms my heart.

I pass by the dining room on the way to the kitchen and find the table set for the whole family. Claudia stands at the stove, a frilly apron around her waist and Gizmo circling her feet. Queen Boudica has a much better plan, hiding behind the black coffee machine and swiping a paw at the mixing bowl as soon as Claws turns toward me.

Gizmo bounds over, happy to see me. She pounces into my arms, and I bury my face in her soft fur. Cats always know exactly what they want. Sometimes I wish I could be like them.

"What's going on here?" I come up behind Claudia and wrap my arms around her tiny waist, nuzzling her neck. Gizmo squirms between us.

"I cooked," Claudia says, a little testily. "I can cook, you know. A little bit. Don't get used to it. But I thought we could have a little celebration tonight, for you."

"For me?"

"Harvard. Yale. Berkeley. You worked so hard, Eli." She lifts the spoon to her mouth and tastes the sauce. "I know it's hard letting go of our old lives and our old dreams. We're building something amazing here, but what's that dumb phrase Ms. Drysdale says sometimes? Rome wasn't built in a day."

She's talking as if it's obvious I won't study at Harvard, as if I won't accept any of my college positions at all. As if a nice meal and a congratulations cake make up for what I'll be missing. She's probably right. I probably will turn them all down to stay here in Emerald Beach with her, but it grates on me that she expects it, that she's not *talking* to me about it the way we've always discussed everything.

But I don't want to start a fight. Not tonight, not when we found the treasure and my head is full of cobwebs tangled together. So I kiss her forehead and wander away, hugging Gizmo close to my heart.

Later, Claudia calls us to dinner and we all gather around the table. The only person who isn't there is Antony, who's been working every spare minute trying to get the fights off the streets and back into the club. I exchange a glance with Noah. Gabriel downs his drink in two seconds flat and reaches for mine, a sure sign that he's certain something's up. Claudia dishes up creamy tagliatelle with salmon, telling us the story of how her father used to prepare this dish for her whenever she felt sick. It smells like garlic and happiness, but when I take a bite all I taste is cardboard.

"I have some news to share with you all. I've found a buyer," Claws says. "It's done."

I stare at her. How can it be done? What about everything we said about the documents being her legacy? What about gifting the treasure to a museum?

"Why?" I ask.

"Why?" she frowns. "For all the reasons I've already said. Because we need to get rid of Nero. Because this might be the only way of drawing Mackenzie out into the open in a situation that I control. Because I need power more than I need a bunch of dusty old tomes. Because I'm the Imperator and I don't have to explain my decisions."

Her words grated against old wounds. I put down my fork. "But *why?* Why do you have to destroy Nero? Why can't you be happy with the empire you already have? We don't need any more power."

"Because we're not safe." Her perfect face screws up.

"You're a crime boss. We'll *never* be safe. You said yourself – the documents will just go back into the underground. They'll be lost forever. Do it some other way. You said Cali knows where Mackenzie is hiding—"

"If I send Cali after Mackenzie and she gets away, we won't get another shot. Instead, she's going to force my sister to come to us, on *my* turf, under *my* terms. I want to protect my family. This is how I do it." Claudia shoots me a look that turns my blood cold. *She looks just like Mackenzie.* "This is not a discussion."

My eyes flick to Noah, who shifts in his seat. He saw it too.

"So that's it, then? We're not your equals, your partners? We're soldiers in your war against Nero. Against your sister. We'd better fall in line or you'll cut us off? Stuff us inside a brass bull and boil us alive?"

At the end of the table, George sinks lower in her seat, a look of utter misery on her face. Yara looks like she's ready to jump to Claudia's defense. Gabriel hums under his breath. I'm making everyone uncomfortable, but I can't stop. This is too important. This is our *lives.*

This is our family, all of ours. And I thought that when my father went to jail I was done doing things I didn't want to do for the good of a family. I was done listening to people who thought they knew better than me. Even if they are my beautiful, stubborn girlfriend.

Claudia shakes her head angrily. "That's not fair. Everything I've done has been for you."

Noah fixes me with a stare across the table. Years of friendship means I read his features perfectly. He's with me. He thinks this is too far.

"No one's saying you don't care about us," Noah says. "But isn't this risky? You're relying on Cali to come through for you.

She tried to kill you in the ring. What's to say she's not preparing to betray you?"

"Cali and I have an understanding."

Noah fists his knife. "Forgive me if I don't trust her. What if we lose the treasure, and you?"

"You said you needed me to be your moral compass," I say. Tears prick at the corners of my eyes. I feel like I'm talking to my father again, trying to get across how much I didn't want a Reality TV film crew in our house. I'm not talking to my beloved girl anymore, but to a wall of brick and indifference. "You said you need someone to point you north. Well, I'm not just pointing this time, I'm a fucking neon sign blinking TURN BACK. Don't do this. Let us figure out another plan, *together*."

"Why did you go to Harvard?" Claudia barks at me.

"You know why. I had that meeting—"

"You went because you're still holding back," she says, an edge of triumph in her voice. As if she wanted me to disappoint her. As if she *relishes* it. "You still believe that after everything that's happened, after everything you've done in my name, that you can still have that Ivy League life, that you can go back to being legitimate. You gave me your word, your blood, Eli. That world is closed to you now. You are *mine*."

"That's not what love is," I shoot back. "That's control. That's what my father did to me and what Noah's dad did to him and what Gabriel's dad did to him. You are becoming everything we raged against, everything we ran from."

Claudia's face clouds with rage. "You didn't just fucking say that."

Even Noah looks shocked. George has slid so far under the table the only thing visible is the top of her blue hair.

"Damn right I said it. And if you really loved me you'd be willing to hear me. We're not mindless clones who rush to fulfill your every command. You said that I was the angel on your shoulder. Well, here I am, flapping my fucking angel wings. Love means I can tell you when you're being pigheaded and foolish and making the worst of the mistakes your father made."

Claws looks around the table, at Noah, at Gabe, at the top of George's head and Yara and me. She fixes each of us with her Ice Queen glare, searching our souls for the blind loyalty she demands of us. My blood turns to stone. There's no love or respect in that gaze – only cold, hard rage.

"Is that what you all think?" she hisses. "You all think I'm making a mistake?"

Gabe stares miserably at his drink. Noah's eyes search hers, those dark chasms now shallow and fragile.

"Then I don't need any of you. Get the fuck out of my house."

Claudia turns on her heel and storms out.

41

CLAUDIA

I watch from the eyrie as Eli's Porsche takes off down the road, followed by Noah's Lambo, Gabriel's arm hanging over the passenger door.

I swipe angrily at my eyes, blotting away the tears before they fall.

They left.

I can't believe *they left.*

This is all Eli's doing. He can't leave anything alone, even after everything he's been through. Doesn't he think I've considered all possible solutions? He's too busy trying to push his own moral code on me that he can't see that his own is jammed as fuck.

As if he has some kind of high ground with his father the illegal body broker – the man who helped make my father disappear.

He said I was as bad as his father. As all their fathers. How can we ever come back from that?

And Noah and Gabriel... Don't they see that everything I've done has been for them?

Noah's always stood by me. His hands are stained with the

blood of my enemies. So why is he going to die on a hill for a bunch of old documents?

And Gabriel...

He got what he wanted. I'll give him his child, but it's not enough. It's never enough.

I sniff back the pain bubbling inside me, that terrible yearning void in my chest, like I'm one of Aristotle's beach-ball, doll-legged people torn down the middle.

If they're so weak-willed that they'll stand with him against me, then good riddance. I thought they understood me. I thought when they tattooed my mark on their skin, they were agreeing to be mine. To trust me.

I thought I'd finally found a family.

But I forgot.

I forgot that only those you love can truly betray you.

Daddy's words echo in my head. And even though I've lived through the aftermath of his own betrayal, even though he's not really my daddy at all, I never for a moment imagined that I'd feel the same sting from my three princes.

They've kept me strong through this hellish year and now... and now I'm right back where I started from. Alone in an empty house, caged by a legacy I wanted to escape.

My phone beeps. It's Livvie. *The drop is set up. You good?*

I'll never be good again. I brace my hand against the glass, suck in a few shuddering breaths.

I'm good, I text back.

I'm Claudia August. I have to be good. I don't have time to fall apart.

42

CLAUDIA

*I*t's the Ides of March.

Not an auspicious day for a plot to capture my sister, but I've already been betrayed by the people I loved most, so what's the worst that can happen?

I pace across the ballroom, flicking my knife from my sleeve, barely noticing the blade nicking my skin. Blood trickles from my palm, dotting the marble with specks of claret.

It's five days after the boys walked out, George and Yara at their heels. I haven't left the house, haven't showered, barely slept. All I do is drag furniture and statues into the rage room to smash and scroll through videos on my phone of the fighting in the street.

A bunch of Cali's haters blew up Constantino's gym. Luckily, Cali and her assassins were out on jobs, but the workers in the Korean restaurant downstairs all died. I stare at the footage of the smoldering wreckage and feel nothing but a giant, gaping hole in my chest.

I'm made of glass. Cold and hard and as if one wrong move will shatter me to pieces.

I look at the clock again, even though it hasn't changed since ten seconds ago when I last looked at it. Today is the big day. The day of the drop. The day I lure my sister out of her cave. I should feel triumphant, nervous, *something.*

But I feel nothing.

None of it makes sense without them. I was doing all of this for them, for us, for our future. But they're not my future anymore.

I'll have to get to the drop-off point soon. To face my sister. I can't even muster up any enthusiasm. After all her crazy attempts to finish me off, I'm the one who blew up my life all on my own. It's better this way. I was a fool to think I could rule a cruel world with love in my heart.

And yet...

And yet I dared to hope.

I don't have a ride. I sent them all a text this morning. I didn't tell them what I needed. I *asked.* Because that's what this is about, isn't it? I've been acting like their ruler instead of their equal. So I asked for their help. I offered the olive branch.

And they're not coming.

They're not coming back to me.

The three people I wanted at my side, the ones I trusted to always have my back, and they won't be there when I finally take down my sister.

It's over.

I've been holding so tight to them that I didn't even know I was holding sand until it trickled through my fingers.

I don't want to do what I'm about to do. I wanted to keep him out of this. He's the person I've turned to again and again. He told me I'd regret bringing so many people into our world, and he was right. And I can't bear looking into his dark eyes and knowing that I cost him his chance to escape this life because of a lie.

They didn't come. It's over.

If my chest is empty, if my heart has shriveled into a dead, broken thing, then how can the cavity ache so much?

I'm running out of options. I hit the CALL button on my phone.

"What now?" Antony sounds annoyed.

"It's me." My voice wobbles. I'm dangerously close to crying. What a fucking day. "I don't have time to explain, but I've laid a trap that I think will lure Mackenzie out of hiding, but I need some backup. Will you get over here and drive me to the docks? Come armed."

Antony can already tell exactly what I'm planning to do. "I told you not to go after Mackenzie on your own. She's danger-ous. And clearly a little unhinged—"

"I'm not on my own."

"Then where are your three Musketeers? Can't they play chauffeur?"

I close my hand over my bleeding heart. "They have some-thing else to do. Look, I have it all sorted. I found the treasure and—"

"You *what?*"

I have to hold the phone away from my ear so Antony's screech doesn't burst my eardrum.

"Look, sorry I didn't tell you, but you haven't exactly been around lately." I used to lob those words at him with such venom, trusting his guilt would get me what I want – the way I used to make him bring treats when he left me alone in the house for too long. But hearing them on my lips only makes my hollow chest burn with shame. "Can you get over here and give me a ride or not?"

I hear a door slam. "I'm already in the car. See you soon, Claws."

I hang up and toss the phone on the sofa. Queen Boudica

bounds after it, then shoots me a glare when she realizes it's not edible. I resume pacing. Livvie texts again.

We're in position. Just waiting on Cali to get her shit together. Where are you, girl?

I hit a little snag with my ride, I type back. *Be there soon.*

I tap my phone against my palm. *Fucking hurry up, Antony.*

I watch Casper play outside the patio doors, waiting for the sound of Antony's car to rumble down the passage. The tiny white tiger paws at the glass, wanting to come in to play on Queen Boudica's cat castle. My kitty winds around my legs and rubs along the glass, anxious to get outside to her friend. She's been lonely since Eli and Gizmo left.

That makes two of us, little kitty.

Eli found homes for the monkeys and most of the reptiles, but the big cats were proving to be a real problem. All the zoos and sanctuaries were full right now – something to do with increased awareness of big cat mistreatment because of some weird Netflix show. In between everything else, he'd been desperately trying to find them a forever home. He couldn't stand the thought of any innocent creature living without love. He cared *so much* and now—

BANG.

A gunshot?

Fuck.

I flatten myself against the floor, pressing Queen Boudica beneath me so she won't run headlong into danger. My veins pulse with adrenaline.

Where's the shooter? Who is in the house?

The boys blocked off the tunnel entrance. I've got a state-of-the-art lock on the maintenance shed. George searched this place from top to bottom and found no other secret tunnels. So how the fuck did someone get in—

No, it wasn't a gunshot. It's the ballroom door slamming

against the wall as someone storms inside. I lift myself onto my elbows, letting Queen Boudica dart away. I'm ready to strangle Antony for scaring the shit out of me.

But it's not Antony.

The figure stalks toward me. I try to scramble to my feet, but I'm too slow. A foot slams onto my back, a stiletto heel digging into my ribs.

"Hello, sister," Mackenzie purrs.

43

CLAUDIA

I twist my neck to look up at my twin. Her blonde hair tumbles over her shoulders in golden waves, her smile frozen like a doll, making a dimple in one of her cheeks. Her eyes eviscerate me.

She's me.

Maybe I've been wrong all this time. Maybe Noah isn't my mirror. Maybe it's her. Maybe my twin sister reflects my own brutality back at me.

I'm suddenly aware of how completely *alone* I am. How alone and empty. If she's come to cut out my heart, she's too late – it's already long gone.

Malloy Manor has been teaming with people for so many months, I've almost forgotten the crushing weight of loneliness.

Now, it's just me and her.

And isn't it fitting? It was always going to come to this – fighting to the death against my reflection.

Mackenzie twists her lips into a terrifying smile as she grinds her heel into my spine. "Where are your three little boyfriends? They're not going to leap in and save you this time?"

"Why do you care?" I shoot back. A cold dread settles in my

stomach. And suddenly I don't give a fuck what she does to me, but if she hurts Eli, Noah, or Gabriel...

"Relax, sis. You look so spooked. I'm not going to hurt them. Why would I break up that sexy sandwich? After I kill you and assume your life, they will become *my* boyfriends. I must congratulate you on your excellent taste. I always knew Noah Marlowe would be dynamite in the sack, and even drippy Eli Hart sure grew up good." Her cold eyes twinkle. "But Gabriel Fallen? *Nice.* I'm going to enjoy breaking him."

At first, I don't understand what she's talking about, but as she digs her nails into my wrist and her hair tickles my cheek, it hits me.

She's not just here to kill me, she's here to insert herself into my life.

Mackenzie Malloy will die tonight, by my hand or hers, and one of us will get to keep living as Claudia.

I jerk my body, trying to knock her foot off so I can get up, but she digs a knee into my back, pinning me good. It's a move that would do Antony proud.

"Atta girl." Mackenzie trails a finger down my cheek. "You understand now. I'm here to take back what's mine, the life I was supposed to have, the life you *stole* from me. But don't worry, I promise I'm going to enjoy every minute of being Claudia August."

I try to curl my legs under my body to get some leverage, but she presses my cheek into the cold marble. Something sharp jabs into my neck.

"Ow, fuck. What are you doing?"

"You mean this old thing?" She glances at the syringe in her hand. "I stole it from Eli. It's some kind of tranquilizer for the animals. I figure if this will bring down a lion it'll probably kill a tiny, insignificant human girl. Goodnight, sister. Thank you for building an empire for me. I'm so excited to step into your life. *My* life. Kisses."

She air-kisses my cheeks as she jams her thumb down, emptying the syringe into my neck. I try to kick, to scream, but a grey fog envelops the edges of my eyes and makes my tongue flop about uselessly. The last thing I see before the fog takes me is my own reflection laughing at me.

Then everything goes black.

44

CLAUDIA

I'm underwater, chest heaving, bubbles escaping my mouth. My whole body screams for oxygen, but I don't want to go up just yet. I like being down here where it's quiet, where no one expects anything from me.

Where my father can't hurt me.

Eli's calling me. I look up and see him silhouetted against the harsh sunlight – a skinny boy of eleven, eyes wide as he begs me to surface, to stop scaring him, to stop pretending I want to give up. He plunges into the water, wrapping his arms around me and pulling, pulling... and I don't want to go...

Wait, *no*. Those aren't my memories. This isn't my life. It's the life I stole from Mackenzie...

The hands around me aren't Eli's. The arms are thick, veins standing up beneath intricate tattoos, the skin on the hands rough from fighting. I sink deeper into the warmth of those familiar arms. A name dances in front of my face, but I'm not sure if I say it aloud or just dream it.

"Antony?"

"C'mon, Claws." He drags me – a dead weight, my feet scraping on rough stone. "It's this way."

"Wha…" I fight to keep my eyes open. I'm no longer in the swimming pool, no longer cocooned in that calm, cool water. I'm assaulted by everything that's *wrong* – the throbbing in my neck, the damp, thick air of the tunnels, the concerning fact that I can no longer feel the cavity where my heart used to be. I can no longer feel anything at all below my neck.

"It's okay, cousin," Antony murmurs as he drags me like I weigh nothing at all, which to him I probably don't. "Everything's going to be fine. I sorted it out, like I always do. I spoke to the guys. They're waiting for us at Colosseum. I just have to get you out of here before she finds us, so do me a favor and move those legs."

I focus every thought on supporting my own weight, but Antony's moving too fast and my legs have become two strange floppy things that aren't attached to my body. I sink back into his arms, letting him drag me where he needs us to go.

Antony's here. The guys. Everything's okay.

We emerge into the round room where Mackenzie left her parents' bodies. *Our parents.* It's exactly as I remember it, except that my foggy, grey-tinged mind registers two differences – a rope ladder now hangs from the hole high on the other side. And there seems to be a giant hole and a pile of dirt, and two more coffins in the room, even though Galen and Tiberius dismantled them and disposed of the Malloys weeks ago.

No. That's just my double-vision. I rub my eyes. Moving my hands makes my whole body lurch to the side. I grab onto Antony to keep from toppling over.

Two coffins, or one?

"Immmmooooo…" I try to say that I'm never going to be able to climb that rope ladder, but what comes out is a strangled moan. My vision swims.

"You don't have to climb the ladder," Antony says as he drops me. I can't control my arms to break my fall. My face slams into the dirt floor. "You're not leaving this room."

Antony's fingers grip my arm, twisting it so roughly I cry out. He kicks out his leg, shoving the lid off the coffin. I expect to see Howard's decomposed body, but instead, it's empty, the sides lined in fancy fresh satin colored ice blue to match my eyes.

A Walter Hart original.

"What's going on?" I cry, although I'm not sure if I say the words out loud or just in my head. I can't feel my lips anymore. "Where's Howard Malloy?"

"This isn't his coffin any longer," Antony says. "It's yours."

45

CLAUDIA

With a tenderness I didn't know him capable of, Antony lays me down inside the coffin. In my head I'm screaming, pummeling him with my fists, hitting him with everything I've got. But my limbs won't move. All that escapes from my mouth are incoherent moans.

I sink down into the plush silk, betrayed by the drug that's pulling me under.

Betrayed by my cousin, by the closest family I have.

"What are you doing?" I try to say as Antony arranges my hands at my sides, positioning me like an Egyptian mummy at a museum. But my lips refuse to work. The words don't materialize – only a low, anguished cry that I can't believe comes from my own lips.

Antony peers down, smoothing back my hair. "I know you're trying to speak, but the drug will keep you quiet. This won't be like last time, I promise. You'll just slip away into nothing. It's more than you deserve."

He steps back, looking satisfied. Mackenzie falls into Antony's arms. He wraps her body in his, holding her close as he lays a kiss on the top of her head.

What?

Why is he looking at her like that, like she holds the stars in her eyes?

Somewhere back in the recesses of my mind, the pieces are fitting together. But I can't access them through the fog of drugs. I don't even know if I can trust the blurred, dreamlike images before me.

Antony and Mackenzie? What the fuck?

Mackenzie peers down at me, her eyes sparkling with satisfaction.

"Look at her face all twisted up," she smirks. "She's trying to understand. Should we explain?"

"That might make you a villainous cliche, babe." Antony looks at his watch. "On the other hand, Nero's still cleaning up at the docks, so we've got time. Whatever you want to do."

"I want to tell her *everything*. I want my sister to understand exactly how we fooled her. I want her to die knowing how the real queen took back her throne."

Mackenzie leans against the side of the coffin, trailing her finger over my arm. I can see her doing it, but I can't feel it.

"Once upon a time," she says in a singsong voice, "there lived a wicked king and queen in their castle on the hill. The queen became pregnant, and the wicked king wasn't happy with the size of his empire, so he sold one of his children to a criminal in exchange for some treasure."

He sold me.

My birth father didn't want me. I wasn't a person to him, just a commodity.

The pain of it slices through my chest, as raw as the first day I found out about it. I didn't think I could feel pain after the guys left and my sister pumped me full of animal tranquilizer, but the human body is amazing, right?

Mackenzie continues, "One princess was left behind – the

unlucky one. While her sister went off to live a magical life in a far-off land, the princess endured years of torture at the cruel king's hands. She thought there was no way out of her fate, until one night when she helped the drunken queen into bed. As the queen tossed and turned and ranted and raved, she admitted everything. That she'd given birth to twins. That the king had drugged her and taken her baby and she only knew about it because she kept a secret diary. That the princess had a sister she'd never ever met, who lived across town with the handsome crime lord.

"So the princess went to find her sister. She just wanted to meet her twin. She'd been so lonely, you see, trapped in the castle with only the evil king and queen for company. She wasn't allowed friends, not even the Golden Boy who wanted to save her and make her good, even though she knew she could never be good. But then the princess saw her sister's life."

Mackenzie isn't stroking me like a cat now. She scratches her nails along my arm, drawing deep rivulets of blood. Claw marks.

"I spent months following you," she hisses, dropping the sing-song voice. "Your father thought he was oh so clever hiding you away, but you weren't hard to find. I rented a shitty apartment opposite your house. I even got a job as a waitress to work some of the August parties. And do you know what I saw? I saw a girl who didn't appreciate how fucking good she had it. A mopey, sulky little shit whining that she couldn't go outside or go to school like normal kids because she was just *too special*. Because the handsome crime lord kept her in a gilded cage. Well, fuck you very much, Claudia. You got the life that I deserved, and you squandered it being sad and bitter. They weren't even your real parents, but they *loved* you. Why should you have that and not me? So I took them away from you."

She… wait, what?

But I can't interrupt Mackenzie. I can barely even see her

now – thick, grey fog is closing in around my eyes again. It takes all my will to keep my focus on Mackenzie and not give in to the bone-deep weariness in my limbs that calls me back to oblivion.

"But first, I needed a way to get close to you," she says. "I needed to know what I was dealing with. So I went down to Colosseum one night and introduced myself to the man of my dreams."

Mackenzie throws her arms around Antony. Pain stabs at my chest. How ironic that the only part of my body with feeling can feel the sharp twist of Antony's treachery.

Never forget that only the ones you love can betray you.

"She gave me a hell of a fright," Antony says, holding Mackenzie close. "I thought you'd somehow figured out a way to sneak out of Uncle Julian's house. But Mackenzie explained everything. She showed me the evidence she'd found – the doctored birth certificate, the mysterious disappearance of a midwife and two doctors at the exclusive facility where both mothers gave birth. And there was the evidence of my eyes – she looks exactly like the cousin I'd grown to hate."

No, Antony. It's not true. You were my friend. You looked out for me when I had no one else. You don't hate me. It can't be true.

It can't...

"That's right." Antony leans over the coffin and spits on my face. I don't feel his saliva roll down my cheek. I'm too numb now to even feel the knife of his betrayal twisting in my chest. "I *despise* you. I have ever since the day Julian told me you would be his successor, and that my job was to watch over you always. All the time he'd been training me, giving me tests, showing me how the empire worked, I thought he was molding me in his image, ready to adopt me as his heir the way his precious Roman emperors did with their successors. But instead, he takes me aside and tells me that he's training me to be your tribune, your advisor, your protector." Antony wrinkles his face. "Your *babysitter.*"

No.

Nonononono.

All my life you've been by my side, you've watched out for me. You pulled me out of the grave that night. How can you hate me? How can you...

He continues, "But I'm much smarter than you. I know not to wear my hate on my sleeve. It's far better to bide your time, to let the world believe you're the dutiful soldier, the loyal cousin, the one who will clean up Julian August's mess. So I raged in silence, and I waited for my chance to strike. And then Mackenzie Malloy burst into my life like a cheerleader out of hell and dropped that chance right in my lap."

"We bonded over our mutual hatred of her, didn't we, babe?" Mackenzie squeezes Antony possessively, her lips pursed.

"We did." He kisses her, long and slow, until each stroke of his tongue lashes against my oblivion, whipping me back to the present, holding me in this moment so he can torture me further. "At first, when Mackenzie came to me with this revelation, I went along with her plan simply because I wanted revenge. Julian loved me like a son. I should've been his heir. I thought for sure one day he'd see I was born to rule, that he had made me into exactly the leader he is. But he kept on with his foolish charade that this weak child he'd hidden away from the world would one day be fit to rule it. I wanted Julian to know what it felt like to be buried under the weight of obligation. I wanted him to know true fear, to reach for me to save him and see on my face the moment he realized that I was the one who'd condemned him. I wanted him to *pay.* Mackenzie and I formed a plan to get exactly what we both wanted, and over the months we worked on the plan, we fell in love."

We fell in love.

How many years have I wished my cousin would find someone who'd appreciate his loyalty, his strength, his cunning? What a laugh. Alanis Morissette should write a song about me.

"First, we had to deal with the Malloys," Mackenzie says, happily snuggling into Antony's shoulder. "They deserved to pay for what they did to me, to *us*. And we needed Daddy to give up the location of the treasure. We knew we'd need money to start over, and Daddy's money would be tied up in the company and all his creditors would come knocking, so we couldn't count on that if we wanted to disappear. So I knocked them out with drugs I brought from Cleo St. James, and I dragged them down into this very tunnel. Our mother died on her knees, begging for her life like the weakling she is. I took my time with dear old Dad. I even had a bucket of water down here to throw over his head when he lost consciousness. I had to make sure he learned his lesson. You would have been proud of me. I punished him for both of us, sister."

In some deep, dark recesses of my fog-addled mind, I feel a tug of solidarity with my twin. Women like us get our justice on the business end of a blade. Our father deserved everything she did to him.

"Daddy was so stubborn. He kept saying that he lost the treasure. It had been stolen from him. What a silly lie to tell. Such a drag! That was not what I wanted to hear." She pouts and stomps her foot for emphasis. "Poor Daddy thought I would spare his life if he gave me some other secret, so he kept on talking. He told me all sorts of useful things about his deal with Lucian August, about how the Triumvirate worked, about the deal he had with Senator Marlowe and how that was falling apart, and about *exactly* what Walter Hart was doing over in Tartarus Oaks. I got him to record the message that I played on the maid's voicemail. Then I stomped on his head until he popped like a balloon. I emptied the safe of cash, drove their car out, and made that phone call. We had time before people would notice the king and queen were missing. Antony wanted us to take Howard's money I stole from the safe and go off somewhere, but I couldn't leave Emerald Beach without doing what I set out to do. I want the treasure my father hid from me. I want my inheritance." She beams up at Antony. "This is fun, babe. I love reliving these old memories. I wish I'd taken more pictures for a scrapbook. I think I'll start one now."

She's insane, which I guess is how I know she shares my DNA.

Mackenzie pulls something from her pocket and holds it up. Through the encroaching haze I can just make out the sparkling pink heart on my phone case. *Mackenzie took my phone... all the guys' numbers are on there...*

What if she tries to contact them? What if she lures them somewhere and hurts them?

Mackenzie holds the phone over the coffin, but Antony knocks it out of her hand.

"Not a good idea, babe. You don't want any possible way her harem will figure out what happened here today."

Still weird hearing Antony call someone babe.

Why is that the only thing I can think about right now?

My sister pouts, but she replaces the phone in her pocket. "Pity, but I guess I'll remember this day without a selfie. Anyway, where were we?"

"The night we buried Julian August alive," Antony says, his voice dripping with pride.

She claps her hands gleefully. "That's right! So, there we were, Antony trying to be sensible, me wanting to burn everything down. But I won, because I always win. We lie low in Tartarus Oaks for a few weeks – enough time so that the disappearance of the Malloys and Julian August's death won't seem connected. We needed more men, so Antony went to Constantine. He didn't reveal the whole plan, but there'd been an undertow of dissatisfaction about Julian's reforms, and Antony played on that. He said that if Constantine helped him get rid of Julian – made it look like an international hit from a disgruntled client – and supported Antony's claim for Imperator, August and Dio would have an alliance and push Nero out. Constantine agreed. He drew up a contract and gave us the men we needed, and we were ready for revenge."

Oh, Daddy, I'm so so sorry.

I hadn't believed that contract Nero showed me was real, but it was. Only, it wasn't between Constantine and Brutus, but Constantine and Antony. I don't even blame Constantine for agreeing to help – I would've done the same thing in a heartbeat to wrestle power from Nero.

"Julian taught me how to disable the security at your house," Antony says. "We knew your parents usually left early from Triumvirate parties—"

"—Mr. and Mrs. Parent of the Year wanted to be home to kiss their baby girl goodnight—" Mackenzie sniffs.

"—so we waited outside until they got back, then we let ourselves in."

"I slashed your mother," Mackenzie grins. "I enjoyed cutting her perfect skin. I *especially* enjoyed watching your face when you saw her."

The figure in the window.

It wasn't my reflection. It was Mackenzie's face, splattered with my mother's blood, watching as Antony dragged me away.

I think of other times when I'd seen my reflection in strange places, or a face in a crowd who looked uncannily like me. There was this time Antony took me to Colosseum for my birthday... I thought it was a trick of the light, a combination of too much alcohol and seeing Brutus again, but it was *her*. It had always been *her*.

How did I not know she was watching me? Characters in

books always feel a prickling on their neck, eyes boring into their back. But I felt nothing. All Daddy's security guards and extra precautions never picked up that my sister was stalking me. And he paid the ultimate price.

Antony puffs out his chest as he explains the next part of the story. "We took you and Julian to Beaumont Hills cemetery, where Constantine had arranged with Hart for two fresh graves to be left open for us, two fresh coffins waiting for their corpses. I threw in the first shovels of dirt myself. Mackenzie and I laid a picnic blanket under the oleander bushes and fucked to a soundtrack of muffled screams. Julian was the first to fall silent. We were waiting for you to die when Constantine called to check up on things. I'm shooting the breeze with Constantine and out of the blue, he tells me he's fucking *sorry*, but the plan has changed. Brutus went to Malloy Manor after that party to have it out with his brother. He saw us enter Julian's house, saw Constantine and his team cleaning up. He knows what we did, and he wants in. And Brutus has support within the family *and* a blood claim. Constantine decides it's better if Brutus claims the killing as his and he becomes Imperator with the full support of Dio. But this isn't what we fucking agreed." Antony smashes his fist against the side of the coffin, which rocks on its stand. "*I'm supposed to be Imperator.*"

He sounds exactly the way he used to sound when we were kids, bitching after he lost a fight in the ring and thought it was because his opponent cheated. He never could stand to be second.

I should have known. I should have seen that he couldn't handle being second to me.

"So now, we're in trouble, because Brutus knows, which means if I don't toe the line he'll tell the world what we did. Without Constantine's support, it would be the brazen bull for both of us." Antony hugs Mackenzie to him. "Not to mention the fact that a few days earlier, Constantine casually mentioned that one of his soldiers, Brentwood, was at Malloy Manor looking for something for a client – it can only be the treasure, which means the client could only be Senator Marlowe. Only instead of finding the cache, he found the mangled, decaying bodies of Howard and Ainsley. Brentwood knows that without his resources, only someone with intimate knowledge of the house would be able to find that underground room – the only person not lying dead within it. My girl." Antony's voice grows fierce. "Brentwood knew Mackenzie killed her parents. And he told Marlowe, the tough-on-crime senator. That meant Mackenzie couldn't show her face in Emerald Beach – especially not on the arm of an August soldier – without Marlowe slapping her with the full force of the law. Our entire plan was shot to shit."

"But Antony came up with a new plan." Mackenzie nuzzles her head in her shoulder. "With a little help from me."

"I had to move quickly," Antony says. "You'd stopped making noise. You'd be dead in minutes. I told Mackenzie to hide, and I pulled you out and took you to Malloy Manor. I told you whatever I needed to tell you to make you cooperate, because you were our scapegoat, our life insurance. The real Mackenzie Malloy needed to disappear, and the fake Mackenzie would squat in her house like a termite, burrowing in deep until Brentwood returned to finish her off. Except that he never did. And all the while Brutus grew more powerful, and although I looked every chance I got, I never found the treasure."

"So instead of ruling my beloved city by Antony's side, I had to leave without my inheritance," my sister pouts, as if this is somehow so much worse than what she and Antony did to me. "Can you imagine how horrible it's been? Laying low, having to work menial jobs, living in dingy squats and gross hostels, missing Antony like crazy, eating food not fit for human consumption, watching news stories about the interloper living in *my* house. No wonder my eyesight started to deteriorate."

Holy shit. The contact lenses Noah found in Antony's bag – they weren't his. They were *hers*.

It was *Mackenzie* who tried to shoot me and Noah. This explains why she missed, why she got me confused with Odette in the darkness...

How close has she been to me this entire time?

How did I not sense she was there?

Mackenzie leans in and taps my cheek, her nails not registering against my numb skin. "And then you had the *nerve* to enroll at Stonehurst Prep."

Antony sighs. "I tried to stop her, babe."

"I know you did, but she is my sister. She has to do things her way and screw the consequences for anyone else." Mackenzie smiles indulgently down at me, like I'm a child who's colored on the furniture. "But it worked out okay in the end. I came back to Emerald Beach as soon as I heard. I didn't tell Antony I was in the city at first. I knew he'd try to send me away again—"

"—for your own good." Antony touches her cheek.

"Is he always this overprotective of you?" Mackenzie giggles. "I mean, *obviously* he was. Otherwise, you wouldn't be alive now, not with all the people who wanted you dead. But as long as you were still alive, still the ghost of Malloy Manor, it meant my enemies hadn't made their move." She kisses Antony's cheek. "You did the best you could, babe, but you haven't taken care of things like I would. You weren't *proactive*. So I came back to make everything right again. Starting with Brentwood. He was so surprised when I showed up for tea, and too busy staring at my tits to notice the drugs I put in his drink. Antony was *so* pissed when he found out what I did—"

"—you're too impulsive, doll. It's your greatest flaw. Claudia was sniffing around, and I couldn't have her find out the truth before I became Imperator."

"Luckily, Antony had the clever idea to make it look like Brutus killed Brentwood. And I took his gun," she rubs her shoulder. "It was *so* heavy. It hurt my arm when it kicked back. I was so close to you and Noah, but I still couldn't hit you."

"You shouldn't have tried," Antony coos. "You were such an adorable klutz. I had everything under control."

They're both insane.

Mackenzie pouts again. "I was just so tired of *waiting*. Of being the good little girl while my sister lived *my* life. And I wanted to find the treasure before you did. Practically every day you were at school I snuck in and searched for it – I used the maintenance shed at first, but then you locked it up, so I started using this tunnel." She wrinkles her nose. "I hate it down here. It's so filthy. And there are spiders. But it would all be worth it if I could find the treasure. I saw all the things you'd done to *my* house. You let an animal sleep in my bed. There was fur everywhere. Muddy pawprints on the marble. Scratches in the Hermes sofa. Such disrespect for my things. All my favorite dolls broken. I needed to teach you a lesson," she smiles, miming her slicing the knife into Queen Boudica.

My veins surge with rage. I try to throw myself out of the coffin. I imagine my fingers sliding around my sister's neck and squeezing the life out of her for what she did to my kitty. But of course it's only in my warped, grey-tinged mind. I'm glued in place, weighed down by the drug that's slowly dragging me into oblivion.

"You should have seen Claudia after you sliced that fleabag cat of hers." Antony kisses the top of Mackenzie's head. "She went to war against an innocent boy. She was so easy to fool."

Alec LeMarque was far from innocent.

"The only reason I agreed to go to Germany was to give my

babe time to search the house top to bottom," Antony says. "But she still couldn't find the treasure. We were starting to think Howard might've been telling the truth."

I remember walking into the house after getting back from Germany and everything feeling strange, just slightly out of place. I put it down to jet lag, but it was *her*. That's been the only time she slipped up, the only hint that something wasn't right before she showed up at Vault and at school pretending to be me.

Antony peers down at me, his breath hot on my cheek. "You're still conscious in there, aren't you? You're hearing every word of this but you can't do a thing. How does it feel, Claudia? How does it feel to be completely helpless? And we have so much more time left with you before we kill you. I kept telling Mackenzie to be patient, that I'd make sure she'd be able to savor this moment once it arrived. She's been waiting so long, you see. So long for her real life to begin."

Antony kisses Mackenzie's head again. "I kept telling her to stay away, that you'd get yourself killed within a week of stepping outside that house. But you kept fucking making trouble, getting the wrong side of every story, telling those boys the truth about you, digging us deeper and deeper into this mess. Meanwhile, I solidified power so I could advance to Imperator and Mackenzie got rid of Brutus, but then you fucking show up at Saturnalia and declare yourself the new ruler of August."

"Antony was so *pissed*," Mackenzie giggles. "You should have seen him storming around, slamming doors, cursing your name to any god that would listen. But I pointed out that this was all actually perfect. We just had to be patient a little longer. We let you build our empire for us. And you've done even better than we ever could have imagined."

"And while you were alive, standing in the firing line, my babe was safe," Antony says. "I decided to see how long you'd last, how much of your father's empire you could reclaim before someone took you out. Which was inevitable with the chaos you were bringing down."

"You were so distracted with your plans for world domination and your little harem and your hatred of Brutus that you didn't notice us maneuvering you behind the scenes," Mackenzie grins. "If you knew all the times I've pretended to be you, steered you in the direction of your own self-destruction. I've even fooled your boyfriend into kissing me."

Eli saw right through you. Because he loves me. He protects me—

He used to love me.

The loneliness hits me like a brick, shattering the rage and hurt that's keeping me conscious. Eli's not coming for me. No one will save me now. The pain of it hurts *too much*. It's more than pain – it's a brittle emptiness in my bones. Grey oblivion wobbles on the edge of my vision, and I long to commit to it, to sail over the edge of the world and never come back.

Eli, Noah, Gabe, I'm so so sorry.

"Brutus was such a convenient scapegoat," Antony says as he leans over the coffin. "All I had to do was add that note to Brentwood's body, and you created an entire mythology about him in your mind. In reality, he had no idea you were still alive. He didn't even know what you looked like. I just wanted to fuck with you. I wanted you to *pay*."

He didn't even know what you looked like.

Antony leans right over me, his body filling the space I need to keep breathing. His lips brush mine, and even though I can't feel his touch, something in that kiss, in his crushing presence, stirs a darkness inside me, a locked box I'd pushed beneath the surface bobbing on the edge of my consciousness.

"How do you think it felt, *cousin*, being around you every day knowing you were living the life I was supposed to have, that my

Mackenzie should have had?" Antony rasps against my lips. "*You* were the impostor. It was never supposed to be you, but you mocked me with her face. And one day, I got tired of pretending. I got tired of waiting to have my chance with her. You know what teenage hormones are like. I was going *crazy*. I couldn't be inside her, but I had the perfect Mackenzie sex doll right down the hall from me."

No. Please, no.

The chains shatter, the box of secrets in my mind blows open, and Antony's scent assaults me. His heavy body presses against mine, the way it had done that night when he pinned me to the bed.

The scream starts in my toes and rises up through my body until even my skin itself is screaming. A scream that can't leave my lips, that struggles against the drug for freedom as I writhe in the truth of what he says.

It wasn't Brutus in my room that night. It wasn't my uncle who violated me.

It was Antony.

46

CLAUDIA

My stomach churns, desperate to disgorge its contents. But I can't move. I can't push the demons Antony's unleashed back into their box. They press against my skull as the full horror of it rolls over me.

And in that moment, something inside me snaps.

I lost everything.

All those years I lived alone in this house, I dreamed of a family, of people who had my back no matter what. And through chance and happenstances and sheer dumb luck, I got everything I dreamed of. I had friends who cared for me, and I had three princes who loved me, who worshipped me. But I blew it. They put me on a pedestal, and I showed them that I was no goddess, but a demon in disguise.

I cost them everything – their futures, their college plans, their families, their innocence. Noah lost *Grace* because of me.

I piled up the house of sand that crumbled around us.

No wonder they left me.

No wonder they *hate* me.

I'm too broken to see that my beloved cousin is my rapist.

I'm too selfish to realize that everything I dreamed of was right under my nose.

I'm too corrupted to understand that the freedom I sought was in their arms the whole time.

I took three guys who had bright, brilliant futures and pulled them into my nightmare. I made them give up everything they are for my love, and never did the same in return.

I'll never be able to right the evil I've done to them. But they gave me so much of themselves, it's time for me to give something back. To give them their dreams back. They deserve that much from me. They deserve so much more.

I close my eyes – the only part of me still able to move – and I picture their faces. Sweet Eli with that too pretty smile. Dark-eyed Noah who mirrors my soul. Gabriel with those sinful lips that sing the stars.

I give them the only gift I have left to give.

I let go.

I stop fighting the grey fog. I sink into nothingness, letting the drug take me. I welcome oblivion. I greet death as my father, Julian August, would have done – with open arms.

In my death, they will live again.

They will truly be free.

Antony's voice courses through my thoughts as a new kind of numb warmth shoots up my legs. "When I got your call today, I couldn't believe our luck. I knew it was time to act. I rang Mackenzie and told her to wait for me, but of course she's too impulsive. She ran straight over here to finish you off. But don't worry, the legend of Claudia August won't die with you. Your empire will live on. It's time for you to retire and the true queen to take over."

"Mmmmmm. Mmmmmmf." A faint cry manages to penetrate my lips. I try to say that I'm ready to go, that Mackenzie can have my savage empire if she wants it so badly, that it's a curse she will regret for the rest of her life.

"I think she's trying to say that someone will come to save her," Mackenzie trills. "She seems to believe that if she doesn't show up at the docks, one of her handsome, loyal boyfriends will come to save her. But we have that all taken care of. Nero's at the docks now with some of his top soldiers. He'll make quick work of your people and secure the treasure, which he's promised to halve with me. I'll take over, and I'll move in here with your three boyfriends. They'll never know that I'm not the real Claudia. I'm going to have so much fun with them."

"Now that we have the treasure," Antony says, "we don't need you anymore."

"We really *do* appreciate everything you've done for us," Mackenzie purrs, gripping the edge of the coffin. "But now it's time to say goodbye, sis. Antony's already dug you a nice deep grave. It'll be such a pleasant way to go with those drugs in your system. You won't feel a thing. Just close your eyes and slip away."

I can't do a thing as my sister lowers the lid. The last thing I see is Mackenzie Malloy's ice-cold eyes glowing in triumph as the world disappears into darkness.

47

CLAUDIA

*a*s soon as the lid slams down, terror pulls me back from the edge.

No, no, no, no.

This can't be happening again.

I'm ready to die. It's right that I die, but not like this. Shoot me in the head, cut my throat, strangle the life from my veins. But not this. Not the way my father went. Not knowing that Mackenzie is going to go out there and drag my princes back into my empire.

If she gets her claws into them, they'll never be free of her.

Too late, I see how stupid I am to let go. I haven't set my princes free of me.

I've doomed them.

I try to fight, but my brain can't make my limbs move. I draw up the images of their faces again, letting the love I feel for Noah, Gabe, and Eli swell inside me, focusing all that love on balling my fingers into a fist. And I do it! I do it! My fingers curl up, and I've got a fist that I can pummel against the wood, if only I can move my arm. But there are scraping sounds and faint voices. They're preparing to lower my coffin into the grave Antony dug.

They're going to bury me alive.

Again.

"Help, help," I cry out, but I know my voice is only in my head. "Please, Gabe, Noah, Eli, I love you."

I can't die in here like this. I can't I can't I can't—

The terror is so raw and hot and real. It's not even about my horrible impending death. It's terror for the people I love.

She's taken my sight, my body, my ability to fight back. And now she's going to take my family.

And I never would have fallen into her trap if I'd listened to Eli. If I'd paid attention.

I'm the tiny bird pulling out my own feathers so I can squeeze through the bars of the cage. And all this time, the door was fucking open. I was *free.* I had love that poets would envy, and I threw it away because of my own stubborn pride. And now I was going to drown in a cage of my own making.

I'll never see them again. I'll never be able to tell them how much I love them. I'll never be able to bury my face in Eli's golden hair and tell him how much I needed to hear that shit he said, even though I hated it at the time. I never should have accused him of betraying me when all he was trying to do was make me *see.*

I know what real betrayal is.

I know what real love is.

The coffin rocks dangerously, slamming my head into the walls. I have no control over my body, can't even throw up my hands to protect my face. I hear the creak of wood and a thumping noise, and then I'm hurled against the lid.

The coffin slams into a hard surface and drops again. My neck snaps back, dancing white stars across my vision. My stomach lurches and I throw up, the puke bouncing back and splattering across my face.

I land facedown in a pile of my own vomit, the coffin wood splintered around me. A faint stream of light burns through the crack.

What happened?

I can't lift my head, can't get a better view of what's going on out there. I can hear footsteps, scuffling, thuds and thumps. I focus every atom of my body into my eyes, trying to clear the haze in my mind so I can interpret the shadows dancing on the other side of the damaged coffin.

Something flies from high up on the wall – from the entrance to the tunnel – and lands hard on a large lump near me that I assume is Antony. My cousin cries out as he falls hard, sliding into the grave he dug for me. The shape on top of him reels up, and a familiar golden head flashes across the hole as the figure pulls back a fist, slamming it into Antony's face.

Eli.

Eli's here?

Of course he's not here. I'm in worse shape than I thought if I'm hallucinating things. Because it really truly looks like my Golden Boy pummeling Antony's face until it's a mess of blood and bone.

"Where's Claudia?" the Eli-hallucination yells in Antony's face. "What did you do to her?"

Eli's voice breaks something inside me. I don't care if he's a hallucination. If this is my last moment on earth before oxygen deprivation pulls me into an eternal sleep, then I want my Golden Boy with me. Even though it's not real, I can die with a smile believing that I was loved.

The coffin shakes again. A board above my head flies away, spinning through the air. Rough hands reach inside, shaking my numb body. I'm dimly aware of my limbs wobbling, my neck snapping back and forth.

"Claudia? Claudia, fuck." Noah's voice reaches my brain. Beautiful, dark Noah. He's here with me, too. Maybe I did something right, after all. Maybe this is what heaven is, having my princes with me as I pass into the afterlife – my guardian angels.

Noah rolls me over. The splintered coffin digs into my back, but it feels like a light massage. I stare up into his eyes, and something in those shadows reaches through the fog and grabs me, shaking me from the inside out.

He wants me to live.

He wants me to fight.

"Something's wrong with her. I think they gave her drugs or something." Noah slaps my cheek. It feels like a feather trailing across my skin. "Claudia, can you hear me?"

"Mackenzie got away," Gabriel drawls from somewhere in the darkness behind Noah's shoulder. "I forgot that girl was head cheerleader for a reason. She's *fit*."

Eli's face appears above Noah, shoving him away. "I'll take care of her. Check Antony. I think he's dead, but we'd better be certain."

Something in the depths of my addled mind, I resurrect the lyrics of Gabriel's song. They repeat over and over as I peer up at the impossible scene.

I've sharpened my steel. I've made my sacrifices. I'm unleashing war.

"Claudia." Eli rolls me into his arms, cradling me against his body. Tears stream down his cheeks. A salty drop falls on my lips, and it rolls into my mouth. The saltiness dances on my tongue. And I know. I fucking *know*.

This isn't a dream.

They're here. They came for me.

The knowledge surges through my body like molten lava. My lips tear open a crack, and a sound escapes. "EEeeeeee..."

"That's right. It's me." Eli touches my cheek. "Shit, shit, what have they done to you?"

"Trraaaaaan—" I can't get the words out. The grey fog waits at the edges of my eyes, waits to claim me.

Eli's brow furrows. He touches my forehead, lifts my sagging eyelid to peer into my eyes. "I think they gave her animal tranquilizer. I keep a bunch in my room for the lion. This is bad. We have to get her to Galen—"

"She threw up," Noah says. "There's puke all inside the coffin. It probably happened when I knocked it over."

"It won't make a difference if she's been injected. We have to keep her awake." Eli's fingers continue to touch and press all over my body, like he wants to make sure every inch of me is still intact. "Claws, can you move at all?"

I try. I try so hard. I manage to straighten my middle finger and point the gesture in the direction I last heard Antony's voice. I'm quite proud of myself, but Eli doesn't see it.

"It's really important that you try to stay awake, you got that? I'm going to get Galen over here to help you. But first, we have to take care of Mackenzie and your cousin."

"Antony's sorted," Noah says. "We'll come back and fill in the grave later. We need to get back to the house."

Eli staggers to his feet and throws me over his shoulder. I can feel his hands on me, but they're like bricks, they don't feel like hands at all. I get a weird, upside-down view of Noah climbing out of the grave, his forearms streaked with blood. He shoves past Eli, raising a rifle in his hands.

I bob along the tunnel, the only sound Noah's heavy footfalls and Eli's ragged breath.

And Gabriel, humming the melody to his song.

We've sharpened our steel. We've made our sacrifices. We're unleashing war.

We emerge into the drawing room. Noah's already at the window, his rifle aimed outside as he peers across the grounds. Eli drops me into Gabriel's arms and picks up his own weapon.

"She can't hardly move or talk," Eli says to Gabe. "I need you to keep her awake."

Gabriel places a kiss on my shuddering eyelids. His rich, pagan scent reaches my nostrils, dragging me back from the brink of sleep. "Stay with me, beautiful. We're here for you. We went to the docks because Noah had this feeling something would go wrong, and we saw Nero's men and figured it was a distraction. We came straight here for you."

He sings in a low voice, his lips pressed against my ear, the same lyrics running on repeat in my head. The song reaches deep into my bones, burrowing into the marrow and forging me anew.

They're here.

After everything I did, they came back for me.

"Mackenzie's outside, opening the gates." Noah frowns at the window, his finger drumming on the trigger. "If it weren't for that fucking garish fountain, I'd have a clear shot."

"Why is she opening the gates?"

"A car's driving up. It's Nero. He's got men behind him. They're surrounding the place. We can't take all of them. Fuck, *fuck.*"

"We could go over the back fence?" Eli suggests. "They don't know the paths through the trees like I do. But we'll have to go fast, or they'll see us."

Noah's mouth twists into a frown. His shoulders hunch. He wants to fight. But even he has to know we can't shoot our way out the front gate. "Claudia wouldn't want us to leave the house. She'd stay and fight."

And you know what? He's right. I've lived and died a thousand times for this house. It's the hill I would die on, the place we'd make our final stand.

But that's the old me.

Now I know that none of this shit matters without love.

They came back for me.

My three princes could have walked away from all of this. They could have left Emerald Beach and the Triumvirate behind and gone on with their lives as they should have been. But they came back for me.

And I'll never, ever let them go again.

I manage to pry my lips open. I push the air from my heavy lungs. I form a single, shaky word. "Run."

Let Mackenzie have the house, the empire. It's only fair. I stole her life – she can have it back, curses and all. The four of us can make something different. Something better.

Gabriel brushes my face with soft kisses. "That's the sweetest word I've ever heard from these perfect lips."

Noah hauls himself away from the window. "They've stopped to talk. No one's seen us. We'd better go now."

Noah darts into the hallway, looking both ways. His weapon swings through the air as he checks for Nero's men. Gabriel jogs after him, cradling me against his body, still singing those beautiful, haunting melodies even though I'm now so fully awake and alive that not even the drugs could pull me back.

My boys are in danger.

Eli takes up the rear, backing down the hallway as he keeps his gun trained on every closed door, every bulletproof window. We pass by the drawing room, the dining room, Howard Malloy's office—

The treasure.

Minus the two cylinders I sent with Livvie for partial payment to make our trap appear real, the documents are still locked in the panic room. My heart aches. Before I know what I'm doing, my fingers reach out for it, grasping thin air.

"It stays here," Eli says firmly, hurt flashing in his eyes. "We came back for *you*, Claws. You're our treasure."

In that flash of a moment, I see my father. He would have wept to see this treasure go to Howard Malloy, who cared not one bit for its true value, who saw only dollar signs when he should have seen knowledge. Eli saw what my father saw, which is why he wanted to give the treasure to a museum. And now, Mackenzie will take the house and find it in the panic room and it'll go back on the black market and the world will never get to learn what those scrolls contain.

Answers. Questions.

The ancient wisdom my father loved.

His legacy.

Gone.

Even as I think the word, I feel lighter, like I'm floating away. *Gone.*

I let go of the hold the treasure has on my heart. *Gone.*

I already had the greatest treasure of all. I had three broken princes.

I have love.

I drop my hand and we pass by the office, creeping toward the ballroom. "The cats," Eli whispers. Noah's face hardens. We don't have time to mess around, but he doesn't stop my Golden Boy as he slips into the ballroom. There's a howl, and a few moments later Eli emerges again holding Casper by the scruff of his neck, and Queen Boudica curled around his shoulders, her claws digging into his skin.

"Hurry." He holds the door open with his foot as Queen Boudica takes a swipe at his face. "They're moving around the side of the house, but this way looks clear."

The boys crouch low and crawl across the ballroom floor so

we can't be seen through the French doors. I lay over Gabriel's shoulders as he wriggles forward on his elbows like a WWI soldier. "The things I do for you, gorgeous," he grunts as he scrapes his skin raw on the hard marble. "You should shoot a video of me looking like a plonker. You could sell it to *The Sun* and make a fortune."

Eli reaches the other side first and lifts the latch, pushing the door open as silently as he can. Noah crawls outside and ducks behind a concrete planter box, his weapon resting over the top. "Go," he hisses. "I'll cover you."

I groan. I can't even support my own body weight. I'm never going to be able to hoist myself up that wall. I'm no Mackenzie – I was a terrible cheerleader for that brief time, and now I'm a half-dead sack of potatoes.

Gabriel hoists me higher up his shoulders, dropping my arms down his front and wrapping his arms around my legs. "I know you can't hold on, but hold on."

We fly out the patio door, Gabriel cursing as he staggers under my weight. Eli jogs ahead of us, his runner's body perfectly at ease as he ducks and dives around the patio furniture. He weaves around the pool, heading for the spot in the wall where the barbed wire is torn away. The same spot he used to sit and watch the house. That's Eli, always watching out for me.

Eli shoves a lawn chair against the wall and staggers backward to take a run-up. He surges forward, arms pumping, golden hair gleaming in the brilliant sunshine—

"I wouldn't move another step if I were you."

Gabriel whips around. My head falls against his shoulder, my view blocked by a curtain of his dark hair. But I don't need to see to know who's stepped off the path that leads around the side of the house and now stands defiantly on my patio.

Nero Lucian.

"Hello, Claudia, Eli." There's a smile in his voice, and I can tell from the way Gabriel stiffens that he has a weapon trained on us. "I heard there was some trouble at the house, so I thought I'd pop over to see how you were faring. Now, step away from the wall and put your weapons down before I'm forced to put a hole in your friend's skull."

48

CLAUDIA

Gabriel's breath comes out in ragged gasps. I assume Nero's talking about shooting *him*, but then he whispers, "Claws, he's got George."

Eli freezes mid-stride. He lowers his gun, pointing it at the ground, but he doesn't let go of it. Gabriel turns, holding me tight even as he waves his hands to show he's unarmed.

I finally see Nero. He stands near the lounger where we played our spin-the-bottle game, holding a struggling George with a beefy arm around her neck. He holds his Glock to her temple.

"I had a very interesting phone call today, inviting me down to the docks to see what my daughter was doing with two Imperators and Howard Malloy's famous treasure," Nero says pleasantly, like we're discussing the weather. "I know we haven't always seen eye-to-eye, Claudia August, but I think our differences can be solved very amicably, as long as you do exactly as I say. First, drop your weapons. Both of you."

"Don't listen to him," George cries. "He's got *mmph mmmmpha.*"

Nero covers her face with his hand.

Eli's mouth sets in a firm line. He tosses his gun away from his body. It sails through the air – the perfect athlete's throw – and lands in the spiky bushes on the other side of the pool. Queen Boudica hisses at Nero, trying to be useful, and Casper cries in fear and cowers behind Eli's legs.

Noah steps out from behind his planter – I see one of Nero's stupid sons at his back, pointing a weapon at his head. The French door is open, and I see another two soldiers running through the house. Noah skids his gun across the concrete, and it comes to a stop beside Nero's foot.

"Very good." Nero's eyes remain fixed on Eli. "Thank you for listening to reason, Elias Hart. A good leader knows when he's outmaneuvered. I must say, I'm impressed at the depth of your loyalty. Not many men would have come back for such a woman after she spurned you. Unfortunately, you fell for the wrong sister. Mackenzie has been a step ahead of you this entire time."

Hearing my sister's name on Nero's lips draws a strangled wail from deep in my chest. How was this going on and I didn't see it? How could I have been so clueless?

I think about that time weeks ago, when Eli told me Mackenzie had been to Vault. We thought it was just her messing with us, but she must've been there to see Nero. The answers were right in front of me, but I've been too distracted, too cocky, to see what I needed to do.

"Mackenzie and Antony came to me some time ago and explained everything," Nero says. "I admit, it was a pretty crazy story, but it became obvious they told me the truth. Initially, I was prepared to string them along until it became convenient for me to expose them to you, but then you became trouble-some. Unpredictable. When you took my girls, I found a grey hair right here." He taps the side of his head. "No matter how often I plucked or dyed them, the greys kept poking through. I wasn't about to let you turn me old before my time. My life will be easier with the new Claudia August."

"What's the point in telling us this if you're going to kill us anyway?" Noah snaps. "Just get it over with."

Maybe don't encourage him, Noah.

"I'm not going to kill all of you." Nero's eyes flick to Eli as he tightens his grip on George. "Become my heir, Eli Hart, and I will spare this girl. I'll even spare the two boys, the Barbarian and the rockstar, if you want them. They are certainly loyal. If you refuse, I have no other option but to kill you all. Claudia must die so her sister can take her place. You have to understand that, but you can avoid more bloodshed if you agree to my terms."

"Your terms?" Eli grabs Queen Boudica from his shoulder and sets her down beside Casper. He takes a casual step toward Nero. He keeps his mouth slack, his voice even. Is he actually considering it, or is he psyching himself up to do something brave and foolish?

I try to yell at Eli to do what Nero asks to save their lives. But all I can get out is a zombified moan.

"It's all very simple. I've arranged everything," Nero says. "Mackenzie will take over the August family, and the marriage between you and my daughter Olivia will go ahead as planned. Mackenzie tells me the two of you used to be friends – for the good of the empire, you will be friends again."

George's eyes are wide and terrified as she watches Eli. Nero jabs the barrel against her cheek. Eli's gaze flicks to something behind Nero's shoulder. I can't see what he's looking at. But I *can* see his features fold into his Sherlock Holmes Orgasm Face – the face he makes when he's figured something out.

Eli Hart has a motherfucking *plan.*

"George," Eli calls. "Gym class."

George's eyes darken with recognition. She clasps her hands

together and drops her body weight, becoming a narrow, dead weight in Nero's arms. He leans forward to attempt to drag her up again, and that's when a dark shape barrels from the garden behind him.

Livvie.

She's covered in bloody scratches and quills from crawling through the succulent garden, but the grim look in her eyes is terrifying. She raises a blood-soaked hand that clutches something round and red. At first, I think it's someone's heart, but then I see its surface is covered in long, terrifying spines. It's a cactus she's ripped from the garden bed.

Nero howls as the cactus collides with the side of his face. Spines stick from his skin, his ear, his eye. He throws his hands up to claw at the plant, dropping his gun behind him. Livvie catches it easily, spins on her heel toward Noah, and takes out her brother with a bullet between the eyes.

Noah wastes no time. He lurches forward and grabs his own weapon, swinging around to shoot Nero's next son as he storms through the ballroom toward us.

Eli strides toward Nero, and Casper skids after him, desperate to get to Livvie. He sinks his teeth into Nero's leg.

"Argh!" Nero stumbles back, shaking his leg to get Casper off. But the tenacious little dude is chomped tight. Queen Boudica mews her encouragement.

Nero's foot clips the edge of the swimming pool. He swings his arms in a vain attempt to keep his balance.

It doesn't work.

He falls.

He hits the netting on top of the pool. The netting that keeps the lion inside.

The netting snaps.

Nero crashes into the pool. Eli runs across the patio, wrapping his arms around George. Gabriel lumbers after them, still holding me over his shoulder. Queen Boudica leaps back onto Eli's shoulder, and Casper jumps into Livvie's open arms. We crowd around the edge of the pool. Gabriel slides me off his back. My legs still won't work, but he and Eli hold me upright.

I want to see this.

Nero lies on his back, his legs flailing uselessly. He still tears at the spines in his face, his cries broken by coughs and gasps as he struggles to regain his breath. In the corner, the lion rears up, stirred by the cries, by the tang of Nero's blood in the air.

"It looks like you've been indulging in too many pasta meals, Imperator," Eli laughs.

"Daughter, help me out of this pool." Nero's face contracts with fury. "I command it."

"Fuck you," Livvie calls down to him cheerfully. "I've spent my entire life trying to impress you, but you never saw me. Well, the great Nero Lucian can fucking see me now. I'll be the last face you see before that lion tears you to pieces."

Nero turns then. He sees the lion at the same time the beast pounces. Nero's screams echo across Harrington Hills. They're beautiful – wild in their torment. They're the screams of a man finally doing what he should have done right from the start – bowing to Claudia fucking August.

I etch every beautiful moment of it to memory. There will be many moments in my undoubtedly short life where I will need to recall this bloodletting, and revel in it, and learn from it.

When it's done, when the screaming stops, when all that's left is a red-lined pool and bloody chunks of meat, I let out a breath. A great weight lifts from my shoulders. Gabriel brushes his lips across mine. The lion drags the stump of a leg across the bottom of the floor, drops down, and gnaws at the end.

"Is it safe to leave this open?" George touches the snapped netting.

"I think so," Livvie says. "He'll be too full now to want to move anywhere for a while. Plus, I don't think he can jump out of this pool. The hole is over the deep end."

"Thaaaa—" I moan.

Livvie frowns at me. "Why's she all limp and zombified?"

"Mackenzie got her with a tranquilizer," Eli says. "She can't speak."

"I prefer her like this." Livvie pats my head affectionately. "And you're welcome, Claws. Always a pleasure to save your ass."

"It *is* a damn fine ass," Gabriel quips.

"I have only one request – when you're feeling better, the first thing you need to do is pull out that damn succulent garden." Livvie winces as she pulls an evil-looking spine from her palm. "When you didn't show up at the docks, I figured you were in trouble. So I pulled everyone back, not a moment too soon, by the way, just as Nero's men showed up. They got the two cylinders you sent, but none of us were there. Then they got a call and packed off to come here, obviously."

Eli gazes at her with awe. "But Nero has the house surrounded. How did you fight your way through—"

Another figure steps out of the garden. Cali. Blood plasters her long hair to her back, and an array of knives on her belt jingle as she strides over to us. Her bloody hands grip a small crate. "Sorry I was late to the docks." She drops the crate at my feet. "I wanted to get you a present."

She kicks the lid off the crate. I peer down at a human head, its mouth open in a silent scream.

Gabriel's father, the Duke of Blackwich.

"Bloody hell." Gabe staggers back. Noah has to grab him before he joins Nero in the swimming pool.

"This fool showed up demanding to see me, wanting to make a deal on Grey Death that would cut you and Nero out." Cali makes a face at the decapitated duke. "I would've killed the girl too, but she's pregnant. I figure we could hold her until she pops, and then we can have our fun with her."

I open my mouth again, trying to push the words in my brain past my unyielding lips, but Cali glares at me. "Save your strength," she says, nodding toward the house, where I'm sure Mackenzie is waiting. "*Et in morte fidelitas.* We're not done with the slaughter yet."

49

CLAUDIA

Gabriel carries me back into the house. We move as a group, clearing each room as we go. A trail of dead bodies paint Cali's path to us, their throats slit, bleeding Rorschach patterns across my marble floors.

We move through the dining room, past the kitchen and the billiards room. Noah turns toward the front of the house – probably to secure the wide-open gates – but I mumble something and he stops in his tracks.

"Offfff…" Damn, why can't my stupid mouth work?

"Claws, what are you saying?" Noah's fingers dig into my shoulders, his dark eyes boring into mine as if he can read my thoughts through my retinas.

Eli frowns. "I think she means Howard Malloy's office."

His eyes meet Noah's in one of their silent conversations. They know the treasure is there. And the treasure is what Mackenzie wanted all along.

Noah steps over a decapitated body and heads down the hall, placing his feet carefully on the carpet so as not to make any sound. Eli and Livvie follow him. Gabriel hangs back, and I don't have any choice but to do what he does. George holds on to Gabriel's sleeve, rubbing her neck, which is covered in bruises from Nero's gross hands.

"Come with me," Cali waves her gun at us. "We'll head around the other side."

We sneak back along the hall and pass through the ballroom again. Malloy Manor is silent – the kind of silence I always tried to fill with Gabriel's music, with my dreams, with my pain. The kind of silence that's been absent for so many months thanks to my family. It feels as though the house itself is trying to restore equilibrium.

Fuck you, house. You belong to me. It's time to rid you of your ghosts, once and for all.

We step out of the French doors and move around the back of the house. Howard's office also contains French doors that open out onto a smaller patio area. The blinds on them are drawn, but I usually keep one of the windows cracked open to let in fresh air. As we near the doors, I hear low voices inside.

Cali gives us a signal to spread out and hide. Gabriel bends down behind a planter, while Livvie takes cover behind a hideous Cupid statue. Cali drops down beside us. The sunlight glitters off her array of knives. I admire a beautiful curved blade as I strain my ears to listen to what's going on inside.

I hear Noah's voice, and then Mackenzie's. She's exactly where I thought she'd be, in Howard's office. I can't hear what they're saying.

The door thumps open and my sister backs outside. A backpack slung over her shoulder clanks with cylinders. Noah and Eli crowd through the door after her, their weapons raised. For some reason, they don't fire.

What are you waiting for? Kill her.

As one, we stand up and surround her, but she doesn't seem

to care. Mackenzie calmly swirls around to face me, holding out her fisted hand.

"I'm surprised by you, sister," she says to me. It's surreal watching her move and talk – my mirror image, and yet everything about her feels *wrong*. "You expended all your resources going after the men, and you let little old me sneak in here and collect my treasure. People are always underestimating us, aren't they? I expected more from you."

Cali flicks off her safety, but Noah makes a hissing noise and she holds fire.

"Good girl," Mackenzie grins, nodding to the device in her fist. "This is a grenade. If I lift my finger off this switch, I go bye-bye, and take all of your boyfriends and the precious treasure with me."

Shit. *Shit.*

Gabriel takes a step back, moving me behind Cali as if her body could somehow shield us from an explosion. Mackenzie hoists the bag higher on her shoulder and nods toward the garden wall. "If you'll all excuse me, I'll be climbing over that fence with my prize. Don't try and stop me. Don't send anyone after me. You have no idea what I'm capable of. You may still have your life and my house, Claudia, but I'd sleep with one eye open if I were you. Now, get out of my way."

She steps toward the wall, her pert lips set in a determined line. As Cali steps back, she brushes against me. My fingers slide over the hilt of her curved knife. Cali starts to jerk away from me, but she sees something in my eyes and snaps her hand back. "Take it," she mouths.

Close your fingers, I command my body. Slowly, achingly slowly, my fingers obey.

Mackenzie waves at us with her free hand as she takes another step toward the wall. The backpack is heavy and ungainly, and she wobbles on spiked pumps as she walks.

I drag the knife from Cali's belt and press my feet into the ground, hoping I can hold myself upright. Every movement is heavy, weighed down by the drug clinging to my veins. I raise the blade and stagger forward just as Mackenzie swings around to face me.

"Oh, no you don't..." With her free hand, Mackenzie reaches for her nearest weapon – the syringe of tranquilizer she shot me with. I know that another dose of that stuff will kill me. Mackenzie thrusts her other hand out, reminding me of the grenade she's just crazy enough to detonate.

Only I'm too slow and too committed to stop. I summon every ounce of strength left inside me, every atom of love and trust for my family, and I wind the blade the way I've seen in Medieval-sword-geek YouTube videos as my body half-barrels, half-topples toward my sister.

The blade connects with Mackenzie's arm just above the elbow. My weight sinks down on top of it, giving the weak swing the power it needs to slice through her flesh and find the bone, which splinters and shatters as my weight bears down on it.

Mackenzie reels in slow motion, her face collapsing in horror. Blood drenches her golden hair, the light catching on the shimmering strands as they're splattered in crimson.

Her arm flies through the air, the finger still pressed firmly on the grenade.

Something else flies through the air and reaches it. George slides across the ground. Her elbows scrape raw as her hands fold around Mackenzie's severed fist. She pushes her fingers down on the trigger.

"Fuck, fuck, fuck." George screws her eyes shut. "Someone take this thing away from me."

Mackenzie turns to stare down at me. Blood rains from the stump on her arm. She doesn't even bother to touch it. She's gone to another place. Her white teeth glitter from within her bloody mask. "Well done, sister. I'd salute you if I could."

The backpack slides off her shoulders. Metal cylinders roll across the patio. Blood spurts from her severed arm, painting Eli as he rushes to George. Mackenzie turns her head to smile at him.

"Sweet little Eli. So earnest. So easily manipulated. Nero was wrong about you – you never had it in you to run his empire. And Gabriel Fallen," she grins at my beautiful, broken angel as he tugs me under the shoulders, dragging me back from her. "I had such plans for you. I was going to enjoy breaking your mind."

She drops to her knees. It's a struggle to keep her head upright.

"And little Noah Marlowe who grew up so good," she smiles. "You hated me so much. You were the only one who saw through the mask I wore. You always see the truth. I'll leave you with this last truth, which I think you know in your heart even if you haven't said it aloud. I knew exactly what they were going to do to your brother. I knew that drug wasn't tested. I knew it was dangerous. I *enjoyed* roping Felix in, knowing I had the power to destroy your family."

An inhuman roar tears from Noah's throat. He lunges forward.

But I get there first.

As my sister pitches forward, I jam the knife into her back, twisting the blade with all my strength. Her blood splatters my face, my eyes. It's in my mouth. I taste my sister's life as it leaves her body.

My sister turns her face to me. She bares her teeth, and her nails dig into my flesh, and she tries to lift the syringe but her body doesn't work any more and I *know* that if things had been different, I could have loved this crazy bitch.

"Goodbye, sister," I say.

Mackenzie Malloy is still holding on, still clinging to her final, bloody battle, as the final spark of life fades from her icicle eyes.

50

GEORGE

I wait in the drawing room while the boys bury Mackenzie and Antony in the grave they dug for Claudia. There isn't much of Nero left, so we leave him in the empty swimming pool and let the lion finish off his meal. He's earned it.

My arm screams from holding down on the trigger. Luckily, Cali knows all about explosives – she was able to take the grenade and disarm it. I'm coated in Mackenzie's blood, which sucks because I liked this shirt. But even when I tug it off and Eli offers me one of his, I don't feel clean.

I doubt I'll feel clean again.

I sit with Claudia, squeezing her hand and talking a mile a minute about nonsense because my job is to keep her awake and I don't fucking know what you're supposed to say to someone who's been shot full of animal tranquilizer and chopped off her own sister's arm and learned that her rapist was her cousin.

She doesn't cry, and I know that's because she has no tears left for Antony. All the hate in the world for what he did to her can't erase the love in her heart.

And it's that love that will make her queen of this city again, that will steer her to make the right decisions for our family, and rule her savage empire with a just and iron fist.

The boys drag Claudia to her bedroom. I send Galen in as soon as he arrives at the house. It feels wrong to be in the room with them, so I pace around the kitchen. Yara bustles around, laying out platters and containers of food from the fridge.

"You should eat." She shoves something lumpy into my hands.

I push the dish away. "You're probably right, but not that. That's Noah's lasagna."

"Lasagna? But it's orange…"

I nod sadly. Yara picks up the dish and dumps it in the trash.

Galen emerges some time later, his face lined in shadows. He slumps at the table and Yara hands him a coffee. I glare at him until he sighs. "She'll live."

"She will?" Relief floods me. I know Galen doesn't like to be optimistic with his diagnosis.

He downs the rest of his cup and holds it out for more. Galen looks tired. He'd known Antony since he was a kid, and Antony had managed to keep all of his betrayals a secret. I worried when I called him that Galen and Tiberius might be in on Antony and Mackenzie's plot, but he knew nothing about it. "I've given her a dose of tolazoline, which reverses the effects of the tranquilizer she was given. She'll be on an IV for at least the next seventy-two hours, and someone will have to stay with her to make sure she's conscious. She was given a hefty dose, and she's not out of the woods – I'll need to monitor her for long-term side effects."

"That's amazing news."

"Is it? Brutus, Constantine, and Nero have all been knocked off in such a short period. A trusted, high-ranking soldier has been unmasked as a traitor. The entire institution of the Triumvirate is in jeopardy." Galen slams the glass down on the table. "This is going to create a power vacuum. We thought we'd seen how bad things can get in recent weeks, but this is nothing. The streets are going to run red with blood. It's already starting."

He shoves his phone toward me, showing me the breaking news. There are articles about a spate of arson attacks, with a picture of a fire engulfing Vault, and a bloody gunfight in a busy street in Tartarus Oaks.

I swallow my coffee. Drink and be merry, for tomorrow we bathe in blood. I think of the phrase Claudia liked to say whenever we had one of our family meals together. I don't know if I'll ever be merry again.

After everything we'd been through, I thought this was over. But it looks like the battle is only just beginning.

***

"Hey," I slide into the chair beside Claudia's bed. "How are you feeling?"

"Like an elephant sat on me and farted." Claws looks up at me with wide, haunted eyes. Galen has tubes sticking out of her and monitors crowded around her bed. She looks so tiny, so vulnerable. She's such a force of nature it's unsettling to see her like this – I forget she's only a couple of inches taller than me.

Eli, Noah, and Gabriel crowd into the window seat, trying to give us a moment to speak in private without leaving her. They should be taking it in shifts so they can sleep, but none of them can bear to be parted from Claudia.

"You look amazing," I smile down at her. "Blood of the guilty looks good on you."

"Don't lie." She cracks a smile, then breaks down coughing. "And don't make me laugh. That's an order. Tell me what's going on out there."

She's talking in full sentences now – that's already a massive improvement. I debate whether I should tell her what Galen showed me. "Not great. News of Nero's death is circulating. There are some people outside who want to speak to Eli."

"Is Livvie still downstairs? Cali?" I nod. She curls her fingers into a weak fist and waves it around. "Get them in here."

Eager to do something to help, I go downstairs and tell Livvie that Claudia wants to see her. Cali went outside for a cigarette, stole Noah's car, and drove off in a cloud of dust.

"Presumably, she's gone to calm things down in Tartarus Oaks," I say as Noah and I stare at the empty spot where his Porsche used to be.

"More likely, she's off to incite violence and mayhem," Noah growls. In the end, he gets on the phone and tells her Claudia might be on her deathbed, which gets Cali to come back. She may have come through for us, but that doesn't mean she won't relish the chance to gloat over Claudia's corpse.

When Cali arrives, Claudia asks me to bring them to her room, and to crack open Howard's oldest bottle of Scotch (that she'd cunningly hidden from Gabriel in the pocket of Mackenzie's headboard) and pour a drink for them all. I hand Livvie and Cali their drinks and drop a box of juice in Claudia's hand. She frowns at me but sticks the straw into her juice and sucks, like a good Imperator.

"Shit, girl, you look terrible." Livvie slides into bed beside Claudia. She doesn't look so hot herself – dressings cover her skin where she was scratched by the spines.

"Want me to finish you off?" Cali slides her knife from her belt. "I'll make it painless. An honorable death."

Claudia smiles at them. "You're both awfully excited to sign my death certificate. I'm not done yet. And neither are you."

Cali flicks her gaze to the window as she sips her drink. Something hardens in her gaze. "I don't have enough knives to put down the chaos out there. My days are numbered as Imperator. I just hope I take as many bastards down with me as possible. Would that Constantine's soldiers had but one neck."

"I've spent too long trying to wrestle more power from Nero and Constantine," Claudia glances at each woman in turn. "I thought the only way to be safe was to own this city. But I learned the opposite is true. You're never truly safe, and if you can't trust anyone, then all the power in the world means jack shit. One person shouldn't have absolute power in Emerald Beach. I'm no better at wielding it than Nero. I think what our world needs is to cleanse this city of the old ways and build something fresh – a new Triumvirate. One made up of the three of us."

Cali spits Scotch all over her leather skirt.

"But Nero'd already announced his successor—" Livvie starts. Claws cuts her off with a raised hand.

"Eli," she calls. He looks up from his seat in the window, between Noah and Gabe. "Do you want to run Nero's empire?"

"Fuck no."

Claudia turns back to Cali. "There's your answer. I mean, look at that Golden Boy. Do you think he's got the cajones to stop what's happening on the streets? No, he doesn't. None of them do. It *has* to be us. We link arms, we show solidarity, and we march out there and end this war with as little bloodshed as possible."

"What makes this Triumvirate any better than the last one?" Livvie asks. "We might shake hands now, but Cali will be trying to slit your throat in a month's time."

Cali twirls her knife in her hand and catches it. She doesn't argue.

"What's different is that we get to decide the rules. No more of this pureblood nonsense. We can nominate the best successors for our jobs. And maybe instead of trying to get the best of each other, we work together. Maybe we strike deals that benefit all of our families, instead of trying to plunder from each other." Claudia reaches across the bed and picks up one of the cylinders. "And maybe we start by sharing this."

She tosses the cylinder to Livvie, who uncaps it and slides out a scroll. "What are we supposed to do with this?"

"Whatever the fuck we want," Claudia grins.

Cali flicks a knife from her sleeve. She slices across her hand. The blood drips onto the sheets as she hands the knife to Livvie, who winces as she makes a tiny cut in her palm. Claudia takes the knife and cuts herself. She holds out her hand. "Nam si violandum est jus, regnandi gratia violandum est: aliis rebus pictatem colas. In the words of Julius Caesar, If you must break the law, do it only to seize power. In all other cases, observe it."

"Can I break necks to seize power?" Cali grins.

"Why not? We make the laws now," Livvie says.

The three women shake.

My chest swells. I feel like I've just witnessed history remake itself. Emerald Beach has its new rulers.

They will not be kind.

They will not be gentle.

They will grant no mercy.

But they will be *brilliant*.

I'm DOWNSTAIRS in Howard Malloy's office, using his big desk to put the finishing touches on the inventory of the document cache, when Gabriel and Claudia walk in. I jerk from Claudia's seat, but she waves me back down and has Gabriel ease her into the sofa under the window. She leans against his shoulder, breathing hard.

"I thought I might come down and do some work," she offers a weak smile. "Now that I'm here, all I want to do is go to sleep."

"There's not much work left to do." I point to the chair in the corner, where Eli is slumped, sound asleep. "He spent all night working on the shipping timetables. And I've made a complete inventory of every scroll, including the title if I know it, the language, length, and the state of preservation. Some of them I can't name without a Latin or Greek scholar, and there are some Egyptian texts that are a complete mystery. But now we at least know what we have."

Claudia's eyes are ringed with red. Her eyelashes flutter as I read down the list. It's a treasure trove of forgotten texts, so much lost wisdom just waiting to be uncovered.

"Thank you for doing this. You're amazing, George. You'll be an incredible asset to the Triumvirate—"

"See, here's the thing." I pull a skinny white envelope from my pocket and set it on the desk. Claudia glares at it like it might explode.

"What's that?"

"My acceptance letter from Blackfriars University."

I expect the words to taste like soot, to feel like a betrayal of my friend. But they feel good. They feel *perfect*.

Gabriel was right. The four of them were in this one hundred percent. There is no going back from the August family, not while they have to clean up Emerald Beach. They're happy to throw their lot in with their beautiful, brilliant crime boss. She gives them everything they never knew they needed – Noah has an outlet for his rage, Eli has the resources and freedom he needs to make a difference in the world, and Gabe... Gabe has someone who loves him unconditionally.

But even though I love them all as my family, this isn't the life I'm meant to have.

It all became clear to me when I was lying on the patio, hands clamped on the grenade's trigger. I don't want to take back anything that happened over the past year. I don't regret passing my fork under the bathroom stall to help another lonely soul. I'll never forget what Claws did for me that night in the arena. The sweet sound of Alec LeMarque's screams will always be with me when I need strength.

But I can't be part of rebuilding her savage empire.

I'm done.

Claudia leans forward, those ice eyes boring into me. She lurches out of her chair and barrels toward me. For a flicker of a moment, I'm back in seventh grade and Mackenzie Malloy is bearing down on me with some fresh cruelty. I flinch away from her. But she wraps her arms around me and hugs me fiercely.

"You're going to be amazing, George Fisher," Claudia whispers in my ear.

"And you're already amazing, *Imperator.*"

"Don't you forget it." She pats my arm. "Now come help me. I saw Noah heading for the kitchen."

CLAUDIA

THREE YEARS LATER

"I'd like to propose a toast," Livvie holds her glass of pink champagne high. Her nails tap the stem – pink sparkles that catch the light. "To us. The most badass bitches in Emerald Beach. And to Claudia, for bringing us together."

"And to Livvie, for your well-placed aim of a cactus." I lift my own glass. "And to Cali, for not skewering me with your blade when you had the chance."

"What is this shit?" Cali glares at her drink like it's about to launch itself from the glass and choke her to death. "Can't we drink Cutty Sark like normal gangsters?"

"We're anything but normal," Livvie shoots back. "Try it. It's delicious. It's the first batch from my new winery."

Ever since she cracked open Nero's books and saw how much the halt on the skin trade hurt his bottom line, Livvie has been proving herself a savvy businesswoman. She's reinvented the Lucian brand as a top-tier wine merchant, buying up failing wineries and distilleries across California and turning them around. She's practically legitimate and has even been profiled in *Harper's Bazaar*. Just don't look too closely at her acquisition methods or the overseas markets where she makes her biggest profits, courtesy of my contacts.

Cali, in contrast, has doubled down on what Dio does best – killing people as brutally and efficiently as possible. She's rebuilt and expanded Constantine's training school, luring the top martial artists to the city with impossible salaries to train her soldiers. She's now recruiting assassins from all over the world and taking contracts from Italian crime families and foreign governments. She just got back from a trip to Monaco to dispose of a troublesome prince – she's quite proud of that one. She even brought the prince's head back on ice to mount above her fireplace.

But Cali isn't all brutality and bloodlust. She's full of surprises. When Cleo gave birth to her baby – a son – Cali and I spent a delightful three days together torturing her before we finally killed her. Call it female bonding, Tartarus Oaks style. We were going to put the boy up for adoption, but then Cali announced she was keeping him, and I'm not going to argue with her. That girl is *terrifying*. She's named him Gaius, and she's counting the days until he's old enough to grip a knife. Blood-thirsty assassins make the best moms.

As for me, I've been strengthening our alliances in foreign markets and digging up the secrets we use as currency to smooth the path of our business endeavors. I've learned that a smile and a toss of golden hair can get me quite far with grizzled old crime lords and corrupt officials. I have Mackenzie Malloy to thank for that little life lesson.

I've also been putting plans in place to donate the documents to the city. We're working out the details of a state-of-the-art museum to house them, designed by my girl Yara, of course. They'll be a gift from three prominent citizens to a city we love.

We make quite a team – Cali, Livvie, and me.

The new Triumvirate.

Today marks three years to the day that we forged our alliance. It's been tougher than we expected to clean up the streets. Who would've thought a bunch of tough criminal soldiers would struggle to accept three powerful, accomplished women as their leaders? We had to pull out the brazen bull a few times, but they got the message.

The Triumvirate has had a feminist makeover, and they either get with the program or are boiled alive inside the belly of a bronze bull. Dealer's choice.

We've kept some of the old traditions – Saturnalia and Lupercalia are too much fun, and we like to manage our own separate corners of the business. But we formed a new joint company that shares all profits equally, and we crafted a new list of rules. Number one on that list is doing away with the need for blood ties – you no longer have to be related to one of the families to gain power in our empire. We want to promote our best people based on what they achieve, not who their parents chose to fuck.

Don't get me wrong – we're still ruthless bitches. Just last week I had a soldier beheaded in the arena for double-crossing me. But we have our code and our honor, and the Triumvirate's business has never been better.

I'd like to think Daddy would be proud.

We finish our drinks, go over a bit of business, and make some final arrangements for tonight's party. We're hosting a celebration at Colosseum – an anniversary party of sorts. Anyone who's anyone in the crooked underbelly of Tartarus Oaks will be there. Noah's gone all out with the entertainment – everyone's favorite fighters will make an appearance, including the return of the Barbarian. I've heard he's even flooding the arena with water to stage a pirate battle.

The Imperators leave, propping the door open so Queen Boudica can slink inside. She settles herself into my lap, purring like the buzzsaw Cali used to chop up the Monaco prince. I stroke my kitty's back, my gaze turning to the French doors. Outside, Eli's talking to a willowy dude with a long beard and leather sandals, who's brought over two pythons he rescued from a roadside zoo.

I watch Eli's face wrinkle in concentration. The Sherlock-Holmes Orgasm Face strikes again. He bends down to look in the cages, then pulls out his phone and flips through something. I'm about to call out to him when—

—two hands clamp over my eyes. "Guess who?" a deep voice rumbles against my ear.

"Gabe?" I whirl around. He plops down beside me and settles my foot in his lap, sliding off my shoe to massage my feet. "You should know better than to scare me like that. I was about to go for my knife."

"Please. As if you can reach your knife in your current state." Gabe smirks. I whack him with a cushion, but I'm too happy to punish him. He's been doing a string of shows with Broken Muse on the West Coast for the last two months. I haven't been able to get away from the empire to see him play. I've watched a few shows via live feed, but it's not the same. I've missed him like hell, and now he's here – my fallen angel came back to me.

Gabriel kisses me, and all the stars fall to earth. No matter how many years pass and how many times his sinful lips touch mine, I still can't believe this beautiful man chose me.

I pull back for some air, tucking a strand of his dark hair behind his ear. "I thought you weren't supposed to get home until tomorrow?"

"Our last show got canceled. The headlining band – this bloody excellent metal group from Europe called Blood Lust –

had a personal emergency. I think they ran out of groupies willing to let them drink their blood."

"You're ridiculous." I whack him again. "They're not vampires."

"Want a bet?" Gabriel lets go of my foot to tick off his fingers. "They're as pale as death. I never see them outside of their bus during the day time. I also never see them eat. They only ever drink red wine. They don't have reflections—"

"You're making that up."

"Maybe," Gabe grins. "*But* they do have this strange, hypnotic power over the audience. When they play, they send everyone in the room into this wild frenzy. It's delicious. Not even my rakishly good looks can compete with vampire magic."

He tells me more about the tour as his skilled fingers work the knots out of my feet. I lay back in the plumped cushions and think about how lucky we are. I know it's too much to believe I'll be able to take things easy as the ruler of a criminal empire, but so far, everything is working out okay.

Tiberius went straight, if you can believe it. He and Ms. Drysdale moved to Scotland so Angel could attend a special school. They both teach at that school now and walk the stark, beautiful countryside on the weekends. Tiberius sends me selfies every now and then. I've never seen that monster look so happy.

Malloy Manor is ours, free and clear. After my soldier Selene at City Hall went through my DNA test and paperwork and determined I am indeed Howard Malloy's daughter, his ill-gotten fortune was transferred to my coffers.

I gave all the money to Eli.

And Eli took that money and made something wonderful.

I offered to kill Walter Hart, but Eli didn't want that. Instead, he made his dad Cali's bitch – after all, bodies still need to be disposed of – and forced him to hand over the Everlasting Hart ranch. Eli transformed it from a dilapidated shithole into a first-class wildlife sanctuary. He now spends his days traveling up and down the country, buying mistreated animals from sideshows and private zoos and giving them a second chance at life. Some he's able to rehabilitate and reintroduce to the wild, but those that can't will live out their days in luxury at the ranch. The lion has a prairie to wander, the monkeys an enormous enclosure. Even Casper is there, delighting visitors with his antics.

Not even Malloy Manor has escaped Eli's ambition. We renovated the wing of guest bedrooms into a luxurious cat palace. Now, women who are fleeing domestic violence and other bad situations in Emerald Beach can house their cats indefinitely while we help them get to safety, and we also take in strays and abandoned animals and try to find them loving new homes. Eli and Yara run this part of the business. Most of the time, I think Eli's happier pretending that the other side – the drug shipments, the nefarious deals Noah and I make on the daily – doesn't exist.

Not me, though. I don't want to deny who I am. I may not be related by blood, but I *am* Julian August's daughter. I have his ruthless streak, his eye for business, his love of possessing beautiful, ancient, rare things. And I have Noah at my side, my loyal soldier. My tribune. I don't need Eli to be someone he's not.

"Claws." Eli taps on the window. "I need a hand with these cages."

"Sorry. Cat gravity." I point to the two cats asleep in my lap.

Eli pokes his head through the doorway. "And what about you, Gabe? Your arms look like they work perfectly fine."

"I'm doing important queen maintenance," Gabriel murmurs as he slides his hand over my swollen foot, digging the pads of his fingers in just the right places to make me moan.

"I'll help." Yara appears at the corner of the garden and heads after Eli.

Yara's been amazing. I offered her all the money and resources she needed to start a new life anywhere in the world, but she chose to stay here with me. She acts as my personal secretary, managing my spreadsheets and doing all the boring admin stuff I hate. She doesn't like to get blood on her hands, but she's a ruthless negotiator and a steady presence in any room.

Gabe casts his eyes to the champagne sitting in the ice bucket on top of the bar, which is now covered in a layer of dust since I can't drink anymore. Gabe's not drinking, either. He went into rehab as soon as we took back the city, conveniently missing all the hard work we had to put in to return peace to the streets and get the animal shelter running. It's been a long road – Gabe's had to dig deep into his past to deal with the issues that made him want to hide behind alcohol. He was terrified of therapy, thought that if he spilled his darkest feelings to a shrink, he'd have nothing left for his music. Instead, the opposite has been true. Now that he's back and clean, he's writing new music every day and his new songs... they're amazing. They tell the rise and fall and rise of an empire in notes of pure pain and beauty. He's captured everything perfectly, just as I knew he would.

But no new tours for a while yet. Gabriel Fallen is about to have his hands full as a new daddy. All the guys are.

Yup. I'm pregnant. I'm nearly four months along now with a beautiful baby girl. Gabe supplied the bonkjuice that gave her life, but she's all of ours. Our miracle. Our legacy.

Many of my soldiers already know, but we're announcing it to our family tonight at Colosseum. It'll be pretty tough to hide now   in the last two weeks, I've ballooned to three times my normal size. I feel like an elephant. I can't sleep. That tranquilizer Mackenzie shot me with is starting to sound like a brilliant idea.

Queen Boudica stretches her paw across my bulging stomach, her eyes meeting mine. *I'll protect this baby with my life,* she seems to say. *Just like you protected me.*

Everything comes full circle. This baby is our future, our hope. Instead of cruelty, she'll know love and kindness. Instead of being so completely alone, she'll have an amazing family to teach her everything.

I'm still afraid about bringing a daughter into our world. Our daughter will be baptized in bloodshed, and one day she'll have to choose between our kingdom and her own path. I don't know what the future will bring for me or for her.

I cast my die in with this lot. I may have lost the only family I've ever known when I found out about Antony's betrayal, but I've gained so much more.

I raise my glass of alcohol-free pink champagne and toast Gabriel with a wink. "Pour yourself a glass of this, Fallen. Drink and be merry, for tomorrow we bathe in blood."

THE END

Claudia's empire may be secure (for now) but George is about to bring down a world of trouble on their heads. Find out more in book 1 of her series, Pretty Girls Make Graves.

https://books2read.com/prettygirlsmakegraves

Don't go outside on Devil's Night.

I'm always the good girl. I never stand out. I follow the rules.

At Blackfriars University, there's one whispered rule: Stay inside the night before Halloween. Hide under your blankets and hope the Orpheus Society isn't the monster outside your window.

If they get you, you won't just be humiliated. They'll put you six feet under.

But I've screwed up.

I found bones in a shallow grave. Another good girl, just like me.

Now I'll do whatever it takes to get to the truth.
I'll catch the eye of the cruel aristocrat with a haunted gaze.
I'll tempt the dark priest with forbidden tastes.
I'll be their shameful little secret. Their plaything. Their sacrifice.

Maybe I don't want to be a good girl anymore.

Maybe it's time to break all the rules.

Pretty Girls Make Graves is a dark romantic suspense and part one of the Dark Academia duet. If you enjoy tales of clever heroines, ancient rites, secret societies, cruel princes and wicked priests, dusty libraries and decadent parties, twisted relationships and buried secrets, then prepare to enter the halls of Blackfriars University. You may never return.

READ NOW: https://books2read.com/prettygirlsmakegraves

Turn the page for a sizzling excerpt.

Get your free copy of *Cabinet of Curiosities*, a Steffanie Holmes compendium of short stories and bonus scenes. To get this collection, all you need to do is sign up for updates with the Steffanie Holmes newsletter.

http://www.steffanieholmes.com/newsletter

FROM THE AUTHOR

Claudia came to me in a dream. She is... not like any other heroine I've ever written. Even though I've sworn up-and-down that I'd never write contemporary romance (imagine, romance *without* vampires? What even *is* that?) she wouldn't shut up until I told her story.

I wrote her for *you*. Because the world is scary out there – it feels like we're on the cusp of empires rising and falling. I know when I'm scared I so often find myself in the pages of a book. Sometimes I even borrow a little strength and a little audacity from the characters I love. I think we all need as much of those as we can get right now.

I'm in awe of the incredible health workers and other essential staff who've kept the world running and done their best in an impossible situation. If you're one of them, there are no words I can say to thank you enough for your contribution.

I'm just a teller of stories. I can't save lives or keep food on tables or make sure businesses stay afloat. But if I can give you a new world and a new life and a strange mystery to lose yourself in for a few hours, then that's some small way I can help you survive this wild and crazy world.

Writing *My Savage Empire* has been a joy and a pleasure, but as always, it takes a village to bring a book to life. I'd like to thank my cantankerous drummer husband, for reading this manuscript and giving me so many ideas to make it better. And for being my lighthouse. And for making me so many bacon butties and keeping the house stocked with chocolate during lockdown.

To Kit, Bri, Elaina, Katya, and the Noodles, for all the writerly encouragement and advice. To Meg and Eveis for the epically helpful editing job, and to CJ for the stunning covers. To Sam and Iris, for the daily Facebook shenanigans that help keep me sane while I spend my days stuck at home covered in cats.

To you, the reader, for going on this journey with me, even though it's led to some dark places. If you're enjoying *Stonehurst Prep* and want to read more from this world, Claws' BFF George has her own series, set at the prestigious and mysterious Blackfriars University. Start *Pretty Girls Make Graves* here: http://books2read.com/prettygirlsmakegraves.

You might also dig my dark reverse harem bully romance series, *Kings of Miskatonic Prep*. HP Lovecraft meets *Cruel Intentions* in this dark paranormal reverse harem bully romance that's definitely not for the faint of heart. Hazel is the most badass FMC I've ever written, and I think you'll love meeting her. Read Shunned now: http://books2read.com/shunned.

Every week I send out a newsletter to fans – it features a spooky story about a real-life haunting or strange criminal case that has inspired one of my books, as well as news about upcoming releases and a free book of bonus scenes called *Cabinet of Curiosities*. To get on the mailing list all you gotta do is head to my website: http://www.steffanieholmes.com/newsletter

I'm so happy you enjoyed this story! I'd love it if you wanted to leave a review on Amazon or Goodreads. It will help other readers to find their next book boyfriend (not Gabriel, though – he's mine).

Alea iacta est. The die is cast.

I love you heaps! Until next time.

Steff

Nothing shatters the magic of my first day at Blackfriars University quite like a naked priest swimming the backstroke in the water fountain.

Until the moment I come face-to-dong with Father Sebastian Pearce, I've been enraptured by this place. Blackfriars is everything my life in Emerald Beach, California was not – I love the gothic arches and ancient, cobbled pathways, the hidden nooks and lichen-covered stone fountains. I love the storybook British names and customs for everything. I love lining up with the other students in our black subfusc robes for the matriculation ceremony, and looking up at the blackened church spires piercing the grey sky.

And turrets. I *adore* the metric fuckton of turrets (a 'fuckton' is the only thing I can correctly measure using the metric system, but I'm learning) at my new university.

Blackfriars is all my Hogwarts dreams come true.

At least, that's how I felt this morning. But then I tripped on the uneven cobbles and tore my skirt, and *then* squirmed for two hours on a hard church pew while a dusky-haired priest performed the High Mass. In Latin. My initial enchantment gave way to boredom and a numb ass. I've never attended a High Mass before (or a Low Mass or even a Medium Mass). My sole exposure to the Catholic Church has been watching scenes from my father's horror movies, and they usually end in someone summoning a demon and getting their brains sucked out through their nostrils.

A little nostril-sucking might've livened up this ceremony.

Blackfriars University is very *into* religion. The campus used to be a Benedictine monastery before King Henry VIII went on a bit of a beheading spree. There's a whole story about the so-called 'Black Monk,' Benet of Blackfriars, who made a last stand against the king before the monastery was closed. Since it reopened as a school, Blackfriars has stubbornly held onto their Catholic heritage despite numerous attempts to convert it to Church of England. As far as I can tell, there's not much difference between the two churches except that a CofE matriculation ceremony would be five minutes long instead of three hours, and in English. And my father never made a movie about it – not demonic enough for his tastes.

Not that I spent my summer memorizing the school's history. Not at all.

Because that would be a dorky thing to do. The sort of thing the *old* George would do – the George who got straight A's and whose only friends were dead punk rock musicians. The George who ate her school lunches in a bathroom stall and never said two words to anyone in case they landed her with her head down a toilet.

And I'm not that George anymore.

New school, new country, new me.

I can be whoever I want to be. And if the students at Blackfriars – the most insane, over-the-top liberal arts school in the world – can't accept me, then I'll have a blast anyway.

That sounds depressing. I swear it's not. I'm so excited about this year.

All around me, students whisper to each other or stare at their phones as the priest drones on. I try to talk to the girl next to me, but she wrinkles her perfect nose as if I smell bad. I probably do smell bad. I arrived by train from London with only minutes to spare before the ceremony, so I haven't even been able to take my bag to my room before they called us to enter the church. So I stare straight ahead with my suitcase wedged awkwardly on my lap and think about all the classes I'm excited about this semester.

Not semester. *Term*. I'm learning the lingo.

We're finally dismissed, and I discreetly massage my numb ass as we shuffle outside. The main quad – Martyrs' Quad – fills with students, leaning against the historical fountain and snapping selfies with their friends. How do they have friends already? We only just got here. The porter barks at one group to get off the immaculate green lawn, but they ignore him.

"I don't know who he thinks he is, trying to tell Orpheans what to do," a girl scoffs to her friend as she walks past. They throw the lawn-ruining students an admiring look.

Now I'm curious. *Orpheans?*

There are ten of them – five guys, five girls – standing around on the grass and completely ignoring the porter as he hops about angrily and jabs his finger at the STAY OFF THE GRASS sign. I've never seen anything like them before, and I come from Emerald Beach, so I have seen a *lot*.

They look like characters from a story – some twisted gothic tale of crumbling estates and rich widows filled with longing. The girls wear floaty, calf-length dresses and blazers with the sleeves rolled up. The boys' trousers have pleats that could draw blood. Their tailored jackets and wing-tipped shoes drip with a certain kind of wealth and power. In Emerald Beach, if you're wealthy, you shove that wealth in everyone's face. But this lot look like they couldn't care less about fashion. They're pale with flushed cheeks, like they've just come from tending the horses or whipping a recalcitrant servant.

Two of the guys in particular stand out. One leans against the fountain, his arm slung casually around the waist of the prettiest girl. Angular and elegant, he has one of those petulant mouths with a full lower lip that my friend Claws would say is begging to be bitten, and eyes the deep blue of the ocean at midnight. The other, despite his starched shirt and black tie, has a kind of messy, sloppy look, with a mop of golden hair falling over one eye and a smile that might be called cheeky if not for the cruel twist at the edges. He takes a long drag from a cigarette and – with carbon grey eyes trained on the porter – grinds the butt into the grass with his heel.

The girl who called them Orpheans catches me staring, and breaks off into giggles.

I hurry away. The hope that's fluttered in my chest since graduation takes a beating. *It's going to be exactly the same as high school.* If people like that are the norm, I'm out of my league. Everyone here already knows each other. They met at their fancy boarding schools or yacht races or private clubs or wherever the fuck rich people make friends.

I'm on the outside.

Again.

But you know what? That's fine with me.

I squeeze the handle of my suitcase as I think about my best friend, Claws. I need to channel her attitude. She wouldn't give a fuck if no one liked her – but then, she runs a crime empire so she's probably not the best example.

It took me until senior year to make a single friend, and I left them all to come here. I left my mom, my house, the Brawley theatre – all the places in the city that remind me of Dad. And I deluded myself into believing things would be different. Despite its Catholic leanings, Blackfriars is supposed to be a bohemian, artsy-fartsy college. There's got to be at least a few kids here like me – the lonely, weird outsiders...

Yes, I know you want to hear about the naked priest. I promise I'm getting there. Existential crisis stuff first, okay?

I can't bear another minute in the quad, being the weird American who's laughed at by strangers. I know it's only in my imagination because I'm tired and raw, but it's ruining my new school buzz. So I do something I've never done in my life. I slip away into the shadows, and bunk off the orientation seminar.

Claws will be so proud.

As the students are being herded into the dining hall, I dart along a covered walkway, peering into the open doors of small lecture theatres and classrooms beneath gothic stone arches. Everything is so old and grand and *cool*. I wonder what kind of ghosts linger in these walls. My bright-red New Rocks make a clomping sound on the cobbles.

I pass under an archway and along a rose-lined walk into St. Benedict's Quad, thinking I'll head toward the college meadow for some fresh air, when I spy a narrow gap in the towering hedge. I step closer. An iron gate hangs open an inch, revealing a secret garden.

A covered walkway of gothic arches frames the hidden court-yard, which bursts with tall herb bushes and scraggly orange trees that obscure my view across to the other side. It's so different from the neat roses and manicured lawns of the rest of Blackfriars. There's something forbidden about it, something wild. Somewhere deeper in the garden, I hear water trickling and splashing.

I can't contain my curiosity. I push the gate open and step through.

The path steps down as I enter the courtyard. I breathe in

the fresh, herby air, and feel some of the tension slip from my shoulders as I push through the overgrown—

Oh.

Oh.

My hand flies to my mouth.

A man floats on his back in the central fountain, spinning in lazy circles as the spray from the tip of Orpheus' lyre cascades off his chiseled body. And what a man he is – probably in his early thirties, and built like a Greek god. Everything about him *glistens*, like his skin is dipped in gold. His smoky black eyes contemplate the heavens, and his strong jaw is relaxed, his lips falling open in silent reverie. A smattering of ink along his abdomen draws my eye down to that lickable V of muscle, and below that, to a package that any god would envy. Heat flares in my cheeks.

He's so perfect it makes my throat hurt.

Beside the pool is a pile of clothes – a black shirt folded neatly on top of what looks like designer jeans and some chunky boots, and a white collar nestled on top.

It doesn't take a true-crime podcaster to figure out this guy is a priest.

A very naked, *very hot*, priest.

Turn away. Just turn away and run back the way you came and he won't even see you—

Too late. The man lifts his head, and his anthracite eyes widen as they see me. I expect him to flail about for something to cover himself, but he seems to sense it's pointless. I've already got an eyeful of the goods.

Instead, the corner of his mouth quirks up into an amused smile.

"Hello, there," he says.

It's the most anyone has spoken to me all day. His voice is

rich and deep and friendly. It crackles at the edges, like a blazing, cozy fire. And that British accent...mmm...

Pity I'm about to be struck by a lightning bolt for having such thoughts about a priest.

I can't speak. My face burns with fifty shades of get-me-the-fuck out of here.

The priest flips over and dog-paddles to the side, resting his hands on the edge. "I don't suppose," his voice is so perfectly British, all clipped and fictive and wonderful, "you'd mind *terribly* passing me that towel."

I nod, still unable to form words. I pick up the towel from the corner and hold it in front of me like a medieval shield protecting me from the power of his peen. The priest pulls himself out of the water, swinging his legs as he dries his face. *Holy father.* Droplets roll down the Celtic cross tattoo over his heart, and my throat dries as I imagine licking them off.

Which is insane. That's not a George thought at all. That's something Claws with her three besotted boyfriends would say.

This must be what jet lag does to my brain.

"You came up today? You're supposed to be at the orientation," he says without shame as he rubs the towel in his hair. He has great hair, I notice. It's longer than I'd expect from a priest, down around his shoulders, with a little curl. It's dark like his eyes, and hopelessly disheveled. I'm a sucker for long hair.

And British accents. And sexy tattooed priests swimming in fountains.

I'm going to hell.

"I...I..."

He slides a pair of boxers over his hips. I'm transfixed by the material of his trousers as he pulls them on.

"The pool in the rec center is closed for renovations at the moment," he says, which I think is supposed to be an explanation.

I nod, as if it's totally normal to swim in a fountain instead of, say, going for a run instead. Maybe it is normal in England. I don't know.

"I'm Sebastian Pearce." He buttons his shirt, hiding away that beautiful ink. "I'm one of the dons here at Blackfriars. I believe you've had the pleasure of meeting my colleague, Father Duncan, at matriculation."

I manage to choke out some words. "Was he the old man chanting the lyrics to a Cradle of Filth song?"

He laughs at this, his whole face crumpling with joy. "We do love dead languages around here. And religion. There's a persistent rumor that a student will receive automatic graduation if they can recite the gospels from memory in their original Greek. And you are?"

"An atheist."

"Ah, excellent. I do love a challenge." He cracks his knuckles. "But I was actually asking about your name."

"Oh, it's Georgina. Georgina Fisher. But everyone calls me George."

"George. I love it. A nice British name. Well, George Fisher, if you ever need to talk about this harrowing experience, you know where to find me." He grins as he slides his feet into a pair of immaculately-shined dress shoes. "I mean, I'll be at the church, not usually in this fountain."

I swallow. "Right."

Silence stretches between us. He seems utterly comfortable with it, but I'm desperate to fill it so I don't keep picturing his body. "What do you teach?"

"History of Religion." He fixes the collar around his neck. With his sleeves rolled up to the elbows, I notice the tattoos on his arm depict figures from Greek mythology – Theseus slaying the minotaur, Cassandra witnessing the fall of Troy. He sees me staring at his ink. "Not just Catholicism. All the religions, new and old and everything in between. I'm only picky when it comes to the salvation of my own soul. Are you lost? Would you like me to walk you to the dining hall?"

I shake my head. "Not lost. I...I guess I was feeling a bit overwhelmed."

"It's hard being away from home, especially if your home is across the ocean." He makes it sound as though I've come on some epic quest, like Odysseus making his way over the seas from Troy, instead of drowning my nerves in daiquiris on the ten-hour flight. "I'll tell you what, I'll show you to your room and then you'll have a bit of time to get used to the campus at your own pace."

Sebastian walks me back through the secret garden to St. Benedict's Quad. It's no longer empty of people, and it takes us forever to navigate to the other side because he's stopped every few feet by senior students or fellow dons. Sebastian has a heart-melting smile and friendly words for every one of them.

We finally reach the opposite corner and head through another gothic archway into a quieter quad with another immaculate lawn and an ancient-looking stone well in the center. "This is Cavendish Quad. There are four staircases, and each one has its own scout, who cleans the rooms and looks after the students."

In the far corner of the quad, Sebastian introduces me to a stony-faced woman named Sally, who is my scout. "You're supposed to be at orientation," she snaps at me.

"George's train arrived late. She'll catch up on the details from the other students. You know what those lectures are like – most of it is self-explanatory. Dining hall hours, library usage, instructions for the laundry machines, how not to get recruited by a secret society with designs on taking over the world." Sebastian asks Sally about her new border collie puppy, and the woman's sour expression dissolves into smiles. Sebastian Pearce has that effect on people. I drag my suitcase up the wheelchair ramp, my cheeks flushing with heat. I can feel strands of hair whipping around my face and yup, my pits could knock out an elephant.

He's a priest. It doesn't matter what you look like or smell like because he's not interested in anything except your immortal soul.

"Goodbye, George Fisher." Sebastian's eyes twinkle as he takes my hand in his. My fingers tingle with the warmth of his touch. "I hope Blackfriars is everything you wished for."

Me too.

I stand awkwardly at the foot of the staircase, waiting for the scout to return from her office to give me the key to my room. As I watch Sebastian's perfect ass stroll back across the quad, I'm seized by an overwhelming and uncharacteristic urge to be reckless.

Before I have time to think about what I'm doing, I pull out my phone and navigate to the Blackfriars app, which lists my class schedule. I slide my finger across the screen, deleting 'Gender and Social History of Popular Music' from my schedule. I click another button to enroll in the 'History of Religion.'

Yup. Booked my one-way ticket to eternal damnation.

Read Pretty Girls Make Graves
http://books2read.com/prettygirlsmakegraves

DON'T GO OUTSIDE ON DEVIL'S NIGHT

I'm always the good girl. I never stand out. I follow the rules.

At Blackfriars University, there's one whispered rule: Stay inside the night before Halloween. Hide under your blankets and hope the Orpheus Society isn't the monster outside your window.
If they get you, you won't just be humiliated. They'll put you six feet under.

But I've screwed up.

I found bones in a shallow grave. Another good girl, just like me.

Now I'll do whatever it takes to get to the truth.

I'll catch the eye of the cruel aristocrat with a haunted gaze.
I'll tempt the dark priest with forbidden tastes.
I'll be their shameful little secret. Their plaything. Their *sacrifice*.

Maybe I don't want to be a good girl anymore.

Maybe it's time to break *all* the rules.

Pretty Girls Make Graves is a dark romantic suspense and part one of the Dark Academia duet. If you enjoy tales of clever heroines, ancient rites, secret societies, cruel princes and wicked priests, dusty libraries and decadent parties, twisted relationships and buried secrets, then prepare to enter the halls of Blackfriars University. You may never return.

START READING NOW
http://books2read.com/prettygirlsmakegraves

OTHER BOOKS BY STEFFANIE HOLMES

Nevermore Bookshop Mysteries

A Dead and Stormy Night

Of Mice and Murder

Pride and Premeditation

How Heathcliff Stole Christmas

Memoirs of a Garroter

Prose and Cons

A Novel Way to Die

Much Ado About Murder

Kings of Miskatonic Prep

Shunned

Initiated

Possessed

Ignited

Stonehurst Prep

My Stolen Life

My Secret Heart

My Broken Crown

My Savage Kingdom

Dark Academia

Pretty Girls Make Graves

Brutal Boys Cry Blood

Manderley Academy

Ghosted

Haunted

Spirited

Briarwood Witches

Earth and Embers

Fire and Fable

Water and Woe

Wind and Whispers

Spirit and Sorrow

Crookshollow Gothic Romance

Art of Cunning (Alex & Ryan)

Art of the Hunt (Alex & Ryan)

Art of Temptation (Alex & Ryan)

The Man in Black (Elinor & Eric)

Watcher (Belinda & Cole)

Reaper (Belinda & Cole)

Wolves of Crookshollow

Digging the Wolf (Anna & Luke)

Writing the Wolf (Rosa & Caleb)

Inking the Wolf (Bianca & Robbie)

Wedding the Wolf (Willow & Irvine)

Want to be informed when the next Steffanie Holmes paranormal romance story goes live? Sign up for the newsletter at www.steffanieholmes.com/ newsletter to get the scoop, and score a free collection of bonus scenes and stories to enjoy!

ABOUT THE AUTHOR

Steffanie Holmes is the *USA Today* bestselling author of the paranormal, gothic, dark, and fantastical. Her books feature clever, witty heroines, secret societies, creepy old mansions and alpha males who *always* get what they want.

Legally-blind since birth, Steffanie received the 2017 Attitude Award for Artistic Achievement. She was also a finalist for a 2018 Women of Influence award.

Steff is the creator of *Rage Against the Manuscript* – a resource of free content, books, and courses to help writers tell their story, find their readers, and build a badass writing career.

Steffanie lives in New Zealand with her husband, a horde of cantankerous cats, and their medieval sword collection.

Steffanie Holmes newsletter

Grab a free copy of *Cabinet of Curiosities* – a Steffanie Holmes compendium of short stories and bonus scenes – when you sign up for updates with the Steffanie Holmes newsletter.

http://www.steffanieholmes.com/newsletter

Come hang with Steffanie
www.steffanieholmes.com
hello@steffanieholmes.com